MINION OR MASTER

MARTIN SMITH

authorHOUSE®

AuthorHouse™ UK Ltd.
1663 Liberty Drive
Bloomington, IN 47403 USA
www.authorhouse.co.uk
Phone: 0800.197.4150

© 2013 by Martin Smith. All rights reserved.

No part of this book may be reproduced, stored in a retrieval system, or transmitted by any means without the written permission of the author.

This book is entirely fictitious. Any resemblance to real people, living or dead, places or events past or present is coincidental and completely unintended.

Published by AuthorHouse 09/25/2013

ISBN: 978-1-4918-7876-7 (sc)
ISBN: 978-1-4918-7877-4 (e)

Any people depicted in stock imagery provided by Thinkstock are models, and such images are being used for illustrative purposes only.
Certain stock imagery © Thinkstock.

This book is printed on acid-free paper.

Because of the dynamic nature of the Internet, any web addresses or links contained in this book may have changed since publication and may no longer be valid. The views expressed in this work are solely those of the author and do not necessarily reflect the views of the publisher, and the publisher hereby disclaims any responsibility for them.

Acknowledgements

I am very grateful for the encouragement received from many friends and clients whilst writing this book. In particular I would mention:

The Aberdare Scribblers. They listened to my readings every week for months.

Alwyn Roberts, Novanna Richards, Maureen Williams and Steven Graham for reading the draft and giving me feedback.

Jay Young who commented on my cover design idea.

Especial thanks to Hester my life partner who read every piece as soon as I had written it, made comments and has given me her support throughout the process.

Thank you all

Any mistakes or errors are entirely my responsibility.

Martin Smith

Preface

The man sitting on the park bench on a fine Sunday morning attracts no attention.

Dressed in a gabardine raincoat, chequered scarf, corduroy trousers and brown casual shoes his clothes are timeless classics whose colours merge into the background shrubbery in the park. A brown trilby hat covers his thinning hair. His attentive grey eyes peer through thick horn rimmed glasses as he sits quietly watching the birds chase each other then stop to preen their feathers in the lake.

The ducks and geese are especially active today he thinks. The coming of spring, the bringer of life forces, encourager of procreation, must be the reason he muses.

A clock strikes 12 midday. George Howden rises from the bench and proceeds out of the park walking due east past the bandstand where workmen are sprucing up the paintwork in readiness for the spring concerts. A keen listener of Classic FM George expects to attend some of the concerts. Walking at a brisk pace George passes through Queen Marys Gardens then, at Broad Walk he crosses the park heading in a south easterly direction. After 300 metres he reaches the entrance to his apartment block overlooking Regents Park. The concierge, a retired corporal, looking spic and span in his uniform of navy blue with red piping, sees George entering into the neat front gardens of the apartment block and with a flourish opens the dark varnished mahogany front door.

"Good afternoon Sir . . . I hope you had a nice walk?"

"Yes thank you Harris very pleasant indeed" replies George speaking in a quiet yet clear and crisp voice.

"While you were out this arrived by courier for you Sir" Harris hands George an A4 sealed envelope addressed to Sir George Howden, 4 Cambridge Terrace Mews, Regents Park NW1. George studies the envelope which provides no external clue as to its contents.

In his apartment he places the envelope on the Chippendale hall stand table hangs up his coat and hat then proceeds to the kitchen to prepare his lunch. At 69 years of age he is in good health but a recent check up indicated his cholesterol level was up from 6 to 7. George plans a lunch of smoked mackerel and salad with a glass of Chateau Latour-Martillac one of the finest Bordeaux Graves. Whilst some adjustment to his lifestyle is necessary in the interests of preserving a healthy body George considers that the enjoyment of a good wine will not be one of them.

Replete from lunch George moves into the sitting room to his favourite high backed red leather arm chair positioned near the bay window. The chair's position enables George to look into Regents Park whilst the sun's rays shine through the window to gently caress his face. In seconds he is asleep. After 30 minutes of deep slumber he awakes and feeling refreshed he fetches the envelope from the hallstand.

Seated at the 18th century Hepplewhite style bureau he acquired from Sotheby's he gazes up to admire one of his pictures showing the foreboding mass of Pen yr Ole Wen in North Wales. He picks up a solid silver Georgian paper knife. He handles the knife delicately and with reverence, this was the last gift he ever received from

Minion or Master

Leonora. With his fine long perfectly formed fingers, such as those belonging to a surgeon or musician, he opens the envelope. He has a good idea what the contents might be so is not completely surprised to take out a further sealed envelope marked from Sir Adrian Cuthbert, Permanent Secretary, H M Treasury, Strictly Private, for the Addressee Only.

Here we go again what this time he wonders.

Chapter One

Chrome Ore

Costas Tinopolis heads up one of the biggest shipping fleets in the West.

How he got finance to get started is shrouded in mystery.

It is nineteen sixty six. Costas has quoted keen prices to ensure he is awarded the United Nations contract to carry grain from the eastern seaboard of the USA to Mozambique, East Africa. His ship will do more than carry grain. Costas has made a deal with Jamil El Hassan.

Costas needs to find a minion, the perfect patsy, to take the wrap if his secret illegal activities with Jamil El Hassan are discovered.

Mid May 1966

A Voyage

Captain Agios Kato is feeling pleased with himself. His ship, the bulk ore carrier "Ocean Star", has completed her voyage to Africa on time. The sealed envelope he opens from his employer orders him to make contact with Jans Smutt the manager of Torreshippes in Lourenco Marques the capital city and port of Mozambique.

Captain Kato allows his Somali crew shore leave. They will make for the bars and sample the delights of the notorious red light district whilst Captain Kato goes ashore to meet Jans Smutt.

"How was the voyage?" asks Smutt looking up from his paper strewn desk.

"The kind I like best, uneventful and on time." replies Kato.

Smutt, a South African Boer retired from the military police, gives Kato a sullen stare before getting up to fetch a file from the safe.

"We have a special delivery of ore coming in from South Africa by train tomorrow which has to be off loaded onto your ship that night." Smutt advises.

Captain Kato stares back at Smutt. A seasoned, experienced sailor, he has worked for Costas Tinopolis since they took delivery of the first new carrier in nineteen fifty. Now, after sixteen years, he is one of the most trusted captains in the Tinopolis fleet. Nothing can fluster or surprise him.

"My ship can't load ore at its present berth and we are not due to move for another three days." Kato responds.

"That's taken care of," Smutt grins, revealing tobacco stained teeth.

"Whisky?" he asks taking out a bottle of scotch and two tumblers from his desk drawer. Kato nods his head slightly to accept and Smutt pours out two slugs of the amber liquid.

"Only decent thing the Brits have ever brought to Africa." Smutt declares.

"Now we have a bloody trade embargo on Rhodesia just because some liberal do gooders in the UK have forced the United Nations to vote this crazy sanction. Every one here knows the white Rhodesian farmers supply most of Africa with food. Now the UN has to get the likes

Minion or Master

of you to carry the food thousands of miles whilst good food rots up north just a few hundred miles from here. I tell you man its crazy!" Smutt spits out the words with venom in his voice.

"What's the plan?" asks Kato. Smutt takes another slug of scotch and offers the bottle to Kato who declines.

"It's a high tide tomorrow night so at dusk you have permission from the harbour authorities to move two miles upstream to the old rail head where the ore will be loaded by conveyor. We have the loaders and diesel powered conveyors all on board the train so it should be possible for the loading to be complete in two nights and you moved back to the normal iron ore berth to load the balance of your cargo by Thursday. The main thing is to stop the bastard Brits in the High Commission from knowing what's going on here. My sources tell me most of the staff has been summoned back to London for briefings." Smutt advises.

"Do you have the move permit from the harbour master?" Kato asks.

"This should pass scrutiny if you do get inspected up river." Smutt passes the permit to Kato.

"Just in case you have any other problems you can use these." Smutt throws over a bag containing a stash of US dollar bills. Kato inspects the contents, around one thousand dollars he reckons. He pushes the bag back towards Smutt and stares hard at Smutt who stares back.

"This is not enough to ensure everything runs smoothly and you know it. Where's the rest?" Kato demands. After a few seconds of stand off staring Smutt opens his desk drawer and produces a roll of dollar bills secured by a rubber band.

"There's another grand in there Captain. That should see you through." Smutt smiles. Gathering up the money Kato stands up to leave.

"Nice doing business with you and thanks for the scotch." Smutt holds up a hand and whispers.

"Just one more thing, you have to deliver this to the agent in St. Helena." He hands Kato a small boxed package which is sealed with wax.

"Good luck Captain."

Loading

As dusk is falling "Ocean Star" leaves her berth on the high tide and steams slowly up stream.

Jans Smutt has sent a local river man to help Captain Kato navigate Maputo river. There is no moon. The ship creeps past ranks of Acacia trees growing down to the river bank. The air is humid and full of noise from cicadas and animals going about their business in the impenetrable forest. Kato has had to part with a hundred dollars for the river man's help. He is banking on the river man's local knowledge to keep them afloat and safe. The last thing he wants is to run his ship aground.

As the river widens a dim yellow light can be seen flashing on the port bank. The outline structure of an old wooden jetty appears out of the dark. Kato orders the ship's engines to reverse. "Ocean Star" slowly loses way. With guidance from the river man Kato slowly negotiates the vessel along side the jetty. As soon as "Ocean Star" is secured to the jetty the load master comes aboard. He has a gang waiting at the rail head. First he has to agree his fee with Kato. After a few pleasantries Kato agrees a price of three hundred dollars per day. Kato calculates that loading at the rate of one thousand tonnes per hour will take at least two nights work.

In minutes the jetty becomes a hive of activity as the gang set to work connecting three conveyor chutes to discharge ore into the central holds of the ship. At the rail head one hundred rail trucks await their turn to tilt their cargo of two hundred tonnes of finest Rhodesian chrome ore into a massive hopper where gravity feeds the ore onto the main conveyor belt which connects to the chutes loading the ship. Every twenty minutes Kato orders the position of the chutes to be altered so that the cargo is equally distributed in the hold to avoid the ship listing.

At three in the morning, after several hours of trouble free loading, a land rover roars up to the jetty carrying four soldiers armed with automatic weapons. Work stops on the jetty as the sergeant demands to know what is going on. The load master takes the sergeant in charge to see Kato. The sergeant inspects the harbour move permit which now has two hundred and fifty dollars folded into the document. After removing the money he hands the document back and says.

"Captain your papers appear to be in good order I wish you good night and good luck."

Three days later, with her holds topped up with iron ore, concealing the bottom layer of chrome ore, "Ocean Star" sets sail for New York. At St. Helena she will pick up provisions and Captain Kato will deliver the package handed to him by Smutts.

Information

The senior officers at the British High Commission in Lourenco Marques have been summoned to London for a high level briefing over the Rhodesian crisis. Britain's interests all over Africa and her standing in the world are at risk. The winds of change foreseen by Harold Macmillan e now blow at gale force. However sympathetic to the white settlers cause in Rhodesia top civil servants and government ministers are, in public, they must be seen to be against white Imperialist supremacy. The last thing wanted is another South Africa.

A junior diplomat, Bertie Mannering, has been left in charge whilst his seniors take advice from their masters in London. The day after "Ocean Star" left port a young Mozambique lad comes in to the Commission asking to see "the boss man".

"I rather suppose that's me at the moment." Bertie shouts into the intercom to reception.

"You'd better wheel the blighter in." A slight, cowering individual clasping a canvas bag is brought in to Bertie.

"Yes what can we help you with?" Bertie shouts in his imperial voice. He stares intently at the trembling lad.

"What's that you have in that canvas bag? Show me!" Bertie barks at the lad. The lad shuffles over to the table with his eyes still gazing at the floor not looking at Bertie. He unties the bag and empties the contents onto Bertie's desk. Two dusty red rocks emerge scattering fragments all over the desk.

"I say steady on you young savage. You'll ruin Her Majesty's desk. What is this all about" Bertie bellows.

"*Please sir engleeesh no vera good, roca hya from up riva on ze ship gone, you giva me?*" The lad holds out his hand for money.

"No such deal old chap this looks like common iron ore to me. Get out of here stop wasting my time!" orders Bertie.

The lad looks agitated. Suddenly his eyes light up as he sees a silver coloured ash tray on the desk. He points at the ash tray and then at the rocks. He looks at Bertie and repeats the movements.

"What the devil are you doing?" Bertie exclaims.

"I've told you its iron" Bertie pauses in mid sentence. His eyes take in the chrome plated ashtray, then they cross to the rock, then to the lad, who has his begging hands outstretched. Placing both hands on the desk Bertie stares intently at the lad.

"Are you telling me this is not iron but chrome ore?" Bertie points to the ash tray then the rocks.

"*Si sir, now money please sir, yes please?*" the lad pleads.

"You say you got this from up river from a ship that has just left port?" Bertie asks more politely now his interest aroused.

"*Si yes sir, yes money please, yes sir?*" the lad repeats himself.

"Wait there. I'm going to check something!" Bertie orders and then asks reception to find out the names of the ships which have left port with ore cargo in the last week.

After a fifteen minute wait reception phone and give Bertie his information.

"I see just two ships have left this week. Thank you. Can you find out from the harbour people if either ship were up river at all please? Thanks awfully." Bertie places the phone down carefully.

"O K laddie here's what I propose. I will buy your rocks for one dollar. Here see." Bertie has pulled out a US dollar bill and shows it to the lad. The boy nods and takes the money.

Martin Smith

"Good. Now if you hear any more about these roca. What's your name laddie? Bertie enquires.

"Your name, what's your name?"

"*Me call Ali sir.*" the lad says brightly.

"Well now Ali, if you hear any more on these roca you come and see me straight away, may be another dollar for you. Good lad. Now let's get all this down in writing before you forget it Ali there's a good chap." Bertie sighs and reaches for a pad of paper.

Chapter Two
Wayne and Adrian

Beginning of May 1966

Opening Account

After a shower of heavy rain the air in Bermuda is laced with the sweet fragrances from poinsettias, oleander, hibiscus and freesias. George Howden walks purposefully through the lush well manicured gardens leading up to the old plantation house which is now the headquarters of the Bank of Pembroke. His mind is concentrating on the forthcoming meeting so he does not notice or appreciate the scents and colourful garden.

Aged twenty four, with golden hair and a muscular thick set body George has been in Bermuda working for an international firm of accountants. He is on a two year posting. Having qualified in London just nine months ago as a numbers man he has come to Bermuda hoping to make his fortune.

George's leather shoes echo off the stone floor as he walks up to the reception desk. An attractive Bermudan girl with a fine featured face, coffee coloured perfect skin, dark hair tied in a bow at the nape of her neck and pale brown eyes looks up and smiles at George enquiringly. Her lips are coloured with a pale beige lipstick and as they part George sees perfectly formed ivory white teeth.

"*Gud morning saah, can I help you?*" she enquires in a soft Bermudan lilt. George eyes the receptionist with more than a hint of interest and gives her his most charming smile which transforms his face from a serious young businessman into a carefree handsome young man.

"Hello dear lady it is a lovely day and I have an appointment to see your Wayne Luther." The girl consults her diary then looks directly into George's eyes

"*Ah yes Meesterr Howten, Mr Luther he be expectin you.*" she guides George to a large leather arm chair.

"*Please to take seat I tell him you heeyah.*" George makes him self comfortable and watches the girl display her shapely calves and pert bottom as she climbs up the cedar wood staircase to fetch Wayne Luther.

After brief hellos Wayne Luther and George make their way up to room three situated off an overhanging balcony on the first floor, the room has cedar wood panelling and double windows overlooking the grounds.

The walls of the office have oil paintings of trading ships in ornate gilded frames. Captions under each picture announce that the ships have been owned or chartered by the Rucker family who own the bank.

"What a fine room this is." George remarks looking at the extra large wooden sign on the over size desk that proclaims in bold letters:

Wayne Luther Executive Vice President.

"Why, thank you kind sir, father in law insisted I should have this room once me and Mary Jayne got hitched. Kinda like an extra wedding present you might say." Wayne replies his voice betraying his Deep South upbringing.

Minion or Master

Dressed in a maroon jacket white shirt and yellow tie with Bermuda shorts and long socks Executive Vice President Wayne Luther has a small podgy face. His hooded eyes and thinning mousy brown hair make him look older than his age of thirty two. George ponders whether his cream linen lounge suit and a Sea Island cotton shirt with a colourful striped tie and slip on black leather shoes might be a tad conservative.

"Well now Mr Howden, may I call you George?" Wayne asks opening his file of papers.

"I have studied your business plans carefully and have run the whole thing past our back room research boys." Wayne looks at George and smiles.

"George, we like your ideas and subject to a few points the bank wants to back you." George is pleased at this initial response from the bank. He had worked hard to make the Tinopolis plan of chartering the bulk carrier ship look financially attractive. Aframe Shipping was to be the operating company. The company name had been chosen to reflect the sailings between Africa (Afr) and America (Ame).

"Wayne I am delighted" George responds.

"That takes care of the formalities!" Wayne cries enthusiastically.

"How about we have some lunch to celebrate?" Wayne winks at George.

"The Princess Hotel is just down the road a piece and they do a real good Lobster"

"Lead on Wayne" George laughs.

"You bet your sweet ass I will. I think you and me is gonna get on just great." Wayne responds as the two walk out of the bank.

Sweeteners

After lunch George and Wayne move from the dining room to the lounge area overlooking the open air salt water pool. They order coffee and brandies.

"*Sooo now George how do you like our little ol' island?*" Wayne asks with a slight slur to his voice and a leer on his face.

"Have you been native yet?"

"How do you mean Wayne?" asks George rather taken aback at the direct line of questioning.

"*Weeell now, I guess even a hard working young Limey like you whose not been here too long can't help noticing the lovely black ass around. Take Leonora, the chick you saw at reception. She told me you gave her an eyeful.*"

"She was rather attractive I have to admit" George blushes.

"*Weeell she told me she likes the look of you an she wouldn't say no to a social meet sometime. Now as it happens we are havin a Barbie down on the beach at Horseshoe Bay at the end of the week. A few beers, a swim, some food, a relax an chill day. Why not come over? There may be a few people from the bank might be useful for y'all to meet. Leonora an her sista will be coming. Wow her sista m mm she sure is a good lookin chick. So what dya say, George?*"

"I'd like that very much thanks, Wayne" George replies looking a little uneasy.

"Wayne you mentioned in the bank there were a few loose ends to tie up with the deal. Can you give me some idea so I can get back to Mercator and his father?"

"*Sure thing George, what is it you have with the Tinopolis family? 'Cos you know the bank's mighty interested in further development there.*"

"Well I met them in the office a few weeks back. I've been working on one of their off shore subsidiaries and had some queries. They were on the island for another meeting so they came in to see me directly. This was when the old man Costas asked if I would be interested in looking after the ship charter venture based here in Bermuda."

"*That's my boy,*" Wayne cries in excitement.

"*I knew you had something special goin on. You're in with the Tinopolis family jess like me with the Ruckers an' I tell you we alls like bein treated as family.*" Wayne pauses and looks out of the window behind George.

"*I was thinking George my boy that as I'm gonna be personally lookin after you, kinda like family, that maybe some of that contingency fund in your business plan might be diverted to security costs? What do you say to that tying up the loose ends?*"

"I hadn't considered a security cost, Wayne," George replied cautiously.

"But now you mention it that might be an idea. How much will it cost?"

"*Weeell now, le me see.*" Wayne drawls as his eyelids droop to cover most of his piggy pupils.

"*There are contacts for business and leisure. Then there's makin sure all the paper work is tied up with the bank and the Government. Y'all know pa in law is a Council representative so he got quite a bit of heavy pull in these parts. So all in all I would say a half of the contingency should just about cover the annual expense an' that will also get y'all my personal attention.*" Wayne waits his face expectant with greed waiting for George's response. George sucks in his breath and whispers.

"Yes, I see, that will come to around thirty thousand US Dollars" George pauses for effect.

"And for that sum I would require priority treatment. Call it a sweetener for both of us if you like."

"*Goddamn name it George jus name it,*" shrieks Wayne. Looking straight into Wayne's sweaty face George makes his request and a deal is struck.

"Hello George? Is everything sorted?" Mercator Tinopolis phoning from Europe enquires.

"Tell your father the plan is accepted, Mercator. Everything is ready this end. Have the money telexed to the Bank. Then the charter can go ahead."

"OK George that's great I'll tell him. He's in the Monte Carlo office this week. Ciao see you soon." Mercator ends the call

George's Deal

George is pleased. He has made a useful friend in Wayne Luther. Mercator Tinopolis has arranged with his father to have fifty thousand dollars transferred by secure telex to the Aframe Shipping account. The bank loan of one hundred thousand dollars agreed by George at the meeting with Wayne Luther will finance the full charter hire for "Ocean Star".

The ship is chartered to complete two return voyages From the US eastern seaboard to South East Africa.

George is the local company director in Bermuda. The involvement of the Tinopolis family in Aframe Shipping is confidential. George's profit share from Aframe Shipping will exceed his full year's salary. George must sign all company papers which will come from various companies owned by Costas Tinopolis.

Life feels good. George is on his way to making a fortune.

Meeting Adrian

The early morning clear blue skies with a gentle sea breeze promise another fine day in Bermuda.

Before the sun rises too high George walks from his apartment in Spanish Point to a local beach for a leisurely swim. The morning sun soon dries his skin leaving evaporated salt, looking like white tide marks, on his back as he returns to his apartment.

After breakfast George rides his Lambretta scooter into town to collect mail from his post box. With a balmy climate, fed by the Gulf Stream, and a maximum speed limit of twenty miles per hour George finds a scooter to be the perfect form of transport to get around the twenty two mile length of the island.

From Hamilton town centre it is a short journey along lanes flanked by coral rock walls with flowers sprouting from the rough crevices to the tennis stadium.

George enjoys tennis not just for the fresh air and exercise. A game for individual participation rather than team involvement suits him, a game in which he can test himself against a variety of opponents and learn something about himself as well.

Since coming to Bermuda George has become a "freelance" player at the tennis stadium. Most Saturdays and evenings when he can get to the stadium he makes himself available to make up numbers for doubles matches or to give visitors from the United States a game of singles.

At five foot nine inches tall his powerful body delivers a strong first service when he gets the tennis ball thrown to the perfect height and angle. Light on his feet, his fine delicate hands provide a deft and delicate touch with the racquet when required.

As he walks into the reception area the stadium manager shouts.

"Hey George there's an English guy just come in looking for a game of singles. He's just gone into the locker room."

"Thanks Freddie I'll catch him right away. Any other guys in yet?"

"No not yet just you two, shall I book Court one for you?"

"Yes please. Make it for just the hour and I'll see how we get on." In the locker room George sees a tall, dark haired slim man getting changed.

"Hi I'm George Howden." Walking up to the man George extends his hand.

"Freddie says you are looking for a game this morning. I shall be happy to oblige if you want?" Taking George's hand and giving him a very firm hand shake the man greets George speaking with a pronounced public school accent.

"Adrian Cuthbert. Pleased to meet you old chap. Yes I would love a game. Only just arrived last week and I could really do with some exercise. I do hope I can give you a decent game as I haven't played for a while, since Oxford as a matter of fact".

"No problem Adrian. Let's just give it a go and see how we get on. What brings you to Bermuda?"

"Boring stuff, work and all that you know, I have been sent out from London to Government House, helping out with the office. Keeping files tidy and generally being

Minion or Master

dogsbody to the Governor, it's my first assignment in the Civil Service. How about you George what is your line?"

"I am office based like you Adrian, I have a two year contract, nearly half way through with Robinsons the international accountancy firm. I came over from the UK straight after qualifying. Get some sun and make some money is my plan"

"Jolly good old chap. Best of luck. Shall we play?"

The knock about before a game is usually where George can spot opponents weaknesses. Going through the full range of strokes and watching their movements gives an idea of what sort of game is likely to develop. With Adrian the knock about revealed very little to George. George thought he was a little stiff in his run ups to retrieve base line shots but his overall play was inscrutable. His strokes were sound but not brilliant. He missed a few serves and volleyed several shots into the net. George had the feeling Adrian was holding back, playing very much within him self.

The first set goes to four games all with each player holding serve. The ninth game is with George to serve. By now each player had warmed up and was seeing the ball well. George takes the first two points with an ace first serve followed by a netted return of serve from Adrian.

"Thirty love!" shouts George across the net.

"OK." replies Adrian taking his stance some three feet inside the base line. George thinks Adrian is too far in to take his first serve. George bounces the tennis ball on the base line and throws it into the air for his racquet to smash onto at the perfect angle. The ball speeds just an inch over the net right into the corner of the junction box past Adrian for an ace.

"Great shot George forty love I think?" Adrian responds walking over to the other side of the court to receive George's next bomber serve. This time Adrian stays on the base line, alert, on his toes with his body crouching in anticipation. George serves another screamer but Adrian moves to anticipate the line of the ball and plays a forehand shot past George landing an inch inside the base line. The next point George misses his first serve. Adrian takes advantage of the slower second serve and returns to George who smashes the ball into the back corner. Somehow, Adrian scrambles at full speed to the back of the court and seeing George running into the net he makes a perfect lob to the back of the court to win the point.

"Forty thirty old chap" shouts Adrian.

I must take this next point

George looks up to see Adrian on his toes ready to receive. Again, George's first serve is a good one which Adrian returns by playing a back hand to the base line. George plays the shot back with all his power but Adrian runs into the front of the court and volleys the ball into the centre line. All George can do is to get his racquet to the ball and play a high lob shot which is heading to the back of the court. Turning on a sixpence Adrian races back and as the ball bounces he bends his knees gracefully, and with his back still to the net returns the ball to the opposite side of the net taking George completely by surprise.

"Well played Adrian, deuce" Says George. Before the players can line up for the next point a cloud carrying a heavy shower arrives. A torrential downpour of warm rain lashes onto the court as George and Adrian race for shelter.

"It's now twelve thirty. We've got just five minutes court time left. Do you want another hour for a second set Adrian?" George looks steadily into Adrian's eyes.

"Awfully sorry old chap, must dash, the Governor's putting on lunch for a few big wigs from Blighty. I have to be back. I did enjoy the game though. May I call you at Robinson's sometime for a return game?"

"Please do, that will be great. It's a pity we can't finish off this set. You seemed to be getting into your stride in that last game. That final point was outstanding. I never thought you would reach the ball let alone return it."

"I think it was a bit of a fluke old boy." Adrian shrugs his shoulders in a gesture of surprise and disappears out of the stadium.

Chapter Three

Beach Fun

Sunday morning Early May 1966

Beach Party

At Horse Shoe Bay the sun is shining high in a clear blue sky, the sand feels hot to George's bare feet as he picks his way over to a group of people sitting around an open marquee. Some are jiving to a Dionne Warwick song blaring out from a portable radio. Others are sitting around talking and drinking.

Wayne Luther is not difficult to spot. Crouching over a massive barbeque set up in the marquee Wayne is turning beef burgers and chicken pieces. He has a large fork in one hand and a can of beer in the other. Wayne is wearing tartan Bermuda shorts and a baseball hat which has the words "Bank on me!!" embroidered on the front. George observes that Wayne's bare torso is turning pink. As Wayne turns to look out of the marquee he spots George closing in on the group.

"Hey George glad you could make it. Come and get a beer from the ice box! Then I'll introduce you around. Mary Jayne this is George from England." Wayne waves his fork in the direction of George. Wayne's gaze turns towards a white faced lady sitting under an umbrella just outside the marquee.

"George this is Mary Jayne Luther my very good lady wife. Mary Jayne would y'all mind takin over heya for a while on the barbie whilst I introduce George around?"

"No sweetie pie, leave it to me!" Mary Jayne answers as she gets out of her chair and looks at George.

"I am honoured to make your acquaintance George." Mary Jayne gives a demure curtsy holding the skirt of her cotton floral pattern dress out with her right hand.

"I am delighted to meet you dear lady." George says and taking her left hand he bows his head so that his lips just brush her knuckle.

"Oh a proper real English gentleman I declare." Mary Jayne blurts out, her cheeks flushed with excitement.

"George an me has done some fine business this week Mary Jayne so he needs real good lookin after. Come on George bring your beer! Come and meet the crowd!"

"Thanks Wayne. I'm amazed how you managed to bring all this equipment here?" queries George.

"That's no problem George. We pack it all in "Pembroke Lady". Then we just cruise around from the bungalow. See there she is!" Wayne points out over the breakers to a sleek white painted speed boat moored about thirty metres from the shore.

"Wow I see she's fitted out for game fishing." George enthuses as he looks at the twin rods stacked at forty five degrees on the out riggers and at the spacious cabin topped with the latest Decca radar dome.

"You betcha George, "Pembroke Lady" is available for game fishing and with her twin Volvo Penta marine engines there's not much around these parts that can catch her. It was a difficult job to get Pa Rucker to part with near on three hundred thousand dollars for her over in Miami. But now with game fishin and a regular monthly charter the "Lady" is paying her way. We can go for a spin after lunch if you want?"

"That will be great" George declares.

"By the way I can't see Leonora here." George looks at Wayne with a hint of disappointment in his face. George is wearing a colourful calypso style shirt, a cream coloured boater hat, sand coloured Bermuda shorts under which he has a pair of shorts which can be used as a swimming costume.

"Oh boy I can see you've taken a shine to her. She's not here 'cos she's over there in the sea swimming with her sister Jasmine. Why don't you take a swim? The water is real nice."

"OK I will. See you later." George shouts as he removes his shirt and shorts and races down to the sea. As George dives into a breaker Leonora and Jasmine begin their graceful exit from the sea. They dodge the odd Parrot fish swimming in the breakers then walk gracefully together up to the marquee.

"Hey Leonora didn't you see the English guy who was in the bank this week. He's just gone in for a swim?" Wayne, with his hands on his hips, queries. Leonora picks up a towel and wraps it around her well shaped body and shakes her hair.

"*No Wayne me an Jasmine we been getting a bit too much sea an de salt water is stingin mes eyes so wes come out for lunch. Be vera nice to see him at lunch. He seemed very nice he done give me a lully smile at da bank.*" Leonora looks up and winks at Jasmine who giggles back.

"*OK, so, after lunch, how's about y'all comin' on "Pembroke Lady" with George an' me for a lill ol trip*" Wayne asks the girls. Mary Jayne is rubbing cream into his back and gives the girls a look that says you can go if you want but you'd better behave or Leonora will be history in my Pa's bank.

"Wayne I'm a sorree I has to be back home for tea. I'm playin with Pa at ze Harbour Club dis evening. But Jasmine can go wiz y'all." Leonora apologises looking a little disappointed. She has caught Mary Jayne's stern look and feels that to upset her might be pushing her luck a bit too far today.

"Ok some other time for you Leonora. Is that OK for you Jasmine" Wayne queries as Mary Jayne finishes the back rub on his pink flesh and gives Jasmine an unfriendly stare.

"Dat's great Wayne I'm game to come for a ride on de boat." Jasmine replies in her throaty seductive voice.

"Now, I gotta finish cookin on this here barbie for y'all." Wayne says backing in to the marquee his eyes transfixed on the ample cleavages displayed by the two sisters.

Sunday Afternoon Early May 1966

Boat Ride

After lunch Wayne sidles over to George

"Ok George, Leonora says she's real sorry not to be comin out for a ride on "Pembroke Lady" but she's singing at the Harbour Club this evening. Maybe you could go over tonight catch the music. It's a real cool place my man. Any how, Jasmine, her older sister, is coming with us."

"No problem Wayne. As a matter of fact I have had a chat with Leonora and her sister over lunch. Jasmine says I'm welcome to go with her and her friend to the Club tonight. I'm really looking forward to it. I'm mainly a classical music man but it will be interesting to hear Calypso and Caribbean music live."

"Fantastic let's get out to the boat."

"*Y'all be careful now ye hear Wayne.*" Mary Jayne cries giving Jasmine a withering look.

Wayne drags a rubber dinghy down to the shore and holds it steady for George and Jasmine to clamber in. They wear swimsuits so getting wet is no problem as Wayne rows out to "Pembroke Lady".

On board, "Pembroke Lady" is more spacious than she appeared from the shore. Her forty five foot length and fifteen foot breadth with the latest hull design give her stability in the Atlantic waves. Below deck there are bunks to sleep six and a spacious sitting area as well as the usual heads and galley. The cabin has two large white leather seats for the skipper and his mate. The seats are designed to give maximum visibility forward and aft. The dashboard is fitted with every navigational aid available.

The twin exhausts make a throaty, bubbly, throbbing roar as "Pembroke Lady" heads out to sea. Jasmine, standing between the two seated men, suggests they head out to Carver Island. Looking in the rear view mirror George spots a mischievous look on Jasmine's face. Two years older than Leonora her dark brown eyes in a well defined face, fulsome lips and long raven black hair hanging loose down to her tiny white bikini pants give her a wild gypsy look.

Wayne anchors "Pembroke Lady" in a small cove.

"Fancy a little fishin George?" asks Wayne as Jasmine disappears into the heads below deck.

"Sure Wayne, this looks like a good place." George says helping Wayne fix up some small rods with bait on the port side. As they busy themselves with the tackle they hear a splash from the starboard side.

"Did you hear that where the hell is Jasmine?" Wayne asks as he and George drop their rods simultaneously and rush to the starboard side. George beats Wayne and peers over into the crystal clear turquoise blue waters where he sees Jasmine completely naked floating on her back. Her body is slim and lithe the same coffee colour all over except for the black curly mound rising between her legs. She sees George staring and gives him a grin then turns onto her front and swims a few metres away.

"*JEEESUS*" shouts Wayne "Did you see that? What are you playing at Jasmine come back here!" Jasmine turns onto her back again and gives both men a view that makes them blush.

"*Why don y'all come on in boys the waters lovely an there's plenty of room?*" Jasmine taunts the men.

Wayne briefly thinks about Mary Jayne and the wrath of the Rucker family if they find out about this. However, unable to control himself, he drops his bathers throws off his "Bank on Me!!" cap and belly flops into the water. His mid quarters are pale white contrasting with the blotchy pink of his back. Jasmine spies Wayne. She swims gracefully away keeping him just out of distance. Desperately Wayne tries his best crawl to reach her but like a sleek seal Jasmine keeps just out of reach.

George notices that Jasmine's eyes seem glazed. He is mesmerised by the scene but some instinct tells him to be careful. Jasmine's look is strange. On his way down to the heads George spots Jasmine's bikini and waterproof bag discarded on the deck. Bending down to look closer he spies a small open plastic envelope containing traces of white powder. As he wonders what it is he hears desperate shouting from Wayne. Sprinting up the stairs he sees Wayne about ten metres from the side frantically turning and tossing his body in the water before his head goes under.

"Hang on Wayne I'm coming in!" George races to the stern and quickly releases a life buoy which he hurls over the starboard side in the general direction of Wayne. With no further thought George dives into the water and swims towards the thrashing figure.

"What's the problem?" George shouts.

"*Craaamp ahhhhh*" Wayne screams before going under once again.

George reaches the life buoy floating a few metres from Wayne and lunges towards him. Wayne has swallowed a great deal of water and is panicking. George manages to get the buoy over one of Wayne's arms but he is struggling so much that George cannot get the other arm through to fit underneath his shoulders. Holding Wayne's arm with the buoy George turns the rope attached to the buoy around Wayne's torso and with a turn of the rope ties in a knot to secure the buoy to Wayne. George swims back to "Pembroke Lady" as fast as he can. Struggling up the ladder at the stern George hauls the rope with the buoy and Wayne attached to the side. Wayne is now lifeless in the sea. Immediately George dives back in. He heaves Wayne over his shoulder. Carefully he carries him up the ladder and drops him onto the deck where he places him in the recovery position. George checks for a pulse. He feels a throb in Wayne's neck. Urgently he slaps him on the back. After a few hard slaps Wayne splutters and spews up sea water onto the deck.

"Are you OK?" George asks

"What in the hell happened there?"

Minion or Master

"You dived in after Jasmine and got cramp surely you remember?"

"*AHWWW yeaah, George, pleeeeasse I beg you not a word to Mary Jayne about this or I'm done for*! Y'all saw the look on Mary Jayne's face when we left?"

"Well you don't sound too bad now old chap. Can you stand up?" As Wayne starts to drag himself onto his knees a voice taunts

"Hello boys what are you two playing at?" Jasmine, now, back in her bikini, looking as innocent as the day is long, has come up from the lower deck.

"*Wayne you really should put some clothes on or y'all get sun burn.*" Jasmine continues

"*I had a real nice swim. Did y'all go in as well?*"

"*You're a minx Jasmine y'all knows I went in.*" Wayne cries trying to look dignified as he pulls his shorts up over the creased crinkled and shrunken pride of his manhood.

"Surely you remember taunting us?" George queries.

"*I remember no such thing. Although I can see that Wayne has been a bit naughty skinny dippin. What's your Mary Jayne gonna make of that Waaaaynie?*" Jasmine taunts.

"*AWWW Jasmine. Pleease don't say anythin! Let's just all keep this to ourselves can we?*" Wayne pleads on his bended knees looking at George then Jasmine.

"Well I guess no harms been done. If George agrees then I will just say we had a nice swim. OK with you George?" Jasmine asks giving George her most beautiful smile.

"Absolutely fine by me no problem at all. Let's just forget it and head back. Are you OK to operate "Pembroke Lady" Wayne?" George queries giving Jasmine his most gallant smile and looking rather concerned at Wayne.

"*Yea I'm fine. Glad that's all cleared up, howsa 'bout some coffee down stairs before we set back?*" Wayne asks.

"Good idea" George and Jasmine shout together.

Sunday evening Early May 1966

Harbour Club

George enters the Harbour Club with Jasmine and her friend from New York. Set in half an acre of gardens situated at the end of the Great Sound the Harbour Club has a reputation for good food and local music. Jasmine's friend, Sammy Santino, explains to George that he makes regular visits from New York in connection with the import export agency he runs in New York. Sammy is dressed in a grey silk suit with black shirt and white tie. Jasmine looks cool and elegant in a figure hugging white cotton dress and red high heeled shoes. Not having had much chance to build up a wardrobe, George is wearing the same suit he wore for his meeting with Wayne Luther.

Leonora has reserved a table alongside the pool just a few metres from the patio area where she and her father will play for the club's guests. Leonora, wearing a red dress with a thick black belt around her hour glass waist joins the table with her father.

"Hi Pa Pa" Jasmine says and stands up to give her father a kiss on his cheek.

"Pa, you know everyone except George here from England. George meet our Pa, Charlie Rucker. Pa this is George." Jasmine looks at George.

"Hi Charlie very pleased to meet you." George gets up and shakes Charlie's hand.

"Lovely to see you again Leonora you look stunning this evening." George looks admiringly.

"*Why tank yu vera much. Did y'all have a nice ride on de boat wiv Wayne? Sorree I couldn't come had to get back to rehearse with Pa for tonight.*" Leonora smiles at George.

"Why yes, a very interesting trip. To Carver Island I think we went. Didn't we Jasmine?" George looks at Jasmine who is blushing a little.

"*Yes George. It was a nice trip and I had a good swim. It might be me last for a while. Sammy he done fixed me up wiv some fancy modelling work in New York, ain't you Sammy?*" Jasmine looks at Sammy as she blows out smoke from a small black cheroot.

"That's right baby. I reckon you could really make it big with your looks. This could be your big chance baby." Sammy grins around the table.

"*Y'all be careful in that sin city you hear Jazzy.*" Charlie says with a little note of caution in his gravely voice.

"*Don y'all worry Pa. I'll be OK. Sammy got me a real nice place to stay. I'll be fine, y'all be seein mes in the fashion magazines one day.*" Jasmine responds whilst she stubs out her cheroot.

After eating, Charlie and Leonora leave to prepare for their performance. When they return the crowd give them a thunderous cheer then everyone lapses into silence as Charlie playing guitar sings a Calypso song "Bananas and Yams" accompanied during the chorus by Leonora. The next song is another local song in which everyone sings the chorus: "I wish I was a Fishin, Dats de life for me". Leonora then sings solo with no accompaniment. George sits still, like a monk in prayer, transfixed by the soul filled husky voice of Leonora. When the two return to the table George, gushing with enthusiasm, congratulates them both

"Leonora, that was fantastic. You have an amazing voice. Have you had any musical training?"

"*No none I jus sings wiv Pa at home. Sometimes he plays de piano but he prefers de guitar 'cos he can stand for de singing when he do play de guitar.*"

"Well, I play the piano. I found it a great source of relaxation when I was studying. The music took me away from all my cares." George muses.

"*George! Maybe you'd like to come around our house sometime. We could try a trio. Leonora can sing, me play on de guitar and you on the piano. What d'ya say?*" Charlie asks looking at Leonora who smiles at Charlie enthusiastically. Before George gets out an answer a voice comes from another table.

"Hello George old boy, nice to see you, what brings you here?" Adrian booms.

"Adrian? Hello. These are friends I've met with work. We've come to see Charlie and Leonora. How about you what are you doing here?"

"I'm entertaining government big wigs over from Blighty old boy. Congratulations to Charlie and Leonora, a first class show tonight. We must finish that game from yesterday sometime." Adrian says as he disappears out of the Harbour Club with his guests.

Chapter Four
Drugs

Mid May 1966

Secret Deals

Costas Tinopolis is lying out on a padded deck chair besides his pool in Monte Carlo. A servant brings the telephone. Costas ushers the servant away. He does not want to be overheard.

It is now one week since "Ocean Star" left Lourenco Marques with her central holds half full of chrome ore from Rhodesia. Smuggled into South Africa, then into Mozambique, the ore is an illegal cargo, carried in breach of the United Nations trade embargo on Rhodesia.

"Hello!" growls Costas into the phone.

"Who is it?"

"It's me Jamil. Costas, can you speak freely?" Jamil questions in a quiet but excitable high pitch.

"Go on!" Costas replies cautiously.

"The goods in the package have arrived with the agent and they have been converted. So the merchandise can be forwarded at the next available sailing. Please advise the arrival time as soon as you can."

Jamil has blurted all this rapidly. Costas looks up to the sky and gives a little smile of thanks to his ancient Greek gods.

"This is good news Jamil. I will let you know as soon as I have the details. Good bye old friend." Costas places the receiver down. The plans are starting to come together, Costas enthuses.

Jamil and Costas have arranged for "Ocean Star's" manifest to declare her carrying iron ore, sourced from South Africa, into New York from Lourenco Marques. US customs will be satisfied with the declaration. The smelting works are desperate for chrome ore, to supply the ever increasing demands of the defence industry, will ask no questions. Jamil's company Hassan Import and Export will be paid a cash premium into an offshore account. Costas will get a generous cut for arranging shipping.

The big deal is that Jamil has secured the funds to supply the Mozambique freedom fighters "Freelimo" with arms. Costas must arrange for "Ocean Star" to receive the arms, in two large crates, in secret, from Jamil's New York contacts. The crates will be marked agricultural machinery.

"Ocean Star" will disclose grain being carried on her return voyage from the USA to Africa. The paper work will be sent by Costas to George Howden at Aframe Shipping in Bermuda. There will be no mention of the arms crates.

I must make sure Kato is looked after now he has delivered the blood diamonds to our St Helena agent. I'd better see him in New York Costas thinks to himself.

Costas feels excited. He is tapping in to a high octane game of power and thrill seeking. It is addictive. He wants more.

Monday Late May 1966

Government House Intelligence

"Good morning Adrian! Please do sit down! Pour some tea if you want." Sir Jeremy Mannerby Watson greets his young assistant in Government House, Bermuda.

"We have some interesting intelligence from London. It seems our people in Lourenco Marques have found out that a ship registered here is carrying Rhodesian chrome ore into the USA." Sir Jeremy puffs on his pipe and looks at Adrian for a reaction.

"Sounds intriguing Sir, what are we going to do?" Adrian enquires in a polite neutral tone.

"It's complicated. It is clearly in breach of the UN trade embargo. Normally we would get the navy boys to go on board, arrest the crew and impound the ship. In this case, however, the Americans are putting pressure on London to hold off. Uncle Sam wants this cargo delivered. Apparently, they are increasing their weapons build up for Vietnam. They need all the chrome they can lay their hands on. There's a world shortage. London is keen to keep on side with Uncle Sam. So officially we take no action." Sir Jeremy turns his eye balls up to the ceiling looking disappointed.

"Perhaps London gets something back in return from the Yanks but I have no information about that."

"How about unofficially, Sir, do we take any action at all locally?" Adrian asks looking a little exasperated.

"Well you know jolly well I can only authorise official action Adrian. Here's the file. If you can come up with anything let me know." Sir Jeremy hands over a manila file headed "Aframe Shipping".

"Thank you Sir. I'll see what I can do." Adrian tucks the file in his attaché case.

"One more thing Adrian, again, relating to our American cousins. It seems that the FBI are concerned that The Bahamas and Bermuda may be used as jumping off points to get drugs into the USA. The FBI has linked up with Scotland Yard. They are planning raids in the near future at which time our local Bobbies will be advised. Have a look at the file! Bring yourself bang up to date. No doubt we will need to move fast to make sure everything is co-ordinated when they do decide to take action." Sir Jeremy then hands over a thick manila file headed "Operation Narcotics".

Back in his office Adrian reads through both files.

So much for the special relationship between the USA and us Brits, it all seems to be in favour of the Yanks. Damned if I like it.

The Aframe Shipping file has a copy of a report from the Lourenco Marques High Commissioners office giving names of two possible vessels of which only one "Ocean Star" had been up river where the ore was reported to have been loaded. There was a witness statement from a local named Ali. London had carried out a search at Lloyds Shipping. This revealed that the ship was registered in Panama to a local company. The ultimate owners of "Ocean Star" were not revealed. The Lloyds Shipping enquiry recorded that voyage insurance was covering a Bermudan company Aframe Shipping. Putting the file away Adrian made a note to check on the public ownership of Aframe Shipping at the Company records office.

The first thing Adrian read in the "Operation Narcotics" file was a memorandum from Scotland Yard advising that as Bermuda was a Crown Colony action on the Island could only be legally initiated by the British. However, the airport land had been leased to the Americans. This enabled FBI agents to act without British consent on the airport land. Both Scotland Yard and the FBI accepted the airport was a security risk due to passengers not being controlled after going through US Immigration.

Adrian knew there were plans to rebuild the commercial part of the airport. The stumbling block was who was to pay for the work. He had attended countless meetings and sent off report after report arguing why it was American responsibility to pay for the work on their land. The Yanks argued that the British Government and the airlines using the terminal should pay because it would benefit tourism and commerce.

The file had several other papers indicating various ways by which drugs could be smuggled on to the American mainland. The most likely methods were by boat or seaplane into remote coastal areas around Virginia and North Carolina. The regular weekly cruise ship sailings from New York by the Franconia and Arcadia were also mentioned. These ships could easily conceal drugs which might be off loaded just outside territorial waters for small boats to collect.

The conclusion of the FBI report was that drug trafficking was being organised on a global scale by criminal gangs who were becoming increasingly sophisticated and ruthless in the methods they employed.

Adrian has been so engrossed in his studies that he lost track of time. A blast of the Franconia's horn entering harbour brings him out of the intense concentration he has devoted to reading the files. Walking out for some air he smiles as he thinks he might get the Americans to stump up for the airport building costs using the drugs trafficking argument.

In the afternoon Adrian goes to Company records office. A very thin file is delivered to him that reveals that Aframe Shipping had been formed this year by the Bank of Pembroke. The signatories to the Act of Parliament creating the company were Henry Rucker witnessed by Wayne Luther. Nothing unusual about that thinks Adrian. He has met both Henry Rucker and Wayne Luther at Government House parties. He quite liked old man Rucker who was polite and courteous with an eye for business, very much an old school colonial type. Adrian had not been impressed by Wayne Luther on the two occasions they had met. A rather coarse, unsophisticated individual Adrian thought. Looking at the company officers Adrian gets rather a surprise to see the name of George Howden.

My tennis opponent, how is he involved? Another game of tennis would be an opportune time to quiz him about this.

The Flight

The taxi drops Sammy and Jasmine outside McKinley Airport's civilian building. They check in at the Pan Am desk.

"Miss Jasmine Rucker your return flight to New York is on time Ma'am. Just the one case to check in?" the check in clerk enquires.

"Did you pack the case yourself Ma'am?" Jasmine nods to the clerk.

"Thank you Ma'am. Here's the boarding pass. Please check in with US Immigration. Your flight leaves in forty minutes".

"Good day Ma'am may I see your passport please. Is your trip for business or pleasure?" the immigration officer queries.

"Business officer here's my contract letter from Astra Agency". Jasmine says handing over her letter.

"Thank you Ma'am I hope you have a nice flight and trip. Welcome to the United States of America." the immigration officer smiles handing Jasmine her passport with the visa insert. Jasmine walks back into the terminal building where Sammy is waiting.

"O K baby you all fixed to go? I'll be following on the next flight in twelve hours. I've just got to finish some business here. I'll see you in the apartment tonight. In the meanwhile here's a little something for you." Sammy gives Jasmine a kiss on her cheek and hands her an envelope.

"*Sammy dat's great.*" Jasmine giggles. Looking in the envelope she sees two one hundred dollar bills and two small packets containing white powder.

"*I took da one packet on da boat. I done jess like you say Sammy. Oh my gawd, Wayne's face, it was a real picture.*" Jasmine laughs out loud.

"Baby you gonna be a Hollywood star some day I can see it. So now Artie, from my agency, is gonna be at the airport to collect you. He asked for some rum. So you can give him this bag." Sammy hands Jasmine a local store carrier bag containing four sealed cardboard cartons marked "Island Rum."

"O K Sammy that's no problem. I'll see you tonight." Jasmine grins and saunters off to the departure door. Sammy watches as Jasmine walks across the tarmac. That's a real nice piece of ass I'm looking forward to getting to know he thinks.

Pick Up

Sammy hurries out of the airport and orders a taxi to drive to the Bank of Pembroke.

"Hi Leonora, any chance I can have a quick word with Wayne" Sammy asks smiling at Leonora who looks up in surprise.

"I thought yose and Jazza were in New York Sammy. Is Jazza OK?"

"Yea she's fine. She got the morning flight an I'm taking the evening flight. I got a colleague picking her up. No worries there. I just need five minutes with Wayne?"

"OK. He got no clients at de moment. Shall I fetcha him down. Or d'ya wanna go up to his office?" Leonora asks.

"Down here is fine. We'll take a walk in the grounds." Sammy says watching Leonora run up the stairs.

"Saammeee my boy how ya doin, hows the import agency doin my man" Wayne asks running up to Sammy both hands extended.

"Hi Wayne, yea business is real good. Now we've landed a contract to ship out your "Island Rum". That rum it's catching on. Can we take a walk outside?" Sammy asks guiding Wayne by the elbow towards the cedar double doors.

"Sure Sammy what's up?" Wayne cries trying hard to keep up with Sammy's fast walk.

"I want to hire your boat for the afternoon Wayne. No paperwork. Cash just between me an you. What do you say?" Sammy asks stopping outside to look Wayne directly in the face.

Minion or Master

"*Sammy Sammy the boats in da bank's name, iIt's gonna be real difficult with no paperwork.*" Wayne responds holding out his hands and closing his piggy eyelids into slits.

"I'll make it easy for you Wayne. Why don't you take the afternoon off? You charter da boat in your name! I'll pay the charter and give you the same amount in cash. That's a great deal." Sammy says. Seeing Wayne looking hesitant he continues.

"I heard from Jasmine what you got up to out at Carver Island. No worries Wayne your secret's safe with me and Jasmine. Don't want to foul up Mary Jayne with any of this do we now?" Sammy slaps Wayne on the back noting the worried look on his face.

"O K Sammy I'll do it. But the price is double. I'll sort out the papers I can't let Mary Jayne down. She'd make life real hard for me." Wayne responds grimacing from the slaps on his back.

"Good man I knew you'd see sense. Take me down to the quay and give me the keys" Sammy orders walking swiftly towards the end of the gardens.

Casting off from the quay at the bottom of the Rucker's garden Sammy negotiates "Pembroke Lady" through the Great Sound out past Ireland Island. Once through the coral reefs he pushes the engine throttles to full power. From his pocket he gets out a strip of paper which has his co-ordinates written down.

After one hour speeding at forty knots Sammy throttles down to half speed to study the radar screen where a faint bleep is registering. Sammy resets the compass bearing directly towards the object on the screen and sets up full power again.

After fifteen minutes with the engines screaming at full power ""Pembroke Lady's" thrusting bow slumps down into the water as Sammy throttles the engines back. Sammy has a transponder which is displaying a direction arrow. Cautiously he eases "Pembroke Lady" to follow the arrow. The transponder's bleep gets louder and louder as the speed boat follows the direction until the sound becomes continuous.

In the swell Sammy spies a large floating package wrapped in polythene sheets with a battery powered signal mechanism attached. Quickly Sammy pulls the package to the side with the aid of a gaffing pole strapped to the outriggers and hauls the package on board.

Returning at full speed to his Import Export warehouse situated at the far end of Hamilton Harbour Sammy secretly unloads the package.

Sammy returns "Pembroke Lady" just as the bank is closing for the day. At seven o clock he is in the airport checking in for the eight o clock flight to New York. After immigration he walks out of the terminal to a waiting taxi car. He collects a carrier bag from a man with tattooed arms. The carrier bag contains four cartons of "Island rum".

Chapter Five

Reilly

Monday Late May 1966

New York

As Jasmine enters the airport lounge she sees a middle aged, short, stocky man wearing a baseball cap, bomber jacket and jeans holding up a placard saying "Astra Agency—Jasmine Rucker". Jasmine walks over to the man.

"Hi are you from Sammy?" she enquires.

"That's right baby. I'm Artie. I see you got my rum. Let's go get a cab!" Artie takes the Island Rum carrier bag and leads Jasmine out of the airport. The taxi drops them off at a Manhattan apartment block. They take the elevator to the fourth floor. Artie opens the door to apartment twelve.

"OK baby here's the keys. There's food and drink in the fridge. Sammy wont be here 'til gone midnight. The rest of the day is yours. A cab will pick you up at nine sharp tomorrow for the shoot. Any questions honey?" Artie asks moving towards the door.

"No thanks Artie. I'll be fine. I'll clean up from the flight. Then maybe get some sleep. Will I see you tomorrow?" Jasmine asks her eyes wandering around the apartment taking in the luxury furnishings.

"Yea see ya tomorrow baby. Have a good day." Artie winks at her as he closes the door.

Jasmine is excited to be here at last. After inspecting the apartment she fixes herself a coffee and snack. She takes a bath then flops into bed and falls asleep. She wakes four hours later. There's no time to waste she thinks to her self. She dresses in a black cocktail dress. In the bathroom she takes half the powder from the packet Sammy gave her at the airport and puts it in two lines on the vanity table and snorts it up. Now I'm ready for anything she thinks as she goes down stairs and takes a yellow cab over to Times Square. So girl let's see what this big city's got to offer.

Artie meets Sammy at La Guardia airport in the evening and drives him to their warehouse at Pulaski Street Upper Bay Bayonne.

"What did you think of the broad?" Sammy asks looking at Artie as they sit around the office desk.

"*Yea good looker alright, my opinion, we still got work to do. If the broad is gonna be a winner for us. Did you get the package?*" Artie asks looking at his fingernails.

"It's safe and sound in the warehouse. We have to get the stuff in the "Island Rum" Franconia shipment scheduled for next month. It takes too long to ship everything via the airport. Today we've brought in eight bottles which is five pounds of pure stuff. To bring in the whole package would be another forty flights. Another load is due next month so we gotta carry volume. We got the contacts with the unions here so there shouldn't be any hitches this end." Sammy hands over his "Island Rum" carrier bag to Artie.

"I got the rum package the broad brought mixed this afternoon. It gives us street value of forty grand. Oh and by the way. We got a message from the boss saying the machinery has got to be loaded on a ship called "Ocean Star" due in this week. That needs to be fixed with the union as well." Artie says still inspecting his fingernails.

"OK leave it with me. You get this load mixed and on the street!" Sammy points at the carrier bag which contains four boxes. Each box should house a bottle of rum but has been replaced with a plastic bag containing pure cocaine.

"I'll make a call to the union guy. Then I'll head over to sixty eighth street. Make a start with the broad." Sammy grins at Artie who responds with a tired world weary look and heads into the gloomy warehouse area to start diluting the pure powder into another twenty five pound package for street consumption.

Sammy picks up the telephone and dials. The call is answered by a man with a heavy Brooklyn accent.

"Reilly"

"This is Sammy. Meet me at the usual place tomorrow at eleven on your own!" Sammy hangs up before Reilly can answer.

By the time Sammy reaches the apartment it is gone midnight. He fixes himself a drink and looks in the bedroom expecting to find Jasmine fast asleep. The bed is empty. Her suitcase is on the floor. In the bathroom he sees traces of powder on the vanity table.

"Ah Shit" Sammy shouts.

"Where have you got to you little minx?" Sammy decides to call it a night and sort out Jasmine in the morning. He gets into bed and within minutes is fast asleep. At five thirty Sammy is awakened by the sound of music coming from the kitchen. He stumbles out of bed and peers around the bedroom door to see Jasmine dancing to the music.

Martin Smith

"Where the fuck did you get to last night?" Sammy asks. Jasmine seems not to hear. Her dress lies discarded on the floor. In her flimsy petticoat and stocking feet she keeps on dancing. Getting angry Sammy races over and grabs Jasmine by the shoulders.

"You got a photo shoot this morning with Artie. You stupid bitch!" Sammy screams and stares into Jasmine's eyes. She has a floating appearance her pupils are tiny. Still gyrating to the music Jasmine presses her body against Sammy's bare thighs. He is dressed only in his boxer shorts. Sammy feels his blood rising.

"I'll teach you . . . you bitch!" Sammy roars and bundles her onto the bed. He tears off her petticoat and mounting her he presses his thickset hairy body against her. Now, fully aroused, no force on earth can stop Sammy from entering Jasmine. He pounds away thrusting deeply into her soft sensuous tissue. Jasmine moans and grips Sammy's back, her long red painted nails claw into his tensed body. This gets Sammy even more aroused. He increases the depth of his penetration. At last he feels his love juices flowing along his member.

"Take this" Sammy shrieks as he ejaculates a heavy load into the depths of Jasmine's womanhood. Sated Sammy rolls away.

Jasmine is starting to come off her high and creeps to the bathroom. As she applies balm to her abused body in a soothing bath she wonders whether getting involved with Sammy was such a great idea. On the other hand she really loves the feeling from the powder he gets for her. Maybe it's worth sticking around she thinks.

"OK here's the deal today." Sammy speaks serving coffee in the kitchen as if nothing had happened.

"At nine the cab takes you to the studio for the shoot. You better put good make up over those bruises on your shoulders! 'Cos it's a lingerie shoot today. Is that clear?" Sammy looks over at Jasmine who is drinking her coffee.

"*Yes Sammy. I'm sorry for going off but I got excited being here in New York an all. Can you give me some more stuff? I used up what you gave me last night?*" Jasmine pleads with Sammy pouting her lips.

"No deal baby. You got work today. Maybe you'll get some tonight. Thing is you gotta be nice if you want Sammy to give you the stuff. Understand?" Sammy gets up from the table and looks at Jasmine who nods in acceptance.

"*Now I gotta get dressed and out for a meeting. So I'll see ya tonight baby. Enjoy your shoot.*" Sammy backs away from the table and with a forced smile on his pock marked face he blatantly exposes himself in his stained boxer shorts before he enters the bathroom.

Tuesday morning Late May 1966

Union

Sammy's taxi drops him off just before eleven o' clock at a cafe on Pulaski Street near the connection to the New Jersey Turnpike. Sammy orders a coffee and sandwich and sits down at the rear of the cafe with his back to the wall. From this position he can see who is coming and going. Sammy is just about to take a mouth full of coffee when a bull of a man well over six foot tall and weighing two hundred and fifty pounds enters the cafe. Sammy acknowledges Reilly with the briefest of nods. Reilly is wearing a blue stevedores jacket he orders a coffee and strolls over to sit opposite Sammy.

"So what's up Sammy?" Reilly questions pouring sugar and cream into his coffee mug.

"We need some co-operation in the next few weeks. Are you still in control of the situation?" Sammy asks. Looking at Reilly's hard nosed face, then, down at the huge rough hands Sammy doesn't doubt that Reilly is very much in control. Reilly, through his amazing strength and swift ruthless actions is in control of the Brooklyn docks unions. There is not a single dock worker who will refuse the orders given by Sean Reilly. If a man fails to comply with orders from Reilly's minions that man never works in Brooklyn again. Drivers, crane workers, stevedores, harbour police and customs men all do Reilly's bidding.

"If the price is right I'm in control Sammy. Give it to me!" Reilly Stares and takes a sip of his coffee.

"Sure thing Sean, we got two crates with agriculture machine parts going out on a ship called the "Ocean Star" later this week. I got copies of the loading papers for you. We need the load to get on board with no inspections. The usual fee is with the papers. Is that OK?" Sammy asks rather tentatively.

"What dock is she coming into?" Reilly asks.

"*Yea its Red Hook. She's discharging iron ore then the crates gotta be loaded into the hold. Then she'll be taking grain which will cover the crates for the voyage*". Sammy responds.

"That we can handle, is there something else Sammy? You look uncomfortable. What you really carrying in those crates?" Reilly whispers looking straight down at Sammy's hands which are fidgeting with his coffee cup.

Minion or Master

"Ask no questions and I'll tell you no lies Sean." Sammy responds looking a little sheepish.

"There's a new deal coming up. We got stuff coming off the cruise ships from Bermuda in a couple of week's time. We need to get the goods out into a secure location with no inspection." Sammy advises looking at Reilly expectantly.

"What sort of goods we talking about Sammy? I need to know." Reilly barks.

"OK, OK no problem. We got a big shipment of rum coming in. We need to isolate 25 boxes from the main cargo. The boxes we need will have a special label and will be on top of the pile." Sammy advises Reilly.

"Well Sammy I don't know about this. First off the cruise ships come into Manhattan, not Brooklyn. That means I gotta give out favours to the Manhattan boys Comprenez?" Reilly looks at Sammy who is nodding thoughtfully.

"Then there's the booze element. You know how hard the customs are on liquor Sammy. That's gonna mean more big favours." Reilly sighs and places his huge calloused fists on the table.

"I'm gonna have to get back to you when I've checked out a few things. In the meantime I need a favour from you on account of this new deal Sammy."

"What kinda favour are you talking about?" Sammy enquires.

"I need one of your class broads to do a trick on a guy that's giving us a little grief. The guy is with the Harbour Authorities. He thinks he can boss us about. I need some photos for back up, the sooner the better. You know the kinda thing." Reilly smiles and then gives Sammy a hard stare.

Martin Smith

"OK, give me the details of this guy and I'll get on to it. In the meantime I'll wait to hear from you on the cruise ships." Sammy gets up from the table and walks out leaving his newspaper on the seat. After a few minutes Reilly drains his coffee mug and walks out with the old newspaper folded to conceal the loading papers and five thousand dollars in used notes.

Chapter Six
Model Work

Tuesday Late May 1966

Breaking In

Jasmine is applying make up to her face in the marble finished bathroom in Sammy's luxury apartment. Sammy has gone. Looking in the mirror she wonders if she is getting in a little deep with Sammy and New York. She had a great time last night at bars and clubs enjoying the music and dancing. Yes, she had taken some more dope and she had put off quite a few handsome guys. Then, when she got back, Sammy had been so hard with her. I'm not a virgin. He knows that. There was no need for him to be so rough with me, she decides, as she feels her bruised inner thighs.

It would be nice to have another fix before I leave. Sammy was mean not giving me anything. He'd better come up with something tonight.

The taxi promised by Artie arrives on time. It leaves Manhattan crossing over the Hudson River into New Jersey picking up the turnpike. Jasmine is let out at a modern warehouse building on Pulaski Street. She notices the sign "SS Enterprises Inc".

Inside the building Jasmine waits at a reception area consisting of a two seated mock leather settee and a table with some tacky magazines. Not having a fix to be going on with she lights up one of her black cheroots and puffs away nervously.

"*How ya doing baby*" Artie greets Jasmine.

"Come on through to the studio!" Artie leads Jasmine through a side door then up a flight of stairs onto a landing and through a double door with a name plate "Astra Agency-Glamour models." They go into a room with no windows. The walls are painted white. Jasmine sees several cameras and lights set up on tripods.

"O K lets take a look at you!" Artie says moving in close to Jasmine's face.

"Wow did you have a rough night? You don't look like you got much sleep. Guess you and Sammy had some fun Huh?" Artie looks at the film equipment and lets out a dirty guffaw.

"So, let's get to work baby. Go through the back and you'll find a bathroom. Get yourself dolled up with red lipstick, plenty of mascara around those eyes and put these on!" Artie throws Jasmine a set of lacy black lingerie and stockings.

After a few hours of filming and numerous changes of clothes Artie shouts out from behind the camera

"OK baby let's take a lunch break. There's a cafe over the road, just under the fly over, get yourself a sandwich! After lunch we got a few more models with you."

"What happens to all these photos? Where will they go, Artie?" Jasmine wants to know.

"It's like this baby. I choose the best ones and they go in our brochure. Then, if a client likes the look of you, you get to meet them. You make money. We make money. The client is happy. It's the way of the world. I got chicks just like you making thirty, forty grand a year tax free.

Minion or Master

Hey that's great money. You might make five grand in an office and for that you'd have to be nice to some schmuck working there. Some of our clients they are in television, films and theatre. You got a chance to make it big. All you gotta do is look good and be nice to them." Artie walks out of the studio.

As Jasmine gets dressed she recalls that Sammy said the same thing about being nice. Forty thousand dollars that would buy a real nice place in Bermuda or perhaps I'll make it big here she dreams.

On her way out she looks through a window on the landing. She sees a large warehouse floor area with a fork lift truck. The truck is stacking a wooden crate against the wall close to the window. The crate is marked in big bold black lettering:

"CONTENTS:AGRICULTURE MACHINE PARTS
DESTINATION: TORRESHIPPES,
        LOURENCO MARQUES,
        MOZAMBIQUE
VESSEL: "Ocean Star"
        RED HOOK TERMINAL
        BROOKLYN NY".

Without taking any great notice Jasmine walks downstairs to the cafe. After lunch Artie brings in another model girl and a man.

"So Jasmine, meet Dolores and Randy, these guys have worked in the agency for some years. They can fill you in on the work. First we need a few shots for the brochure. Dolores get in close on Jasmine look like your gonna eat her up. Put your hands around her waist. Randy stand behind Dolores right in close to her ass, Jasmine bring

Martin Smith

your face in towards Randy's lips. Look in his eyes and pucker those lips. *Yea . . . Nice . . . real nice.*" Artie directs gesticulating with his arms and staring into his camera lens.

The three work up various poses under Artie's direction until three thirty in the afternoon when they are released with Artie proclaiming that they did some great shots which he will print up. As the two girls get changed in the bathroom Jasmine asks Dolores

"So what's the work like? Do you make much money?"

"Honey let me tell you something, the moneys not bad if you are nice to the clients. Do what they want. You know what I mean. Me I need the dough. My kid she's eleven and wants to go to College. She's a clever kid. S o I do what the clients ask. I sometimes get presents. Artie gives me fifty per cent of the cash. I still make six hundred bucks a week and get two nights off with my girl. It could be worse. But you watch yourself with Sammy and Artie. Those guys can be real mean. Keep them sweet or get the hell out before it's too late." Dolores implores Jasmine.

"What about Randy? Does he go with clients as well? He was getting a bit aroused with us didn't you think?"

"Randy he's a stud. Sometimes clients want to watch and Randy does the business. He'll do whatever Sammy asks him to do. Well I gotta run to pick my kid up. I have a client over in Manhattan at eight tonight. See you around Jasmine." Dolores waves her hand in sympathy as she leaves the bathroom.

Back at the apartment at East sixty eighth street Sammy is waiting for Jasmine.

"So was it OK at the studio?" Sammy asks pouring himself a drink.

"Artie said the photos should be good and I met Dolores and Randy this afternoon." Jasmine says in a fairly neutral tone of voice.

"That's good baby. After supper Randy is coming over here. He's gonna teach you what you need to know. You do what he says and you'll get another of these." Sammy throws her an envelope containing one hundred dollars and one fix.

Tuesday night Late May 1966

Randy with Jasmine

Sammy leaves as soon as Randy arrives saying he has business with Artie. Jasmine now has the chance to study Randy in greater detail. In the studio this afternoon she was pre-occupied, heeding Artie's instructions, so she didn't take a lot of notice of Randy's looks. Aged twenty nine Randy is 5 foot nine inches tall, she guesses he weighs over twelve stone with no sign of fat around his middle area. He has thick black hair and is wearing tight designer jeans over cowboy boots. The open necked white silk shirt shows off his tan. A gold medallion glistens in his black chest hairs. Not bad, if you like the Italian stud type of guy, Jasmine decides.

"So Jasmine how did you think the day went at the studio?" Randy gives her a warm smile as he sits down on the leather settee and lights a cigarette.

"I guess it was interesting. Artie and Dolores gave me quite a bit of information. They both said I should be nice to clients. What does that mean? Can you tell me Randy?" Jasmine asks as she sits down on the settee and lights up one of her black cheroots.

"That's what I'm here to go over with you baby. I will act like a client with you. First we go to dinner, then, maybe, a night club or casino. After that you might go with a client to his hotel or to private rooms. You'll be told with each client whether it's just dinner or more. Tonight, it's all the way baby. You'r gonna learn what the clients like and how to look after yourself." Randy explains as he blows smoke rings up to the ceiling and grins at Jasmine.

"So let me get this straight Randy. We are going out tonight. Then we have sex. Are you going to be rough and violent? Sammy was real rough with me and I didn't like it." Jasmine looks angry as she crosses her legs and flicks ash from her cheroot into the silver ash tray on the coffee table in front of her.

"Okay baby. Here's the bottom line. Most clients will want sex. That's where the big money is. Clients ain't gonna pay big bucks just to go out to dinner. They are looking for the full works. You gotta give em what they want. Most of the broads enjoy it and make good money. The girls stay on average two, maybe, three years. Some make it big and move on. Artie and Sammy they need at least a year from each broad to make it worth their while. Is there a problem?" Randy queries in a voice that doesn't sound too concerned.

"So what if I want to leave early? Sammy didn't say there was any minimum period?" Jasmine remarks getting agitated.

"You should get used to being here baby. Some girls I know, real cuties just like you, they've tried to leave and it turned out real bad for them. One girl, a Mexican, Juanita, she ended up in jail for three years. The word is Sammy got one of his cop contacts to raid her apartment. They found a shed load of dope. Another broad she got hit by a car on Pulaski Street. Then we heard one girl was tricking Artie out of money. Her face was cut up so bad she'll never work again. You best stick around. Keep everyone sweet baby starting with me tonight." Randy advises as he places one hand on Jasmine's breast.

Through out the last two days since arriving in New York Jasmine has been going over her options, should she tough it out and see if she could make it as a model over here? Can she "be nice" to everyone then get out later without being hurt? Would she end up like one of the girls Randy had mentioned? She didn't know what to think. She knew when she took the dope nothing seemed to be the same. She could float through situations feeling she was in control. She had stuff for tonight. Randy was not bad looking and had, at least, been honest with her. He didn't seem any worse than some of the guys she knew from the wrong side of the tracks in Bermuda. Perhaps, as Artie said, she might meet some rich guy who would sweep her off her feet. She was starting to realize that the longer she stayed the more difficult it would be to get out. Should she cut her losses and get out or take a risk? So much has happened since Wayne introduced her to Sammy at the Island Rum launch party just over a month ago. She had flirted a little with Sammy to get Wayne off her back. Later, Sammy had taken her out to dinner. He had given her a little sample just to try he said. The intense feeling as the chemicals entered her blood stream and flowed into the brain was something she had never experienced before. Sammy talked about New York and the opportunities there for a good looking girl. He made it easy; he swept her off her feet.

Martin Smith

"O K Randy show me what New York's got to offer this girl. Give it your best shot." Jasmine declares deciding that at least for tonight she is going to take a chance that lady luck will be there for her.

Chapter Seven
First Kiss

Tuesday morning Late May 1966

Adrian's Call

George is reviewing the voyage accounts for Aframe Shipping. It is over three weeks since the account was opened at the Bank of Pembroke. George has co-ordinated "Ocean Star"'s voyage to Lourenco Marques. Now the vessel is in bound for New York with its cargo specified as iron ore. At Brooklyn Docks, New York she will collect another load of grain for Africa.

As George is thinking how everything is going so well with the project the phone on his desk rings.

"Hello! George Howden speaking, can I be of help?" George asks.

"Ah George, hello again, it's Adrian from Government House here. I was wondering if we could finish our tennis game. Left it a bit late getting in touch I know. Thing is I've been inundated. So awfully sorry, I know its short notice but how about tomorrow evening can you make it old chap? It would be splendid to see you again. What do you say?"

"Hello Adrian thanks for the call. Good to hear from you. I am free tomorrow. I was planning to work on a bit. I could do with a game. It will make a nice break from the office, how about six?" As George thumbs through his diary he is reminded that tonight he is going to Leonora's house to play the piano. Charlie will be playing guitar and Leonora will sing.

"That's great. Perhaps we can have supper at Government House after? The least I can do for being so long in getting back to you. Do say yes!" Adrian pleads.

"Fine supper it is. See you at the stadium." Replacing the receiver George wonders why Adrian is so keen to play tomorrow. Why not at the week end? No accounting for others he thinks as he packs away his records. He wants to get home for a shower and change before going over to see Charlie and Leonora.

Tuesday evening Late May 1966

Charlie's House

Charlie's house is hidden away in a small cul de sac about 10 miles out of Hamilton. George arrives promptly at seven. Charlie leads George through the house to a large veranda overlooking the sea.

"This veranda is where we do most of our entertaining." Charlie points for George to take a seat at the large table which will seat ten comfortably.

"Used to have a whole lot of people come regular when my dear wife was here, sadly the Lord called her away four years back. Not a day goes by when I don't miss my Emilia." Charlie sighs showing George a picture of Emilia.

"Oh I can see where Leonora and Jasmine get their good looks from Charlie. She is quite a stunner. I am so sorry for your loss." George smiles sympathetically and hands the picture back.

"You never get over the loss George. But I have Lenny home and she is a wonderful daughter to me. She'll be down here in a tick. Then we'll have supper before playing. I'm looking forward to hearing you play." Charlie points to an upright piano in the corner, looking a little neglected. George gets up and walks over to the instrument. He plays a few chords with casual aplomb.

"I can see you've got nifty fingers. There's some music in the box under the seat. Take a look see if there's anything you like. I'll just go and check on our chicken stew and give Lenny a shout." Charlie walks into the house whilst George looks over the music sheets. He selects some calypso music and jazz.

"*So how's Misteer Howteen tonight?*" Leonora enquires.

"*Sorreee to keep you waitin I had to stay late at de bank tonight so I only jess got home.*"

"If we are going to spend the evening playing music and eating together, please call me George and I'll call you Leonora, how's that?" George smiles at Leonora and extends his hand in a handshake.

"*My frens dey call me Lenny, what do your frens call you?*" Leonora ignores the offered hand and instead gives George a peck on his cheek. George blushes.

"Generally it's George. In school I was called Howdy from my surname." George laughs and grins at Leonora.

"*Well dats settled when yous here I gonna call you Howdy. Howdy . . . hmmm dats a real nice name an easy for me to remember. Pa did you hear? We's to call George, Howdy, from now on.*" Leonora grins from ear to ear as she looks at George then at Charlie who calls them to supper.

After supper the three get around to making music. In no time, they agree to try some of the jazz music George selected. If anything, George thinks Leonora's voice is even better than when she sang at the Harbour Club. That's because she is relaxed in her own home he thinks.

"I must say Charlie, Lenny has the most fantastic voice. It's soulful and rich. As good as any professional female jazz singer I've ever heard. She should take it further you know."

"I know she's got talent. But I am real afraid. See, Howdy, I don't want her getting into bother over there in New York like our Jazzy." Charlie looks at his daughter then gives her a protective hug.

"Oh! I'm sorry to hear that. The last time I saw you all was at the Harbour Club. Jasmine was excited about her trip to New York with er Sammy wasn't it?"

"Dat Sammy he's takin Jazzy away from us. She's afraid to speak to us case she upsets Sammy. I don like it at all." George detects anger in Leonora's voice. He thinks back to the boat trip out to Carver Island with Wayne and how strange Jasmine had acted and that look in her eyes.

"Did you notice any changes in her before she went?" he enquires looking directly at Charlie.

"She seemed like more up and down. One day she is bright and cheerful then a few days later she'd be moody and sulky. I jess put it down to her being impatient to get her model work going. Why do you ask Howdy? Do you know something? May be about Sammy?" Charlie asks looking puzzled.

"Oh no it's nothing, I only met Sammy with Jasmine the once. I say look at the time it's past eleven. I must go. It's been a fabulous evening I've had so much pleasure with you two tonight." George gives Charlie a hug.

"Our pleasure Howdy, let's do it again, how about next week?" Charlie asks smiling at George and Leonora.

"*Oh that's great Pa. I love that jazz especially now you and Howdy are playing so well. Say yes Howdy!*" Leonora implores.

"Lenny how could I possibly refuse such a charming request. Of course I will be delighted to come." George grins and gives Leonora a peck on the cheek.

"I'll see Howdy out!" Leonora says to Charlie.

Outside the moon is reflecting silver patches onto the Atlantic Ocean. A faint noise comes from the waves with a louder clicking sound from the nearby cicadas calling in the trees.

"*Thanks for comin Howdy. You don know how much it meant to Pa playin tonight. It's a long time since I seen him laugh like dat.*" Leonora stares straight into George's eyes. George stares back and thinks how exquisite Leonora looks, an innocent raving beauty with the potential voice of a jazz diva. As he dreams away Leonora moves her face in closer. Their lips meet and touch. George feels the warmth of Leonora's body brushing against his thigh. Their lips press together tenderly as they kiss goodnight.

"I hope that won't be the last of those." George says taking Leonora's hand in his.

"*Now Howdy I'm sure you can wait 'til next week. See what comes along. Good night now.*"

Tuesday night Late May 1966

Discovery

George's heart is racing as he rides home. The good night kiss from Lenny makes him feel tingly. Is he in love or is it infatuation? Only time will tell he thinks to himself.

Jasmine seems to be in trouble. Could that white powder he had spotted on the deck of "Pembroke Lady" be part of the problem? How does Sammy fit in? George wants answers but isn't sure how to get them. He recalls Sammy saying he has a warehouse nearby. George decides to take a look on his way home.

Just as his scooter is coming into the harbour area he spies a sign "SS Import Export" with the slogan underneath "Supplies to the Island from the mainland-Our speciality." This must be the warehouse George decides. He parks his scooter under a tree and walks along a moonlit lane to a large single storey building situated alongside the harbour jetty. From the shadows two men emerge carrying a large package. They bundle the package through a side door at the rear of the building. George, more than curious, creeps up to the edge of the building. He notices that all the windows are boarded and shuttered. There is an iron ladder fixed to the wall which leads to the roof. He starts to climb the ladder. Half way George feels the ladder moving in its rusty stanchions. The air is still. There is silence all around. Any noise will easily be heard by the men in the building. Beads of sweat come onto George's brow as he considers whether to risk carrying on. A US Air Force helicopter flies over the harbour. George takes advantage of the noise and swiftly climbs onto the roof.

Cautiously he moves towards a faint yellowish light coming from a skylight window in the centre of the roof. Peering through the dust grimed glass George can see the package the men carried in, now opened, set out on a large bench. All around the bench are cardboard cartons

Minion or Master

stamped Island Rum. One man, wearing sun glasses, is filling plastic bags with white powder which he is extracting from the opened package. Then the other man comes into George's view at the end of the bench. His arms are tattooed. He picks up the plastic bags and stuffs them into Island Rum cartons. Why is this going on here at midnight George wonders.

Before he is able to think it through a car comes into the lane and stops outside the warehouse. George decides to make his escape. When he reaches the ladder he hears voices from inside the building. He rushes down the ladder whilst the men are talking. He reaches the bottom rung and moves quietly away. He notices the parked car number plate is 2650.

Chapter Eight

Meetings

Wednesday Late May 1966

Costas meets Kato

As the pilot comes aboard "Ocean Star" to take command for the last stage of her voyage from Mozambique he hands Captain Kato a sealed letter. Opening the letter Kato reads a note:

My Dear Kato

Please join me for dinner tonight. My car will collect you at seven thirty.

Costas Tinopolis.

What does the boss want? Kato contemplates if he has done anything wrong. It's more likely to be about the funny business with Jans Smutt and the ore loading, he concludes it must be good news or else there would be no dinner invite. Costas was not known for throwing his money about even for senior employees like Kato.

Kato goes over the program for the rest of the week in his head. Today is Wednesday by Saturday we should have discharged our cargo and be ready to take on grain.

Minion or Master

Kato is taken to the fiftieth floor of the Park Inn Hotel where Costas Tinopolis has a suite.

"Agios my old friend how was your voyage? Welcome to New York. I have taken the liberty of ordering a buffet. Please help yourself to food and drink. How long since we last met? Can you remember Agios?" Costas slaps Kato on the back as he takes him over to the buffet.

"It must be five or six years now Sir. There was the problem with the ship, Pacific Venturer, chartered by Hassan Import. We were in the Indian Ocean. Pirates took the ship, left us for dead on the high seas. We got picked up by a passing fishing boat. I always wonder how lucky we were to be picked up so quickly. It was strange that the fishing boat's radio couldn't get a signal and we had to wait two weeks before we could get to land in Saudi Arabia." Kato reminisces.

"Ah yes indeed so very lucky. Of course the ship was never found. We were well reimbursed by the insurance I recall. I was so glad you all made it safely. Now of course you are one of the senior captains. So many experiences eh Agios?" Costas muses remembering well how he and Jamil El Hassan had staged a great coup. Jamil got paid for the cargo which his pirates sold on the black market. The ship had been disguised in Mumbai by one of Jamil's company's and was still earning good money in the China Seas for both of them. Those were the days he dreams.

After the meal Costas ushers Kato over to some comfortable chairs near the window where they can see the New York skyline.

"So now Agios I have been checking up. You are forty seven. You have been with the Tinopolis Group for sixteen years. You have a fine record with us. One of my most respected and trusted officers. It is why you have command of "Ocean Star"." Costas lights a Havana cigar.

"The "Ocean Star" is a fine vessel." Kato replies waiting for Costas to get to the point.

"You have done fine work in Lourenco Marques and with a package for our agent in St Helena. Have you discussed these things with any one? You know how much I value discretion Agios?" Costas murmurs turning to look directly at Kato and blowing out a stream of cigar smoke.

"No Sir certainly not, the only person is Smutt in Lourenco Marques Sir." Kato splutters through a cloud of smoke.

"Good, good it is very important that the next voyage runs to plan. I have arranged for two crates to be loaded here. The crates must be covered over with your grain cargo. It is essential that only you know about this Captain. The crates will not be in your manifest. Smutt will take charge when you reach Lourenco Marques. You will be well rewarded for this service and your absolute discretion. What do you say?" Costas looks intently at Kato.

"This is a surprise to me Sir. What is in the crates? I should know."

"My dear Agios it is OK. The crates contain agricultural machinery. They are for the hard pressed white farmers in Rhodesia. Smutt will get the crates to South Africa and then it will be easy to get them into Rhodesia. All you are doing is helping people to feed themselves. After all you have done a similar thing on this last voyage have you not?" Costas says with a tone of malevolence in his voice.

"You know that you have carried chrome ore from Rhodesia against the United Nations trade embargo. The stuff is sitting in your hold right now. All it takes is one call and your career will be over and you could end up in jail in the USA for a long time." Costas continues in a soft menacing voice.

"All Smutt told me was that it was special ore. I assumed it was a higher grade iron when we moved upstream to load it." Kato says with concern in his voice.

"Well now you know otherwise Captain" Costas responds firmly.

"But I had no idea about this Sir. Would you see me go to jail after all my years of service?" Kato pleads looking hurt at Costas.

"Of course not Agios, however, you must realise your predicament as master of the vessel. I will make it easy for you. You complete the voyage to Lourenco Marques with the crates. After that I will retire you making up your pension service to twenty years and you will get a bonus of ten thousand dollars cash. What do you say Agios? Is this not a good offer?" Costas purrs in his most silky voice and puts his arm around Kato's shoulder.

"Sir, I too am a Greek. I think a good offer will be for you to give me ten thousand dollars now and another ten thousand in Lourenco Marques plus my full pension to be twenty five years. What do you think?" Kato says in a firm voice.

"Now that's what I like. It's trade. We Greeks are born for it. I will give you five thousand dollars now and seven thousand five hundred at the end of the voyage. Your pension years will be made up to twenty two. That is as far as I will go Captain." Costas booms enjoying the cut and thrust of negotiations.

"If you make that call the ship will be impounded, maybe for several years if a trial takes place. I don't think you will like that Sir. How about seven thousand five hundred dollars now and again in Lourenco Marques and my pension is twenty three years?" Kato calls out triumphantly believing he has trumped his boss. As Kato awaits his bosses answer he remembers that he still has over a thousand dollars from Smutt, which, after this development he thinks he will keep.

"OK Captain it's a deal. I'll get you the money. Wait here!" Costas walks over to the safe and fidgets with the combination. Kato watches and thinks that it is unlikely his boss will honour the pension or the Lourenco Marques cash promise unless he can get some more leverage.

"Here you are Captain, your cash. I wish you a good voyage next week."

"Thank you Sir, nice doing business with you." Kato pockets the cash and walks out of the suite.

Wednesday evening Late May 1966

Tennis and Supper

At the tennis stadium George feels Adrian is somewhat pensive as they change. However, out on court Adrian proves to be more than a worthy opponent. It seems as if Adrian is coaxing him along, allowing him to keep in the game. Then, when a crucial point comes, Adrian wins with consummate ease. As the match progresses Adrian is becoming more playful with George. Adrian keeps rally after rally going making George run all over the court chasing balls only for Adrian, eventually, to administer the coup de grace with a well timed shot. The sun is shining powerfully making the evening temperature over seventy degrees. After two hours of play George is feeling the pace

Minion or Master

and the heat. He hasn't been worked so hard on a tennis court for a long time. Sweat is pouring from his head then running down his neck then soaking into his shirt. His hands are greasy as the sweat reacts with his racquet handle. After another long rally which leaves George breathless the players walk over to sit on a bench in the shade.

"I think you have done for me tonight Adrian. You are playing great tennis." George gasps between taking great gulps from his water bottle.

"Thanks old chap. Sometimes Lady Luck smiles on me. Perhaps this is one of those evenings. How do you feel about finishing now and coming up to Government House for some supper?" Adrian enquires giving George an inquisitive look.

"Yes I think I'm ready to concede this match to you." George admits. Adrian looks as though he could carry on playing for hours more.

Adrian takes George into a small private room in Government House where they eat Maryland chicken with salad washed down with a few bottles of Heineken lager.

"Ah I needed that. Thanks Adrian. Where did you learn to play tennis so well?"

"At school we had a very good teacher. He was a professional player before retiring and coming to Malvern. I was lucky enough to gain a blue for tennis and hockey at Oxford. I haven't played serious tennis for quite a while but I felt the old technique coming back tonight. Hope I didn't give you too much of a run around?" Before George can answer Adrian carries on.

"Actually, old chap there's something I want to have a wee chat to you about. It's rather embarrassing but we have had some information passed to us about a ship called "Ocean Star". On checking records we find that George Howden is the director of the company that is chartering her. Could that possibly be you" Adrian looks directly at George who appears to be having difficulty taking in exactly what Adrian has said.

"It is a simple enough question. What's your answer" Adrian keeps up the pressure on George just as he did on the tennis court.

"Well yes, I am a Director of Aframe Shipping, and the company is chartering "Ocean Star". I look after the records and accounts. What on earth is this all about Adrian?" George asks looking very concerned. George is now feeling ill at ease and uncomfortable. Not only has Adrian smashed me at tennis tonight now he's querying my work. He must have planned this. The tennis match was just pretence to get me here.

"I am hoping you might be able to tell me why you, a United Kingdom citizen, are in charge of a company that is chartering a ship which is carrying goods in flagrant breach of United Nations Security Council resolutions 216 and 217. We have information, from a reliable source, that "Ocean Star" is loaded with chrome ore from Rhodesia". Adrian explains patiently and with some sympathy in his voice. He likes George and his actions, so far, indicate that the accusations have taken him completely by surprise.

George is trying hard to maintain his composure.

"Well I can tell you that the ship hasn't been to Rhodesia she sailed from Mozambique and her manifest states she is carrying iron ore. That is what all my papers in the office specify." George explains wondering desperately where this is going to lead. With the adrenalin

Minion or Master

surge from the shock of Adrian's accusation easing, George's usual cool, calculating brain gradually comes back into play.

"What evidence do you have to back this up Adrian?" George demands looking reproachfully at his tennis opponent now turned accuser.

"We have a witness statement from a resident in Lourenco Marques who saw the ore being loaded secretly at night. The witness took a sample of the ore and gave it to our people. Pretty much cut and dried. Think very carefully. If this goes to trial you will be branded as a racist international criminal. You will get a lengthy jail sentence. Your life will be in ruins. Are you sure your telling me everything you know about this?" Adrian demands his voice getting a little less controlled as the tension in the room mounts.

"Yes of course I am telling you the truth. The papers from the ship's owners and the agents will confirm what I am telling you. If you know so much why hasn't the ship been stopped by the navy or someone?" George asks in a slightly more aggressive tone and is surprised to see a faint reaction from Adrian who ignores this question.

"I need to know your contacts. Who are the owners? Let me see your paperwork. If you are innocent then someone is using you. Are you happy about that?" Adrian responds rapidly taking another line of questioning. The last thing he wishes to give away is how impotent he and the government are to take any action, London having bowed to pressure from the Americans.

"I must say you have delivered a bombshell accusation. You must believe I had no idea about this chrome ore. I need some time to investigate. Will you consider meeting again in say seven days? I hope I can find out some more by then. What do you say?" George looks at Adrian who is toying with the fork on his empty plate.

"I accept if you are innocent, as you say that this news has come as a surprise, possibly a shock, to you. I am prepared to give you seven days to report back. Between you and me I am under pressure from my boss over the drugs problem. Putting you on the shelf for a week will suit me. However, don't think this is the end George. I will want some hard facts next time we meet. Are you clear about that old chap?" Adrian gives George a thin smile and a reproachful look.

"Yes understood. I didn't realise there was a drugs problem here. There's been nothing on the news about it." George responds to Adrian wondering if he has stumbled on something at Sammy's warehouse.

"It is to do with our American cousins. Being so close to their mainland we sometimes get lumbered with their problems. Something to do with the special relationship we have with them." Adrian confides speaking with a slightly sarcastic tone as he leads George out of the building.

Chapter Nine

George Decides

Thursday Late May 1966

Going to the Bank

George spent a sleepless night tossing and turning going over the events of the last few days. He was not prepared for last night's meeting with Adrian. He knows his life is not yet in ruins but he is in trouble. He realises for the first time in his life he is being compelled to look at the real world, a world where not everyone is honest. He has led a sheltered life. He has trusted everyone and been naive. Now he must face facts and act. He must take the first painful steps on his road to maturity. Adrian's message has been the catalyst. For George this is his "Damascus road."

George now realises Costas has used him. Who else? Is Wayne Luther involved? He isn't sure. What about Jasmine and Sammy? Could they be drug dealers? Now he worries that this might ruin his budding friendship with Lenny. Lenny works with Wayne at the bank. Are they working together? Who can he trust? In less than a day his business and social relationships are in turmoil.

George feels some affinity with Adrian despite the way Adrian questioned him. I want him as an ally rather than an enemy George decides. Now, he has seven days to get answers. The clock is ticking.

The first thing George sees in the office is a cheque from the United Nations for the grain shipment. He decides to bank this cheque and settle the security payment with Wayne.

In the bank grounds a car is parked discreetly at the side of the building, a white Austin Cambridge registration 2650. George peers through its windows. There is nothing to see on its seats or any clue from the windscreen as to the owner.

After banking the cheque George goes to reception desk to arrange to see Wayne Luther.

"*Hello der Howdy nice to see you. Are you O K? You don't look right.*" Leonora gives George a concerned look.

"Lenny it really is lovely to see you. I'm not ill just got a few things on my mind. How are you and Charlie? I'm looking forward to coming over next week." George smiles his best at Leonora.

"*It will be great to see you again. Pa can't wait. It will take his mind off Jazzy. We done heard notin since she left on Monday. Is it Wayne you want?*" Leonora asks putting on her business voice.

"Yes, but also, I wondered if you are free lunch time. We can have a sandwich in the park. There are a few things I want to check with you about next week?" George blurts out, surprising himself by his boldness.

"*Wayne he not back until this afternoon. So if you like we can meet for lunch, then after you can see Wayne. I'll see you in Par la Ville at one. OK Howdy?*" Leonora smiles at the thought of seeing George on her own.

"By the way Lenny, do you know who the white car outside belongs to? It's the sort I'd like to buy. You know

Minion or Master

how difficult it is to get a car here on the Island?" George enquires feeling a little more confident in him self.

"*Yea dats Wayne's car, he left it here 'cos him and Mister Rucker have gone to a beeg meetin this mornin.*" Leonora replies.

At lunchtime George strolls into Par la Ville Park and sits on a bench under a large cedar tree. Deep in thought he is pondering why Wayne's car was at Sammy's warehouse when Leonora joins him on the bench.

"I'm sorry to hear Jasmine hasn't been in contact yet. Do you know where she is staying?" George asks as he brushes away some crumbs off his Bermuda shorts.

"*She left a note. It's somewhere in Central New York. Why Howdy? Do you wanna go see her?*" Lenny asks in a reproachful voice.

"Something's come up with business. I might have to go out this week end. If I do I could look her up for you and Charlie. Maybe put your minds at ease?"

"*Dat would be real kind Howdy. Not like dat Sammy he never even went out wiv Jazzy. She flew out Monday mornin on her own. I know 'cos Sammy was here dat mornin said he was flyin out in the evening. Den he was all over Wayne in the grounds. Dey went off down to the jetty. Sammy he done come back just as I was finishin work. He was in such a hurry dat he never saw me wavin 'cos I wanted to give him a message to take to Jazzy.*" Leonora says, her voice taking on a bitter tone.

"That is interesting Lenny. So how did Jazzy meet Sammy in the first place?" George asks. He is also wondering now about the relationship of Sammy and Wayne.

"That was Wayne. He took Jazzy to the Island Rum party last month. He introduced her to Sammy. Wayne and Sammy are both involved in the company. Wayne has fancied Jazzy for some time but Jazzy doesn't really like Wayne. Besides he is married to Mary Jayne. Jazzy is ambitious. She felt Sammy was exciting. So she has strung along with him. Why are you asking?"

"No sorry I don't mean to pry. It might be useful information if I do see Jazzy in New York. I didn't know that Sammy and Wayne were business partners." George replies quickly and looks anxiously at Leonora checking if she looks upset.

"*No problem Howdy. I know you mean well. Sorry if I sounded angry. You know I likes you vera much.*" Leonora places her hand on George's and gazes into his eyes.

"The feelings mutual Lenny, it's nearly two, we had better get back to work." George squeezes Leonora's hand as they walk from the park hand in hand.

What is Wayne Up To?

Wayne Luther sees George entering the Bank and rushes over.

"*How ya doing George, great to see you again, come on up*" Wayne gushes at George in his usual full on way. As they settle in room three George hands Wayne an envelope.

"There you are Wayne, your first security payment for two thousand five hundred dollars. We got our first cheque from the United Nations today. Sorry I haven't been around before. I nearly stopped you in the car on Tuesday night near the harbour but I thought it was a bit late." George remarks in his most casual sounding voice noticing Wayne appears slightly flustered.

"Tuesday, hmmm Tuesday, I can't recall. Ah yes . . . I remember . . . I lent my car to Sammy. See Sammy is not an island resident so he can't have a car of his own here. Every now and then he borrows mine." Wayne explains in a subdued voice as he makes sure his cheque is in order.

"Just as well I didn't stop the car then. I hear you are both involved with Island Rum. It seems to be getting quite a lot of attention over here." George thinks Wayne is hiding something about the car but he can't be sure.

"Sammy is an investor. He has got a big order from his contacts in New York. He also got us a much better deal for printing the boxes and cartons. Since he's been involved things are looking good for the company. If we get bigger maybe you and the Tinopolis's might want to invest?" Wayne gives George a look with raised eyebrows.

"That might be a possibility Wayne. Perhaps I could have a look over sometime. Whilst I'm here would you happen to have Sammy's New York address? I have to go over to New York this week end. I promised Leonora I'd drop by and say Hi to Jasmine. She's over there with Sammy did you know? I heard you had a bit of a crush on her once. It looked like it was re kindling on the boat the other week." George remembers how Wayne reacted on the boat.

"Don't you start about the boat? It's causing me pain. Sammy was taunting me about it on Monday. Jasmine must have told him what happened. He threatened to tell Mary Jayne unless he could hire the boat." Wayne raises his voice getting slightly hysterical as he hands George one of Sammy's cards.

"Wayne, you know I won't say anything. I wonder what was so important for Sammy to have the boat. Was it a fishing trip perhaps?" George tries another tack.

"I don't think so the rods were not used. He used up nearly all the fuel. The tanks were full when he took it, didn't offer to pay for it neither. Said he might need her again. If he does I'll make him pay for da fuel up front." Wayne cries out defiantly staring at George.

George reviews the situation in his office. There is a connection between Wayne and Sammy with Island Rum. What is going on with "Pembroke Lady"? Why did Sammy want the boat in such a hurry? Did Wayne lie about the car? Sammy flew to New York on Monday evening according to Leonora. So he couldn't have been using Wayne's car when I saw it at the warehouse on Tuesday night, unless, maybe, Sammy flew back to Bermuda on Tuesday. Jasmine can tell me. She might know more about the drugs too. If I can get some useful information on drugs, I might be able to do some kind of a deal with Adrian. George concludes he has to go to New York to talk with "Ocean Stars" captain and Jasmine.

George arranges a flight for early Friday morning and books a hotel on Lexington Avenue. He confirms his hotel is about eight blocks south from the address Leonora had given him for Jasmine. He hopes to make contact with Jasmine on Friday and check out Sammy's Bayonne address. On Saturday he will visit "Ocean Star" and see Captain Kato.

Thursday afternoon Late May 1966

Reilly's Deal

It is two days since Sammy requested help from Reilly. They meet again at the Pulaski Street cafe.

"We got your mark all set up for Saturday night. Seems he likes the casino near Rockefeller Centre. We got contacts there. My broad will get chummy with him and set him up for some nice shots. You'll get them on Sunday. How goes the cruise ships angle?" Sammy whispers to Reilly who is loading his coffee with sugar and cream.

"That's good Sammy. Make sure his face is nice and clear. About the cruise ships, we got lucky. One of my customs men is transferring from Brooklyn to Manhattan Pier next week. He says he can be on duty if he knows the time of arrival of your ship. The Manhattan union boss is a guy named Straker. We did some business a while back. He's into antiques from the Middle East. You might remember we got some stuff from your boss to him about three years ago. He's happy to help us for some more antiques. So we take the rum off the ship intact. Straker will sort that. Remove the marked boxes for you to collect then let my customs man pass the crate through into bond." Reilly looks at Sammy.

"So that's very good Sean, what's the damage gonna be? I need to get back to the boss y know for this." Sammy asks.

"Yea it's gonna be twenty big ones Sammy, that's ten for me, five for Straker and five for my customs guy. Straker says he will take his cut in antiques. If he can see the photos of the goods like you did for him before." Reilly, waiting for Sammy's response, moves a toothpick from side to side of his mouth. Sammy looks down at the table cloth calculating the score in his head.

The whole package will gross three million bucks. With his twenty five per cent that's seven hundred and fifty for him and Artie before costs should leave them at least half a million.

"It should be OK Sean payment will be when the goods are delivered into Pulaski Street. I'll get the antique photos and give you the shipping details as soon as I can. Where are we with "Ocean Star"?"

"I'm going over there now. We got to change the trucks when we start unloading the central holds. That's gonna delay us half a day. We should get the crates in on Saturday. Then the grain will be pumped straight in from the silo, should be a piece of cake. See you Sunday with my photo shots." Reilly puts a great mitt into Sammy's hand and squeezes just hard enough for Sammy to know he had better deliver on his promises.

Iron Ore Unloading

On board "Ocean Star" Captain Kato is busy overseeing the discharge of iron ore. Three overhead grabs are extracting ore at the rate of ten tons a pick. The grabs drop the ore into a hopper which feeds a conveyor connected to waiting rail trucks lined up at the end of the wharf. Unloading has been going on since Wednesday evening. Almost half the cargo is unloaded. Kato wonders if there will be any change in procedures to deal with the ore in the lower central holds which is about to be exposed. How many people in the docks are aware of the chrome he wonders?

The meeting with his boss Costas is playing on his mind. Kato worries whether he will be left high and dry after the voyage. Costas will deny everything. I need some hold, some evidence to tie him in. It will be difficult Kato thinks. He comforts himself in the knowledge that at least he has over eight thousand five hundred dollars.

A harbour vehicle stops alongside the steps to the ship. Reilly gets out of the vehicle and waves to the Grab

Minion or Master

operators. As soon as the grabs finish discharging their loads the men climb down from the gantries.

"What's happening down there?" Kato, seeing the men leaving their grabs, runs out from the bridge and shouts down to Reilly.

"Can I come aboard?" Reilly shouts back.

"Do you know what's happening with the Grab operators? Any long delay and we will incur demurrage charges." Kato says, in exasperation, as soon as Reilly is on board

"I'm Sean Reilly in charge of the dock workers Captain. There's going to be a delay here. We have orders to discharge from holds four and five into a special train. So we have to empty the hopper before recommencing with the grabs. In the meantime I've sent the operators for a tea break." Reilly glances at Kato looking him up and down trying to gauge what reaction he will get.

"I see Mr Reilly. How much extra time will this all take?" Kato asks politely. He now knows how the chrome will be separated from the iron. He wonders how much this great hulk Reilly knows.

"I guess we are looking at a half day taking account of only two grabs can work and the downtime in closing the hopper. Not too bad eh Captain?" Reilly counters surprised he hasn't had any more of a protest.

"I'll require a copy of your dispatch orders for my owners. If they are charged half a day's demurrage they will need to pass it on to the rail company." Kato demands looking Reilly straight in the face. Kato is hoping he might get some more information from this paperwork.

"No problem Captain. By the way have you been advised about the two crates coming on board after the ores been unloaded?" Reilly asks nonchalantly.

"Yes I have. If it's all the same to you I want those crates put straight into holds four and five to help with ballast." Kato instructs, hoping he might be able to take a look inside them before the grain is loaded. Reilly is taken aback at this. He was planning to put the crates in on Saturday. He scratches his head in deep thought. So what difference does it make? Let's do it Friday instead he decides.

"*I got no problem wiv dat Captain. Here's the paper work for the crates. They'll be loaded around nine thirty tomorrow morning. The Grabs should get going again by six thirty tonight. You got time to get some grub. I can see myself off.*" Reilly chuckles and walks off the bridge leaving Kato studying the loading papers for the crates. Still engrossed in the papers Kato is disturbed by the telex machine starting to chatter. The message reads:

Attention Captain Kato

I will be coming on board "Ocean Star" on Saturday at nine am to go over the voyage paper work. Please be available.

George Howden
Aframe Shipping
Charterers of "Ocean Star"

"What does this guy Howden want? Charterers don't normally bother us." Kato wonders.

Chapter Ten

New York

Friday morning Late May 1966

George goes to New York.

George's flight is due to take off at nine in the morning. The flight time is two hours. Because New York is on Eastern Standard Time it will still be nine o 'clock when he lands. George will collect a hire car from La Guardia airport.

As he queues for U S Immigration two people appear familiar but he can't identify them. He thinks no more about it. His mind keeps going back over the events of the last few days. George sees the two men again. They are walking in front of him across the tarmac to board his flight. They are carrying Island Rum carrier bags. Suddenly, it hits him, like a great flash of light shining into his over worked brain. They are the men he saw through the sky light window of the warehouse on Tuesday night. He had put that incident into a far recess of his mind as he concentrated on trying to work out who used Wayne's car and what did Sammy want the boat for. The common thread with Sammy, Wayne and these two might be Island Rum. He recalls those two packing rum cartons in the warehouse. It might be a false trail: but I shall follow these two off the flight George decides.

George keeps a safe distance from the men as they disembark and walk towards the baggage area. They walk straight past the baggage carousel and out of the terminal building.

Damn it, they didn't check in any luggage! George curses to himself. He decides to leave his own case and pick it up later. The two men walk briskly to the taxi rank and into a yellow cab. George gets into the next cab and in the time honoured custom he shouts to the cabbie:

"Follow that cab in front please."

"You got it Buddy," the cabbie says.

"You must be a Limey with that funny accent. No one says please here. What's the big deal? Are you one of those James Bond guys?" the Cabbie enquires as he shifts from neutral into drive and steers out into the traffic.

"Oh, no, it's nothing like that. I am a writer for a British magazine. Every month we do a story called *"Follow that Cab"* in a different City. Next month it's on New York. I will just write about the area wherever the cab takes us." George explains feeling rather pleased with his off the cuff explanation.

"Sounds real crazy to me, hey did you know the Beatles just been here? They caused mayhem, kids screaming and fainting all over Manhattan." The cabbie asks looking at George in his rear view mirror.

"No, I didn't. I'm more of a classical music man: although, I am getting a taste for blues and jazz music. Oh look! We are heading for Manhattan according to that sign, should be good for the magazine article." George enthuses getting into the spirit of his deception of the cabbie.

"You are out of luck on that score buddy. Looks like we're heading for Holland Tunnel could be we're heading for New Jersey, Newark or maybe Bayonne. Whatever, you're gonna be on the west side." The cabbie remarks sounding as though he might be getting interested. Ten minutes later the cab they are following stops to pay a toll for Bayonne Bridge: then, after a mile, it turns into Pulaski Street and lets the two men off at a warehouse.

"OK pal. This is it. Where do you want to be dropped?" the cabbie asks losing interest in George.

"Over there opposite at that cafe will be fine." George orders as he watches the two men go into the warehouse.

In the cafe George wastes no time in ordering a mug of coffee and a bacon and egg roll. The time is ten fifteen. He is hungry. Sitting at a window seat he has a good view of the warehouse. The building has a door entrance into what looks like a small reception area. At the side there are two roller shutter doors. The sign on the building says "*SS Enterprises Inc*". Now, that is more than a coincidence George proclaims to himself as he ferrets in his wallet for Sammy's card that Wayne gave him. The card reads *Sammy Santino, SS Enterprises, Pulaski Street, Bayonne*. This is Sammy's address. George wonders if he can get a look inside.

Before he can take any action there is movement at the warehouse. The roller shutter doors open. A large truck and trailer emerge. The combination rig is so long it has to ease out of the warehouse coming across the road to the cafe window to turn. The trailer is loaded with two large wooden crates. George is dumbstruck when he makes out the crate markings in big bold black lettering:

**"CONTENTS:AGRICULTURE MACHINE PARTS
DESTINATION: TORRESHIPPES,
        LOURENCO MARQUES,**

MOZAMBIQUE
VESSEL: "Ocean Star"
RED HOOK TERMINAL
BROOKLYN NY".

That is just not possible! There must be some mistake. George mutters under his breath.

"Ocean Star", that's my ship. Its carrying ore and grain not machine parts. What is going on? What has Sammy got to do with my ship? This is getting so complicated.

George pays the cafe bill but the rig has driven off. The roller shutter doors are still open. Hurrying across the road he walks in to the warehouse and creeps to the far end. This area is poorly lit. In the corner there is a door which looks as if it leads to a store room. Very carefully and slowly George opens the door and pops his head in.

"Who the fuck is you?" a voice shouts from inside the room. George's eyes are now getting accustomed to the dingy light. He can just make out the two men from the plane. The man who shouted appears middle aged. He is short and stocky but moves with lightening speed towards George who has just enough time to observe a table topped with a stainless steel tray full of white powder.

"How did you get in here? What do you want? This is private property pal!" The man explodes with rage.

"Oh I'm really sorry. I'm George Howden from Aframe Shipping and I'm looking for a forwarding agent for my ships. The door at the front was open so I just came in." George says showing his business card.

"Well you came in through the wrong door pal. Go out and into reception at the side! They might see you today but not if you ain't got an appointment. Now beat it!" The man pushes George away from the door. George has seen enough and goes without a murmur. As he gets to the street he hears the man screaming at the other two to get the doors closed and can just make out a *"Sure thing Artie"* response.

George decides he should get away before he gets into any more scrapes. He orders a cab from the cafe and goes back to La Guardia to pick up his suitcase from left luggage and his rental car. It is midday as he drives the car out of the airport towards Red Hook Terminal in Brooklyn. George wants answers about those crates.

Friday morning Late May 1966

Loading the Crates

After breakfast on Friday morning Kato gives all but three of the crew permission to leave the ship for the day. Kato orders the three left to oversee the discharge of the chrome ore in "Ocean Stars" holds. One of the grabs had needed repairing during the night. Holds four and five will not be emptied until mid day. Reilly has telephoned to advise that the crates will be in the docks by mid day to be loaded.

Kato spends some time on his own. First he studies the paper work for the crates then the dispatch order for the discharge of the chrome ore from holds four and five.

The shipment order for the crates is probably a work of fiction Kato thinks. The purpose is to make everything look genuine for any snooping customs or harbour official. The contents are described as engineered machine parts for tractors, harvesters and bulldozers. The supplier is named as Ace Machine Factors, Detroit, and the receiving forwarding agent is SS Enterprises Inc. Bayonne.

An export certificate is attached with various stamps and signatures from the US Trade and Development Agency. That looks genuine Kato thinks feeling the paper quality before holding the document up to the light to see the watermark logo of the Agency.

"*There's going to be trouble over these crates.*" Kato mutters to himself.

The dispatch order for the chrome ore came from the Docks Authority. The instructions advise that the final eighty per cent in volume of holds four and five from "Ocean Star" must be discharged separately from the remainder of the cargo. The order is signed by Marshall C Brumbell, Vice President, Bulk Handling, Brooklyn Docks Board.

If that order is genuine it must mean that someone in authority knows about the chrome. Costas has been feeding me bull shit about going to jail. Kato feels anger welling up from the pit of his stomach. *How could Costas be so cynical towards me after all my service? What a mess.* Kato recalls his conversation with Costas in the hotel on Wednesday evening. He wonders if perhaps the Pacific Venturer hi jacking was no co incidence. Maybe the fishing boat was in on the plot.

Costas was so quick to re call the insurance claim was a success. If I can prove that Costas put my crew's lives at risk deliberately then he will be dead meat. I will tear him to pieces with my bare hands before he rots in hell. Kato swears to himself.

Kato is interrupted by the leading sea man reporting that holds four and five have been emptied. The seaman tells Kato that the Grabs will now be inactive until the hopper has been emptied. Kato orders the crew to take two hours off for lunch and to report back for duty at two o'clock to resume the discharge from the other holds.

Within minutes of the crew leaving the ship Reilly telephones Kato to say that the crates are in the docks. He is arranging for one grab to be fitted with a hook system. By one o'clock both crates are in holds four and five. The crates will not be concealed by grain until Sunday.

Friday midday Late May 1966

Seeing "Ocean Star"

It takes George thirty minutes to get to Red Hook Terminal. He follows the taxi drivers route from earlier but goes south instead of west through Holland tunnel. At the gates he shows his Aframe Shipping card and tells the gate man he has business with "Ocean Star". George drives the hire car along the main dock road from which each wharf extends at ninety degrees. He carefully negotiates the car between trucks and Lorries loading and unloading whilst watching out for dock workers who are popping up everywhere. As the car arrives at wharf twenty nine George thinks he will be less noticeable if he is on foot. So he parks up the Pontiac in a disused lot next to a warehouse. He walks towards Wharf thirty, where "Ocean Star" is berthed, trying to keep out of sight as much as he can without making it too obvious.

The first thing he notices is the lack of activity at this wharf. The overhead conveyor has stopped. The area around the wagons is deserted. On one line, the wagons are full, whilst on a second line they are empty. George walks across to the full wagons and pockets a sample of ore which has fallen onto the line. He takes a photograph of the wagons using his Kodak Instamatic camera and one of the names *Consolidated Smelting—Newark* stamped on the side of each wagon.

Looking down the length of the wharf the only activity to be seen is about 400 metres away where a crate on a trailer is being hooked up to a grab for lifting into "Ocean Star". *That has to be the crates I saw this morning,* George exclaims.

A cold breeze is coming off the Upper Bay waters. George is thankful that he chose to wear Jeans held up with a leather belt and a thick long sleeved sweat shirt worn underneath a Grey Jersey Knit pullover. Sneaker shoes and a baseball hat complete his wardrobe. His camera along with passport, money and papers are held in a compact ruck sack along with a thin rain proof anorak.

Cautiously, George makes his way down Wharf thirty using the overhead ore conveyor as a cover until he reaches the gantry legs of the discharge hopper. He is now within 100 metres of the truck. As the crate is winched up by the grab George takes a photograph. A bright flash of light comes from the camera. Not thinking, George has taken his photograph from the dark shadows thrown down from the hopper. This has caused the automatic flash light to go off.

"*Damn it!*" he exclaims as he sinks back further into the shadows.

Within seconds George hears voices shouting as two men run towards the hopper. Shouldering his ruck sack he retreats to the rear of the hopper looking for cover. He cannot see any hiding place on the ground so he climbs to the top of the rear gantry leg and rolls himself into the empty hopper. He grasps the top lip with his bare hands and grips onto the angled side with his sneakers. Out of breath from this exertion he hangs on praying no one has seen him. "*Thank God for the sneakers. They were quiet and are giving me some grip inside here.*" George whispers.

"Sean I could have sworn that light came from just here." a voice down below proclaims.

"Yea me too, take a look around the back Mickey!" Sean Reilly barks out in his thick Brooklyn accent.

George hears footsteps coming under the hopper. The man called Mickey has now walked right out beyond the hopper and is looking intently all around.

"There's no sign of any one here Sean." Mickey shouts.

"OK we can't afford any problems with this, here's what you do. Stay here and keep an eye out for anything suspect! I'll finish off the crates with the drivers. Give me a shout if you see anything!" Reilly orders and walks back to the lorry.

In the hopper George is covered in ore dust. His hands are losing their grip on the top lip. If he lets go he will fall several feet down to the feeder mouth. This will be heard by Mickey on guard under the hopper. Dust is irritating his nose and eyes. George is worried the dust will make him sneeze. His eyes are watering. He can't let go of the hopper edge to wipe them. After several minutes of hanging on the feeling in his hands goes. His arms start tingling. George knows he cannot hold this position any more. He starts to slide down the hopper. He knows that when he hits the bottom the game will be up. The man called Mickey is still on guard underneath the hopper. As soon as George's tumbling body hits the hopper's mouth the sound of him crashing onto the bottom of the hopper floor will give him away. With seconds to go before he hits the bottom a passing ship blasts out on its fog horn masking any other noise for hundreds of metres. George crumples up at the bottom of the hopper in a pile of dust. He rubs his hands to get circulation back and then wipes the dust from his eyes.

That's done it. How can I get out of here? The sides are too smooth and just a little too high for me to climb up. George ponders his predicament. *If I wait in here I'll be crushed to pulp by rocks. If I can't get out I'll have to try and attract some attention and risk giving the game away.*

Chapter Eleven

Escape

Friday afternoon Late May 1966

Inside the Hold

Right let me get down to the bottom of hold four to take a look before the crew get back Kato says to himself.

Before going into the depths of hold number four Kato changes into overalls and heavy duty boots. He puts on a safety helmet. He takes a crow bar, a large insulated torch, a heavy duty claw hammer and industrial gloves then proceeds to climb down the series of steel steps welded into the side of the ship's hold.

The atmosphere in the hold is dusty. The dust is clinging to the steps and rail guards. Soon Kato's overalls are covered in the reddish grime. He sees that the crate has been strapped to the deck to secure it from rolling.

Once at the bottom of the hold he walks over to the crate. He estimates it measures 20 foot long by ten foot wide and is eight feet tall. He walks around the structure: examining the construction method: looking for the easiest way to get inside. *Let's see what Costas really has to deliver. I'll bet it isn't agricultural machinery.*

Kato climbs onto the top of the crate thinking it will be easiest to prise open some of the wooden slats with his crow bar from there. The top is made from unseasoned softwood cut into planks measuring four foot by one foot. They are nailed into the frame of the crate and are covered at the edge and centre with hardwood securing planks.

Kato goes to work with his crow bar on the leading edge hardwood plank. The ten foot long plank is fixed into the frame by six inch nails set every six inches. It takes Kato several minutes to lever the whole length up. The wooden slats then prise up with the aid of the crow bar. He removes half a dozen slats. Now he has access into the crate. The first object he sees is a wooden box measuring three foot by two foot. Kato grabs the rope handles on each side of the box. He hauls the box onto the top of the crate. The effort of opening the crate and hauling this box out has made Kato sweat. The lid of the box is nailed down. There is lettering on the box. Kato does not understand the writing.

He prises the lid of the box off with his crow bar. The open box reveals a Soviet RPG-7 rocket grenade launcher.

Not agricultural machinery. What devilry are you up to then Costas? Kato asks himself as he lifts the launcher out of its box to get a closer look.

As Kato goes to replace the weapon back in its box a flash of light comes from the top of the hold. Kato looks up towards the top of the hold and is blinded by another flash of light.

"Who is that up there?" Kato shouts. There is no answer.

Quickly Kato replaces the box in the crate, nails the lid back down and scuttles up to the top deck to investigate the flash. By the time he reaches the there is no sign of any one on board. Kato looks at his watch. It is one forty five. He operates the mechanism to shut down the hatches covering holds four and five. The hatches will not be re opened until the grain is loaded which will bury the arms crates at the bottom of holds four and five.

Out of the Hopper

Ten minutes after dropping to the bottom of the hopper George hears someone shout to Mickey to return to the truck.

Tense with every sense on full alert George waits. There is no sound in the immediate vicinity of the hopper. It is now ten minutes past one. George tries to scramble up the side of the hopper to get a grip on the upper lip. Whichever way he attempts he falls short by at least four feet. He cannot get out through the bottom feeder because the trap doors are locked shut by hydraulic rams. When the doors open George knows he will be crushed by tons of rock. He will be dead meat.

The only way out has to be up but how?

George wracks his brains if only there was a ladder or some kind of step he might be able to get higher to reach the lip top. There is nothing. His prospects are bleak. He looks up again at the out of reach hopper lip. For the first time he notices that all along the lip plate there are bolts protruding up securing the plates.

Will my belt buckle hook over one of those bolts so I can haul myself out?

George removes his thick leather belt. It has a strong buckle which, with luck, might fit over one of the bolts. He tries swinging the belt over head but the length is too short to reach the bolts. In vain he tries to scramble up the side of the hopper. This gives him extra height to swing the belt: he is unable to maintain balance and ends up sliding back into the base of the hopper. With his clothes covered in grime and dust George sits down nursing his bruised and battered body wishing he had bought the six foot belt instead of the four foot one when he had the chance.

Is this the end? Dumped in a hopper, escape thwarted by a mere few feet of belt.

George ponders: sitting: staring disconsolately down at his filthy trainers.

You idiot! He curses to himself.

I can get another three feet from my trainer laces.

Swiftly he removes them. He threads one lace through the top hole of his belt securing with a heavy knot. He ties the other lace to the end forming a hoop for his hand to hold. His first swing sees the belt buckle go over the lip but misses the bolts. After several tries the buckle snags on a bolt and with gentle pulling it finally slides over the bolt. Tentatively George gives the makeshift rope his full weight and ascends the hopper side climbing hand over hand. When he finally reaches the top lip, he lies still for a few seconds, saved from being crushed by rocks, thankful to be in fresh air.

From the top of the hopper George can see that the wharf and "Ocean Star" are deserted. There is no sign of activity any where. It has seemed like an eternity to George trying to get out of that damned hopper but looking at his watch he sees that it is twenty past one. He replaces his trainer laces and using his belt as a brake around the steel hopper legs he rappels down the gantry to the dock floor.

With adrenaline flowing freely George dusts himself down and races up the wharf towards "Ocean Star". He makes for the mid ships area where the boarding ladders are secured and races up towards the top deck. Still no one in sight, he reaches the top deck. Peering into hold five he sees a wooden crate lying at the bottom. Quickly George takes out his camera from the ruck sack and takes two shots of the crate. He moves on to hold four and again peers over the side into its depths.

Visibility is poor but George makes out in the bowels of the hold another crate. This one has part of the wooden top removed. A man is standing on top of the crate holding a rocket grenade launcher and peering down into the crate. George aims the Instamatic camera. Again the flash goes off. He takes another picture. He hears a shout coming up from the hold. George races away as fast as he can down the boarding ladders and races to the hopper to take refuge there. No one has come on deck. The wharf is still deserted. George sprints towards the rail wagons at the end of the wharf using the overhead conveyor as cover. At the rail head there are signs of activity. George determines his safest option is to walk nonchalantly out towards Wharf twenty nine. In five minutes he is back in the Pontiac. He drives out of the docks heading for his hotel on Lexington Avenue.

He checks his watch the time is one forty five.

Friday afternoon and evening Late May 1966

George meets Jasmine

On the way back to Manhattan George stops at an out of town super market. He cleans himself up in the rest room. He purchases work clothes: a cheap business suit: a blue shirt and tie: industrial boots: a pair of spectacles: a make up box and a black hair wig. He pays a premium price to have his Instamatic photographs developed in one hour and orders some business cards with a leather identity wallet from the stationery store. Whilst waiting for the photographs and cards he devours a burger, fries and soft drink from the supermarket cafe. The excitement of the last few hours has made him ravenous.

George parks the Pontiac in the underground car park and checks in to his hotel on Lexington Avenue. He wastes no time in showering and changes into the business clothes he bought earlier. He walks two blocks and finds a photo booth where he has several passport pictures taken, some of his normal likeness and some whilst he wears the black wig and spectacles. Satisfied he hails a taxi to take him to the corner of Fifth Avenue and Sixty Eighth Street. From there he walks the two blocks to the address Lenny has given him for Jasmine. He isn't expecting to see Jasmine but walking allows him to form an impression of the neighbourhood, comprising mostly up market hotels, restaurants and apartments.

If this is where Jasmine is living she must be doing alright.

The apartment block has an elegant nineteen thirties look with a small wall gardened entrance. It has ten floors. Each floor has three apartments. George looks at the fourth floor where Jasmine's apartment should be. There are lights on in one of the windows but he cannot tell if the lights are from Jasmine's apartment. There is no doorman in the foyer. George takes the elevator to the fourth floor. He gets no answer from the apartment. He stands by the door considering whether to wait. The elevator starts to descend summoned from the ground. George does not want to be seen lurking so he walks down the stairs which encircle the lift shaft. As he gets to the second floor the elevator is on its way up. The lift cage has small triangular windows on its wooden front doors and side panels. Although the cage passes in a split second George gets a glimpse of a man in the cage. He is staring straight ahead and doesn't notice George.

"That's the guy who ejected me from the warehouse this morning." George mutters under his breath as he walks briskly out of the apartment entrance. From across the street a yellow taxi cab turns across the traffic to the sound of car horns blaring. The cab drops its woman passenger outside the apartment block.

"Jasmine is that you?" George gazes at a very sophisticated woman dressed in a grey suit with white blouse and black stilettos who has exited from the cab. With a hand on each of Jasmine's shoulders George stares into Jasmine's face. Her pupils are dilated and there are dark shadows under her eyes.

"I'm on business over here. Lenny and your Pa are worried about you. They haven't heard from you. I told them I'd look you up. Is everything alright Jasmine? Are you OK?" George asks trying to keep his voice as natural as he can still holding Jasmine by the shoulders.

"Oh George," Jasmine says quietly "I miss Pa and Lenny. I think I might have made a mistake. Sammy won't let me leave now. I'm scared George." Jasmine looks down at the pavement and starts to cry. George moves his hands from Jasmine's shoulders and wraps his arms around her and comforts her with a hug.

"Can we go somewhere to talk?" George asks, his voice getting more urgent.

"I can't get away now. Artie is waiting for me in the apartment. I have to go George." Jasmine still sobbing breaks away from George's hug.

"Jasmine listen to me please. I will be at the Palace Hotel on Lexington Avenue. I'll wait there all night. Promise me you will come over tonight. Here is the hotel card with my room number. I'll wait for you all night. Please promise me!" George looks into Jasmine's eyes his voice urgent and insistent as he places the card in Jasmine's hands.

"Ill try George, thanks for coming. I have to go or Artie will be suspicious." Jasmine breaks away and rushes into the Apartment block foyer. George watches Jasmine walk away wishing he could do something.

Deep in thought George walks the one block back to Sixty Seventh Street where he catches the sub way back to Lexington Avenue and his hotel.

Friday evening Late May 1966

Artie pays Jasmine

Jasmine is still upset as she enters the elevator. She has been surprised and taken a back to see some one from home. She sobs into her tissue. As the elevator ascends to the fourth floor she starts thinking what will Pa and Lenny think of her if they find out what she is doing here. It's all happened so quickly. Maybe, if she can get away for an hour, later, she could at least speak to George. How can he help her? She's seen how cruel and ruthless Sammy and Randy have been during the week. What chance has she and young George got against the likes of them? Can she make do with out Sammy's drugs? She places George's hotel card carefully into her purse before she enters the apartment.

Artie is sprawled on the settee watching television as Jasmine enters the lounge.

"Baby how is it going" Artie asks getting up from the settee and walking to the table to pick up an envelope.

"You've been pretty popular with the clients since Randy gave you the special training tour around town last Tuesday." Artie says in a gloating tone handing her the envelope.

"Let's see," Artie takes a pocket book from inside his jacket and opens it up.

"Two on Wednesday, Two yesterday, one today, so far, and one tonight at nine, not bad, not bad at all." Artie concludes watching Jasmine open the envelope.

"What's this? I expected a lot more than this there's only two hundred dollars here Artie. Where's the rest?" Jasmine complains looking at Artie with suspicion.

"You got expenses to pay Baby." Artie explains with his hands outstretched.

"What are you talking about? What expenses?"

"First there's the cost of the shoot on Monday. Then there's Randy's expenses on Tuesday, your flight over here, Sammy's expenses for looking after you, plus your rent for this apartment. It's not cheap baby. You still owe the best part of a grand, I'm being considerate giving you as much as two hundred bucks." Artie shrugs his shoulders.

"But I never agreed to any of this. No way was I expecting to pay. Are you telling me I have to pay you for Randy to crawl all over me last Tuesday? Are you kidding me?" Jasmine screams. She is getting so angry she has completely forgotten her upset over seeing George just a short while ago.

"Take it easy Babe. You got one more client today. Then tomorrow there's a real special client for you to see over at the Casino in Rockefeller Centre. That pays triple money baby. The way I see it by the end of next week you should be clear, home free." Artie says in the most pacifying tone he can muster.

"So this triple money client tomorrow, what is that all about? What's so special about this client? What do I have to do?" Jasmine wonders whether she can work her way out of this tyranny.

"That's more like it baby. He's a special client. He wants pictures taken but he wants to be with you in private. No cameras or anything in the room to spoil the atmosphere. So we got this special room in the Casino all lined up. It's a piece of cake, easy money." Artie continues in his pacifying tone.

"I need some stuff if I gotta do this Artie. Sammy usually gives me some but I haven't seen him since Tuesday. Can you get me some stuff Artie?" Jasmine pleads trying hard to act nice.

"Yea I'll see what I can do. Come over to the studio around eleven tomorrow. I might have some stuff then. So are you all fixed for tonight?"

"Tonight, oh yes, I have the paper in my bag. Yes nine o' clock at The Palace Hotel, Lexington Avenue, its dinner then a night club with this business man. I got his photo here. Just like a passport picture. That reminds me Artie. When do I get my passport back from Sammy?"

"You will get your passport back when you are clear with paying your expenses baby, probably next week sometime. Listen I gotta go. See you tomorrow at the studio." With his back to Jasmine Artie waves his hand in the air as he leaves the apartment.

Jasmine is still looking at her booking sheet wondering why it is bothering her. She rummages in her purse and pulls out the hotel card George gave her. Her client will be at the same hotel that George is staying at. What kind of a coincidence is that?

Chapter Twelve

Sammy

Sammy Santino

Brought up in Queens District in New York City Sammy is an only child. His Italian father worked in hotels and restaurants and his mother of mixed Mexican and African blood took in laundry work and did some cleaning. They worked unsocial hours. Except for Friday nights Sammy had little contact with his parents. When his father came home drunk Sammy would hear him cursing and swearing followed usually by the sound of him puking. It was Sammy's job to clean up. Sammy would see his father collapsed in a slovenly heap after trying to have sex with his long suffering mother.

It was not the best up bringing. Sammy was a bright kid but formal schooling did not appeal to him. He saw no future in books.

By the time he was eleven Sammy had more of a relationship and a feeling of belonging with the bookies and pimps he ran messages for. He was a fast runner and kept his mouth shut. A dollar a run was not bad. Sammy was making enough to feed and clothe himself by the time he was twelve.

He was thirteen years old when one of the pimps took him to Manhattan. Sammy had never seen such luxury. The comparison with the scruffy, smelly, dirty hell hole of

Minion or Master

a dump he lived in was stark. The carpets were pure silk. There were flowers in vases on tables. Everything smelled nice. Sammy wanted to live in a place just like this.

The man in the Manhattan apartment liked young boys. The pimp told him the man would unzip his trousers and show Sammy what to do. The pimp said he wouldn't get hurt. The man gave him twenty dollars.

Sammy was taken to see the man once a week for six months. After that he never saw the man again. Sammy never knew the man's name and never spoke about it to any one. He had saved five hundred dollars which he hid in a tin under the floorboards.

At fourteen years old Sammy left home. He lived with one of the pimps. He was never asked to go with a man again. He learnt the pimp's trade. He learned how to dish out violence when necessary. Sometimes the girls allowed him to experiment with them. Sammy was a fast learner. By the time he was eighteen he was running his own girls.

He never questioned why a stranger offered him the lease on the Pulaski Street warehouse or why this stranger arranged delivery of cocaine to the warehouse. Sammy was told to dilute the drugs from one hundred per cent purity down to twenty five per cent. Pushers were introduced. They paid market value less twenty five per cent in cash. Sammy kept one third. The stranger never gave Sammy his name or a contact address, the takings from the pushers was collected every day. Sammy would be telephoned with a password an hour before pick up. The caller never introduced himself. Sammy and Artie referred to him as *the boss*.

From time to time Sammy would be instructed to make a call from an outside call box. It was from one of these calls that Sammy was given information to help him set up his import export business in Bermuda. Another call told him there was an apartment available for rent in Manhattan. When Sammy went to see the apartment on East sixty eighth street near second avenue he remembered the pure silk carpets. He still did not ask any questions. There was no need. He was becoming rich.

Artie took the call from *the boss* instructing them to arrange for the crates of machine parts to be loaded on "Ocean Star". Sammy was given the day, time and coordinates for a drop off of drugs in the Atlantic Ocean. Sammy wrote the details down on a piece of paper.

Friday evening and night Late May 1966

Palace Hotel

It is six thirty in the evening by the time George gets back to his hotel room. Flopping down on the king size bed he tries to make sense of an eventful day.

Starting with the photographs, the first shows a crate being hoisted from the truck onto "Ocean Star". George studies the four men in the photograph carefully. Their faces are not clear; the shot is out of focus, but, George thinks one man looks like Sammy.

George concentrates on piecing together everything he knows about Sammy.

Sammy has a warehouse in Bermuda and one here. Everything points to that white powder in both warehouses being an illegal drug. So, there are drugs in Sammy's Bermuda warehouse being couriered over here in the rum packaging. I must have disturbed those three in the warehouse this morning. They must have been working on the drugs.

Minion or Master

He racks his brains for any other clues. *That man in the lift was at the warehouse. Jasmine said she had to see Artie and that was the name shouted in the warehouse. So this Artie chap is involved with the drugs and Jasmine.*

George takes a long time studying the photograph of "Ocean Star's" hold showing the man standing on the crate holding what looks like a weapon. He doesn't recognise the man and again the picture is slightly out of focus. When he took the shot this morning everything happened so quickly. George had not taken in the full implications of what he had witnessed. Now, looking at the picture, his body shivers involuntarily. A cold sweat breaks out on his forehead. He now appreciates the enormity of the situation and his involvement.

George now has doubts about his actions. He had close calls at the warehouse and the docks today. *I saw that crate come out of Sammy's warehouse this morning. Jasmine said she was afraid of Sammy. He won't let her leave.* George now realizes he is involved in something dangerous. Should he take more risks to find more answers? He is out of his depth. He has never taken drugs or even come across them until now. It is all a bit of a mystery. Now weapons are involved. His head spins with all this detail. The situation is outside his control. Sammy is involved in everything. That much George is sure about.

George wonders if he can get out of this mess by finding out what Kato knows at his meeting tomorrow then passing everything on to Adrian next week. *Let him sort it out, if he can, after all he has the Government connections.* This thought is superseded by another as George looks into the future. He imagines the look of horror and disappointment in Lenny's eyes as he tells her he didn't help her sister; even though he spoke with

Jasmine, who told him she was scared and unhappy. He can't face that. It would tear him apart. He has to think of some way to help Jasmine. He is interrupted by a gentle yet persistent tapping on his hotel room door.

As he goes to open the door George checks the time on his wrist watch. It shows eight o 'clock. He has been so engrossed in his thoughts he has completely forgotten about dinner. He starts to feel hunger pangs.

"Jasmine you came! Quick come in!" George cries urgently grabbing Jasmine's hands and pulling her into the room. Jasmine almost trips on her high heels as she comes into the bedroom but with a lurch into George's body she regains her balance. She is wearing a skimpy tight red mini skirt and a black low cut blouse. Her neck and shoulders are draped in a red scarf. George takes a good look at Jasmine as she sits on the edge of the bed. He can still detect the mischievous look he saw on "Pembroke Lady" but now she reveals something extra in her demeanour. He can't make out if it is fear, anger or determination.

"Do you want a drink or something?" George asks lamely unsure how to explain what he has discovered.

"No thanks George. I'm sorry about this afternoon. Seeing you was a shock. It upset me. I have had time to think. I haven't got long now because Artie has fixed a client for me to meet here later tonight." Jasmine speaks in a firm voice which is emotionless.

"Will you talk to me please Jasmine? Are you involved in drugs with Sammy? What do you know about Sammy? I can help you but you have to tell me all you know." George blurts out unable to keep back the tide of emotions he has experienced today.

"Yes I am taking drugs. I guess I am hooked. Sammy gives me them. At first it was exciting. Now I need them.

Minion or Master

I have been fooled. I thought I was going to be a fashion model. They have turned me into a hooker. It was only tonight after seeing you, then talking to Artie, that I started to realize the truth. I'm stuck. I got no real money. Sammy's got my passport. If I make a run for it they will get me. Some of the girls have been beaten up badly. Some are in Jail. The way I see it I have to stick it out. But, I really don't want Lenny or Pa to know about this. So, how do you propose to help me?" Jasmine lights up one of her slim cheroots.

"Well I have contacts with the British Government who have contacts here with the US Government. They want to stop the drugs. If you can help put Sammy away they will help you. Where does Sammy get the drugs?"

"I don't know where the drugs come from honestly George. I just get supplied by Sammy. Artie has said he will give me some tomorrow if I go over to the warehouse. So are you some kind of secret agent?"

"No I am not an agent of any kind. You are the second person to ask me that today. Like you, I seem to be caught up in some kind of web of deceit with Sammy, only, my web is much more complicated than yours. What about that incident with Wayne on the boat? What was all that about?"

"That was Sammy's idea. He thought it would be fun to goad Wayne. I played along. I didn't like Wayne that much. He was always pestering me. I thought it would be a way to get him off my back. So, George, Sammy's got a hold on you as well, how?" Jasmine asks with a quizzical look on her face.

"You will have to trust me about that. It is too complicated to explain now. Maybe later I will confide in you. Did you see Sammy in New York on Tuesday? Do you know if he went back to Bermuda? Wayne said he lent Sammy his car on Tuesday night. I think Wayne may be lying."

"Well Sammy was definitely here Tuesday evening he left about 7.30 said he had business with Artie." Jasmine says looking puzzled and bewildered at the questions.

"Did you know that Sammy threatened Wayne he would tell Mary Jayne about you on the boat? He used it to force Wayne to hire him the boat. I don't know why but somehow I think Wayne is mixed up in all this." George smiles to himself. He has been puzzling over how the drugs get to Bermuda and has now realized that Sammy was using "Pembroke Lady" for collecting drugs. Yes that would make sense he smiles again.

"Why are you smiling George? I can't see anything funny in any of this. I am not surprised if Sammy threatened Wayne. Sammy scares me." Jasmine shivers and wraps the scarf more tightly around her self.

"Oh sorry Jasmine, I am not smiling about your situation. I think I have answered a question that was puzzling me. Who is Artie I saw him going in to the apartment block just before I bumped into you? Does he live there with you?" George wants to know thinking that the apartment might provide fresh information.

"Artie is a slimy toad. He does a lot of Sammy's dirty work with the girls. I guess he does whatever Sammy wants. Mostly the apartment is empty, except for me. Sometimes Sammy sleeps there; he uses it to make calls. He has his own room. I can't see how telling you all this is helping. Like I say I am stuck. Please just don't tell Lenny and Pa! George, I have to go soon. Promise me you won't tell them." Jasmine pleads as she gets up from the bed preparing to leave.

"The last thing I want to do is hurt Lenny or your Pa Jasmine. I have a crucial meeting tomorrow morning which will throw light on this mess. In the meantime will you lend me your apartment key? I might find some clue or information there that might help us both. I'll be back before midnight. You can collect the key then. What do you say? You know I am on your side. Let's work together on this." Jasmine is taken aback at George's suggestion she takes her time staring into George's eyes, for what seems like minutes rather than seconds to George, before responding.

"I am going to trust you on this George. I don't know why but somehow I believe you. Please don't let me down. Here is the key. I'll see you later." Jasmine takes the key from her purse hands it to George and with a last stare she leaves.

Friday night Late May 1966

The Apartment

It has been dark for over an hour. Turning up the collar of his work clothes and keeping his head down George walks into the foyer taking the stairs to the fourth floor. He rings the bell at apartment twelve and waits a few minutes. There is no answer. He enters using the key from Jasmine. There is sufficient light from outside for George to see as he moves from the hall through an open door into the lounge. He finds nothing of interest in either the kitchen or bathroom. The first bedroom has make up and lipsticks on the dressing table. The drawers are full of lingerie.

This must be where Jasmine sleeps.

Outside the walls are covered with ivy. Some of the vines clinging onto and into the masonry are as thick as a man's arm.

That other room must be where Sammy sleeps.

The door is locked. He retraces his steps into Jasmine's bedroom and opens the window fully. He pushes his head out and craning his neck sees that the window in Sammy's room is slightly open. Carefully, George lowers himself out of Jasmine's window; holding on with his hands gripping the window sill, gradually he allows more of his body weight to be held by the vines. His trainers are standing on the vine trunk. He must let go of the window sill if he is to get across to Sammy's window. Tentatively he removes a hand from the sill and holds on to the nearest vine. The vine moves slightly with the extra weight but is still holding. George feels his legs shaking as the fear of falling and his predicament start to fill his thoughts.

If I stay in this position for much longer I will fall.

Without further thought he takes a deep lungful of air and lets go of the sill putting his full weight onto the vine. The vine gives slightly with the extra weight. Now committed, George crab walks across the masonry towards the window. He grabs the sill with one hand whilst the other hand pushes the window fully open. Hauling himself in through the open window he tumbles head first onto the floor and collapses in a heap.

Sammy's room is much bigger than Jasmine's room. There is a massive bed underneath a mirrored ceiling. On the wall opposite the window is a bureau and telephone. The bureau drawers are not locked. George opens each one in turn, the bottom drawer contains a New York telephone directory and various opened and unopened brown envelopes stuffed into the drawer in no particular order. Picking up the telephone directory George flicks through the pages but finds nothing. Looking at a sample of the brown envelopes George sees that they are letters and bills concerning the apartment.

The middle drawer contains three A4 sized envelope folders. The first folder contains bank statements for an ordinary checking account in the name of Samuel Santino. George flicks through the pages and sees there is a regular monthly transfer of three thousand dollars from SS Enterprises with no unusual outgoings. George takes a photograph of a statement with his Instamatic camera.

The next folder contains four bank pass books. Flicking through each one he is staggered to see balances in the hundreds of thousands.

The third folder leaves George open mouthed. There are three passports each having Sammy's photograph but made out in different names.

This is hard evidence.

George feels his hand trembling with excitement.

The top drawer contains a vicious looking flick knife, a stainless steel revolver marked "Smith & Wesson M 60" and a folded sheet of paper which has numbers hand written on it.

Worried that he might get caught George takes photographs of the last two pages of each bank book and the passports. As he takes the last photograph of the sheet with numbers written down he hears a noise coming from outside the locked door, then, he sees light coming from underneath the door.

Moving carefully George climbs out through the window backwards with his feet dangling over the sill. He reaches up and pulls the window down. Now he is precariously perched with his knees balancing on the edge of the sill. He grips the sill with his hands and drops his feet and lower body into the vines letting go of the sill. He falls a few feet into the vines which he grabs and clutches at as he shimmies his way down to the garden court yard.

Concealed in the shadows from the shrubbery in the courtyard he brushes off bits of vine and leaves from his clothes. His hands are scratched and bleeding: his clothes are stained from the ivy: walking the twelve blocks back to the hotel he avoids street lights and stays in the shadow.

It is midnight when George gets to the hotel. He is excited at his discovery and thankful that yet again he has managed to avoid discovery. At one o'clock Jasmine returns for her key and George tells her what he has discovered in Sammy's room.

Chapter Thirteen
Saturday in New York

Saturday morning Late May 1966

Visiting Kato

George had little sleep. He talked until three in the morning with Jasmine making plans. He will meet her at the hotel this afternoon. His stomach is churning as he quietly eats his breakfast of scrambled eggs on toast. His muscles are aching. His hands are sore. He forces himself to eat to replace the calories he used up yesterday. He is confused. What exactly has he discovered? There is some sort of conspiracy going on.

I must trust no one.

Aware that today's meeting with Captain Kato will be crucial if he is to discover what is going on with "Ocean Star" he feels apprehension and a tinge of excitement.

Fearing his Pontiac might be recognised from his escape at the Docks yesterday George has hired a Ford Taunus car from the hotel. He leaves the dented Pontiac still covered in red dust in the hotel garage.

At seven thirty, dressed in his business suit, he drives out of the city to the out of town super market where he arranges for the photographs of the documents taken in the apartment to be developed. He orders duplicate prints of all the other pictures. In the rest room George disguises his appearance with the black hair wig and spectacles.

At Red Hook Terminal there is a different gate man from yesterday. Wearing the wig and spectacles George presents his identity wallet which has his passport picture and a business card in the name of Thomas White, Marine Insurance and Salvage, London. George advises the gate he has business at Wharf twenty seven. Once through the gate George stops the car in a concealed position and removes his wig and glasses. He changes into work clothes and industrial boots then drives to wharf thirty.

In contrast to yesterday the wharf is a hive of activity. The conveyor is working and the four giant grabs are feeding the hopper. As he passes the hopper George shudders, remembering yesterday's incident. He stops the car alongside the boarding ladders of "Ocean Star". As he gets out of the car Reilly wearing a blue stevedore's donkey jacket rushes over.

"What's your game pal? You can't leave that car there!"

"Oh I'm sorry I have an appointment with Captain Kato at nine o'clock. Where can I park up?"

"See those grabs. There's ten ton of rock in each. You're in the firing line. If one slips you and your car is pulp. Back up behind the yellow line over there." Reilly waves his hand pointing to an area away from the ship and the feeder hopper.

"O K thanks." As he climbs back into the Ford Taunus Reilly places one of his huge rough hands on the door stopping George from closing it.

"What's your name buster? I ain't seen you before. We don't get many Limeys here." Reilly bends his bull neck and peers into the car staring intently at George.

Minion or Master

"No it's my first trip. We have chartered "Ocean Star". I'm George Howden from Aframe Shipping." George blurts out as he re calls the similarity in this voice to the one he heard under the hopper yesterday.

"You don't say. Well Mister George Howden. I got my eye on you. Nothing happens in this dock with out Sean Reilly knowing about it." Reilly gives George a final stare and slams the door shut. Flustered and upset with his heart racing at this confrontation George clashes the gear change as he moves the Ford over to the parking zone. In the rear view mirror George can see Reilly staring and thinks that he looks familiar.

Did I make a mistake giving a false name at the gate this morning?

Forcing himself to take some deep slow breaths he calms himself down and goes aboard "Ocean Star".

"Captain Kato?" George queries as he climbs the ladder to the bridge looking at the man standing at the open door.

"Yes I am Kato. You must be Mr Howden from Bermuda. I received your telex. This is very unusual for me to see the charter representative. I usually work with my ship owner or the port agents. How can I help you?" Kato looks George up and down.

"I believe there are some most unusual circumstances with this charter Captain. Do you think we can talk somewhere in private?" George gives Kato a hard stare. His heart is thumping inside his chest as he considers the risk he is taking going straight into the attack rather than skirting around with polite small talk.

"Now I am intrigued Mr Howden. Let's go into my private cabin. My number two can supervise the unloading". Kato guides George from the bridge to his cabin which is larger than George had expected. They sit at a table bolted to the deck Kato pours coffee from an electric percolator.

"So Captain I shall come straight to the point. Can you tell me please about your cargoes? Are you aware they are not in accordance with the ships manifest sent to me by Costas Tinopolis?" George enquires with a quiet clipped edge to his voice wondering if Kato will open up to him.

"I am not sure if I understand your question Mr Howden. Are you suggesting that my employer has somehow altered the ship's manifest without my knowledge?" Kato shifts uncomfortably in his seat trying to gauge how much this young upstart knows.

"That is possible Captain. I should tell you I have information to validate this claim. I have been informed by the British Foreign Office that your ship has carried chrome ore from Rhodesia in breach of international law. There are witnesses in Lourenco Marques. Before I take action I want to know whether you were compliant in carrying out this action at the behest of your employer or if you have been used like my self." George hopes he is not pushing Kato too hard. He needs Kato to co operate if his plans are to work.

"Look Mr Howden, may I call you George" Kato smiles.

"You may." George smiles back praying that Kato is going to co operate.

"George I will be honest with you. I knew nothing until Costas Tinopolis told me at dinner on Wednesday. My guess is the U S authorities know about the chrome and are turning a blind eye. I don't know what action you can take." Kato opens up the palms of his hands on the

Minion or Master

top of the table in a gesture of hopelessness wondering if George knows anything else.

"What makes you think the authorities here know?"

"This." Kato pulls out the dispatch order from the Docks Authority signed by Marshall C Brumbell, Vice President, Bulk Handling, Brooklyn Docks Board and hands it to George.

"I got that from the boss of the stevedores Sean Reilly. It looks like the harbour people know or else why give this special unloading order? It doesn't make sense unless they were in on it."

"I think I just had a run in with your Sean Reilly on the wharf. That's him in this photograph isn't it?" George tosses over the picture of the four men with the crate being hoisted from the truck onto "Ocean Star" and watches Captain Kato's reaction.

"How did you get this?" Kato feels the blood draining from his extremities to feed his vital organs as he recovers from the shock of the picture.

"Don't you worry Captain that is just a copy, like this one?" George snarls as he shows Kato the picture inside "Ocean Stars" hold showing the man standing on the crate holding what looks like a weapon.

"That rather looks like you holding that weapon from the crate Captain wouldn't you say?" George presses home his advantage watching Captain Kato place his head in his hands and stare dejectedly down at the table.

"Earlier, you asked what action I could take. Well, to answer you, if I do not get to a certain rendezvous after lunch my associate has orders to contact the U S Authorities. Within minutes of that contact this ship will be crawling with FBI and CIA agents wanting to know all about the weapons in your hold. You will go to prison for a long time Captain." George, now feeling confidence oozing through his body, returns to speaking in his quiet clipped tone of voice.

"However, there are at least three people who I believe are more involved than you in this affair. One is Costas Tinopolis. I do not take kindly to being used Captain, and, I suspect neither do you. So I propose we work together to give these people their come uppance. What do you say?" George enquires in a gentle conciliatory voice.

Kato slowly looks up from the table not believing what he has heard. This young English man has offered a lifeline, perhaps a way out.

If we could put one over on Costas Tinopolis I would not be bothered thinks Kato. *He's used me so let's get the manipulative master together.*

"O K George tell me your plan. I want Tinopolis for getting me in this situation. If I can do him and at the same time secure my way out of this mess I want in with you." Kato looks up at George and gives him a conciliatory grin.

"This is what I need you to do Captain." George walks around the table and sits alongside Kato.

Reilly checks Up

Something troubles Reilly as he watches George park the car. He has an uneasy feeling which experience tells him not to ignore. His instincts had been proved right many times in the past. That guy is trouble with a capital "T" Reilly thinks to himself.

Reilly keeps an eye on George as he boards "Ocean Star" and disappears into the bridge area. He waits a few

Minion or Master

minutes before walking purposefully towards the parked Ford Taunus for a closer inspection. The car is clean inside and the doors are locked. Reilly tries the trunk which, to his surprise, opens. Reilly sees a business suit in a clear polythene bag and in another bag is a black wig. Feeling inside the suit pockets Reilly pulls out a wallet which has a passport picture of George with black hair, glasses and a business card in the name of Thomas White, Marine Insurance and Salvage, London.

Who is this guy? What's his game? Reilly's suspicions are now fully aroused.

Calling to one of the grab operators to keep watch on the car and stop it from leaving Reilly hurries off to the main Docks office which is a half mile walk. By the time Reilly reaches the office it is ten thirty. He goes straight in to the manager's office and verifies that the charterers are Aframe Shipping registered in Bermuda. Reilly tries telephoning the Terminal gate from the office but the line is engaged. In frustration, Reilly slams the telephone down and storms out of the office heading for the Docks gate. He almost tears out the current page of the gate visitor register in his impatience to see the entry for George Howden. He cannot find an entry for Aframe Shipping but he sees an entry at eight fifty for Thomas White, Marine Insurance and Salvage, London. As Reilly questions the gate keeper the Ford Taunus covered in red dust with a dent in its roof cruises past the gate with George driving.

"Stop that car!" Reilly shouts waving his fist out of the window but it is too late. The time is now eleven thirty.

Grabbing at the telephone in the gate office Reilly requests the Docks office to patch him through to "Ocean Star". After waiting for several minutes Reilly is finding it difficult to control his famed Irish temper. At last Captain Kato answers.

"That Limey visitor this morning, what do you know about him?" Reilly yells into the mouthpiece his spittle splattering across the desk.

"Ah yes Mr Howden from the charterers in Bermuda. Not much I've not met him before. He's new and wanted to just check up with me on my paperwork. He left me perfectly happy about forty minutes ago. Why is there some problem?" Kato enquires in his smoothest Greek accent.

"Damn right. The guy is some kind of impostor. He's signed in at the gate as Thomas White, Marine Insurance and Salvage, London. I want to know why."

"Well Reilly I really can't explain that. He knew all about the charter and had all the right papers. He's an accountant so maybe he deals with insurance and got a card mixed up at the gate. I am sure there must be a reasonable explanation."

"Did he say where he was staying?" Reilly shouts.

"No. There is the address in Bermuda. So far as I know he will be heading back there. I really cannot see a problem. Why are you so upset?"

"Call it an Irishman's instinct. We got disturbed yesterday loading those crates, now this today. I like to know what I am dealing with in these docks. Did you find out what is in the crates? May be he's some kind of insurance fraud investigator? The last thing I want in my docks is trouble with some Limey investigator." Reilly replies in a slightly less hostile tone than before.

"As far as I know we have agricultural machinery in those crates and the paperwork validates it stamped by the

US Trade and Development Agency. You should know that. You gave me the paperwork don't you remember?"

"Well I guess you may be right Captain. If you hear anything different get in touch!" Reilly slams down the telephone and orders one of the stevedores coming in through the gate to drive him to Wharf thirty immediately.

Chapter Fourteen
Worry

Saturday afternoon Late May 1966

Afternoon Plans

George is feeling optimistic about the plans he and Kato have made as he walks back to his car. As he reverses the Ford Taunus a rock thumps onto the car roof. Inside the car the noise sounds like a bomb exploding. A split second later there is a tremendous roar sounding like an avalanche. The car is enveloped in a cloud of red dust. An overhead grab has unleashed its ten ton pay load narrowly missing the car. Shocked and disorientated, with adrenaline surging through his body, George drives blindly through the dust. The car swerves then crashes over rolling lumps of iron ore.

After his confrontation with Reilly George's instinct is to get away fast. He doesn't stop to inspect the damage to the car or to find out how the rocks fell so close to him. In his hurry to escape he forgets to change back into his suit and wig for the barrier guard. As he nears the docks exit he is relieved to see the barrier post is raised. Taking a deep breath he presses down hard on the throttle and speeds past the docks exit. Through the dust grimed rear window George sees Reilly waving his fist from the terminal gate window.

Minion or Master

Aframe Shipping can pay for the car damage as well as all my expenses for this trip George reflects as he stops off at the supermarket to collect his photographs.

After taking lunch in his hotel room George examines carefully the photographs he took in the apartment last night. The one that puzzles George the most is the photograph of the paper left in the drawer with the gun and knife. The numbers 5 30 1400 33 468 62 973 mean absolutely nothing to him. George is convinced the numbers are important because they were placed in the top drawer with Sammy's gun. Try as he may he can not make any sense of them.

Next he studies the copy paperwork Kato has given him concerning the ore loading and the export licence for the agricultural machinery. He and Kato now know the agricultural machinery is armaments. George concludes that Sammy is mixed up in a web of criminal activity including drugs, prostitution and gun running. Still puzzling over the numbers George silently pledges to himself that he must try to free Jasmine from Sammy's corrupting world.

A knock interrupts his thoughts. George looks down at his wrist watch and is surprised to discover it is two thirty in the afternoon. He has been so engrossed in his problems he has lost track of time and has forgotten Jasmine agreed to call back.

"Did you find out any thing this morning?" Jasmine asks as she takes a seat on the bed. George sitting at the small desk in the room with the photographs and paper with the mystery numbers spread out looks up at Jasmine and gives her a long stare before replying in a quiet but firm voice.

"Yes, actually, a remarkable number of things Jasmine, I think you might get into serious trouble and possible danger if you stay in New York with Sammy. In my opinion Sammy is involved in really serious criminal activity. You need to leave with me. There will be no chance to get you out later. You will be too enmeshed in Sammy's web. Seize this moment. I can get you away from this nightmare. It is what your Pa and sister would want you to do." George sits silently his whole body gripped with tension hoping Jasmine will see sense and go along with his suggestion.

"I don't know George. I haven't got my passport and tonight Artie has organised a big meet for me at the Casino in Rockefeller Centre. I get triple pay. I need the money George. I need the dope Sammy gives me. Artie has given me some stuff. If I am not there tonight they will hunt me down and hurt me. George I am scared. I can't leave just like that." Jasmine, clearly upset, close to tears, folds her arms across her chest and looks defiantly at George. Sensing Jasmine is at breaking point George gets up from the desk and moves towards Jasmine. He takes hold of her hands and bending down looks straight into her watery eyes.

"You must trust me. I can get you away from Sammy. No one will find you. You won't need your passport. I will get it for you later. You need to break away from these drugs and the first step is to get away from Sammy. He is ruining your life Jasmine. For your sake and your Pa and Lenny make the move!" George grips Jasmine's hands tightly as he continues staring into her face with his cool grey eyes willing her to accede. Jasmine looks into George's face, and, for the first time, she understands and sees as only a woman can the mental strength and resolve in

Minion or Master

George. Instinctively she lowers her head in submission and very softly says:

"OK George. Please help me. I will do what you ask." George lets out a sigh of relief, offers up a prayer of thanks and cuddles Jasmine like a father would comfort a wayward child who has just said sorry.

"Jasmine I need to make a telephone call to organise your escape. Before I do that, do you remember last night I asked if you could find out anything at the warehouse when you went this morning? Did anything look odd or arouse your suspicion?" George asks his brain going back into its analytical cool mode.

"No I can't recall anything George. Sammy and Artie were there and all they talked about was some cruise ship delivering rum to New York next Wednesday. Artie gave me a run down on what I have to do tonight and Sammy said that the guy I had to please was really important to him and he was relying on me. Artie gave me some dope and that was it." Jasmine looking more relaxed, relieved to have made a decision is praying that George will be as strong as his looks suggest.

"Could you go down to the restaurant and fetch us some cool drinks please?" George asks giving Jasmine a re assuring smile. With Jasmine out of the room George requests the hotel switchboard to connect him to "Ocean Star" and after to Government House Bermuda. George considers he has sufficient information to put in a long distance call to Adrian.

Reilly speaks with Sammy

When Reilly arrived at wharf thirty a gang of men were clearing up the pile of ore.

"So what happened? I told you to stop that guy from leaving." Reilly interrogates the grab operator who is looking sheepish and afraid.

"It all happened so quickly Sean. I tried to stop the car with the rocks. I didn't want to kill the guy." The operator whines out his explanation to Reilly who is staring sullenly.

"Mores the pity, there's something real fishy about this guy. I don't like the smell of this at all." Looking over to "Ocean Star" Reilly sees Kato on the bridge preparing to move to the grain wharf.

The sooner the grain covers up those crates the better.

Reilly orders the stevedore to drive him back to the Docks office where there is a pay phone. Reilly telephones the Pulaski Street warehouse and asks to speak to Sammy.

"*He ain't here. Who wants him?*" Artie responds in his rough accent.

"It's Sean Reilly. Tell Sammy I need to see him urgent. He knows where to find me." Reilly slams the telephone down frustrated he cannot speak with Sammy.

An hour later at two thirty Sammy drives into the Docks and finds Reilly.

"What's up Sean? They said it was urgent." Sammy looks at Reilly searching for any clue.

"I got a funny feeling things ain't right with those crates Sammy. There was a guy visited "Ocean Star" today said he was from the charterers said his name was George Howden but he signed in at the gate as another name. I told my guys to stop him leaving but he raced out even though we dropped some rocks around his car. I spoke to the captain of "Ocean Star" who isn't bothered but what with that flash yesterday I ain't so sure Sammy." Reilly scratches his head wondering what further action he can take.

"That name George Howden it sounds kinda familiar to me. Maybe a co-incidence, I'll ask Artie at the warehouse if he knows the guy. I'll get back to you. On another matter we got news that the rum is coming over on the Franconia next Wednesday. She is due to berth at sixteen hundred hours. Is that alright for you and your contacts?" Sammy looks down at the floor not wanting to stir up Reilly with eye contact.

"It should be, provided you come up with my pictures tonight and the cash on Tuesday. Is everything fixed up? I need to nail this guy Brumbell. He is starting to be a pain in the ass at the Docks office asking awkward questions." Reilly gives Sammy one of his menacing looks.

"Sure thing Sean, we fixed up this gorgeous broad from Bermuda she'll have him eating out of her hands tonight. You wait and see." Sammy smiles confidently at Reilly who looks puzzled.

"That's real funny Sammy you know this guy his company is in Bermuda I checked at the docks office. I said we didn't get many Limeys over here." Reilly notices Sammy's face changing colour.

"Jesus Christ Sean I might know the guy. He was with my broad Jasmine in Bermuda when we went to a club. His name was George he didn't give me his last name but he is a Limey. I'll check with her what his last name is. I need a telephone." Sammy chases after Reilly who is sprinting to the coin box near the office.

"Artie its Sammy, is Jasmine there?"

"She left here this morning Sammy. She's probably gone to the apartment. Why what's the problem?" Artie queries getting concerned.

"There was a guy in Bermuda. Sean here reckons it's a guy called George Howden who has been to the Docks today. Jasmine knows him. I want to check if he is the same one, if she comes back keep her there for me." Sammy orders Artie. He is just about to replace the receiver when he hears Artie shriek

"Sammy there was a guy yesterday snooping in the warehouse, a Limey, called himself George Howden from Aframe Shipping said he was looking for a forwarding agent. I sent him out to the office. It was just after you left with the crates Sammy."

"Did he leave an address? We need to find this guy fast. I don't like what I am hearing." Sammy retorts.

"No we got nothing. Maybe Jasmine might know." Artie suggests.

"OK, drop everything and find Jasmine. When you have her let me know and get some of the boys to try local hotels we might get lucky with finding this guy."

"I guess you heard what Artie said Sean?" Sammy looks at Reilly who is going puce with rage.

"I should have sorted this guy out when he was in the car. We need to find out what he is up to. I'll get my boys checking the hotels in Manhattan, we'll get the son of a bitch."

Sammy looks for George

When Sammy returns to the warehouse he hears Artie talking loudly into the telephone.

"Randy I'm telling you I want you to get everyone out checking hotels for the next two hours. A limey called George Howden. We need to locate him fast. Call me back here every half hour so I can keep you updated."

Minion or Master

Artie slams down the telephone and holds his hands up looking guiltily at Sammy.

"So we had this schmuck right here under our noses yesterday. What did he see Artie?" Sammy looks at Artie the way a vulture looks at a piece of carrion.

"Sammy he must have come right into the warehouse just after you left for the docks with the crates. The doors were still open. Me and the boys we were packaging up the stuff for the pushers in the back room. All of a sudden the door opens and this guy pops his head in. It happened so quickly. He seemed genuine, like a business man, definitely not a cop. I would smell a cop from miles away." Artie puffs up his chest trying to appease Sammy.

"The thing is unless we find this guy we are not secure. We gotta assume he knows what you and the boys were up to. He has to be found and silenced tonight. Otherwise I will have to tell the boss next time he calls with the password that this place is not safe. Have you found Jasmine? She might know something." Sammy sits down thinking what his next move should be.

"I ain't seen Jasmine since this morning. She came in the office when we were fixing the Franconia deal for next Wednesday. My guess is she is at the apartment."

"Get one of the guys to get over there and see if she is there. Tell him to telephone either way. If she is there I want him to keep an eye on her until I can get there. In the meantime you and me have gotta make contingency plans." Sammy says in a determined voice.

"OK Sammy what can I do?" Artie gets up ready for action.

"First make that telephone call. Next get all the dope packaged up ready to move out immediately. Then, get some gasoline cans ready to torch this place. We can't leave any traces. I am gonna get all the files and contact papers from the office packed. Let's move!"

An hour later the telephone rings in the office. It is Artie's man reporting that Jasmine is not in the apartment. Sammy orders the man to wait and telephone as soon as she is seen. As soon as Sammy puts the telephone down it rings again. This time it is the man Sammy and Artie call *the boss* giving them tonight's password. The cash is to be collected at six o'clock. Sammy advises *the boss* that they might have a problem. Sammy is told to wait for orders.

At six o'clock *the boss's* collectors arrive and show Sammy a piece of paper which has the password "Bronx Kitten 65" written down. Sammy confirms the password is correct and hands over a brief case stacked with notes and a sealed envelope which confirms the contents is thirty thousand dollars. The senior of the two collectors, who is dressed in a business suit which appears two sizes too small for his bulk, takes out a card and hands it to Sammy saying:

"Ring this number from a call box at seven thirty". Without a further word the two collectors walk out avoiding eye contact with Artie and Sammy.

At six forty five Reilly telephones to advise that one of his men has traced George Howden to The Palace Hotel but he checked out earlier in the day. He left no forwarding address. Reilly has sent a couple of his men to La Guardia Airport to see if they can find him checking in for the evening Bermuda flight. Reilly has also made enquiries with his union contacts at JFK airport in case he takes any other international flight. Sammy tells Artie to get Randy and the other contacts to switch their attention from looking for George Howden to finding Jasmine.

Minion or Master

"So what now Sammy, where do I take this stuff?" Artie points at a large container which holds twenty kilos of diluted cocaine in plastic bags.

"For now put it in the trunk of my car with these papers. Make sure it's all locked up, any news on Jasmine?"

"Nothing, she seems to have gone to ground real well. She should be turning up at the apartment for her clothes any time now. I've told Randy to get over to the Casino in case she has made her way over there early. She is due there by nine to get acquainted with Reilly's mark. I need to be getting over there soon myself to sort out the camera." Artie is gasping as he starts to move the papers and drugs to Sammy's car parked inside the warehouse.

"O K when you have done that. Move the car out of the warehouse and park it a few blocks away. Just in case. Then get over to the casino. I've got a call to make." Sammy sighs looking at the card with the telephone number on.

Chapter Fifteen

Leaving

Saturday afternoon Late May 1966

George leaves the hotel

George is on the telephone when Jasmine returns with cool drinks from the bar.

"Yes Adrian, I see. I will be back tomorrow. Meet me at the airport. I have a lot more information but it will be safer not to use the telephone. See you tomorrow." George hangs up and takes a long sip of the soft drink Jasmine hands him.

"So Jasmine everything is organised, do you have any clothes with you?"

"Only these, everything is at the apartment. Why? Where are we going George?" Jasmine looks worried.

"You will find out in just a few hours. I do not think it is safe for you or me to go back to your apartment. We need to leave. Let's go down to the basement. You can wait in the car whilst I go back and check out." George gives Jasmine a reassuring smile.

Thirty minutes later they are driving towards New Jersey and the out of town supermarket. George takes Jasmine to the clothing department. He chooses a variety of practical warm comfortable clothes and shoes for

Minion or Master

Jasmine who is completely bewildered by the clothes selection.

"George if you don't mind my saying. None of these clothes are my style. They are ugly. I am supposed to be a glamour model not some raggedy work woman. What are you playing at?" Jasmine gives George an old fashioned look and stands with her arms folded across her chest.

"Believe me Jasmine these are right for now. In a few days time you will thank me. Now let's get some provisions for you.

Do you like any particular foods?" George asks as they head for the food hall.

"I get my food in the cafe George. I don't need no provisions."

"Trust me Jasmine. You will be glad of some tit bits. I have to get you away from Sammy and believe me this is the best solution. We have another hour to wait before I can deliver you safely. So what do you say we finish loading the car then let's have a coffee here and go over our plans?" George grins at Jasmine.

"You are a truly unusual man, if I hadn't seen that look in your face back in the hotel. I would be running from you as fast as I could but I still trust you even though I don't understand any of this." Jasmine makes her final protest but instinctively deep down she is excited and intrigued at what this English guy is up to.

Over coffee George goes over with Jasmine what he knows about Sammy and his involvement with drugs. He explains how Sammy's gang has been smuggling drugs in to New York hidden in the Island rum packaging. George is careful not to mention any thing about Sammy's involvement with arms smuggling. He shows Jasmine the photograph of the paper with the numbers on he found in

Sammy's bed room on the off chance Jasmine might just know what they mean.

"I don't know George I can't make the numbers out. The first ones they could be dates but then the other ones I can't make sense of. So this Island rum that is why Sammy gave me a carrier bag for Artie he said it was rum. Then, remember, I told you this morning at the warehouse they were talking about a cruise ship delivering rum to New York next Wednesday." Jasmine talks absent minded still concentrating over the numbers on the photographs. George, just about to drink from his coffee cup, pauses, then emphatically places the cup back onto its saucer and looks intently at Jasmine.

"Hang on just a minute, dates, of course. American dates put the month before the day. I am still not used to that. So if you are correct 5 and 30 might be May 30th and 1400 two o'clock. That is Monday at two o'clock. Even though I consider myself something of a numbers man I still can't figure out the others." George gets back to his coffee.

"I don't know about Monday. Wednesday was the day Sammy and Artie were talking about rum on the cruise ship. May be they are bringing in a load of drugs with the rum." Jasmine suggests.

"That kind of makes sense. Did they say any thing else about the rum can you remember?"

"Not that I can remember. I wasn't paying a load of attention just waiting for Artie to give me some drugs for tonight.

"Jasmine I want you to give me those drugs please. You have to get off this habit. It is going to be hard I know; but, in the next week you will have a chance to do it. I will keep the drugs for emergency use for you.

Now we have to make a move. It is six thirty and I have arranged for your rescuer to meet us for dinner." George explains pocketing the drugs which Jasmine has meekly handed over.

Saturday evening Late May 1966

Sammy 'phones the boss

Two blocks away from the warehouse Sammy is in a phone booth, he dials the number on the card given to him by *the boss's* cash collector. After the first ring Sammy hears a monosyllabic grunt in the receiver.

"Yea it's Sammy I was told to call."

"Be at the casino at Rockefeller Centre at midnight!" The voice immediately closes the connection.

When Sammy returns to the warehouse the telephone is ringing.

"It's Artie Sammy. I'm over at the casino. The room and the cameras are all fixed up but there is still no sign of the broad. Randy suggests we should get some back up in case she has done a runner." Artie speaks fast and urgently. Sammy, holding the telephone receiver to his ear is trying hard to control the anger welling up. Any hint of tender feelings he might have had initially for Jasmine have evaporated in the last four hours. He vows to focus his anger to bring his ruthless sadistic nature up to new unimaginable heights for Jasmine to experience when he finds her.

"Yea OK Artie, you had better get another broad down there for insurance. We can't afford to upset Sean Reilly. I will be over at eleven. Keep looking for the Jasmine bitch though because I have some unfinished business with her." The telephone rings again as Sammy is locking up the warehouse.

"This is Reilly. We may have got lucky with this Howden guy. One of my contacts bribed the Palace Hotel receptionist and we found the guy hired a car from the hotel. A Ford Taunus that was the car I saw him drive this morning. The receptionist remembers the guy well because he had to pay the insurance excess for the car damage. He paid five hundred bucks in cash. Any how he had another car, a Pontiac. He put the car registration in the hotel register. I got my police contacts to do a check. The car is due back at the rental office at La Guardia airport tomorrow. A couple of my guys will be waiting for this sucker to turn up at the rental company tomorrow. Then we will nail him." Reilly says with a hint of satisfaction in his Bronx accent.

"O k that's great Sean. When you get this guy can you keep him on ice for a few days? I will be away until Wednesday sorting out the Franconia deal."

"We got some of these new fangled containers at Red Hook. It will cost you five grand up front and I don't guarantee his condition by Wednesday after I have finished with him."

"I will organise the money tonight for you Sean. Just make sure he can talk when I get back." Sammy hangs up.

Sammy takes a taxi to the apartment. He packs a small suit case and includes the folded sheet of paper with numbers written down and his flick knife. He takes one of the passports and his Bank of Pembroke pass book which has a credit balance of five hundred thousand dollars. Sammy checks his ticket is for the morning flight to Bermuda tomorrow morning from La Guardia airport.

Saturday evening Late May 1966

George delivers Jasmine

Captain Kato with assistance from the harbour pilots has successfully transferred "Ocean Star" from wharf thirty to wharf eighteen at the Red Hook terminal. The feed pipes from the grain silos have been connected to "Ocean Star". The ship will be fully bunkered with a full cargo of grain by Monday. She is scheduled to sail on Tuesday. A taxi drops him off at a Greek restaurant on Broadway. He intends to celebrate his last meal ashore with traditional Greek food and wine with his guests. He orders some meze with a glass of Ouzo and starts to sample the delicious savouries. Kato is so engrossed in enjoying the delicious meze that he does not notice George and Jasmine arrive.

"Agios, may I introduce you to Jasmine, Jasmine this is Captain Agios Kato he will be taking good care of you for the next week or so." George smiles as he looks at Kato who is staring at Jasmine, his mouth wide open with some meze on a fork poised to be consumed.

"My God, George you didn't say how beautiful my guest would be Jasmine what a lovely name." Kato puts down his meze.

"Please seat yourselves. Try some meze and Ouzo. Tonight we celebrate. I have ordered food for all of us. To start, Cretan bruschetta topped with tomato & oregano, drizzled with olive oil & finished with feta cheese. For our main course we have beef stifado all washed down with Domaine Spiropoulos." Kato waves at a waiter and orders more Ouzo and Meze whilst George and Jasmine get settled.

"Did you say Captain Kato . . . . George?" Jasmine enquires looking puzzled.

"Yes, Jasmine; Captain Kato will take you aboard the "Ocean Star" after dinner. On Tuesday you sail for Africa." George grins at Kato and Jasmine.

"We have a spare cabin on board reserved for visitors. You will be comfortable, Jasmine, although the food is somewhat monotonous. We will be in Lourenco Marques, Mozambique two weeks from now. However, George hopes he will be seeing you in St Helena when we stop for bunker fuel. Is there anything troubling you my dear?" Kato enquires as he tucks in to some more meze and Ouzo.

"What happens there, will I be safe from Sammy?" Jasmine looks at the two men with doubt in her eyes.

"If all goes to plan by next week Sammy and his gang will be history. I will see you in St Helena with your passport and in a few more days after that you can be back in Bermuda with your family." George declares.

"Of course I shall be delighted if you stay on board "Ocean Star" until we get to Mozambique, Jasmine. Do not let George whisk you away too soon from me." Kato pleads as he pours Jasmine some Ouzo.

"Sailing to Africa I declare. How things change. Three hours ago I was expecting to be with Marshall Brumbell this evening. Now I know why you got me those ugly clothes George." Jasmine speaks quietly and slowly trying to absorb the changes going on.

"Did you say Marshall Brumbell was the man you were seeing tonight?" George asks with more than passing interest in his voice.

"That's the guy who signed the discharge order for the chrome!" Kato blurts out thumping the table.

Minion or Master

"I was to see him at the Casino at Rockefeller Centre tonight. Artie was to take compromising pictures of us. I was to get triple pay. Instead I'm running away on a ship to Africa." Jasmine stares intently at George and Kato.

"Perhaps I can assist Mr Brumbell avoid his downfall tonight and get some more information about the chrome ore; or, better still make him an ally." George muses.

"If you can get evidence to hook in Tinopolis that will be even better" Kato says with conviction then he smiles at Jasmine and rubs his hands in anticipation as the bruschetta arrives.

"Maybe you can help with this Agios?" George shows Kato the photograph of the paper with the numbers on.

"We think the first sequence of numbers is dates and times but have no idea about the others."

"I don't know. No idea." Kato says having given the numbers a cursory glance before he hands them back to George. Kato is more interested in chatting to Jasmine.

"Come on Captain I solved the first set how about you have another look?" Jasmine gives Kato a stunning smile and pushes the sheet back.

"Of course my dear how could I refuse your very first request? Let's see well now these numbers 33 and 62 could be co—ordinates. Those are the type of numbers we use with marine charts. 33 could be 33 degrees latitude and 62 would be longitude." Kato returns the papers to George eager to get back to his bruschetta.

"So, if you are correct, where would 33 latitude and 62 longitude be in the world? Do you know?" George questions Kato.

"Somewhere in the North Atlantic I guess. I would need my charts to give you a precise location." Kato looks disinterested and transfers his attention to finishing off his bruschetta.

George is secretly delighted with this information and decides not to pursue this any further with Kato. If Kato is correct then George now knows what these numbers mean and can make plans accordingly.

"You know that guy Reilly in the docks he was making inquiries about you this morning George. He said you signed in as Thomas White, Marine Insurance and Salvage, London. Is that true George?" Kato asks.

"Yes I didn't want to give my name at the gate again as George Howden because I signed in as that yesterday. My scheming almost got me into trouble. Did you see the rocks come crashing around the car after I left you? Reilly questioned me before I came aboard to see you. A very unpleasant character if you ask me. I hope I don't run into him again."

"I told Reilly as you were an accountant you had dealings with insurance companies and you got your cards mixed up. I don't think he fully believed me. I wouldn't worry George we will soon be on the high seas and you will be back in Bermuda." Kato grins at Jasmine as he finishes off the last of the Domaine Spiropoulos.

"It's nine thirty; if I am to thwart Sammy and his gang I have to go. I will see you both in St Helena." George gives Kato a bear hug and Jasmine a tender kiss on the cheek.

"Please be careful George." Jasmine implores.

"Don't worry George all will be well. The Gods are with us." Kato waves his arms in a farewell gesture.

Chapter Sixteen
Marshall Brumbell

Saturday night Late May 1966

Casino Rumpus

Returning to his car George removes the black wig, spectacles and make up box from his suitcase. At ten thirty wearing spectacles and with his eyebrows coloured black to match his black wig George enters the casino.

"I am due to meet a friend here tonight, Marshall Brumbell. Has he arrived yet do you know?" The hostess at the booking desk looks up at George and then glances through her register.

"Mr. Brumbell is a regular client here Sir. He has checked in tonight you will find him at the roulette table."

As George walks into the main casino room he sees Artie at the bar talking with a woman and a man. George works his way across the crowded room towards the bar making sure that Artie has his back to him. George orders a gin and tonic and sits on a bar stool with a group of people standing between himself and Artie's group. He watches in the bar mirror as Artie gesticulates to the woman. She is angry. The bar is crowded with casino clients talking loudly: background music is blaring out: it is impossible for George to hear anything they are saying.

After a few more minutes of heated discussion the woman and the man move away from the bar. Artie is joined by a worried and nervous looking Sammy. George decides it is too risky to stay so close to Sammy and Artie at the bar so he picks up his drink and follows the man and woman who are moving across to the roulette table. The man and woman do not know George so he moves in close and overhears the conversation between them and a third man at the table.

"How are you Randy?" the third man playing the roulette wheel opens the conversation and gives the woman an inquisitive expectant look.

"Great Marshall, just great, may I introduce a friend of mine Dolores. She is from out of town and has never played roulette before. I told her you are something of an expert and she was hoping you might show her the ropes so to speak." Randy smiles and moves Dolores nearer to the man.

"Sure thing, Dolores, that's a cute name. Come in here and sit right next to me. Let's play roulette," the man called Marshall grins as Randy moves away.

George feels sure the woman named Dolores is Jasmine's replacement and the man Marshall at the roulette wheel must be the target for black mail. The man is tall, middle aged with thinning hair and is talking animatedly to Dolores who has her hand on his arm. George has seen and heard enough. He moves away to watch a group playing black jack.

Keeping a low profile George spots Reilly walk into the casino and go straight into a private room. Sammy and Artie are no longer in George's view.

A waiter walks across to the roulette table and hands Marshall a note. Soon after he tells Dolores he needs the rest room. He orders drinks for the two of them and advises Dolores to keep betting on the black.

George follows Marshall into the men's rest room. No one else is in the room.

"You got my note then". George says in a nervous whisper.

"What the hell is this all about? It had better be good." Marshall whispers back looking angrily at George.

"You are Marshall Brumbell Vice President, Bulk Handling, Brooklyn Docks Board?"

"Yes I am. How do you know that? Who the hell are you?"

"My name is George Howden. There is not much time to explain. Please believe me, you are the target of a black mail set up. The woman you are with is the bait. Do you know a Sean Reilly at the docks?" At the name Sean Reilly George notices Marshall's face momentarily freeze.

"How do you know that son of a bitch?" Marshall asks his interest now fully aroused. Before George can respond the rest room door opens and two men walk in.

"It's not safe to talk here. I think Sean Reilly is behind this black mail with a gang involved in prostitution and drugs. If you want to stay safe I suggest you leave as soon as possible. Meet me at the Palace Hotel on Lexington Avenue in an hour! We can talk in detail then." Whilst talking George has been washing his hands then drying them on the air dryer.

"I have been trying to nail Reilly for some months now. I am not surprised he is involved. I am out of here. Here's my card meet me at my home at Englewood Cliffs. I'll expect you later." Marshall leaves without a further word.

Walking casually out of the rest room George makes his way to the bar where he orders tonic water. He then moves away cautiously before merging into a crowd watching a high stakes dice game.

"I missed you so much Marshall. I haven't been too lucky with the black honey. If you want we can go and play another game. What do you say honey?" Dolores looks into Marshall's eyes as she places her left hand onto his inner thigh and presses her long red nails into his bulging man hood.

"Gee Dolores. There's nothing I want more baby than to play some games with you. The thing is baby I don't feel too good. I think I'm coming down with a bug. I'm gonna have to take a rain check. I'm real sorry baby. There's one hundred dollars in chips still here. Have a ball baby. Next time you are in town look me up. Here's my card." Marshall takes Dolores hand from his crotch and gives her a peck on the cheek and walks away.

Spying from the crowd George sees Dolores turn from the roulette table and make a sign of exasperation at the man Marshall had called Randy who is now standing at the bar. Randy races over to the private office.

Minutes later Sammy and Reilly emerge from the room with Randy in tow. Reilly is gesticulating at Sammy and looks frustrated and angry. Reilly pushes Sammy across the room. Sammy staggers as Reilly lands one of his meaty fists into Sammy's stomach. In the ensuing brawl two guards emerge from the security office and pounce on Reilly. One of the guards pins back Reilly's arms whilst the other tries to placate him. Having none of this Reilly leans his head back then with lightening speed he launches his forehead on to the guard's nose. Blood spurts from his

Minion or Master

nose; the other guard goes down as Reilly backs his thick skull into his face.

"All deals are off you greasy Wop slime ball!" Reilly shouts as he lunges towards Sammy. The area is now in pandemonium with clients and staff turning to watch the spectacle. More guards arrive. Four manage to subdue Reilly long enough to handcuff him. As Reilly is man handled past the crowd he shouts at Sammy

"That Limey is in on this! He's dead meat when he checks his rented car in. Then I'm coming for you!"

Still merged in with the crowd George has overheard Reilly's last remark.

Forewarned is forearmed.

George decides it is time to pay Marshall Brumbell a visit.

Early Sunday morning Late May 1966

Marshall Brumbell

It takes George forty five minutes to drive north to Highway ninety five crossing the Hudson River onto Palisades Parkway before turning into a very select neighbourhood in Chestnut Street; the address of Marshall C Brumbell. As George gets out of the car Marshall opens his front door and waves to George to come up the tree lined illuminated drive.

"Heard a bit of a rumpus kicked off as I was leaving, you had better tell me what this is all about." Marshall guides George in to a sitting room furnished with brown leather chairs. The low walnut side table, close to the chairs, has a silver coffee pot with cream and sugar jugs neatly set out along with fine china cups and saucers.

Marshall listens intently as George explains how Jasmine had been tricked into prostitution by Sammy Santino and that George had come to New York to find out what had become of her. The whole story takes over thirty minutes to relate to. George outlines the gang's involvement with drugs but holds back on mentioning anything to do with the chrome ore and arms; he is not sure how much trust he can place in Marshall.

"So where is this Jasmine lady now? Is she with you?" Marshall wants to know.

"She is safe for now, the fewer people who know where she is the better."

"Son, she could end up being a valuable witness here." Marshall speaks sternly and continues

"I don't know how much you know; but let me tell you, Brooklyn Docks Board want to clean up the wharves; Reilly's sort have to go; Red Hook is to become a massive container port. I am working with the FBI on this. If we can pin prostitution and drugs on to Reilly a major problem will be solved."

"I don't think Jasmine has any direct evidence that can link Reilly to Sammy Santino's operations. They clearly know each other and have dealings. Tonight's events show that. There may be some incriminating papers at the Pulaski Street warehouse or at Sammy's apartment." George suggests in a rather subdued voice as he fights hard to keep his eyes open. The events of the last two days with their adrenaline surges coupled with lack of sleep are starting to tell on him.

"O K this is what I suggest. I will call my FBI contact let's see if we can get some information on these guys. In the meantime you look all in. You can get some shut eye here before your flight this morning. What time is the flight?"

"It's ten thirty from La Guardia. I have to return the rent car but I overheard Reilly saying they know about me checking in. I suspect they will be waiting for me." George answers feeling drained of energy.

"We will worry about that later. Get some shut eye on the sofa over there. I will make some calls." Marshall throws over some blankets as he leaves the room.

Exhausted, George complies and snuggles up under the blankets on the sofa. He is soon fast asleep.

Sammy gets Orders

Sitting down on the velvet seat Sammy tries to accustom his sight to the lack of light in the cubicle. The curtains are closed. He can barely make out two figures.

"So Sammy you are lucky that my boss has a soft spot for you. After today any one else would be history." The smaller of the figures whispers.

"I have never asked questions always followed orders. I don't know your boss. I've never met him. The operation has run pretty smoothly until today. This guy Howden may have stumbled upon something in the warehouse. Reilly reckons he was snooping around the docks using a false name. Tonight the broad from Bermuda, who, I think, knows Howden, has disappeared."

Sammy whines out his explanation. As his eyes get accustomed to the gloom he can see a thin wiry man dressed in a business suit looking like a banking executive. Alongside is a man in his early thirties well dressed but with a face as cold and hard looking as an Alaskan glacier.

"So what have you done to protect our operation?" Michael Gregory the banker type queries in a cool unruffled voice.

"We got all the stuff out of the warehouse including papers. It's all in my car which is parked away safe. Reilly found where this guy Howden was staying but he's done a bunk. He's got a rental car which has to go back to La Guardia tomorrow, I mean today. After he checks in he's gonna be questioned." Sammy blurts out to the two opposite who show no expression on their faces.

"Give me the keys to your car!" the man with the glacier face orders. Sammy complies. The man pulls back the curtain slightly, hands the keys to someone and whispers

"Move Sammy's cars to our depot, then torch the warehouse. Leave no trace!" Staring hard at Sammy the glacier face says

"You won't need the car again!"

"Me and Artie already got some gasoline cans in ready." Sammy says eagerly, trying to be helpful.

"You have to disappear for a while Sammy. Make sure there is nothing incriminating in your apartment. You have to get our shipment tomorrow. Then make yourself scarce. Take a holiday. We will find you when the time is right." Michael Gregory instructs.

"What about this Howden guy?" Sammy wants to know.

"Leave him to us. If Reilly gets him we will know. Then he won't be a problem. Now you'd better run along. You got a lot to do before you disappear."

Chapter Seventeen
Duane Pickens

Sunday morning 29th May 1966

George Awakes

"George, wake up! It is six o'clock. Breakfast is ready. We need to talk." Marshall Brumbell gives George a gentle shake.

"I'll be ten minutes. Can I use the bathroom?" George asks in a sleepy voice.

"Sure. Watch out for Mrs Brumbell." As George wanders out of the study a lady sitting in a wheel chair comes out of an adjoining room and gives George a smile.

"Oh sorry, I didn't mean to intrude." George apologises.

"Think nothing of it honey. You must be George. I am Martha. I got hit by a truck six years ago, paralysed from the waist down. Hope you don't mind me being so straight talking, best not to beat about the bush. Bathroom's just here honey." Martha points to a door.

"Thank you Martha, nice to meet you." George blurts out rushing in to the bathroom to hide his embarrassment.

"So now you are fair haired." Marshall exclaims as George returns from the bath room.

"I was in disguise at the Casino in case Sammy recognised me. Sorry about Martha. She is so positive."

George sits down to breakfast looking over at Marshall who is sipping at a cup of coffee.

"Yes it was a real shock when it happened. Because of the paralysis Martha and I can't have normal relations. So now and again I take relief elsewhere. I sure wouldn't want some slime ball showing pictures to Martha. So I guess I owe you for last night, seems as though you have caused a stir. My FBI contacts went out to take a look at the warehouse. The place was an inferno. They couldn't get near to it."

"They must have suspected something after Reilly quizzed me at the docks. This prompts me to ask you something else. Can you give me any information about this document?" George hands Marshall a copy of the loading document.

"How did you get hold of this?" Marshall exclaims incredulously now looking at George with respect. George explains his dealings with "Ocean Star" and Costas Tinopolis and how the British had found out about the chrome ore.

"That's why I had to come to New York. Seeing Jasmine was supposed to be a side issue but it turns out to have been more than that. It is a remarkable co incidence that you happen to be the person signing that document Marshall. I really am looking for something to take back to the British to get me off the hook. They are not best pleased." George hopes he hasn't given too much away.

"Well I'll be damned. There is more to you than first comes across. I can't give you any proof and I'll deny it if ever questioned but I was ordered by my FBI contact to prepare and sign that loading document. I was told it was helping the country. That is the truth. I followed

Minion or Master

orders." Marshall declares shifting in his chair appearing uncomfortable at the revelation.

"Thank you for that Marshall. You have confirmed what I suspected. Your Government wants this chrome ore badly and they have leaned on the British to go along with it." George smiles at Marshall.

"Ok I hope it helps. The FBI boys have come up with a plan to get Reilly. One of the FBI who happens to look like you is gonna take your car back to the rental place. If Reilly does kidnap the driver we will be following and then we can put him away legitimately." Marshall utters with a smirk on his face.

"That certainly solves one problem. Here are the keys and documents." George exclaims with a sigh of relief. Pausing, he remembers he still has to find the exact North Atlantic location for 33 latitude and 62 longitude to check Sammy's paper with the numbers on. He asks Marshall who is able to identify the location from his marine charts.

"It's about 150 nautical miles north east from Bermuda. Why do you want to know?" Marshall asks noticing that George has a look of triumph on his face.

"That is the location for a drugs drop off tomorrow afternoon at two o'clock to be collected by Sammy Santino, or one of his gang, in Bermuda. The drugs are then smuggled in to the States in cartons of rum. There isn't much time but if you get the FBI to help I think we can break this operation up." George now feels certain he has cracked the numbers.

"You are right there isn't much time. What is your plan?" Marshall asks as he pours more coffee. After an hour of discussion interrupted with Marshall making and receiving telephone calls Marshall declares

"Its eight fifteen now, the FBI guy has taken your car and plans to deliver it back to the rental company at nine. I will take you to La Guardia and use my contacts to get you through the flight formalities smoothly. We had better move out."

Car is returned

At eight fifty five a fair haired man drives a Pontiac into the delivery compound of Alpha rentals at La Guardia airport and walks into the reception office.

"Can I help you Sir?" enquires the counter assistant.

"Mr. Howden returning the Pontiac, here are the papers." The fair haired man says in a loud voice with an unmistakable British accent.

After signing the car papers the fair haired man leaves the office. As he makes his way towards the shuttle bus stop two men walk up alongside and bundle him into the back of a car which has silently glided up to the side walk.

The two men quickly enter the car sandwiching the fair haired man in the back and the car accelerates away out of the terminal area.

"*Bravo One* this is *Delta One* suspects have been followed to Red Hook terminal they have taken target to a container. No sign of *Alpha One* yet, over." The driver of the FBI unmarked car code named *Bravo One* radios in to his controller. The co driver studies a photograph of Sean Reilly marked *Alpha One*.

"*Delta One* this is *Bravo One* keep watch and wait for *Alpha One*, out."

Thirty minutes later a car pulls up outside the container. Sean Reilly looking grim and angry from his fracas at the Casino gets out from the car and knocks on the container with a knuckle duster.

"*Bravo One* this is *Delta One*. *Alpha One* has arrived, permission to proceed to apprehend. There are three tangos."

"*Delta One* this is *Bravo One* wait for back up before proceeding. Maintain watch, out."

As the container door opens the two men emerge and stand aside to allow Sean Reilly access.

"Who the fuck is you, you ain't the Limey!" Reilly roars. He grabs the fair haired FBI stooge by the collar and hurls him across the container. Although his hands are tied behind his back the stooge gets onto his feet and stumbles out into the day light. Reilly pursues and lands a vicious punch with the knuckle duster encircled fist in the stooges ribs.

"*Bravo One* this is *Delta One* target is compromised."

As the FBI team await instructions they see a motorbike with a pillion passenger roar up to the container. The pillion passenger swivels on the motor bike and in a split second has fired a burst of bullets from an automatic machine pistol.

"*Delta One* this is *Bravo One* proceed. *Delta two* is en route."

"Head off that bike fast!" the passenger in *Bravo One* says to his colleague.

As *Bravo One* hurtles towards the container the motor cycle pillion passenger fires one last burst at the four men now lying on the ground. The motor cycle accelerates away out of Red Hook.

"*Bravo One* this is *Delta One* target and three tangos down, motor cycle with armed passenger heading south out of Red Hook, request *Delta two* to intercept. Send ambulance and medical assistance."

Airport rumpus

Marshall parks his car in a restricted area marked up for Airport security staff. He and George walk into the outer office of La Guardia Airport control room. Marshall shows an identity card and signs George in at the security desk. They go into a secure area which has one way windows. Homeland security officials are monitoring passengers queuing in the roped lanes waiting final processing before passing into the restricted departure area.

"George let me introduce you to my FBI associate. Duane Pickens meet George Howden the English guy I told you about on the telephone. Let me tell you George, Duane and I have been working closely on the Red Hook Docks clean up for nearly two months now. Your help has been much appreciated ain't that so Duane." Marshall has taken George over to a desk near the observation window.

"Sure thing Marshall. Glad to meet you George. I hear you are leaving us this morning? Too bad we could use some more informants like you to bust this case." Duane relates in a Tennessee twang. George shakes Duane's hand and looks into the face of a man who has cool blue eyes; aged in his early thirties; George guesses; but with a world weary look that says here is a man of experience; who knows all the tricks any rogue might play and how to counter them.

"Good morning Duane it is nice to meet you. A real FBI man, I have only ever read about you people in adventure stories. This is quite exciting." George smiles

Minion or Master

at Duane who just stares back his facial expression giving nothing away.

"You might be seeing more of me than you bargained for. The information you have given Marshall on drugs has caused quite a stir with my bosses. I am detailed to fly out with you. We won't be sitting together and I don't expect you to be pally with me. Keep away; it's best if no one knows our status. The local cops and Bermudan Government are in the loop. Our liaison with the local cops is a guy called Adrian Cuthbert, talks like he has a whole water melon stuck in his mouth, says he knows you."

"Now this really is getting exciting. Adrian and I . . ." George pauses in mid sentence his mouth wide open as he gawps over Duane's broad shoulder at the observation window.

"I swear that was Sammy Santino. Yes it's him. What's he doing here?" Before George can say any more Duane has bounded across to the security officer monitoring the passengers and whispers in his ear. The security officer picks up a telephone and after a pause speaks to Duane who strides back to his desk.

"The guy's name is Roberto Marcello, address in Milan, Italy. He is on the flight to Bermuda with us." Duane reports back.

"That's one of the names in the passports I photographed. If Sammy sees me on the flight he will smell a rat for sure." Before Duane can respond the telephone on his desk rings. Duane answers with grunts. George notices Duane's facial expression has changed.

"This is getting real serious. Reilly and two of his men are dead, gunned down at Red Hook just a few minutes ago. Our guy who took your hire car is wounded in the shoulder and leg. Seems his bullet proof vest saved him. The killers got away on a motorbike, as yet no ID and no trace. There is an APB out. We might get lucky and catch them." Duane speaks in a matter of fact tone of voice as if he was giving out a football score then he rubs a hand around his chin in thought before looking up at George and Marshall.

"I'm gonna ask control if we should pull this Sammy or Roberto guy, whatever his name is, from the flight for questioning." Duane picks up the telephone.

"Well at least now Reilly is out of the way we can get Red Hook cleaned up." Marshall declares looking at George who is wondering how all this will play out.

"Yes Captain, understood Sir." Duane puts the telephone down and without a further word races back over to the security officer. After a few minutes of urgent discussion and telephone calls Duane walks back to Marshall and George.

"OK George you are out of here right now. You are to board the aircraft with the flight crew. You will be sitting at the rear of the aircraft. Sammy, whatever his name is, is booked in first class at the front of the Aircraft. He ain't gonna see you. We are gonna let this guy run for a while. See what happens. I volunteered to be up graded to first class to keep an eye on the son of a gun. Some one has to do the dirty work. Ain't that right guys. See you in Bermuda George. The security officer here will take you on board. Take care Marshall." Duane races out of the security office waving his right arm in a farewell gesture.

Chapter Eighteen
Apology accepted

Sunday afternoon 29th May 1966

Welcome back George

The Pan Am flight to Bermuda was uneventful except for the buffeting the Boeing 707 passengers experienced as the jet descended from its normal cruising height. At ten thousand feet the port side passengers had a good view of the southern side of the island as the plane continued its descent into Mckinley Air base located at the eastern end of the Island. George, sitting at the rear of the aircraft, had taken the chance to catch up on lost sleep. Later, his mind was occupied going over all the events since Friday. He could not believe that so much had occurred in such a short space of time. He has a lot to go over with Adrian. He worries whether Jasmine is coping with "Ocean Star" and Kato. He has some explaining to do with Lenny and Charlie about Jasmine and Sammy.

Obeying the cabin crew commands George fastens his seat belt and swallows hard several times to counter act the air pressure change as the aircraft descends rapidly. He feels the inside of his ears squeezing against his skull in protest at the violent change in pressure. As he rubs his ears trying to relieve the pain there is a loud bang from the tyres as they smack in to the tarmac; this is followed by a roaring sound as the pilot puts the jet engines into reverse thrust to assist with braking. In less than a minute the aircraft is taxiing sedately along the runway towards the terminal building to link up with its mobile ladders.

Conscious that Sammy and Duane are in the front of the aircraft George decides to bide his time to be one of the last to disembark. Looking through a cabin window George sees Sammy walking across the tarmac to the terminal building. Duane is strolling nonchalantly close by; trying hard to look like an excited tourist on his first visit. Sammy waves to someone on the balcony of the terminal building. The building is too far away for George to identify the person.

Time to leave

George picks up his ruck sack from the overhead locker. He exits at the rear door and walks across the tarmac with the last of the passengers. As George approaches the terminal building a Land Rover cruises up alongside.

"Hop in George there's a good chap!" shouts Adrian. George is taken aback at this sudden and unexpected move from Adrian but quickly regains composure and climbs aboard.

"What about my luggage?" George asks Adrian in a lame voice.

"All taken care of old boy, let's go to Government House where we can have a bit of a natter. You seem to have been rather busy this week end from what I have heard. There's still some brunch left over from the garden party at Government House. I bet you are famished." Adrian, hanging on to the Land Rover's door strap with his left arm, gives George a grin, as the vehicle accelerates out of the Airport.

Sammy gets a taxi

Looking up at the Airport terminal balcony as he walks across the tarmac Sammy spots one of the gang from the Harbour Road warehouse waving. Carlton is a low life drug user who helps out packing the rum cartons with drugs. He has made a few courier trips to New York. He is easily recognised; wearing a gaudy red and yellow shirt with his Rastafarian hairstyle and the constant sun glasses. What does he want Sammy wonders.

"*Hey boss how ya bin? I saw you cummin. We is going to New York wiv da stuff.*" Carlton greets Sammy as if he had been absent for months not just a few days.

"What's up Carlton?" Sammy wants to know as Sammy starts to walk out to pick up a taxi.

"*Meeser Waaain from de bank he bin pestering me ever since he done cum to de shed tewsday late at nite. He sees me an Churchill packing da stuff. Late at nite he do cum. Wanna see you he say. I say Boss away in New York.*" Carlton blurts out information so fast in his pigeon language that Sammy, whose ears are blocked from the sharp aircraft landing, is rather slow in assimilating what he is being told.

"Wait a minute Carlton! Whoa slow down! Are you telling me Wayne Luther from the bank saw you packing shit at the warehouse last Tuesday night?" Sammy stops Carlton some yards from the taxi rank and turns him so that he can see him talking.

"*Das right boss. Everee day he dun cum to da shed. Where's Sammy he wanna know. Me an Churchill we jess shrugs an say dat we don know where you is.*"

"O K. Are you and Churchill carrying to New York tonight?"

"Yessir boss, we got an hour before da flite. Das when I saw u cumin. I thought I tell u bout dis." Carlton falters wondering if he should have told Sammy and whether this might mean trouble.

"Here's what you do Carlton. You and Churchill take your flight. Artie will meet you in New York as usual. Don't say anything about this to Artie or anyone. I'll handle Wayne at the bank. Do you understand?" Sammy holds on to Carlton by the shoulders checking he understands.

"Yessir boss dat's fine. I go fine Churchill. See you soon Yessir."

On the way to his apartment near Hamilton Sammy wonders if he should call Wayne tonight to find out what is going on but decides to wait until tomorrow. Let's hope this next week goes better than the last one Sammy thinks to himself.

After fixing a drink and something to eat Sammy puts in a call to Artie in New York, he is desperate to know what happened after he left the Casino. The warehouse was toasted. He knew that. Has Reilly got the Limey Howden? What does Howden know about him? The telephone keeps ringing with no answer. Frustrated, Sammy slams the receiver down and pours himself a stiff drink. He decides Artie must have already left for the airport to pick up Eugene and Churchill. He will have to try later.

Duane gets to work

Duane tries hard to look inconspicuous sitting in the first class cabin. Located two rows behind Sammy and on

Minion or Master

the opposite side of the gang way Duane is able to observe Sammy during the flight.

Except when the stewardess brings food and drink Sammy is asleep for most of the flight time. Duane tries to relax and enjoy the idle time. Being a doer, with a reputation as an action man in the FBI, this is difficult for Duane. He is very pleased when the flight lands and he can resume his quiet surveillance of the man George Howden identified at La Guardia.

Sammy has hand luggage only; he is heading for the terminal exit when he gets into a conversation with a black guy. As Duane observes from a discrete distance someone catches hold of his elbow and whispers

"Welcome to Bermuda Sir, Inspector Johnson from Her Majesties Colonial Police Force at your service. Please follow me. Government House advised us to expect you and provide all assistance." Johnson, speaking with a soft Scottish accent, is about to guide Duane across the terminal building to the airport security offices but Duane stops abruptly; he turns to look at Johnson who is about the same age as Duane but looks younger.

"Listen Johnson those two guys over there. One has just come off the flight with me and he needs to be kept under surveillance. We need to know what he is up to. The other guy, the black one has just made contact. Can you find out who he is?" Duane starts to feel his adrenaline levels rising as he gets back to work.

"We already have instructions about Sammy Santino, Sir. We know his address and his business. He can't get far away from us. The Island is only twenty two miles long. The black man has, I believe, just booked in for the New York flight with another person."

"So how in the hell can he mingle with arrivals? Where's your security here man?" Duane queries in a disbelieving voice.

"Ah yes we are trying hard to agree the re build of the commercial wing of this terminal but the finance has not been forthcoming from your Government. You see Sir, this land is on lease to you Americans." Johnson keeps his voice neutral and thinks to himself.

This is not going very well.

"Unbelievable." Duane remarks; looking up to the roof he pauses; regains his composure; he looks at Johnson

"Can you get me to an office with a telephone and give me the details of these two passengers? I want them picked up at La Guardia and followed."

"Yes Sir, follow me please!" Johnson smiles as he walks towards the airport terminal security offices.

Duane immediately settles in to the office Johnston takes him to. In no time he is on the telephone to his New York office briefing his colleagues to follow the two couriers when they get to La Guardia.

"You have a briefing meeting with the Governor's office at seven this evening Sir. Your accommodation has been organised by your own Air Force on the base here. Please make yourself comfortable. I will call for you at six thirty to go to the Governor's office. In the meantime you can contact me on the direct line here." Johnson points to a telephone on the wall and then hands Duane a cup of tea.

"Thanks Johnson. See you later." Duane takes a sip of the tea and screws up his face

"Ugghh . . . ain't you got something stronger? Like some sweet black coffee?" Duane pleads looking hurt and in pain.

"I'll see if I can rustle up some for you Sir." Johnson says as he leaves the room.

Sunday afternoon and evening 29th May 1966

Adrian is briefed

"I say look at the time it's three thirty I don't think brunch is a terribly good idea. How about some tea and scones on the terrace? You can tell me all about your trip." Adrian advises George as they walk from the Land Rover through Government House gardens towards the main building.

"Just a cup of tea will be fine Adrian. I had a meal on the plane over."

"Those flight meals are positively grotesque old boy, all plastic and tasteless. No, you must have some tea and scones. I might even be able to rustle up some fruit cake as well."

As they walk into the building Adrian gives the house boy instructions for tea and leads George out onto the terrace which has a partial veranda giving shelter from the strong sun. They sit at a stone table on wrought iron chairs padded with floral cushions under the veranda.

Before settling down George asks if he can freshen up. He is shown into a marble and cedar wood lined toilet suite.

Looking into the gilt framed mirror George sees something different in his face, a strength he hadn't noticed before. He smiles in to the mirror; he can still see the boyish charm; but now, there is more; the unquestioning innocence is no longer dominant in his persona; a resilient toughness is taking prominence.

As he towels his face and hands he realises that this is the first time since last Friday, just three days ago, that he has been able to relax.

It is truly incredible all that has occurred in just three days. Now is not the time to drop my guard with Adrian. Even though Adrian is giving me that "hail fellow well met" business; I know how canny he can be. The last tennis match was a lesson to be heeded. Adrian is no fool and I need to give him full respect. This is going to be a crunch meeting.

George saunters back to Adrian who is supervising the pouring of tea from a china tea pot.

"Well George I must say you have caused quite a stir. Sir Jeremy normally has a lie in and plays golf on a Sunday. Not today though old boy. I was summoned at eight o 'clock this morning. A Sunday morning! Would you believe it? First we had a long call from the Commissioner at Scotland Yard! Apparently he had been disturbed from his Sunday lunch in the pub. The FBI has pulled quite a few strings; seems your meeting with this chappie Marshall has brought things to a nice head. Is this Marshall chappie some type of sheriff? Never mind. You can fill me in on him in a minute. The Commissioner has given strict instructions we are to give our American cousins the fullest co operation to close down this drugs gang that you seem to have unearthed. Then Johnson, our local CID walla; he arrived; we had a conference call with FBI New York. I barely had time to taste the Fillet steak with that gorgeous Pomerol at lunch before I was dispatched to collect you. Life is certainly not dull. Do try some of this fruit cake old boy. It's made by the Chef's mother the old traditional Bermudan way. You will taste the rum in it." Adrian smiles at George and offers to slice up a piece of the fruit cake.

Minion or Master

"I am pleased that I have been of some help with your fight against drugs Adrian. However, you do remember, it was just last Wednesday not even a full five days ago, that you more or less accused me of being an international criminal and gave me seven days to come back to you. Have you forgotten the little chat we had after tennis?" George speaks calmly, waving his hand to decline the fruit caked proffered by Adrian whose smile is changing into a mild frown with his mouth agape.

"Oh George, no, of course I remember. On reflection I think I was a bit hard on you over that business old boy. Will you forgive me?" Adrian looks slightly uncomfortable as he places the fruit cake back on the table and waits for George's response.

I will not let him off that lightly.

George feels a quiver of self satisfaction.

"It is not quite that simple Adrian. You see Marshall Brumbell, and no, to answer your earlier question, he is not a sheriff, but he does work closely with the FBI. Marshall Brumbell's job title is Vice President, Bulk Handling, Brooklyn Docks Board. Acting on orders from the FBI he signed this loading document." George hands Adrian his copy of the loading document.

"Yes I see, but forgive me, what has that got to do with anything?" Adrian queries in a subdued voice as he studies the document intently.

"Marshall was ordered by his FBI contact to prepare and sign it. Holds four and five on "Ocean Star" held the chrome ore. Marshall was told he was helping the USA and he confirmed to me that the USA wanted the chrome ore so badly that they leaned on us, the British, to take no action, in effect to turn a blind eye. That is why "Ocean Star" was not stopped by the navy. You must have known all this when you gave me the fifth degree last Wednesday." George states in his steady voice as he picks through the facts in a forensic manner gently but firmly giving Adrian a taste of his own medicine.

"I think I owe you a massive apology old boy. I admit I was "fishing" to see if I could get information that might be of help for our Government. I really do object to our American cousins dictating to us. I am truly sorry to have upset you so. Will you please accept my humble and profuse apology and allow us both to move on?"

Now that's more like it. That makes me feel a whole lot better.

"Yes, of course Adrian, your apology is accepted. Let's co—operate and move on. As you can imagine the events over these last few days have been dramatic for me. It's Costas Tinopolis who is behind a lot of this. He should be in the dock, not me. He has taken me for an easy to handle, easy to manipulate simple numbers man. He set me up as his stooge his front line fall guy, his minion. I am not at all happy about it. I want him brought to account. Captain Kato confirmed to me that Costas knew all about the chrome when they met in New York. Will you help me get him?" George looks directly into Adrian's face, which, for a fraction of a second displays a flicker of doubt.

"He is a very powerful and influential man George. Our hands are tied in with the Americans over this chrome business as you already know. I can't see what I can do except possibly make some very discrete enquiries into his business affairs."

"Yes, I can see that it might be difficult. There may be more. The drugs gang has to have a shipping connection. They are picking up their main supplies in the Atlantic. If I am right; Sammy will be picking up a consignment tomorrow; 150 nautical miles north east from here. Perhaps one of Costa's ships will make the drop? Might that make a difference?" George now sees Adrian look slightly more enthusiastic.

"It will be a tenuous connection. Even if we can prove Tinopolis's ships are involved. It will not link him directly. Although I am sure the Yanks will be delighted if we can pin point the supply route and put a stop to it. We might then be able to get them to take him as a serious threat. We will need more if he is to be indicted though." Adrian reflects, thoughtfully rubbing his chin, studying George with his hawk like light brown eyes that miss very little.

Now shall I confide in Adrian about the arms? Can I trust him? It will open up a whole new and much more dangerous phase. Dammit! This is much too big for me and Kato to cope with on our own. I have to bring the Authorities into this play and confide in Adrian.

"What if we could link Costas directly to something like for instance gun running? Do you think that might change the dynamics and get attention?" Adrian sits bolt up right.

"I am all ears George. Better come into my office. Now what have you got." Taking out the photographs George explains to Adrian about the two crates of arms disguised as agricultural machinery "Ocean Star" is carrying buried under tons of grain; and how Costas bribed Kato to take them on board. After carefully questioning George and taking copious notes Adrian looks up from his office desk and remarks

"So the crates came from the Pulaski Street warehouse run by Sammy. He cannot be behind this. There has to be someone bigger than him. Perhaps it is Costas." Adrian stretches back in his chair.

"Can we do a check on Ace Machine Factors, Detroit, named in the export documents? Perhaps that might lead us to the people behind this."

"Yes good point old boy. We also need to find out the end user for these arms. Presumably it's an African gang of some sort. I'll get checking." Adrian mutters making another note on his pad then looking at his watch.

"I think we have covered as much ground as we can here Adrian. I Would like to catch up on some sleep if that is alright with you."

"Yes certainly George. I have a briefing with Inspector Johnson and the FBI in an hour any how. Let's meet again say lunch time tomorrow. Can you come up to Government House at twelve thirty say?" Adrian asks more by way of an order than an invitation.

"I'll check in at the office and confirm by telephone tomorrow morning with you." George responds, deciding to keep his options open.

Chapter Nineteen
Sammy and Wayne

Sunday evening Late May 1966

Sammy talks to Wayne

Sammy puts the telephone down. He has now tried three times to speak to Artie. The telephone rings.

"Yea who is this?" Sammy answers abruptly

"Sammy my man, its Wayne here, welcome back, when can we meet up Sammy I got some business to talk over with you?" Wayne cries out in an excited voice.

"Yea I heard you been down the warehouse hassling my boys Wayne. Tell you what, how about I come around to the bank early tomorrow. I want the boat again same arrangements as before. We can talk then."

"*Weeel now Sammeee it's about lil ol "Pembroke Lady" that I planned to talk to y'all about, cos, see, I knows what you are usin the Lady for. I don't think your same arrangement deal will work, I been thinking more along a partnership type arrangement to maybe smooth the way.*" Wayne puts down his feelers in his sugary Southerner twang voice.

There is a long silence as Sammy thinks through the consequences of Wayne being involved.

"Have you discussed this with any one else Wayne? I might be able to work something good for you. However, it has to be only you, no one else can know. Security is vital in our line Wayne. Guess it's the same in the bank too?" Sammy speaks in a quiet, measured tone which disguises his anger.

"Not a soul knows Sammeee on my heart I swear it. Y'all know you can bank on Wayne."

"O K Wayne. I will have to get my US backers to agree any deal. I can see ways in which you might be real useful to us. In the meantime let's you and me go out on the boat tomorrow. We can discuss your deal whilst I attend to some business. How does that sound?" Sammy speaks in a cajoling way appealing to Wayne's sense of self importance.

"Sounds good to me Sammeee, real good, what time y'all wanna meet?" Wayne relaxes, feeling he is onto something big at last.

"Let's meet early say seven o 'clock and have the Lady fully fuelled. Then we can make a day of it. Remember now Wayne not a word to any one or all deals are off. Understood?" Sammy waits to hear Wayne's gleeful agreement before hanging up.

Should be an interesting day tomorrow

Sammy freshens his drink, the telephone rings again.

"It's Artie. Since you left this morning everything has gone crazy. Reilly is dead. The boss got in touch and has moved operations to New Jersey. The cruise ship deal is suspended until we know who takes over from Reilly. *The boss* says you still got to pick up tomorrow then shut everything down. The cops are all over Pulaski Street and Red Hook wharf. We gotta stay low for a while *the boss* says."

"Whoa Artie, what about Howden remember him? Did Reilly get him?" Sammy interrupts Artie's breathless talk.

"Yea we think so. There were four men shot at Red Hook. One of them was picked up at the airport car rental lot. We think that must have been Howden. Sammy it's difficult to get further info 'cos the cops are screwing everything down tight over here right now."

"What about the broad Jasmine? Any sign of her?"

"It's like she's been taken off the planet. No one has seen her. Her clothes are still in your apartment. I don't get it Sammy. How could she just disappear like that?"

"Well at least if Howden is out of the way that's something I guess. I'll call you tomorrow evening for the latest." Sammy rings off.

Hello Lenny

Adrian arranged for a Government House car to drive George back to his Spanish Point apartment. On the way home George reflects with satisfaction over his meeting with Adrian. It couldn't have gone better he thinks. As they drive into Hamilton past the Harbour Club George hears the sound of music and suddenly remembers he needs to let Lenny know what has happened to Jasmine. He instructs the driver to turn around and drive the ten miles east to Charlie's house.

As the car turns into the cul de sac the time is six forty five, George knocks tentatively on the mosquito netting fixed to the outside of the front door and side steps two scuttling cock roaches who he has disturbed by the front door mat.

"Hello Lenny, Charlie?" George calls feeling a little embarrassed about calling unannounced. Soon he hears the sound of foot steps coming from the rear of the house and the door is opened.

"Howdy! What are you doing here? Me and Pa is jess 'bout to go to de Harbour Club. Come in! Have you seen Jazzy?" Lenny smiles as she grabs George by the hand and takes him through the house to the veranda.

"I'm so sorry to call uninvited Lenny but I thought I should see you and Charlie as soon as I could. I've just come from New York and I have seen Jasmine. I thought you would want to know straight away. That's why I decided to come uninvited. I do hope you don't mind me calling like this?" George is feeling slightly embarrassed; he keeps staring at Leonora; she is wearing a white cotton blouse which reveals a hint of cleavage. The white of the blouse is a perfect contrast to her coloured skin which seems almost translucent. Her blouse is trimmed with crimson to match the embroidered figure of a sea horse on Leonora's black skirt.

How absolutely divine

George dreams away mesmerized by Leonora's innocent beauty

"Did I hear you say Jasmine's name?" Charlie's voice interrupts George's thoughts.

"Charlie it's good to see you. Yes I have seen Jasmine. It's a long story. I have so much to tell you. I'm not sure where to start." George gives Charlie a hug and tries to stop staring at Leonora who is now starting to blush and grin at George's obvious interest.

"Have you eaten George? Come with us to the Harbour Club! You can have dinner with us then watch us perform. You can tell us all about Jasmine." Charlie suggests looking at Leonora who is nodding her head vigorously.

It takes George nearly two hours; first on the journey to the Harbour Club in Charlie's Morris Minor; then, during dinner to relate his story. Leonora and Charlie hardly say a word as they sit at their table open mouthed staring incredulously at George as he unfolds the tale of his week end adventures in New York culminating with Jasmine's escape on "Ocean Star". George, not wanting to hurt their feelings any more, does not mention Jasmine's drug problem.

"Howdy dat's de mos amazin story I eva did hear. I jess can't believe you dun all dis in three days. You are amazin." Leonora finally exclaims as she looks at George with a mixture of feminine interest and complete respect competing in her facial expressions. George looks up at Leonora and then across to Charlie who is sobbing, his head held in his hands supported on the table.

"Me and Lenny we can't thank you enough for all that you have done. I hope Jazzy will be alright now. When can we see her?" Charlie asks between sobs as Leonora gives her father a comforting hug.

"I hope it will be very soon. If all goes to plan. Sammy has to be dealt with first so there is no risk for Jasmine when she returns to the Island." George answers taking a sip of beer and looking across the floodlit pool over to the bar area.

"Oh no!"

"What is it?" Leonora and Charlie both cry out.

"It's Sammy. He's just arrived at the bar. No Charlie! Don't move! You can't let him know anything! It will give the game away! Please keep away from him! Act normally!" George orders in a firm voice as he places his hands down on Charlie's shoulders.

"*He's dun damaged my girl. I can't forgive dat George!*" Charlie cries out.

"Charlie please say nothing. All our safety including Jasmine's depends upon you. If you have to speak with Sammy just ask how Jazzy is. She is still in New York so far as you know. On no account must he know anything before the FBI arrests him. Stay cool. Why don't you and Lenny get back stage away from here? You'll be singing in fifteen minutes any way. Let me handle Sammy!" Charlie and Leonora agree and leave the table.

The time is nine forty five as Charlie and Leonora take to the stage for their usual calypso routine followed by Leonora singing solo. George, sitting by the pool sipping a beer is delighted to hear Leonora sing one of the songs he had selected at the house the other evening.

"Mind if I join you? We met here a few weeks ago remember?" Sammy asks standing over the table.

"Oh, I say, no, of course. Yes. We were all together here. Its Sidney isn't it? Sorry I'm terrible with names and faces." Looking up at Sammy, George hears Leonora's voice tremble, missing a high note she normally hits perfectly.

"It's Sammy from New York. Didn't I see you over there this week end?"

"You must be mistaking me for some one else Sammy." George answers then looking at Sammy with a smile of remembrance George says

"I remember now. You brought Leonora's sister, Jasmine, to the club. We came together. How is Jasmine? Are you still seeing her?" Before Sammy can answer a voice intercedes

"George old man, sorry to interrupt, but you must come and meet Sir Jeremy over here. Do forgive me old chap!" Adrian smiles sweetly at Sammy as he steers George away. As Sammy starts to protest and follow them, a waiter, carrying a tray full of drinks, slips on the pool tiles and crashes into Sammy who loses his balance and falls backwards into the pool.

"Sorry to cause a diversion old man. You owe the waiter fifty dollars. Go home. I'll see to this." Adrian chuckles as he steers George out to a Government car.

As Sammy gets out of the pool Adrian rushes over gushing with remorse over the accident. Apologising, in case it was his fault, offering to pay to have Sammy's clothes dry cleaned, and ordering the hapless waiter to get a taxi for Sammy.

"I have had a belly full of you Limey's this week end." Sammy mutters as the waiter hands him a beach robe and escorts him to a waiting taxi.

Monday morning Late May 1966

Wayne's Deal

Sammy's head is still reeling from the shock of seeing George at the Harbour Club last night.

Nothing seems to be making sense. Still after today I will be out of here for a while.

As the taxi drives through the gates of the Bank of Pembroke Wayne cries out

"*Sammeee*" and opens the taxi door.

"Hi Wayne, we all fixed to sail?"

"*All ready to go Sammeee, "Pembroke Lady" is fully fuelled. So where we going Sammeee?*"

"The faster we move the sooner you will know Wayne." Sammy shouts as he trots over the gardens towards the bungalow and the jetty.

"*You are the boss Sammeee.*" Wayne cries as he tries valiantly to keep up with Sammy.

Once aboard "Pembroke Lady" Sammy orders Wayne to steer a north east course after they are through the reefs.

"*So Sammeee my man what sort of a deal are you giving me here?*" Wayne shouts from the comfort of his white leather seat as he keeps "Pembroke Lady" on the course Sammy has given him.

"Here's the deal Wayne!" Sammy shouts. As Wayne swivels in his seat, to look at Sammy, his podgy face, full of greedy anticipation, changes to a more hesitant, doubtful look. Sammy has a harpoon gun. Without hesitation Sammy fires a spear directly into Wayne's chest. Wayne looks surprised, then, realising what has happened, he screams. Quickly Sammy pulls the wire attached to the harpoon spear. Wayne drops out of his chair onto the deck. Sammy drags Wayne to the rear of the boat, secures the harpoon gun to its fittings, releases the wire brake, then man handles the screaming Wayne over the stern, Sammy watches as Wayne floats away. Fresh blood is spurting from Wayne's chest leaving a trail on the surface of the sea. After Wayne has drifted thirty metres from "Pembroke Lady" Sammy applies the harpoon brake; then he throttles back on "Pembroke Lady's" engines.

Moving forward at two knots Sammy can still hear Wayne's shrieks. Sammy watches the first eleven foot sleek body, topped with a black triangular fin; move in at the scent of human blood. Soon the sea is a throbbing cauldron of white foam and blood as the animals devour every last morsel of Wayne.

Minion or Master

Sammy winds in the harpoon gun wire cleansed of all evidence by the sharks and the salt sea water. After washing Wayne's blood down the decks and out through the bilges he sets course then powers up "Pembroke Lady's" twin engines to full speed.

Chapter Twenty

Intercepted

Monday morning Late May 1966

Boats and Planes

George enjoyed a full night of undisturbed peaceful sleep for the first time in nearly a week. Such a lot has happened since I was playing music with Lenny and Charlie last Tuesday evening he thinks to himself as he walks to the nearby beach for an early morning dip in the warm, salty, Atlantic breakers. George has decided that after Adrian's timely intervention, last night, in diverting Sammy the least he can do is honour Adrian's invitation to meet at Government House this morning.

Nothing much has happened in George's office since Thursday. A telex has come in from Costa's advising he had met with Captain Kati and had paid him a ten thousand dollar bonus.

Funny I thought Kati mentioned a sum of seven thousand five hundred dollars. He will have to wait to be reimbursed for that. Perhaps I'll request a receipt.

As George works through some paper work his telephone rings.

"Ah! Good morning George. Things are hotting up with the FBI and your drugs gang. Would you like to witness Sammy's pick up at first hand?" Adrian enquires.

"Well yes I would Adrian. As I identified him for the FBI in the first place it will be good to see the conclusion. I also want to know he is put away for a long time for Jasmine's sake." George responds, all thoughts of his office paper work have vanished.

"Be at the docks Government jetty at noon! I'll see you there!" Adrian hangs up before George can say anything else.

"This is Inspector Johnson from your local police. He's bin liaising with me. George here has bin real helpful with our operations; so, your Government man has requested him to join us. Can't say I agree with civilians muscling in on our action like this. But I guess it's your territory." Duane gives Johnson an old fashioned look as he introduces George at the jetty. Duane hadn't forgotten the fiasco at the airport yesterday with departing and arriving passengers mingling together.

"I see you've all met, excellent. Let's get aboard quickly as we can!" Adrian orders as he marches purposefully along the jetty to the awaiting Royal Navy motor patrol boat. A naval rating salutes the four men as they clamber on board. The boat heads out of the Great Sound for the thirty minute journey toward the naval base at Ireland Island.

"Are we going to intercept Sammy on his way back from the pick up?" George asks looking first at Adrian; then Duane; and finally at Inspector Johnson.

"We will do a heap better than that." Duane responds pointing at the twin engine Grumman sea plane bobbing up and down at its moorings. As the patrol boat manoeuvres alongside the starboard side of the sea plane the naval rating jumps from the patrol boat onto the plane's pontoon float; he nimbly balances whilst securing a mooring rope to a float strut.

At one o'clock the US Navy pilot receives permission to fire up the twin engines and taxi out of the harbour into the relative shelter of the Great Sound.

"Control this is US Navy sea plane Alpha Foxtrot Niner requesting permission to take off with six souls on board."

"Alpha Foxtrot Niner this is control. You are clear to take off. Wind strength is three knots north east with a sea height maximum of three feet."

"Roger that Control Alpha Foxtrot Niner out." As the pilot steers the plane into the wind and applies the throttle and flaps Duane, seated next to the pilot, tunes his radio to pick up transmissions from Lieutenant Casey Hughes speeding at mach. one point five towards the drop zone.

Snapped

At eight a.m. Lieutenant Casey Hughes takes off from Beale air force base in California. Within twenty minutes his Lockheed SR 71 spy plane is cruising at 70,000 feet heading for the Atlantic Ocean. His mission, code named "Powder Drop", was briefed to him at zero six hundred hours this morning.

At nine forty five am California time Casey will be over the target zone of 33 latitude and 62 longitude. Casey has orders to use the top secret spy cameras to film a cargo ship, the Neptune Carrier. The local time will be one forty five p.m. four hours ahead of California time. Casey hopes he will be back by lunch time to go to see the Padres play the La Dodgers with his best buddy Gary Powers.

Minion or Master

"Base this is "Powder Drop" reporting in position awaiting target,. visibility alpha plus, over." Casey adjusts the settings on his camera pod as he listens for instructions from base and looks down at the curvature of the earth.

""Powder Drop" this is base. Your mission is go, repeat go, over." Casey hears the neutral voice through the ear pieces set in his pressurized helmet and calmly responds

"Roger that base. Out"

Seventy thousand feet below Lieutenant Casey Hughes Neptune Carrier, owned by one of Costas Tinopolis's companies, is steaming towards New York inbound from Hong Kong via the Panama Canal. At one fifty local time two deck hands are ordered by the second in command to discharge a two hundred pound package fitted with a transponder. The crew are Chinese. They ask no questions. They carry out orders. They know any sign of disobedience will result in their loved ones removal to work camps and much worse for them. They quietly go about carrying out their orders; after, they remember nothing.

Costas Tinopolis and Jamil Hassan have influential contacts in mainland China. For substantial sums their contacts ruthlessly order action from chosen vulnerable workers; impenetrable silence from the worker is the only option for them and their families if they are to avoid death. Jamil and Costas consider this to be a perfect system to loot huge sums of money from the West. Drugs from China and Afghanistan are the must have cravings for decadent westerners. Drugs are used to infiltrate and corrupt the young and not so young; thus attacking the soft under belly of the so called free countries. The smuggled drugs are enslaving the citizens in the western democracies; they are making Jamil and Costas filthy rich.

Even better; their Chinese contacts finance conflicts in places such as Vietnam and Mozambique. Arms smuggling make Jamil and Costas even more profits. Right now Jamil and Costas know nothing of spy planes. They have no idea their activities will be filmed from the fringes of outer space.

"Base this is "Powder Drop" have visuals on target, film is rolling." Casey speaks into his communication pod as he brings up the magnification on his quadruple camera pods to maximum.

"Roger that "Powder Drop. Continue observation, base out."

Looking in his monitor Casey sees the package clearly fall from Neptune Trader's stern and float off into the Atlantic.

"Base this is "Powder Drop" package has been released. Over"

"Roger that "Powder Drop" maintain observation on package! Base over."

"Roger that base, out". Casey continues observation; his fuel gages indicate he will be able to maintain this station for another hour before he has to return to base.

Monday afternoon Late May 1966

Wave

George is seated next to Inspector Johnson; Adrian sits with the co pilot of the Grumman HU-16D Albatross on the starboard side of the plane. There is no possibility of conversation whilst the sea plane guns up its powerful engines to full speed then rushes through the sea for what seemed like an eternity. Finally its momentum forces the sea to give up its tenuous grip allowing the craft to rise ponderously into the air. The pilot sets his compass. The Albatross flies in a north easterly direction.

"I say this is all very exciting. As a numbers man I am not used to all this action." George remarks to Inspector Johnson who has removed a Smith & Wesson Model 36 revolver from his coat and proceeds to load five bullets into its cylinder, then, with practiced hands, spins the cylinder flipping it shut with one deft movement.

"From what I heard you haven't done too badly for excitement in the last few days Laddie." Inspector Johnson remarks in his soft Scottish accent then looking over George's shoulder through the Albatross's port hole he frowns.

"Best get the life jackets on Laddie. The sea is a harsh mistress for those that are unprepared." Inspector Johnson ferrets under the seat for two life jackets handing one to George.

"Do you think we will have to go into the sea then?" George ties up his jacket tags.

"One never knows what might happen when the Yanks are playing hard ball. They are determined to stamp out these drug gangsters. Your information has proved invaluable Laddie. Probably it has helped to advance their operation by months I should say. Now, all we have to do is sit tight for the next few minutes, await developments and, be prepared, as my old scout master from Tyndrum would say." Inspector Johnson settles back down in his seat appearing alert but calm.

Having cruised "Pembroke Lady" at thirty knots since dumping Wayne Sammy rechecks his bearings and location. He reckons he is now about ten minutes from the pick up.

The sooner I can get the hell away the better I'll be pleased.

Sammy makes final adjustments to his course.

"Base this is "Powder Drop" have visuals on a white speed boat targeting the package. Cameras are rolling, over." Lieutenant Casey Hughes intones as he watches his monitor screen.

""Powder Drop" this is base. Maintain visuals. Am patching you in to US Navy sea plane Alpha Foxtrot Niner inbound to location, over."

"Roger that Base, out."

""Powder Drop" this is Alpha Foxtrot Niner. Confirm your co ordinates on the speed boat and advise numbers on board, over." Duane speaks urgently into the radio then swivels in his chair and shouts into the cabin

"We have contact with the speed boat. Stay focused everyone!"

Simultaneously to Duane's shout into the cabin the pilot puts the Grumman HU-16D Albatross into a sharp dive from ten thousand feet down to sea level. For five minutes all George can do is hang on to the sides of his seat; he tries to keep his mind focused to block out the intense noise from the engine; the wind roars against the wing struts; the fuselage is shaking and pounding as the pilot places the Albatross under maximum strain.

Sammy has successfully located and loaded the floating package from Neptune Carrier onto "Pembroke Lady". He has plotted his course back to Bermuda. Sitting in the white leather Captain's seat, lately occupied by Wayne, Sammy pushes the throttles requesting maximum power from the twin Volvo Penta marine engines. "Pembroke Lady" responds with a roar as her stern pushes hard into the water and spray lashes the windscreen.

Minion or Master

Feeling relieved with the success of this operation Sammy wants to sort out that Limey Howden when he gets back to Bermuda.

One way or the other he has caused me problems. Howden will wish he never messed with me. He needs to be savaged by sharks just like that little shit Wayne, yea a sea grave is what Howden will get.

As the Albatross starts to pull out of its break neck descent and level off George looks out through his port hole at the endless sea.

It will be a miracle if we can spot anything in these conditions. How can Duane say he has contact?

"Alpha Foxtrot Niner this is "Powder Drop" You are closing on the speed boat there is one occupant, ETA one minute, over."

"Roger that "Powder Drop" we have visuals, out." Duane responds and shouts into the cabin

"Speed boat coming up on the port side!"

Peering through the spray splattered windscreen Sammy is concentrating on keeping "Pembroke Lady" on course. He is watching out for rogue waves which can cause a small craft, even one as well constructed as "Pembroke Lady" to tip right over; especially, at the speed she is making.

The pilot of the Albatross has brought the craft down to ten metres from the sea. The albatross skims over the sea waves at a speed of one hundred and fifty knots heading right for "Pembroke Lady".

The first thing Sammy feels is a rush of wind, then with adrenaline pumping fast to his organs, he sees the Albatross emerging like some monster from the waves heading straight for him. Instinctively Sammy turns the wheel to starboard to avoid collision. At full speed

"Pembroke Lady" responds bouncing over Atlantic waves then dropping into little troughs. Sammy turns around. He sees a dark shadow flash by on his port side then he hears an enormous roar as the sound from the Grumman engines on either side of the Albatross's wings blast his ears.

Mesmerized, Sammy watches the Albatross gaining height. He doesn't see the rogue wave coming from the starboard side. The wave lifts "Pembroke Lady" out of the water. The force of the lift takes Sammy by surprise; as "Pembroke Lady" drops back into the sea the wave lashes over the deck. Sammy is flushed into the sea.

"Alpha Foxtrot Niner this is "Powder Drop" man overboard from speed boat thirty metres on the port side, over."

"Roger that "Powder Drop" we will attempt a landing. Keep us informed. Maintain visuals on man overboard, over." Duane replies.

"Brace yourselves! We are going to surface land." Duane shouts to everyone as he comes into the cabin and takes the seat next to Adrian so that the co pilot can assist with the landing.

"The speed boat occupant is in the drink." Duane shouts to the other occupants as he puts on a life vest.

Before being flushed out to sea by the incoming wave Sammy is first washed against "Pembroke Lady's" instrument panel. Unable to fight the power of the water Sammy is sent crashing into the engine controls. Sammy's body is pushed against the drive mechanism forcing the shift lever into the idle position.

In the water Sammy can see "Pembroke Lady" thirty metres away. He starts to swim towards the boat.

Minion or Master

It takes the combined efforts of pilot and co pilot to nurse the hull of the Grumman HU-16D Albatross into the water. The co pilot takes instructions from Lieutenant Casey Hughes and taxis the lumbering sea plane towards Sammy and "Pembroke Lady".

Sammy is struggling to reach "Pembroke Lady". Every time he makes some progress towards the boat the wind pushes her further away. He has been swimming for ten minutes and cold is starting to creep into his body.

George and Inspector Johnson are first to the door of the Albatross. Inspector Johnson opens the door and throws out a rope ladder attached to the deck; then, a self inflating dinghy is dropped into the sea. Within minutes the dinghy is inflated and George, Duane and Inspector Johnson jump in and paddle towards Sammy who is about forty metres away.

As soon as the dinghy is away from the Albatross the pilot taxis across to "Pembroke Lady". Standing in the open doorway of the Albatross Adrian uses the skill and timing he exhibited on the tennis court to judge the perfect moment when the sea is at its optimum height to launch him self out of the door and land as gracefully as any Puma on board "Pembroke Lady". The co pilot throws out a line and with painters lashed to the hull by Adrian "Pembroke Lady" is secured to the Albatross.

Sammy is relieved to see the dinghy approach. He knows that the wind is preventing him from reaching the safety of "Pembroke Lady"; the cold sea water is sapping energy from his body. As the dinghy approaches he is grateful to be rescued. He is hauled aboard the dinghy in a not too graceful movement. He looks at his rescuers. Seeing George smiling at him produces something like steam in Sammy's blood. The frustrations and set backs of the last few days feed such a powerful anger within his body that he is able to summon sufficient strength to leap across the dinghy and grab the unsuspecting George by the throat.

Before any one can move Sammy has pushed George over the side. With manic strength he is throttling the life out of George who has been taken completely by surprise. Sammy will fulfil his wish. He will give this Limey a watery grave. Sammy keeps a tight grip around George's neck until he feels the strength start to ebb from George.

Now for the end

Sammy lets go with one hand and fishes for the flick knife in his trouser pocket. As his hand clasps the instrument of death he feels a thump in the back of his head. The lights in Sammy's head go out as the thirty eight calibre bullet from Inspector Johnson's Smith & Wesson rips half his head away.

Without hesitation Duane jumps out of the dinghy and swims frantically towards George. His up turned body lies inert in the sea. Quickly he and Inspector Johnson man handle George into the dinghy and urgently apply first aid. Slowly colour starts to come back into George's skin as oxygen feeds back into his blood stream.

"We need to get him on board the Albatross!" Inspector Johnson shouts.

As they paddle frantically towards the Albatross they pass by Sammy who is lying face down in the sea with blood pouring from the crater which was once the right side of his skull. Before they can decide whether to take him back to the Albatross Sammy is pushed right out of the sea. Before his body has settled back in the water it is pushed up again. Looking into the water Inspector Johnson spies a monster grey shark whose malevolent cold staring eye seems to touch a raw nerve with him. Pulling out the Smith & Wesson from his pocket Inspector Johnson takes aim at the beast from the sea. He does not fire the gun.

"I'll let the wee fishy enjoy his supper tonight." Inspector Johnson intones as he and Duane head back to the Albatross with George slowly recovering.

Chapter Twenty One
Love the steak

Monday Afternoon late 30th May 1966

Island Return

"It makes sense for Adrian and me to take the boat back to the Island. I know the seas around here and George needs to get back to shore as soon as possible. He has taken quite a pounding from the sea and Sammy." Inspector Johnson advises Duane as they return to the Albatross. George looks confused and bewildered.

As the dinghy nears the flying boat George seems to be recovering, with assistance from Duane and the co pilot, he manages the tricky manoeuvre from the dinghy onto the flying boat float then into the safe haven of the cabin.

"See you tonight in Hamilton" Inspector Johnson shouts as he jumps from the Grumman's float onto "Pembroke Lady" where Adrian is waiting to help steady him, acting as an anchor from the bobbing of the boat in the waves.

"Make sure the package is intact. I'm gonna need that evidence to try and link this back to the source when I get back to New York" Duane cautions Inspector Johnson.

"Are we taking her in?" Adrian asks.

Minion or Master

"That's right Adrian, take the wheel, put her in cruise speed and steer south west. We should make the reefs in about five hours. Now I want to take a look at the package." Inspector Johnson orders.

As Adrian familiarises himself with the controls the ropes holding "Pembroke Lady" into the Albatross flying boat are released. The Albatross turns away into the wind her engines roaring as she bounces and crashes in the water steadily gathering momentum. From the boat's windscreen Adrian watches as the flying boat rises gradually into the late afternoon sky, then, circling "Pembroke Lady", she dips her wings in a nonchalant salute before the pilot heads the Grumman Albatross south west for Ireland Island.

By five o'clock Duane and George are being transported back to Hamilton harbour.

"I guess I and the FBI owe you. Much as it goes against the grain for me to admit it. You are one hell of a guy, Limey or not. You need anything in the future. You jess call me George you hear?" Duane tells George who has now fully recovered from the shock and violence of Sammy's attack.

"Thanks awfully Duane. It has been a very exciting day. I just never thought Sammy would go for me like that, Adrian steered him away from me last night you know." George recalls.

"Yea I guess you and Adrian "Water Melon Mouth" Cuthbert are a force to be reckoned with when you get together. Limeys, who would have thought they really could play like James Bond, I guess I'll never understand."

"If it hadn't been for your technical gizmos on the sea plane we would never have succeeded Duane. I would say we all worked together, Adrian calls it a special relationship." George answers.

"Maybe you're right George, maybe you're right."

Wayne turns Up

Eugene Jordan skipper of the game fishing boat "Sara's Pride" ties up at the public jetty at Hamilton dock. A crowd of locals eagerly gather around. Eugene has a good catch of nine six footers and one giant eleven foot shark. The meat is considered a delicacy on the Island.

Bidding is fast and rapid as each fish is hung up and weighed; the eleven footer is hammered down to Jimmy Smith a store owner over in Warwick parish. Jimmy reckons he will triple the one hundred twenty dollar bid in meat sales alone once he has cut and dressed the animal's flanks.

With help from his two sons Jimmy gets the monster shark onto his cutting bench. With a nine inch razor sharp fleshing knife Jimmy slices into the beast's stomach to allow the entrails and stomach contents to pour into an aluminium tub. Later the offal will be minced up for animal food. As Jimmy glances down at the blood and offal swirling around he is surprised to see a base ball cap. Picking it out Jimmy can make out the inscription on the front "Bank on me!!" Inside is a name tag reading Wayne Luther Executive Vice President Bank of Pembroke.

Jimmy thinks he should maybe report this to the police. Just as he is about to telephone he is interrupted by his old friend from across the road.

"Hi Jimmy I hear you might have some good shark steaks." Charlie Rucker calls out.

"Just come in now Charlie. I can cut you up some real tasty ones." Jimmy shouts back.

"UM UM sounds like me and Lenny will be eating like kings and queens tonight." Charlie calls out as he waits for Jimmy to fetch him the choicest steaks.

Monday evening 30th May 1966

Lenny sings a message

"See you tomorrow Duane." George says as he walks from the jetty for his scooter.

Duane is returning to McKinley to brief his New York office. He intends to come back to see Adrian and Inspector Johnson arrive on "Pembroke Lady" later tonight.

George decides he should let Charlie and Lenny know about Sammy so he drives out to Charlie's house. The evening sun is throwing red and golden hues over the ocean as George pulls the Lambretta on to its stand at the house. Charlie's Morris Minor is not parked up. George sees that Leonora's Mobylette is leaning against the side door. At the front door he hears abandoned singing coming through the upstairs bath room window. Lenny is singing a Beatles song but with some of the lyrics changed. George listens to Lenny's melodious husky voice with more than a hint of enthusiasm singing

"And when I touch him I feel happy inside
I wanna hold George's hand I wanna hold his hand."

Chorus after chorus is rendered as George stands in the drive feeling a trifle embarrassed but thrilled at Lenny's obvious interest. After silence for a few minutes George attracts attention by revving up his scooters engine. Lenny comes to the front door.

"George, what are you doing here? I have been worried about you after last night with that Sammy. Is everything alright? It is really good to see you, a lovely surprise. I telephoned your office this morning but they said you had gone out for the day. Come in tell me what has been happening." Lenny grabs George by the hands and pulls him into the house.

"Oh I say Lenny I have had such a day. I have been out with the FBI. It was so exciting. Anyhow the main thing I came to tell you is that Sammy is dead. He was smuggling drugs. We caught him dead to rights. He tried to strangle me but Inspector Johnson shot him. It was so strange. I could feel myself slowly sinking away. Sammy had his hand around my throat, next thing I was coming around in a dinghy, now, here I am." George blurts out his tale hardly pausing for breath. Leonora is staring transfixed as George speaks.

"*Oh Howdy, dear Howdy, you dun been through a very hard day. Have you eaten yet? Charlie is out but he dun got some real nice shark steaks. Hows a bout I cook you one with some potatoes and salad? What do you say Howdy?*" Leonora pouts and looks George straight in the eyes giving him no opportunity to refuse her invitation.

"I wasn't expecting food Lenny. I just wanted you and Charlie to know about Sammy so that you won't need to worry when Jasmine does come home that Sammy will be bothering her again." George can see that Lenny is going to start a fracas if he doesn't accede.

"However, I am feeling hungry, ravenous in fact, so let's get to it. This will be a new experience for me. I've never eaten shark before. Where is Charlie by the way?"

"Pa he done gone to see an old friend, Eugene Jordan, over in Smith Parish, he said he gonna be late back. They used to play in a band together years back so I guess they gonna be talking old times until late tonight." Leonora says giving George a knowing and provocative stare.

"Wow this steak is delicious rather like chicken. Thank you so much Lenny." George smiles as he finishes the last remnants of the shark steak.

After clearing the plates Lenny suggests they listen to some music. George selects a few records and starts with a Sinatra hit "Strangers in the Night." After a few bars Lenny stands up, kicks off her shoes and with a flick of her slim hands beckons George to dance with her. George holds Lenny's left hand and places his right hand around her waist. As they gently and softly glide around the room George can feel Lenny's body relax into his. He feels a charge of emotion as strong as a high voltage power shock as Lenny turns her face right into his and finds his lips. They kiss; Lenny's body shudders; their tongues explore each others mouths; their hands feel each others bodies tenderly and intimately. George has his eyes closed as Lenny's body presses closer with power and urgency into his core. She leads him into her bed room.

Lying together naked, time stands still for the two lovers. They touch and fondle, they kiss intimately. It is George's turn to shudder as Lenny's tongue explores his erogenous flesh from base to tip; George's fingers, with the sensitive touch of a pianist, explore all of Lenny's willing body. The two lovers finally bind together. The record has changed. The Byrds are singing "Hey Mr Tambourine Man".

"*Oh wow Howdy you made me shudder and shake all over. You are my true lover.*" Leonora purrs with contentment.

"Amazing, fantastic I am tingling all over. That feeling Oh how wonderful. I wish it could last forever." George enthuses.

"*Well now Mr Howdy lover maybe it will. Right now I am gonna make us some coffee then you is gonna go home for some rest.*" Leonora teases.

Chapter Twenty Two

A new airport

Late May Monday Evening

Evidence Gathering

Adrian and Inspector Johnson bring "Pembroke Lady" alongside the Government Jetty in Hamilton harbour. The sun is turning pale red as dusk descends.

"Have this package taken to Police Headquarters at once." Inspector Johnson orders his men.

"May I go along with these guys?" Duane asks.

"Yes. Of course, help yourself, Duane, although please remember you are on Her Majesty's territory and this package is our property."

"OK, I know the score. I don't want to play hard ball with you guys. We have worked well together. I will be recommending to my bosses that our Drug Enforcement Agency stumps up half the cash for your airport re build." Duane smiles as he presents his peace offering.

"Glad to hear some sense is creeping in to all this chaos." Inspector Johnson remarks.

"Now, in the morning I want to interview "Pembroke Lady's" owners. See how they fit in to this drug running. I have already ordered my men to raid Sammy Santino's warehouse. The Governor signed the order whilst we were at sea."

"Guess I'll stick around for a while and see what you come up with there." Duane replies.

"I say Duane, really glad to hear about this cash. The Governor will be very pleased. I wouldn't be surprised if you get an invitation to dinner." Adrian enthuses.

"You Limeys, you crease me up. I offer you half a million bucks and you invite me for dinner. You guys sure know how to grease the wheels of trade." Duane guffaws as he enters the police car.

Tuesday Morning Late May 1966

Value of the Package

After a good night's rest Inspector Johnson is at Police HQ by seven o'clock. He is eager to hear about the raid on Sammy Santino's warehouse and the contents of the package.

"We found twenty five boxes each containing twelve bottles of Island Rum Sir." The duty sergeant explains and goes on

"But the bottles did not contain rum. Each bottle is filled with diluted cocaine. All in all it is reckoned the New York street value of each bottle is ten thousand dollars. The total for all the boxes comes to a nice round three million dollars." The duty sergeant puffs up his chest and looks incredulous. His monthly salary is just four hundred dollars.

"What about the package from "Pembroke Lady"? What does that amount to?" Inspector Johnson asks in an excited tone of voice.

"So far as we can tell Sir there is two hundred pounds of pure cocaine in the package. If it is diluted similar to the stuff in the bottles you are looking at a street value of three point two million dollars Sir." The sergeant pronounces trying hard to keep his voice on an even pitch as the amounts are so enormous.

"Wow over six million dollars that is quite a haul Sergeant. Any clues or evidence to link back to the source?"

"None found so far Sir. Forensics is on it. They may pick up something."

"I very much doubt it. Let the FBI chappie have access when he comes over; but, on no account is he allowed to remove anything. Now, I am going to have a wee chat with Mr. Wayne Luther at the Bank of Pembroke. I want to know what he knows about the bank's boat being used for drug smuggling, should be revealing."

"That's strange Sir we just had a call from Jimmy Smith out at Warwick. He says he got Wayne Luther's cap out of the stomach of a shark he bought from Eugene Jordan yesterday afternoon."

"Now that is interesting Sergeant. Get someone out to Warwick for that cap and have Eugene Jordan interviewed. Find out where and when that shark was caught." Inspector Johnson orders as he reaches for his telephone and requests the switchboard to connect him to Wayne Luther's residence.

Where's Wayne?

"Mary Jayne is Wayne there with you?" Henry Rucker queries as he knocks and enters the private quarters that Wayne and Mary Jayne occupy in the Rucker's six bedroom bungalow.

"No Pa. I don't know where he is. He didn't come home last night. If he's bin dallying with some girl on "Pembroke Lady" he's gonna be dead meat." Mary Jayne responds angrily with a tinge of worry in her voice.

"I thought as much. He signed out for the boat real early Monday morning. Was that the last time you saw him Mary Jayne?" Henry Rucker asks his voice sounding exasperated.

"He left in a mighty hurry, didn't say goodbye. Pa I'm not happy at all. It's no way for me to be treated." Mary Jayne starts to blubber.

"He is due at an Island Rum meeting in thirty minutes. You jess let me know if he turns up darlin. Don't you worry your dear head over this? Your Pa will be having a few words with Mr Wayne Luther when I catch up with him." Henry Rucker consoles his daughter by giving her a bear like hug.

"The boat has been gone over twenty four hours now Pa. Do you think something has happened to him? Do you think I should call in the police?" Mary Jayne demands panic creeping into her voice.

"Let's just give it a few more hours for him to turn up. If there is no news by lunch time I'll come back and we will decide what to do." Henry Rucker continues to reassure his only daughter with a hug and a cuddle only to be interrupted by the telephone ringing. Pushing her father away Mary Jayne rushes to the telephone.

"Hello, hello is that you Wayne?" Mary Jayne calls not waiting for a first response from the caller.

"Hello Ma'am its Inspector Johnson from Her Majesties Colonial Police calling. Are you Mary Jayne Luther?" Hearing the word Police Mary Jayne drops the telephone and crashes to the floor in a faint.

Chapter Twenty Three

Jasmine

Tuesday Afternoon 31st May 1966

Setting Sail

"Good sailing Captain" the New York harbour pilot bids farewell to Captain Kato. The pilot has navigated "Ocean Star" out of Red Hook Wharf into Upper Bay. The well known land marks of Sea Gate and Coney Island pass on the port bow as the ship enters the deeper waters of the Lower Bay. Once the harbour pilot has safely transferred back to his pilot boat Kato orders the helmsman to steer one hundred and forty degrees and calls for eighty per cent power. This course will take "Ocean Star" past Ascension Island and on to St. Helena a British Protectorate which should be reached in nine days.

"I shall be in my cabin if you need me for anything." Kato informs the watch.

You don't fool me Captain

Petrus, the second in command thinks to himself as he watches the back of Captain Kato disappear downstairs to his quarters.

I wouldn't mind some action with that girl he's got hidden away my self. Still, I am a hundred dollars to the good for letting the boss know about the girl, maybe another hundred dollars in Mozambique if I can find out anything more for the boss.

"So Jasmine we have finally left New York. So for now you are safe. How do you feel about that now my sweet girl?" Kato asks as he pours Jasmine a coffee in his cabin.

"I'm feeling like shit if you must know. My goddamn room it's just like a prison. There's no action. I'm bored. I need a fix. Where's that stuff I gave George in New York. I know he gave it to you. I'm going crazy. It's like I've been shut up here for over two days now. I can't take any more. I really need some stuff to see me through." Jasmine implores as she puffs on one of her black cheroots her hands trembling nervously.

It's time for action

Kato slips two fifteen milligram Temazepan sleeping pills into Jasmine's coffee cup.

"Drink this coffee up Jasmine. It's not as bad as you think. You are away from those gangsters. Now you shall have some stuff just as soon as you have finished your coffee. George said it was to be used in an emergency and I guess we can class your state as being an emergency. There my sweet drink it all up there's a good girl." Kato coaxes Jasmine to swallow the coffee.

"OK you Greek pain in the ass. Where's my stuff. I need it now!" Jasmine screams.

"Yes, yes my child. I will fetch it for you. You don't think I would be so foolish as to leave it lying around do you my child? Give me five minutes to fetch it from the safe. How about another coffee while you wait?" Kato requests in a mild soothing voice.

"Just go and fetch it you dummy!" Jasmine screams at Kato as he leaves his cabin locking the door behind him. Fifteen minutes later he returns to find Jasmine lying on his small sofa; her eyelids are drooping; she looks listless; the drugs have calmed her nervous system and shut down her body.

"Did you get them?" Jasmine asks in a subdued murmur.

"Yes dear girl. Everything is just fine. Just relax. Go to sleep now." In another five minutes Jasmine is in a deep sleep and Kato carries her back to her cabin and makes her comfortable.

Can I keep up this nursemaid job? Kato wonders as he shuts and locks the cabin door.

Tuesday Evening 31st. May, 1966

Toast to Success

"Gentlemen, congratulations on a well executed operation." Sir Jeremy Mannerby Watson raises his glass of port. He looks kindly at each of his guests enjoying after dinner drinks in the cedar panelled ante room in Government house.

"Cheers!" Duane, Inspector Johnson, Adrian and George toast each other and clink glasses one to another.

"I will miss you guys. It's been a real interesting couple of days. I never dreamt we could achieve so much so quickly." Duane remarks looking at each in turn feeling surprised and also be mused at how his attitude to his Limey colleagues has changed from his early disdain to one of growing respect.

"I am so pleased that having seen the problems at first hand you are recommending your colleagues at DEA to stump up the cash to re develop our terminal. That will be the best way to stop the trafficking permanently." Adrian says with conviction edging his voice.

"There's no doubt my bosses are real pleased. Not only have we shut down a major drugs operation but thanks to George we have cleaned up the Brooklyn docks racket. I will be on the case for development of the base real soon Adrian." Duane looks across at Adrian whose face has changed from his usual non committal, taciturn look to almost one of satisfaction as he gives George a look that says he is in his debt.

"I understand that Wayne Luther was involved with Sammy. Can you tell us any detail?" George asks Inspector Johnson.

"Yes it seems that Wayne Luther went out on "Pembroke Lady" with Sammy yesterday. He hasn't been seen since although his cap turned up inside a shark. We obviously can't ask Sammy about it and Wayne's wife and father in law know nothing at all. At the moment he is missing presumed dead. It will be a tricky one for the coroner without further evidence. Duane what I don't understand is how you were able to locate "Pembroke Lady" so accurately from the plane?"

"Yea, well, that information is classified. I don't mind saying though that we have proof that a ship called Neptune Carrier dropped off the drugs. She is part of the Tinopolis fleet. She may not be for much longer though. In twelve hours time the US navy will be impounding her when she enters US waters. What with Sammy's drug money in New York and this ship; our crime sequestration income should be more than enough to finance your airport development." Duane notices that Adrian and George are exchanging weird glances.

"There is some further information about Tinopolis and his operations that has come to our attention here in Bermuda, Duane. We need to talk some more with you and Inspector Johnson." Adrian advises.

"Now that's real interesting . . . ." Duane says looking intrigued but before he can find out any further information a voice booms out

"Adrian, if you are starting up some more work I think I will leave you to it. Do excuse me gentlemen please!" Sir Jeremy Mannerby Watson makes his excuses and leaves the ante room. For the next hour Adrian and George explain to Duane and Inspector Johnson what they know about "Ocean Star" and its cargo of arms heading for the coast of Mozambique.

Wednesday Morning 1ˢᵗ June, 1966

Costas loses a Ship

Costas is puzzled about Kato's secret woman passenger. Kato's, second in command, Petrus could not give him any explanation as to why she was on board. Costas did not believe Kato was a womaniser.

There has to be some other explanation but, racking his brains, he cannot come up with an answer.

It will be useful to get something more on Kato to ensure the arms delivery to Smutts in Mozambique goes without a hitch.

Having flown back to Monaco on Monday Costas has now brought himself up to date with his business affairs. He is angry to find that his request to George for reimbursement of his payment to Kato has been ignored.

I'll have to sort out that impudent young pen pusher. I will send Mercator over.

He notes that Neptune Carrier is due to dock into New York today. Another delivery of cocaine seamlessly delivered to the soft underbelly of the United States Eastern Seaboard by him and Jamil. Costas rubs his hands together greedily anticipating his share from this latest delivery.

Walking through his open plan office he hears the telex machine chattering in the corner. The telex is from the captain of Neptune Carrier.

Probably a routine message advising her safe berth into New York

As he tears the paper message from its roller he gives the message just a cursory glance; about to toss the paper in to the filing tray the word "impounded" catches his attention.

Stopping in mid stride Costas reads the message carefully. The colour drains away from his face as he realises the implications.

My ship which cost me three million dollars is out of action. The ship will earn no revenue. I will have to pay massive legal fees and fines to get the ship back. May be I can with hold the crews wages for the duration reduce my losses. My God, this is looking like a disaster.

Costas hurries to his private office. He tells his secretary he wants no interruptions. He sits down, puts his head in his hands, trying desperately to think of a way to get his ship back to work. Finally, he decides he must obtain more information before taking any action. He must advise Jamil El Hassan.

Chapter Twenty Four
Jamil El Hassan

Wednesday Afternoon 1st June 1966

Costas talks to Jamil

The man is sitting in a Turkish bath. The young boy massaging the hard fibrous muscle and sinew beneath the loose flesh around the man's neck and shoulders has been instructed to comply with any request. He has been told the man has influence. He is powerful. Please him and it will go well for you. Do not upset him. The boy is nervous. The steam combining with the orange scented oil make his hands slippery. The man seems relaxed; his eyes are closed; his stomach falls away in layers hiding his genitalia. The scene reminds the boy of a Hippo in a mud pool. The boy coughs as steam combines with smoke from the jewel encrusted, handsomely carved, houka waft into his throat. The boy feels the man tense up; his eye lids blink open; the eyes give out a cruel look; they lack compassion like those seen in a desert hawk as it pounces on weak prey.

The boy trembles inwardly with fear but continues kneading the man's back and neck and prays to Allah that he has not up set the man. Seeing no danger, the man relaxes, shuts his eyes and takes another puff from the houka.

Outside, music combines with the noise from people hustling and bustling in the Souk—al—Jamil in Beirut's central district. The sounds drift into the baths. Jamil El Hassan is relaxing after lunch and a short siesta. His mind drifts back over ten years to when he was in Manhattan. Then the thirteen year old Sammy was his regular boy.

Such pleasure from one so young, such a pity he had to reach puberty. Still Sammy has been well rewarded through my New York associates. May the will of Allah permit this new boy to provide pleasures anew?

Jamil El Hassan's dream like thoughts is interrupted by one of his aides who enter the bath cubicle. The aide signals the boy to move away and fetch a towel and bath robe.

"Forgive this intrusion on your valuable and respected leisure time master but your dear old friend Costas Tinopolis is telephoning. He begs your forgiveness, as I do also master, but says it is important to your esteemed interests that he speaks to you." The aide grovels, bowing low, averting his eyes from his master's gaze. Jamil El Hassan raises his right arm and locates a solid gold wall handle which he grips with his large powerful hand. He commences a ponderous rise from his bath. Before he is half way out of the bath the aide snatches the pristine white towel made from the finest Egyptian cotton from the boy and wraps it around Jamil El Hassan's broad shoulders. Jamil El Hassan now stands in the bath at his full height of five foot six inches. Before he raises a leg to step out of the bath the aide has placed a Persian rug by the side of the bath, then, kneeling with his head bowed, the aide places on his master's feet embroidered and jewel encrusted slippers made from the finest softest goat skin.

Minion or Master

Jamil El Hassan dries himself with the towel and then anoints his body with frankincense and perfumed oils. The aide now waves the boy over to hand Jamil El Hassan his bath robe, made from Persian silk, embroidered with Jamil El Hassan's motif of two crossed silver scimitars shown behind an eagle, landing with its talons extended.

"Thank you Mustaf, you may go. See to it that the boy awaits me in my rooms." Jamil El Hassan commands, eyeing the boy who is standing demurely in front of him.

The nerve centre of Jamil El Hassan's operations as a merchant, entrepreneur, smuggler, financier of shipping, drug exporter, arms dealer, investor in pornography, prostitution, piracy and breaker of United Nation sanctions lies in the heart of the Souk—al—Jamil. His offices, which from the outside appear to be private residences are on the floor above the Turkish baths. The baths are managed by Lebanese associates. The business is owned by a Maltese company which in turn is owned by a company registered in the Cayman Islands which in turn is owned by a company registered in Panama. There are many such companies and businesses in Jamil El Hassan's empire.

The ownership web is always triple layered and sometimes quadruple layered to form a complex pattern making it difficult for Jamil El Hassan to be directly associated with any of his nefarious activities.

Each company has a front man appointed by an associate of Jamil El Hassan. Any act of disloyalty would result in ruin, followed by torture and finally a merciful release into death. Secrecy, fear and loyalty are his bye words.

Jamil El Hassan leaves the Turkish bath complex through a secret door which opens into a circular courtyard situated in the centre of the building. The door is disguised to look like a framed oil painting of an Arab warrior on a white charger. When Jamil El Hassan presses the right hoof of the charger with his be jewelled finger the door catch is released. Jamil El Hassan climbs up a set of stairs to his private rooms to receive the telephone call from Costas Tinopolis.

Jamil El Hassan is concerned at the news from Costas Tinopolis especially since he has had no pre warning from his contacts in the USA. His associates in New York run a lucrative drug operation. They have contacts in the Judiciary, the Police and Government. Each contact has been corrupted and coerced to be the gang's eyes and ears using bribery, blackmail or fear of violence to themselves or their loved ones.

Jamil El Hassan instructs an aide to contact his New York associates.

Wednesday Morning 1st June 1966

Sammy's Bank account

George found it difficult to get to sleep on Tuesday night. Such a contrast from Monday, following the sensational love making he experienced with Lenny, when he slept deeply, his mind and body completely relaxed.

After the celebration dinner at Government House; then the late meeting with Duane and Inspector Johnson to discuss "Ocean Star" carrying illegal arms; George is unable to switch off and surrender to sleep; he keeps thinking about the plans they have hatched up; he wonders what the next few weeks will have in store for him.

Minion or Master

George is relieved to see the first shaft of faint red light filter into his bedroom. Before the sun has fully risen he is swimming in the salty Atlantic Ocean, warmed by the Gulf Stream.

He thinks about his forthcoming journey to St Helena for Jasmine. Sammy has been the cause of her trouble. Now he is dead. He must have suffered pain and discomfort in his death George believes; but, was it sufficient to atone for all the misery he has caused? George thinks not. Jasmine's misery will continue. As a numbers man George is constantly searching for balance. Whether it be income with expenditure, assets with liabilities, work with reward or Sammy's payment for misery caused.

At the dinner last night Duane had mentioned that Sammy's assets in America were to be seized. George thinks that Sammy's Bank of Pembroke money should be used to compensate for the misery he has caused Jasmine and her family. Some sort of basic justice will be served. The problem is how to make it happen.

The Bank of Pembroke will be the first place I shall enquire. Refreshed, George wades out of the sea, ready for the day ahead.

The Island flag is flying at half mast from the Bank of Pembroke offices. The mood inside is sombre. Wayne's mystery disappearance, in such dramatic circumstances, has shocked the Rucker family and the bank staff.

"*Since de news yesterday we done feel numb. Although Mr. Henry he come to work today. Says we has to carry on for de customers. Some of de people here say Wayne he dun be mixed up with dat Sammy an dats why he not here. Do you know anyting 'bout dat Howdy?*" Leonora, wearing a black arm band, whispers to George at the reception desk.

"Well it is a possibility Lenny. Wayne was not on "Pembroke Lady" when we intercepted her but the Police think it is fairly certain he went out with Sammy in the morning. Trouble is they have no witnesses. Do you think I could speak with Mr. Henry now Wayne is not here?" George is trying hard to retain a business like demeanour with Leonora despite his heart rate going sky high at being so close to her.

"Should be alright Howdy, he got no appointments. It might help take his mind off tings. You not forget dat you is to come to de house tonight. Pa an me is lookin forward to another musical evening wiv you?" Leonora gives George her brightest smile which causes his face to turn red and his heart to race faster.

"So Mr Howden how can I help, Wayne was handling your account and as you probably know he is presently missing." Henry Rucker, looking pale and distracted, greets George with old world courtesy and walks him to his private office.

"Yes I am sorry to hear about Wayne. I wanted to clarify whether it is still in order to continue the arrangements Wayne made with me concerning the Aframe Account. Wayne has been paid the first instalment of an annual thirty thousand dollars. Should we continue these payments?" George looks at Henry Rucker whose face is turning from pale to a red puce.

"Are you telling me, Sir, that you are paying my son in law personally?" Henry Rucker gives George a look of disbelief mixed with horror.

"Why, yes, Wayne requested it when we agreed the bank details last month. Forgive me, Sir. I am new here. Wayne led me to believe this was a perfectly normal transaction for a customer to do. Is anything wrong?"

Minion or Master

George fears he has triggered off a lethal volcano, judging by the look on Henry Rucker's face.

"Most certainly, Sir, in all my years in the bank no one expects you, the customer, to pay anything other than our interest, charges and fees. Wayne has been acting outside my authority in this matter. To hear this makes me sad; on behalf of my family and the bank I can only apologise and say to you this is not the way we do business. After hearing this it might be better for Wayne if he never comes back to this bank. No Sir, payments will cease forthwith. I am obliged to you for bringing it to my attention." Henry Rucker advises George trying hard to maintain a dignified composure.

"Well I am most grateful for your forthright honesty in this regard Mr Rucker and I do offer you my profound apologies for troubling you at such a difficult time. There is just one other matter I would be grateful to have your advice about. A client has died with no relations and leaving no will. There is a large sum in their account. What happens to the account?"

"Of course you will need the death certificate. Then an advert is placed in the paper. If no one responds the account is transferred to the Governor's office." Henry Rucker responds mechanically clearly still seething over his son in laws malfeasance.

"That is very interesting, thank you for seeing me Sir." George bows as he shakes Henry Rucker's hand.

Wednesday Afternoon 1st June 1966

New York News for Jamil

Jamil El Hassan's private rooms are on the top floor of the Souk—al—Jamil. No expense has been spared by him in furnishing his private domain. Every piece of furniture, every carpet and drape has been carefully chosen. All made from the finest materials by the best craftsmen. The rooms are accessed from a balcony running around a central circular courtyard laid out in Italian marble. In the centre of the court yard is a twenty foot diameter mosaic depicting two crossed scimitars with a Pharaoh Eagle Owl landing with its talons extended. The orange yellow eyes of the Pharaoh Eagle Owl, made from diamond and amber, shine ominously from the mosaic. The Pharaoh Eagle Owl is an inconspicuous and secretive bird of prey; this mirrors the lifestyle Jamil El Hassan has chosen. Jamil El Hassan controls his nefarious activities secretly; his enemies will be cut down ruthlessly by the razor sharp blade of the scimitar. Jamil El Hassan is proud of his motif.

Lying on his back he feels relaxed. His body sinks into the soft, king sized mattress. His eyes are open; they look at the crystal chandelier hanging from the gold talons of a Pharaoh Eagle Owl attached to the ceiling by the tip of each outstretched wing. Earlier, he had given the young boy twenty dollars. The price was the same ten years ago. Nothing changes he muses contentedly. His thoughts are interrupted by Mustaf who plugs a telephone receiver made from ivory with gold inlay into an extension.

The front man for the New York operation, Michael Gregory is on the telephone. The time in Beirut is five in the afternoon. In New York it is is ten in the morning.

Jamil El Hassan listens as Michael Gregory explains the situation in his quiet, unruffled, deep tone of voice. Michael Gregory dresses in the style of a Wall Street banker. The dress style and voice give those he meets no hint of the utterly ruthless character he is.

"We got information from our contact at the FBI. Sammy's operation is busted. Our contact doesn't know how they found the drop in the Atlantic. Sammy was left for the sharks. The good news is we got all the dope from Pulaski Street before it was torched. The FBI picked up some of Sammy's couriers yesterday after following them from the Airport. One of these guys is singing like a canary; says Sammy was mixed up with a banker guy in Bermuda called Wayne Luther. Maybe this Wayne Luther gave the cop the tip off, do you want this checked out boss?"

"Yes Michael put your best man on it. I want those responsible for Sammy's death to feel the scimitar, do you understand?"

"OK boss leave it with me, one other thing. Sammy's number two, Artie, got away from the FBI guys. He used a stooge to meet Sammy's couriers at La Guardia. Maybe nothing in it; but, Artie says they were spied on by a guy called George Howden; said he was in shipping from Bermuda. Sammy also mentioned this at the Casino. Seems the guy Howden was mixed up with a broad from Bermuda who Sammy and Artie had in training. We had a tip off so we got a crew to get him. The broad's missing and so far we haven't got a confirmed kill on Howden. We got our FBI contact checking on it right now Boss."

"Get your man to check this Howden in Bermuda with the banker. If he has interfered in our affairs he must feel the edge of the scimitar." Jamil El Hassan places the receiver gently down. Deep in thought he walks purposefully from the bedroom through a connecting door made from Lebanese oak into his office. For minutes Jamil El Hassan sits motionless at his office desk, his fingertips forming a vee shape touching his lips, still in thought. Then, rising he walks across to the inner wall and with his thumb touches the bottom of a central wall light frame made from gold and silver which conceals a recessed button.

The button opens a concealed panel in the wall revealing a wall safe. Jamil El Hassan enters the safe combination and takes out a leather bound note book. He turns the pages in the book until he finds the notes referring to "Ocean Star" chartered by Aframe Shipping, Bermuda arriving Lourenco Marques early June.

Chapter Twenty Five

Mercator

Thursday Morning 2nd June 1966

Mercator calls on George

Mercator Tinopolis brooded and sulked on the direct flight from London to Bermuda. His father had interfered with his social life once more. Mercator and two acquaintances had arranged a long week end trip to Corsica. A private boat was chartered to whisk them out to the Island from the port of Marseille on Thursday evening. Island partying with plenty of wine, women and sun was eagerly anticipated. The curt instruction from his father on Wednesday afternoon had created a mixture of anger and hatred in Mercator. Costas Tinopolis, his millionaire pig of a father, had insisted he fly straight to London to catch the BOAC morning flight. His father's instructions were

"Sort out that trumped up numbers man George Howden. If necessary sack him and get someone like Wayne Luther at the Bank of Pembroke to take his place."

All through his life his father had dominated him. Now at the age of twenty three Mercator's resentment at his father's bully boy tactics was becoming unrestrained. George Howden would be the recipient of the anger welling up in Mercator and spreading throughout his being like a malignant tumour. One day, I will do to my father what George Howden is going to get today . . . . vows Mercator as the taxi pulls up outside the Bank of Pembroke.

The bank officer explains that Wayne Luther will not be available in the foreseeable future. They can provide an alternative to act as a Director for the company once the necessary company resolution has been passed. The resolution requires the approval of the company shareholders meeting after seven days notice. The notice may be waived if all shareholders are present and give their consent. Dammit thinks Mercator I can't get rid of him as easily as I thought. The old man will have to come over. In the meantime I'll go and rattle George Howden's cage.

George is in his office catching up with client work. After lunch he is due to go to the Coroner's office where he, Duane and Inspector Johnson will swear affidavits concerning Sammy's death. Duane has agreed to stay on coordinating plans to deal with the arms on "Ocean Star". He is due to fly back to New York tonight. Adrian has spoken with the Coroner on behalf of the Governor to get things hurried through to produce a death certificate for Sammy so that his money can be accessed. George's work is interrupted by the telephone ringing.

"Mercator Tinopolis? What is he doing here? You had better show him up!" George talks into the receiver.

"Father is not pleased with your performance managing these accounts. He wants you out of the company as soon as possible. It will be best if you resign now." Mercator Tinopolis has wasted no words on social niceties with George who is sitting quietly listening to Mercator's demands. Mercator having blurted out his complaint with some venom is surprised at George's

Minion or Master

reaction. The impression he had formed of George when they first met with his father was of someone who was an innocent pushover. He had expected George to collapse at his accusation allowing Mercator to turn the screw further in pursuing misery for George. Looking at George sitting across from him with his skin tanned from tennis, cool grey eyes looking steadily back Mercator is flummoxed.

"So tell me, what is your answer? Will you leave now to avoid further embarrassment for you with your employer? Or do you want a bad reference as well?" Mercator queries menacingly, trying to throw George off guard. George continues to sit still in his chair considering the situation, his ice cool brain working through the options like a Grand Master eying the chess board. How shall I play this George ponders.

How much does the son know about his father? Can I use this opportunity to get evidence from Mercator which will prove Costas guilty of drug running and arms smuggling? That would be just great.

"So Mercator, how much do you know about your father's business affairs? Has he taken you into his confidence? Do you know why you are here in Bermuda and not him?"

"I am in charge here. I ask the questions not you! My father will see to it you never work again." Mercator shouts losing control and shaking his fists at George. Before George can respond the telephone rings. George listens to the receptionist advise him that Duane Pickens is here for their lunch appointment. Keeping his eyes fixed on Mercator George requests reception to show Duane into the office.

"Duane let me introduce you to Mercator Tinopolis, son of Costas Tinopolis, the owner of "Ocean Star" and

Neptune Carrier." Mercator gives Duane a cursory look; one reserved for someone of little importance or interest. Duane, on the other hand, looks animated and pleased, as if he has found a long lost friend. Mercator now looks confused and put out at having his confrontation with George disturbed.

"This is a private business meeting. Perhaps you would be so kind as to leave us until we have concluded our meeting?" Mercator asks Duane with a look of complete indifference on his face.

"Do forgive me Mercator. May I introduce you to Duane Pickens from the FBI? Duane is investigating Neptune Carrier; your father's ship is it not? The ship is involved in drug smuggling. Quite a haul was taken from her before she was impounded in New York. Did your father mention it to you before you left him? I am sure Duane will want to ask you a few questions about what you know about this very serious crime." George smiles, Mercator's face has changed from indifference to a trembling look of panic, his mouth is wide open; the eyes have the look of a haunted victim; his bottom lip is quivering.

"I know nothing of this. This is a trick. I want to speak to my father before I say anything." Mercator shrieks as Duane moves in close to Mercator's cringing face. Holding him by the arms Duane whispers into Mercator's ear

"Now sonny this is the situation. You are free to leave. You can even call your Daddy; cry down the 'phone to him if you want. But I gotta tell you sonny boy. Listen well now. The airport is US property. As soon as you set your dainty feet in there my boys will be all over you like a rash. Now, me an George is gonna take a bite to eat. You can kick your heels for a while until I decide whether to get the Governor to subpoena you for evidence. Or maybe my pal Inspector Johnson will come and arrest you for disturbin my peace and with holdin evidence. I jess can't decide right now. But, one thing is for sure. Your sorry ass is stuck on this little Island for a good while. On the other hand, if you co operate, I might just let you through the airport with no hassle. Now run along and we'll see you later." Duane lets go of Mercator's arms as he turns him towards the door.

"Real nice to meet you." Duane calls as Mercator walks towards the office door. Hearing the sarcastic comment Mercator turns to look back at George and Duane; his face is scowling with anger. As he goes through the door Duane shouts out

"Now you have a nice day do you hear?"

Thursday afternoon 2nd June 1966

Sammy's Inquest

The Court House clock is striking three in the afternoon as Duane, George and Inspector Johnson accompanied by Adrian walk down the steps from the Coroner's Court.

"That seems fairly cut and dried. Sammy is dead. Cause—misadventure. The verdict couldn't be better." Adrian remarks.

"Yes the last thing I wanted was to be caught up with some Police complaints investigation. I must say I am relieved and pleased everything has been cleared so quickly. It just shows what you can achieve when you can use the Governor's powers so effectively, thank you Adrian.

You have saved me weeks of paper work on this one." Inspector Johnson responds in a grateful tone.

"You jess hold on to your Hoss there Jonno of the Yard!" Duane interjects

"Me an George need you to create some special paper work. Ain't that right George?" Duane grins looking first at George then at Adrian and Inspector Johnson who both look bewildered.

"Please do tell all. Don't keep us in suspense." Adrian orders giving George a stare that demands a response.

"Yes, well, actually it's Duane's idea really. You see Costas Tinopolis's son Mercator is on the Island and Duane wants him extradited to the States to answer charges about Neptune Carrier and the drugs. Duane thinks this will put more pressure on Costas Tinopolis. Under pressure he might slip up and inadvertently provide leads back to who is behind the drugs and arms smuggling. I think it is worth a try." George looks at Adrian who is deep in thought then at Inspector Johnson who snaps straight back.

"Can't be done laddie, nice try though, for extradition I'll need the charges from the States put before the Court here. It will need a High Court Judge from London. It will take months." Inspector Johnson looks smug thinking that a few days paperwork has been avoided.

"Hang on just a second," Adrian intercedes.

"Maybe we don't have to go through the whole process. What if we just hold him for questioning? Scare the pants off him. Maybe he will give us some useful information. At the same time it will put Costas Tinopolis under extra pressure. It is worth a try. I think we owe it to our American cousins to help them all we can now they are going to finance the improvements to the airport terminal. You have already been saved a great deal of paperwork by my speedy actions. I think a little quid pro quo is in order". Adrian finishes by giving Inspector Johnson a cool stare.

"OK. OK. I can see the merit. I can hold him for questioning for forty eight hours. No doubt you will want to have a go at this prey Duane? It will mean cancelling your flight home".

"No Problem Jonno. I'm looking forward to meeting Mercator once more. I've already rattled him and wished him a nice day. Now I feel like helping to make his day get a whole lot worse. Count me in. I'm here on this case for the next forty eight hours."

Costa's is Told about George

Mercator is still shaking after his confrontation with George and Duane Pickens. He telephones room service at the Princess Hotel ordering some lunch and a stiff drink. He is also feeling angry about being out manoeuvred by that impudent upstart George Howden.

God forbid if it means I have to stay here for some time. He shudders at the prospect. The thought of being cooped up on this small island with out his friends just adds to his negative thoughts especially concerning his father. The fact that his arrogant, interfering father has not told him about Neptune Carrier stokes his anger even more. Resentment and hatred towards his father well up.

It is time I made him realise I am not his plaything child to just do his bidding like a lap dog. He will see that my bite can be poisonous.

Mercator broods; he is calmer after lunch; thinking how the situation might best work to his advantage.

Martin Smith

Mercator decides to speak with his father. He has booked a long distance call. The time in Monaco will be nine o'clock in the evening. *Maybe I will interrupt his dinner*

The telephone rings

"Son, this had better be good. You have disturbed my dinner. Have you sorted out that minion Howden for me?" Costas bellows.

"It is not straight forward father. There is a mess here. Howden has been charged by the authorities with fraud. The bank has frozen our accounts. They need your signature here as soon as possible. When can you get here? I need to tell the Bank and the Police. They take shipping fraud very seriously here as there are so many ships registered in Bermuda. They say they will throw the book at the upstart; they are threatening to impound "Ocean Star" when she stops at St. Helena if you cannot come here to sort out the mess. What do you want me to do father?" Mercator pauses for breath; he smiles feeling smug at the deception he is playing; he listens for a response from his father thousands of miles away.

"This is not what I expected. The accounts sent to me so far have been in order. Howden did not pay me for what I gave Kato, fraud? I cannot believe it. Why did I not hear before?" Costas queries his voice sounding suspicious.

"The authorities have only just discovered it Pa. Howden is in jail. They need you to come here. You are such a well known International business man, friend of Princes and Presidents. As soon as you come things will be resolved I am sure." Mercator purrs into the receiver spreading his deceit in thick layers.

"Son, I am impressed with your cool analysis of our situation. I will talk with your uncle Jamil and decide then

Minion or Master

how to best resolve this temporary blip to our complete success." Costas speaks in a placatory manner not sure if Mercator's pleading for him to go to Bermuda is the most sensible option.

"Thank you father, as always, I will abide by your wise decision. I will await your further instructions." Mercator smiles thinking his Father has believed his deception. Before Costas can respond Mercator's room door is opened. Inspector Johnson using the Police powers he possesses has taken a master key from hotel reception he is quickly followed into the room by Duane Pickens

"Hello sonny, are you havin a nice day jest like I wished for you?" Duane enquires.

"Mercator! What is happening? I can hear voices in your room. Mercator!" Costas bellows on the phone. Mercator hears his Father screaming but is mesmerized by the entrance of the two men. Before he can reply to his Father Duane has stretched over and placed the receiver back on its base. Costas is disconnected.

"Mercator Tinopolis. I have reason to believe that ships owned by you or your immediate family are involved in the illegal smuggling of drugs into the United States of America. I request you to accompany me to Her Majesty's Police Station to answer some questions. Do you have anything to say?" Inspector Johnson's voice is barely audible as he whispers in his soft Scottish lowlands accent.

"Come on sonny boy. Come into my den. I want to whisper a few little ol questions to you." Duane whispers into Mercator's ear.

"I want to speak to my lawyer and my Father." Mercator shrieks as he is unceremoniously hustled out of the Princess Hotel.

"You don't need a lawyer. We are just asking you a few questions; hoping you can help us with our enquiries." Inspector Johnson responds giving Mercator Tinopolis a look that implies this will not be just a few routine questions.

George Reflects

Having returned to his office, George has no appetite for routine work. Seated at his desk George's mind mulls over events in the last week, Adrian had been very effective organizing the Coroner. It was clever of him to have over come the "habeas corpus" problem of no dead body. The prospect of close on half a million dollars for the exchequer from Sammy's Bermuda account must have concentrated his mind. On the other hand; once he knew I intended to help Jasmine using Sammy's money; he agreed a generous commission would be paid to me. I guess it is fair. Adrian knows without the information I provided to the FBI there would have been nothing. No, I have earned it George concludes.

I can't think that Wayne's death will be handled quite so easily. There are no witnesses; his body will never be recovered if he was consumed by a shark. It is bizarre that my first taste of shark with Lenny was on the very day that Wayne met his demise by one.

That will not stop me from enjoying another shark steak meal; especially, if it is shared with Lenny. I should love another chance for an after dinner dance to hold her tight once more. Oh yes, I shall definitely be eating shark again if I can hold Lenny like last time.

George was disappointed that there had been no opportunity at Charlie's home for any more romantic

Minion or Master

action with Lenny. Their eyes had met on more than one occasion across Charlie's kitchen table as they tucked in to Fish Chowder. They had played footsie under the table, Charlie, being preoccupied with thoughts about Jasmine, if he did notice any change in their behaviour he made no mention.

Their musical evening had been less spontaneous and joyous than before. Everyone's concentration was poor. It was obvious that Charlie was hurting. He had been brooding over events worrying that it was his fault. He had allowed Sammy to take his daughter away. He said he was worried she might be changed forever. He had lost his little girl. Lenny and Charlie talked about what they would do with Jasmine when she returned.

Sensing Charlie and Lenny needed their private space George left early. Lenny had seen him out; for one lovely moment the magic returned as they kissed good night. Lenny did not pursue the kiss; she was worried about Charlie. George felt tension in his own body for holding back information. The last thing he wanted was to keep secrets from Lenny. Their relationship was still fragile. There were no deep roots of shared experiences forged from a long relationship. One thoughtless action, one misunderstood remark might destroy a budding relationship. George felt in his very core he wanted Lenny. He wanted a relationship, based upon trust, with no secrets. He wanted that relationship to build into a rich, long term, strong and unbreakable bond between them. He had tasted just a soupcon of the full relationship. He was very aware that his actions now might snuff out the tender, fragile romance he was involved with before time could strengthen it. George knew he faced a dilemma; but he did not know how to solve the puzzle without risking losing a future he desperately wished for.

George had still not told Charlie or Lenny about Jasmine's drug problem. He just could not bring himself to be the giver of the hurtful news. Each time he thought about telling them; he bottled out. He was terrified of seeing the look of horror and despair he knew they would feel. He considered Charlie to be a friend. Lenny he hoped was much more than just a friend. He worried that as the bearer of bad news he would be the recipient of any backlash, especially from Lenny. He really didn't want to go down that road. He had tried skirting around the issue. Last night at supper, he had mentioned tactfully about Sammy being a drug gangster. Neither Lenny nor Charlie had cottoned on to the possibility that Jasmine might have been affected. They were upset that Jasmine had been tricked in to a life of prostitution by Sammy. That was bad enough for them to take.

I can put it off at least for the next week until "Ocean Star" gets to St. Helena; then perhaps for another week before Jasmine gets repatriated to Bermuda. So I have maybe two weeks at the most.

Still immersed with his problem over how best not to upset Lenny and Charlie, George decides that a game of tennis will prove a welcome distraction.

Thursday evening 2nd June 1966

Costas Panics

The unexplained interruption to his telephone call with Mercator has caused alarm bells to start ringing in

Costas's brain. His instincts scream at him that something is not right.

Too much bad news cannot be just a coincidence. Problems everywhere I turn. What is happening?

Costas had been savouring every mouth watering flavour from his dinner. The sweet tender taste from saddle of Welsh salt marsh lamb cooked with fresh herbs from Provence. A young Medoc wine, carefully selected from a vineyard situated near the banks of the Gironde, where the alluvial silts from the Dordogne and the Garonne, combine with a humid atmosphere to work a special magic on the grapes. This superb meal had been anticipated with relish by Costas throughout the day. His mouth had salivated at the thought on more than one occasion. Now the meat, encrusted in herbs, is left abandoned on the fine bone china plate. The sauce made from the meat's juices is congealing, revealing small globules of white fat, looking like desert islands marooned in a sea of mud.

Costas paces up and down; impatiently waiting for his staff to connect him to Mercator. He must know what is happening. After thirty minutes a connection is made via the Trans Atlantic cable to the Princess hotel. There is no reply from Mercator's room. Reception desk has no information as to Mercator's whereabouts. Lack of information angers Costas. Like all control freaks he cannot bear to be left uninformed. The uncertainty gnaws away at his confidence pushing him out of his comfort zone. He must know what is happening so that he can influence what is going to happen. Only then can he relax knowing that he, Costas Tinopolis, is in control.

The time is one hour before midnight in Monaco when Jamil El Hassan answers Costas's call.

"Costas this must be serious it is midnight here. What is the problem?" Jamil El Hassan's eyes are half closed in concentration, awaiting the response.

"Please forgive me Jamil but I am very concerned. You know about Neptune Carrier in New York. That is bad for us. It will cost many dollars to change the outcome. Now, my son has reported there is a fraud in Bermuda. A young English man, Howden, is behind it. Jamil, Mercator has warned that "Ocean Star" may be impounded in St. Helena because of this fraud. You know what that means. You know what cargo she carries?" Costas has blurted the story out quickly; Jamil El Hassan takes a long time to respond as he considers carefully every word spoken by Costas. Many times Jamil El Hassan has found that a slow, deliberate, calculated consideration of people's remarks can work to his advantage. It does not pay to answer in the heat of the moment.

"I will speak with my man in Lourenco Marques. He should be warned if there is a delay in delivering the special cargo. Who is this Howden person Costas? Tell me more." Jamil El Hassan already knows that his New York associate Michael Gregory has mentioned Howden. Jamil El Hassan is not going to tell Costas this. He knows, from years of dealing with under world gangsters, never to provide gratuitous information.

At the right time information will be valuable. You never know how or when. Allah will reveal it to me in good time.

Jamil El Hassan is content to await Costas's response.

"He is a worthless numbers man. I engaged him to front the Bermuda shipping company. I shall go there tomorrow to sort him out. In the meantime, Jamil, I thought you should know about this. So many bad things are happening. Perhaps we should work together? There is a lot at stake. I cannot afford to lose two of my best ships Jamil."

"Go to Bermuda Costas. Sort out this Howden. Let me know when it is finished. At all costs "Ocean Star" must complete her voyage. The cargo must be delivered or we all face serious consequences. May Allah be with you?" Jamil El Hassan replaces the telephone receiver and immediately orders his loyal servant Mustaf to contact Michael Gregory.

Chapter Twenty Six
Michael Gregory

Thursday evening 2nd June 1966

To St. Helena

Captain Kato stands on the starboard side of the bridge of "Ocean Star". He is watching the sun glowing dark red spreading its warm coloured hues across the sea as it slowly dips into the Atlantic Ocean. When the weather is clear, and he is at sea, the sight of the sun setting in the west never fails to move him. Reminding him that nature is all powerful. The scene renews his respect for nature's elemental forces. Like all experienced sailors Captain Kato knows that a combination of sea and foul weather can wreak havoc with the strongest vessel.

Since leaving New York "Ocean Star" has covered one thousand five hundred miles. Burning the cheapest oils; evidenced by the clouds of filthy black smoke belching from her funnels; the massive two stroke diesel engines pound away hour after hour delivering enough power to the propeller shaft to maintain a cruising speed of twenty five knots.

Seven more days until he can off load Jasmine at St. Helena, Kato reminds him self. He is not sure if she can be controlled for another week. Yesterday she woke from her Temazepan induced sleep at midday. She refused food but drank coffee and smoked her black cheroots. Then in the afternoon she demanded that Kato give her a fix. Kato pleaded with her to try to do with out. He finally persuaded her to eat some food but within an hour the scrambled eggs on toast had been vomited from Jasmine's stomach. He recalled the pathetic picture of Jasmine, her face contorted as she knelt in the heads spewing out the food. He wished he could do more to help. He wanted to make everything right but he knew that it was only Jasmine that could win this fight.

I'll have to give her some of the drugs soon if she gets any worse, perhaps to morrow.

A tropical storm is building in Mid Atlantic. "Ocean Star" is heading straight for the bad weather. In four hours time the ship's course will take her into the heart of the tempest. Kato considers changing course to avoid the storm but decides not to. The radar picture and weather reports from the US Coastguard indicate that the storm is medium strength with force five and six winds. Kato thinks "Ocean Star" is more than capable of riding through such weather. He orders a check on all hatches to be certain that the vessel is watertight and requests to be called back to the bridge in three hours time. He will take command one hour before "Ocean Star" enters the eye of the storm.

Returning to his cabin for his evening meal he pauses at the door of Jasmine's cabin wondering whether to go in and check on her. Entering her cabin is not an easy decision to make for Kato. Going in to the cabin means he can satisfy himself everything is all right. On the other hand his entry might provoke Jasmine into a fit of pleading for drugs and make her situation worse. Before deciding Kato presses his ear to the cabin door. Listening for any sound to indicate Jasmine is awake and needs attention. Kato hears nothing. There is silence. Kato hopes she is asleep. In this case it is better not to disturb her. Listening for one last time Kato prepares to move away when he catches the faint sound of a muffled cry. Kato decides to investigate.

Peering around the cabin door, at first, Kato sees nothing unusual. He cannot see Jasmine. She must be in the shower or the heads he thinks. Walking into the cabin towards the shower room door he is completely taken aback to see his second in command lying on top of Jasmine. Jasmine is struggling to get away but the man is heavy. His head is buried into Jasmine's neck, his right hand covers her mouth pinning her head to the cabin floor whilst his left hand gropes with her clothes.

"Officer Petrus what do you think you are doing here?" Costas screams. Petrus tilts his head up from Jasmine's neck towards the direction of the voice. Seizing her chance, Jasmine takes a bite at Petrus's hand. Petrus lifts his hand from Jasmine's mouth and screams with pain. Jasmine rolls away from Petrus. She stands up. Petrus is on the floor clasping his hand. Jasmine picks up a heavy ash tray which is full of black cheroot stubs and smashes it down on the head of Petrus. Petrus slumps to the floor. Blood gushes from his skull.

"He promised me a fix." Jasmine cries. She drops the blood stained ash tray on the floor and buries her head in her hands, her body shivering uncontrollably. Gently Kato takes Jasmine to the bed and gets her to lie down. He covers Jasmine's shaking body with a giant sized duvet. Apart from shock and coming off drugs Kato can see no evidence of physical damage to Jasmine. Kato turns his attention to his second in command. Petrus is breathing but unconscious. He smells alcohol on Petrus's breath. Kato bandages Petrus's head and thinks Petrus will need stitches.

The first aid nominated sea man applies sutures to Petrus's wound. Petrus is now conscious and has been confined to his cabin. Kato decides to continue the voyage into the storm. He will discipline Petrus tomorrow. Now with his second in command out of action, Kato will have his work cut out in the next four hours dealing with the storm.

At twenty three hundred hours mid Atlantic Time the storm arrives. The wind strength gradually builds up in intensity. Kato watches the barometric pressure continue to fall.

This is more than a medium intensity storm judging by the fall in pressure.

As a precaution Kato orders a reduction in speed. By midnight the wind force is gusting seventy miles an hour and pressure is still falling. The ocean is a maelstrom of angry water. White frothed waves several metres high continually smash into "Ocean Stars" hull; testing the ships integrity. As the hull survives one pounding another wave arrives. The seas are relentless; whipped up by the air rushing from high pressure to fill the low pressure area. The pressure reduction is creating winds upwards of storm force eight.

Fully laden, "Ocean Star" is at the mercy of nature's power. Alone in mid Atlantic she has no where to hide. The rain is lashing into the bridge. "Ocean Star" is under a cloud burst. It is impossible for Kato or his helmsman to see clearly through the bridge windows. Each wave seems to be building in intensity. One particular rogue wave, fifteen metres high, smashes a massive weight of sea water onto "Ocean Stars" deck. The vessel is being tossed about like a small toy. For the first time on the voyage Kato is afraid. He has doubts. The storm is relentless.

"Ocean Star" can't with stand much more of this pounding.

High up, on the bridge, Kato can hear groans from "Ocean Stars" hull as wave after wave attempt to destroy the vessel by breaching the hull. The storm knows no mercy. Its power is raw and savage.

The storm shows no sign of abatement. It is two in the morning; "Ocean Star" is still intact. For how much longer is any one's guess Kato thinks to him self. Yet another wave surges over the decks. The angry black waters, frothing and sloshing over every obstacle on the deck, are illuminated by the ship's floodlights. The scene is like something from a seaman's idea of hell.

This is my worst night mare come true.

Kato, looking grim and feeling helpless watches the storm kick the life from his vessel.

Another massive wave smashes tons of water onto the hatch of number one hold. The ship lurches in the swell caused by the water from the wave flooding away; "Ocean Star" is struck by another wave. This monster wave has travelled miles; pushed by the storm to find a home on the deck of "Ocean Star". From a height of over twelve metres the waters smash into hold one's hatch and find a weakness. A rivet has worked loose. Within minutes the angry sea is surging into the breach. Hold one is flooding with sea water. The water is flooding grain onto the deck. Each wave forces more water into the hold. "Ocean Star" is under attack. The sea has penetrated her guard. The weight of water entering the vessel might cause the ship to list. She will no longer be responsive to Kato's command from the bridge.

As the men fight the storm and the ingress of water, "Ocean Star" is dealt another blow. The hatch covers from hold one is smashed away from its mountings. Carried by the frothing waters the heavy steel smashes into the hatches of holds two and three. The sea attacks with renewed force. The hatches of holds two and three are breached. More water floods into the holds.

Floating on the crest of the waves the hatch doors from hold one return and smash into "Ocean Stars" hull; the hull is breached below the waterline. Taking on water Captain Kato has no option but to advise the Coastguard of the ship's problems. He is ordered to alter course. Six hundred miles away the Island of Bermuda is the nearest landfall.

Friday Morning 3rd June 1966

Scimitar in Bermuda

Michael Gregory caught the early morning flight to Bermuda. He had already sent his most experienced man on to Bermuda.

Al Corsino arrived on Thursday morning; known as "Ice" to everyone because his facial features never change. Al Corsino's face always looks cold and hard like an Alaskan glacier. Find out who killed Sammy Santino and deliver retribution. Michael Gregory had said. There is a banker called Wayne Luther. Did he grass to the FBI about Sammy? Get the low down on a guy called George Howden in shipping was the final order from Michael Gregory.

"I didn't expect you here so soon boss. I only just got started. What's the panic?" Al Corsino asks as they walk into the Princess Hotel.

"The boss is worried there's something big going on here Al. Too many co incidences he reckons." Michael Gregory speaks fast in his clipped, no nonsense business style voice. They say nothing in the taxi from the airport. They know careless talk in front of strangers can re bound in unexpected ways. The two continue their silence as Michael Gregory registers at the hotel reception desk.

"What have you come up with?" Michael Gregory asks Al as soon as they are on their own in the hotel suite with all doors closed and the radio blaring out.

"Sammy's inquest was yesterday. It made the local paper headlines. Seems like three people were involved; a local cop, an FBI man and this guy Howden you asked about. They said Sammy was disturbed collecting drugs. He fell off his boat into the sea and was taken by a shark before he could be rescued." Al hands over a copy of the Bermuda Gazette to Michael Gregory who sees the headline "Drug baron meets grisly end".

"This Howden guy seems to be turning up all the time. We never made the hit in New York that's for sure. What have you found out about him?" Michael Gregory tosses the newspaper to one side after reading the article in full.

"Not much boss. I don't get why he was with the cops. He's a young punk Limey. If he was under cover he wouldn't have given evidence yesterday. There has to be some connection with Sammy that we are missing." Al shakes his head in puzzlement.

"Find out more about this Howden. Who does he hang out with? Has he got a woman? Remember,

Artie said he was mixed up with some broad they were working with. That could be the link. Dig some more Al. What about the bank guy?" Michael Gregory continues impatient to learn all the detail.

"Yesterday I went to the bank. Wayne Luther has disappeared. There's no trace of him. Local gossip is that he was killed by a shark as well. His cap turned up in one big brute that was landed last Monday; looks like he might be a dead end enquiry boss." Al mutters looking at his boss impassively.

"May be, maybe not, meet me back here this afternoon Al. I've got another shark to mind over now." Michael Gregory looks thoughtful.

Where is my son?

After talking with Jamil El Hassan, Costas feels no sympathy, despite it being nearly midnight in Monaco, in ordering the pilot and co pilot of his Lear Jet 24 to take off from Monte Carlo to Lisbon within the hour.

"Get me to Bermuda by the fastest route" Costas bellows down the telephone.

"Earn the fancy salaries I pay you!" he snarls at the pilot who has started to protest that they need more time.

The Lear Jet is Costas's latest toy. He took delivery just one month ago. It is one of the first off the production line.

Now it can prove its usefulness.

"Do not give me any excuse. Just do as I command." He admonishes the pilot.

"If you fail I will hire another minion to do my bidding."

Just after one o'clock in the morning the jet takes off. At Lisbon the jet takes on fuel. The pilot advises Costas that with just Costas as passenger the maximum range is two thousand miles with full tanks. It will take ten hours of flying time via the Azores to Nova Scotia. There they must re fuel before the final leg to Bermuda.

"I do not concern myself with all this detail. See to it we get there as soon as possible. I will sleep while you earn your pay." Costas advises turning his back on the pilot and entering his private cabin.

Costas finds it difficult to sleep. The information from Mercator worries him. For hours he paces up and down going over in his mind the events of the last few weeks.

My God I might lose two ships. How can this be happening to me? This has all started since Howden; that upstart numbers man appeared on the scene. He will not get away with fraud against me. Does he think he is up against some naive innocent? I will teach him a lesson he will remember for the rest of his life, if he has a life after this.

Costas's mood becomes angrier as he vows revenge on George.

The Lear Jet 24 touches down in Bermuda at eleven thirty local time.

"Take me to the Princess Hotel!" Costas orders the taxi driver.

At the hotel a receptionist advises Costas that Mercator is still registered as a guest.

"Telephone his room! It is urgent I speak with him." Costas demands. Listening to the ringing tone with no answer Costas becomes agitated and shouts excitedly at the receptionist

"We must go to his room. He may be ill."

"Sir, it is not our policy to open our client's rooms to strangers." The receptionist replies softly.

"Dammit. I am Costas Tinopolis, his father. Don't you understand?" Costas shouts at the receptionist banging his fists on the desk in frustration as the veins on his neck bulge out and his face turns a vermillion blotchy red colour.

Other hotel guests are starting to look over to the reception desk to see what the noise and commotion is all about.

A security guard, called by reception, agrees to open the room for Costas but insists he can not leave Costas alone in the room.

"It's better than nothing I suppose. Let's get on with it" Costas screams at the security guard.

Mercator's room has a "do not disturb" notice hanging from the door handle. Impatient to see inside the bed room for himself; Costas pushes the security guard to one side and barges into the bed room as soon as he turns the key in the lock.

The bed room is one of the hotel's luxury rooms over looking the Ocean with a balcony. Costas rushes into the bath room. Mercator has left his wash kit and tooth brush on the bath shelf; his dressing gown hangs from the bath room door; the large wardrobe has Mercator's clothes hanging on the rail; the king size bed is undisturbed.

No one slept here last night.

"My son is not here. He must still be on the Island somewhere. Most likely he has gone off with some worthless money grabbing slut. How could he leave with this mess?" Costas shouts as he leaves the bed room and races down the corridor back to reception where he is advised that his suite is ready for him to move into.

In his suite Costas wastes no time in telephoning his New York lawyers. The news about Neptune Carrier is bad. The FBI has shown the lawyers the film of the drugs drop. Costas is wanted for questioning by the FBI.

"Tell them I know nothing. I cannot be responsible for what goes on in every ship I own. It is ridiculous. Prepare papers to sue the Americans for damages. Get hold of the Greek ambassador! Tell him to call in some favours from his Senator friends. He knows the ones." Costas shouts the instructions down the telephone.

Immediately after Costas banged down the telephone receiver the instrument rings.

"Who is this?" Costas shouts impatiently.

"Sir it's your pilot. We have received a message from Monaco. "Ocean Star" has been damaged in a storm and is making for Bermuda. Monaco request you telephone for up to date information." The pilot pauses, awaiting a reaction from his employer. Costas is silent. Standing at the window gazing at the Atlantic sea breaking on the shore Costas is deep in thought. Eventually he speaks into the telephone to his pilot.

"Have the jet fuelled and ready for take off at a moments notice. Await further instructions from me."

Chapter Twenty Seven

Storm Damage

Friday Morning 3rd June 1966

George raises the Alarm

Playing tennis last evening; then enjoying a few beers with the other players down at the tennis stadium had helped George to relax and take his mind away from his worries over Leonora and Jasmine.

He enjoyed a comfortable night's rest. Arriving early at the office George feels full of energy; ready to get through a mountain of work.

The papers in his "for attention" tray are over flowing. He has been too pre occupied to work on them. Today's mail has been dumped on top of yesterdays. George sets to work with determination; quietly and efficiently sorting his papers into for rubbish bin, urgent and not so urgent piles. One or two letters from clients cause him to leave his desk and confer with colleagues. There are interruptions for client's telephone calls.

It is eleven in the morning when he sees the message from Kato. George scans the text of the message rapidly. This is his usual procedure. Firstly he assimilates the gist of a document. If the first scan suggests a routine document requiring no immediate action he places it in the not so urgent pile. Papers needing more immediate action he will read more carefully, mulling over their implications, before placing the document on the urgent pile.

The message from Captain Agios Kato captures George's attention; he sits dumbfounded at his desk; his body taut; every nerve tensed.

The plans made with Duane, Adrian and Inspector Johnson are now useless. Putting off telling Leonora and Charlie about Jasmine for two weeks is no longer possible. How will this pan out with Costas Tinopolis?

George's mind races through the implications as he continues to stare at the words on the sheet.

""Ocean Stars" hull breached in storm. No casualties, dangerous to continue voyage, making for Bermuda ETA Monday, Kato." George reaches for the telephone to give the news to Adrian.

Adrian takes tea

Adrian's cedar desk, inlaid with leather, is covered in plans and documents for the Airport extension. The Architect's drawings bulge up on the desk; they cover the bone china tea pot along with milk jug, tea strainer with its own bowl, sugar caddy, cup, saucer and plate of ginger biscuits; all sitting untouched on a tea tray buried beneath the papers. Most mornings Adrian makes something of a ritual in taking his morning tea. First Adrian places his hands on the tea pot to establish that the tea is at a suitable temperature; in Adrian's opinion this should be just below boiling point. Next the solid silver tea strainer is held in Adrian's left hand half an inch over the matching Royal Worcester tea cup; his right hand, holding the matching tea pot, gently and carefully pours out the rich dark brown liquid into the tea cup. A small portion of milk might then be poured from the delicate translucent porcelain milk jug. Adrian is fastidious about this ritual. Milk poured in first before the tea was an indication that the perpetrator was from a lower social order. Adrian believes taking more than two spoonfuls of sugar is excessive, an indication of greed and vulgarity. The taking of tea is not only a great pleasure to Adrian but the manner in which guests and colleagues participate in the ritual influences his assessment of them.

This morning Adrian was so engrossed in the airport plans that his tea ritual has been ignored. Following the celebration dinner at Government House on Tuesday evening Duane had arranged for a high ranking official in the DEA (Drug Enforcement Agency) to contact Adrian. The DEA now wanted the Airport to be made secure for passengers as a top priority. Finance was available. The project, which had been delayed countless times because of wrangling between British, Bermudan and US Authorities, now, thanks to George and Duane busting up Sammy's drug gang, has the green light to proceed. The project is now Adrian's top priority. Everyone wants the work to go ahead at top speed.

The shrill sound of the telephone ringing disturbs Adrian's concentration. He frowns with displeasure as he grapples underneath the papers and plans strewn across his desk to reach the telephone.

"Adrian Cuthbert here, who is calling?" Adrian demands impatiently annoyed with this interruption.

"Adrian this is George Howden have you heard the news?" George speaks in an excited voice which instantly gets Adrian's attention as he forgets his annoyance.

"George, good morning, what news old boy, I have been hard at it since yesterday on the Airport plans. A DEA chappie is coming over next week. It is all systems go thanks to your involvement with the drugs bust." Before Adrian can pause for breath George declares

"Ocean Star" with the arms has been damaged at sea. The ship is heading here. She is due on Monday. We need to meet urgently."

"You had better come over. I will alert Inspector Johnson." Not waiting for an answer from George, Adrian replaces the telephone receiver to call Police Headquarters.

Questions

"So now Jonno have you managed to get any useful information from our witness? I guess leaving him to cool his heels last night in your old fashioned gaol might have kinda softened him up nicely for me this morning? Yea, me and Mercator we got a thing going on. He trembles when I get up close and personal to whisper in his ear. I jess can't wait to start the whispering all over." Duane smiles with anticipation at the thought of questioning Mercator as he sits opposite Inspector Johnson in the Inspector's office.

"The wee laddie has been shouting for a lawyer and his father ever since yesterday evening. I thought letting him cool his impetuous heels over night might be the best course. He has been given food and drink but no one has questioned him. Technically he is free to leave. I think now might be a good time to ask a few questions. If we cannee charge him then we have to release him by the end of twenty four hours."

Minion or Master

"So what are we waiting for Jonno? Let's get started!" Duane stands up and rubs his hands together eagerly awaiting the confrontation.

Mercator is brought in to the interview room by the duty sergeant. He is made to sit at a small utility pine table. The room's bare walls are coloured with white lime. There is one small window which is covered by iron bars fitted inside and outside. There is an underlying scent of sweat generated from decades of fearful prisoners being interrogated here. After ten minutes Duane and Inspector Johnson enter the room

"You have no right to hold me like this. I want a lawyer. My father will sue you for wrongful imprisonment. You will be sorry. Just you wait." Mercator's face has turned red flushed with blood rising as he becomes agitated at seeing Duane and Inspector Johnson; he senses the atmosphere of fear from the room's stench.

"Now Laddie, calm yourself down, yesterday I judged you were in no state to be questioned. Perhaps now you are able to talk rationally. I have the power to hold you, without charges, for twenty four hours if I judge it to be necessary to assist my investigations. We know that a ship called Neptune Carrier has been involved with drug running. We also have reason to believe that another ship "Ocean Star" has been carrying goods in contravention of the United Nations sanctions against Southern Rhodesia. Now both these ships are owned by your father. "Ocean Star" is leased to a Bermudan company which must be why you are here on this little Island stuck right out in the middle of the Atlantic. What do you have to say about this Laddie?" Inspector Johnson asks in his softest most comforting voice, observing every twitch and slight change in breathing of his witness. Inspector Johnson is looking for any clue to indicate guilt or innocence, truth or lies, the very meat and drink of his profession. Mercator's reactions will provide clues as to how Inspector Johnson will proceed.

"This is all news to me. My father tells me nothing. I am innocent I tell you. I know nothing . . . nothing do you hear me?" Mercator cries anger and fear in his voice.

"Why have you come to Bermuda then Mercator? Officer Pickens met you with George Howden in his office. What were you doing there?" Inspector Johnson continues his questioning thinking that Mercator might be telling the truth.

"My father, he made me come to sort out Howden. My father is angry because Howden did not pay over some money to him. My father he treats me like a dog. I was going to party in Corsica this week end. Now I am stuck here in this stinking room on this stinking Island because of him." Mercator puts his head in his hands and rests on the table.

"Mr Howden thinks your father has used him as a front man and from what I am hearing he has used you too. Is that right Mercator? Has your father used you?" Inspector Johnson poses the question gently trying to coax more from Mercator.

He is starting to open up

Inspector Johnson watches, waiting patiently.

"Hah I told my father Howden was in gaol for fraud and if he wants to keep his precious ship he has to come here too. Why should I be the only one to be inconvenienced? Now he will have to come. I telephoned him just as he was having his dinner. He loves his dinner more than he loves me. I spoilt the dinner for him." Mercator speaks defiantly; looking pleased at deceiving his father. Duane and Inspector Johnson look at each other in surprise. They had not expected this revelation.

"Excuse me for a minute. I have to check something in my office. Officer Pickens from the FBI will ask you a few questions in my absence." Inspector Johnson hurries away to check if Costas Tinopolis is scheduled to arrive on the Island.

"So now Mercator, let me get friendly with you I am gonna call you Murky. Yea you are a Murky kinda guy. So Murky, do you know a guy called Sammy Santino? See Sammy picked up drugs from your fathers boat, Neptune Carrier. He was bringing the drugs back to Bermuda. Thing is; we caught him red handed. Unfortunately he resisted arrest and he is dead." Duane speaks with menace in his voice.

I jess love playing "bad Cop" to Jonno's good guy

"What I don't get is that your father would send you here just to speak to George Howden. No Murky you were coming for the drugs from Sammy Santino, ain't that right Murky? See Sammy is dead but who is to say he never told us before he died that the drugs were for you and your Pa?" Duane whispers the last sentence in Mercator's ear and is well satisfied with the look of fear and dread coming across Mercator's face as the full implication of Duane's accusation hits home.

I got you going now Murky here's some more pressure

"We got almost six million bucks worth of drugs here. It's not chicken feed Murky. It means twenty years in San Quentin for you once I get you extradited to the States. Don't think I won't Murky. Your ass is mine. Got any more to tell me Murky?" Before Mercator answers, Inspector Johnson returns looking pleased.

"Seems like your father is concerned, his private jet has landed at McKinley. Now what do you think about that eh Laddie?" Inspector Johnson looks at Mercator who does not look at all happy.

"Well I guess, Jonno, young Murky here doesn't like his Pa that much. We had a little chat while you were out. I think young Murky here is gonna help little old you and me sort his Pa out once and for all. Ain't that right Murky?" Duane looks at Mercator who is reluctantly accepting Duane's suggestion. Before Inspector Johnson can answer Duane the duty sergeant enters the room advising that there is an urgent telephone call for Inspector Johnson from Adrian Cuthbert at Government House.

"He's probably gotten us a dinner invite." Duane quips. Inspector Johnson leaves the room again.

"Now let's you and me sort out your future Murky hmm." Duane whispers to Mercator who is looking ill at ease.

Emergency repairs

Captain Kato and his crew toil desperately throughout the early morning darkness battling against the elements to keep "Ocean Star" afloat.

The cargo of grain in holds one to three is being soaked through as the sea rushes in through the breached hatches. The grain, now contaminated by salt water, is worthless. This is of no concern to Kato. He knows insurance will cover the damage. The main danger worrying Kato is from the grain swelling to twice or three times its weight. With water still entering the three hatches this will make the vessel more unstable. At the height of the storm, Captain Kato orders his crew to work on securing the breached hatches to holds one, two and three. The work is dangerous and difficult. The men secure themselves to the ship by safety ropes. This impedes their movements on deck but prevents them from being swept over board by the storm's waves.

Daylight reveals that the makeshift canvas covers roped around each hatch has prevented further ingress of damaging salt sea water into the grain cargo. Now a clean up operation is in progress; the ships powerful pumps suck out the damaged grain and spew it into the Atlantic swell. The storm's most vicious, intense assaults on the vessel occurred three hours ago. Now, the rain has disappeared; a pale sun is rising in the east. A strong wind blows from the south east providing some assistance to "Ocean Star" as she limps towards Bermuda.

The tropical storm has left the ship battered. Kato has more to worry about. The ship's hull is breached just below the water line. After several hours the sea water has succeeded in pushing out grain from hold five. Now the water has finally reached the bilges and is filling the hold.

When he first heard the muffled thumps coming at irregular intervals from the bowels of hold five a cold, icy, shiver crept up his spine This noise is what he has dreaded to hear ever since the rogue solid steel hatch from hold one had been used by the storm to pulverize the double skinned hull beneath the water line. Kato knows, only too well, that each of the eight holds of "Ocean Star" is constructed as self contained compartments. The ship's design for maximum buoyancy requires the integrity between each hold to be maintained.

This noise can mean only one thing. The force of the water sloshing from one side of the ship to the other has broken the retaining straps securing the crate of arms. It's that crate banging against the sides of the hold. It's loose.

How long might it be before that damned crate, with its heavy load of God only knows what sort of armaments, breaches the sides into hold six or hold four where the other crate of smuggled arms is secured? Oh my God! If hold four is breached the sea water could easily force the other arms crate to break free. A domino effect could occur. With all four holds filling with water and two crates full of arms and possibly explosives banging against the sides "Ocean Star" would be doomed.

Kato looks down into the sea and calls on the sea Gods to place a curse on Costas Tinopolis.

Lunch at the Harbour Club

Al Corsino is Michael Gregory's right hand man in New York for good reason. Al Corsino is ruthless. His emotions are buried so deep in his psyche they never surface to disturb whatever action he has to carry out. Such attributes go with the territory of being a gangster. Ruthless, hard nosed gangsters are two a penny in New York. Michael Gregory can have his pick of many to be his number two. It's his discretion and resourcefulness that make Al Corsino stand out from the crowd. Michael Gregory is relying on Al Corsino's resourcefulness to tease out the information they urgently need to understand the full picture surrounding Sammy's death. It is also vital to remain unnoticed. Keeping below the radar of the Authorities will be difficult in a small island like Bermuda.

There was one big discrepancy which puzzled Al. Their FBI snout had told Michael Gregory that Sammy was shot by the Limey cop. The only cop mentioned

Minion or Master

in the newspaper report about Sammy's inquest is this Inspector Johnson. Funny thing, Al thinks, there is no mention of any shots at Sammy's inquest.

Al decides to make his first inquiries down at the docks. He is wearing tartan Bermuda shorts. Long red socks emerge from white sneakers to envelop his thick, hairy, pale legs. His upper body is covered by an extra large tee shirt. A baseball cap sits on his close cropped hair. Both tee shirt and baseball cap are emblazoned with the Franconia cruise ship logo. Al's ice cold blue, snake like eyes, hide behind large dark, wrap around, sun glasses. In any other part of the world Al would stand out. In Bermuda his clothes announce to all the locals that here is a New York cruise tourist. One of thousands let off on the Island for a few days of relaxation before being re packaged in the ship to be returned from whence they came. If he had worn his New York gangster suit, with give away bulges, he would have stuck out like a dog's turd lying on an immaculate golf green close to the tee. In his tourist attire he blends unobtrusively into the background. He will not be noticed. He does not stick out.

At the public dock Al strolls quietly up to Eugene Jordan skipper of the game fishing boat "Sara's Pride".

"Excuse me Sir, my name is Henry. I'm on vacation. Back in New York I'm a journalist. Heard you had some excitement this week with a banker's hat. Maybe a story for my paper when I get back home and some dollars for you, if you are interested Sir?" At the mention of dollars, the skipper stops coiling the rope on the deck of "Sara's Pride" and looks up at Al.

"*Maybe I did, maybe I didn't. How many dollars be you havin in mind?*" Eugene Jordan responds and continues working the rope.

Got ya straight away

"Could be quite a bit if my editor likes the sound of it, course we would need pictures. I'm thinking of something like "Skipper fights killer sharks every day" type headline. This type of story would make you famous in New York, could mean a whole heap of charters for you. If you wanna give me the details I could 'phone my editor see if he likes it. In the meantime I got fifty dollars for your time to talk it through over lunch. What do you say skipper?" Al throws out the bait.

"*Make it one hundred bucks and we can take lunch at the Harbour Club in ten minutes once I dun finished wiv dis rope.*" Eugene Jordan shouts back.

"That is a deal skipper. Come and get your money!" Al fingers a one hundred dollar note.

Chapter Twenty Eight

A Killing

Friday Afternoon 3rd June 1966

Lunch time Meeting

"Well this is a turn up for the books ain't it George. Who would have guessed your little ol' ship would come right here to the Island, saves us a whole lot of travelling." Duane Pickens laughs as he walks over to the side table and helps himself to a ham sandwich. His face wrinkles up, with a look of horror, as he spies the bone china tea pot along with milk jug and tea strainer with its own bowl; thoughtfully provided by Adrian for the emergency meeting at Government House.

"You Limeys crease me. Ain't you got any coffee Adrian? JEEsus it was only last week I had to bawl Jonno out for giving me this poor excuse for a drink. It looks like gnats piss to me. I know you guys went to war over your precious tea. This boy he ain't gonna work on tea, gimme sweet black coffee."

"Do calm down old chap. I am rather partial to tea and this is a particularly good blend. I suppose I will have to make allowances for you, especially as your DEA boys seem to be coming up with the goods for me regarding the airport. I'll see if cook can get you a pot of coffee." Adrian smiles at Duane.

"There is much more at stake here than tea or coffee gentlemen. Not only do we have "Ocean Star" coming here, carrying the smuggled arms, we also have Costas Tinopolis on the Island. It couldn't be better. There seems to be no love lost between Costas and his son. Did you know Mercator boasted to Duane and me how he tricked his father to come here, he told his father that George has defrauded the company and he then gave Costas a cock and bull story how he was needed urgently on the Island to sign papers." Inspector Johnson informs Adrian and George as he tries to bring an air of urgency back to the meeting.

"That is the first I have heard about a fraud. That is an outrageous suggestion." George protests.

"Of course we know it's not true Laddie. There is no need for you to worry." Inspector Johnson re assures George in his calm soft Scottish accent.

"Well I jolly well am extremely worried. My job could be on the line if there is even a hint of fraud against me. You know the saying "no smoke with out fire". I do not want this story to be made public. I had to fight very hard to clear my name over the chrome ore due to Costas fooling me into fronting his illegal dealings. Now his son is spreading malicious rumours about me. I want them both to get their come uppance." George speaks with a firm, confident voice.

"Do we know the present condition of the ship?" Inspector Johnson asks.

"Our naval station at Ireland Island is receiving reports on the status of "Ocean Star" from the US Coast guard every hour. They have flown over the ship twice. The last report advised that the storm had gone. The ship has secured its hatches and is heading on a northwest course

Minion or Master

she should arrive here sometime on Monday. Of course we can't allow her to enter the docks until we know that the armaments crates are secure. She will have to anchor in the Great Sound." Adrian looks up from the side table where he has been pouring tea and carefully walks back to his seat at the table with a cup of tea.

"Well I don't know if I will be able to stay over here until Monday. Me an Jonno set a rat to catch another rat this morning and I hope we get Costas nailed by this time tomorrow. If all goes well I wanna take him back with me. Uncle Sam has a nice cold room jess waiting for him." Duane looking smug now he has his coffee tells his colleagues with great enthusiasm.

"Do please tell. What have you two dreamed up? You both look quite pleased with yourselves." Adrian questions, his hawk like brown eyes not missing anything.

"Well now, I jess gave Mercator; I like to call him Murky, a taste of his own medicine. See Murky thinks that I think his Pa sent him here to pick up Sammy's drugs. Now poor old Murky don't know who to believe. He's a confused and scared son of a gun. If he doesn't bring me something real dirty on his Pa's business by tomorrow morning he thinks I will arrest him on drugs charges. So now me and Jonno have let him go running back to his Pa. His Pa is surely going to find out that Murky lied to him. So with a little bit of family anger mixed up with fear and greed we sure do have a powerful cocktail of emotions working their butts off for us good guys. Who knows what might happen. I hope they make some big mistakes and we will be waiting to pounce." Duane finishes by hoisting his cowboy boots onto the finely polished cedar table.

"That is very interesting Duane. Please do be aware that we have little time. The Tinopolis family have influence in high places. It will not be long before they start to bring pressure on each of us if we can't prove their culpability in drugs and arms smuggling." Adrian gives Duane's cowboy boots a look of disdain as he shuffle some papers and continues "Now, Duane, have your people had any luck with Ace Machine Factors, Detroit the company named in the export documents for agricultural machinery which George got for us?".

Looking a little sheepish Duane hastily removes his boots from the table

"No luck. The business looks legitimate so far as we can tell. IRS forms and business returns are in order. One thing; we have not been able to identify the real owners. There is a network of nominees leading into Switzerland and Liberia which our guys can't penetrate. Our back room boys gave the accounts the once over and they found that they pay a lot of consultancy fees. We are having the IRS check this out but so far no further info."

"I have followed up the link to Jans Smutt, the manager of the Mozambique freight firm Torreshippes, based in Lourenco Marques. Thanks again to George who got the contact from Agios Kato the captain of "Ocean Star". Any how, London seems to be on top of this one. MI5 spooks are working with the Portuguese authorities. There have been rumours and whispers that the Freelimo guerrillas were planning something big. London wants to keep a lid on this part of Africa. Any escalation of trouble could see the whole of South and East Africa blowing itself up. Not good for our business interests or those of South Africa. Our boys have leaned on Smutts in a big way. Before he went back to South Africa he spilt the beans. The Freelimo have ordered rifles, machine guns, as well as RPG's plus a very large quantity of Nitro-glycerine." Adrian pauses for a reaction.

"Nitro-glycerine is one of the most unstable and lethal explosives. That ship is sitting on a time bomb." Inspector Johnson remarks.

"My God Jasmine, I was responsible for putting her on the ship. If anything happens to her I will never forgive myself. Is there any way we can get her off the ship before anything happens?" George pleads looking at Duane who merely shrugs his shoulders in a "Don't ask me it's your ship look".

"It might not be as bad as we think. I am led to believe that the explosive freezes at around 13 degrees centigrade and provided it is kept below that temperature it should be safe enough. The problem might arise if the crates are damaged in the storm and the Nitro-glycerine temperature controls, probably some type of vacuum packing, gets broken. Then there is no hope for that ship or any one near it. That is why if she makes it here safely she will not be allowed to enter the docks area." Adrian advises the silenced group.

After a lengthy period of silence in the room George finally speaks

"Well one way or another Jasmine, Kato and his crew must be rescued before that ship blows up."

Costas finds his son

"So Costas have you sorted out this numbers man Howden? I assume this is the reason for your call." Jamil El Hassan speaks quietly into the telephone. It is eight in the evening in Beirut. Jamil El Hassan hopes this call will not take long; Mustaf has brought the young boy who provided so much pleasure on Wednesday to the bedroom.

"Jamil forgive me. I have bad news. "Ocean Star" has been damaged by a storm in Mid Atlantic she is heading here for Bermuda. My office in Monaco say she will be here on Monday. I thought you should be informed straight away." Costas speaks loudly and quickly into the telephone as he paces across the deep pile carpet in his suite at the Princess hotel.

"This is serious Costas. We cannot allow the goods in "Ocean Star" to be discovered. The ship must not get to Bermuda. Remain in your hotel suite. I will arrange help. Someone will be with you very soon. Do you understand?" After hearing Costas agree to wait in his suite Jamil El Hassan calls Michael Gregory.

Costas continues pacing up and down in his luxury suite. Like yesterday evening he does not know what is happening. He is not in control.

Where is Mercator? Who is Jamil sending?

Costas hates not knowing the answers to these questions.

Maybe I can at least find out about Howden Costas thinks as he telephones the offices of Robinsons.

Costas is dumbfounded to hear from Robinson's senior partner that George Howden is at work and that there has been no question of any fraud.

"Let me speak with him at once!" Costas orders but is told that George left his desk to attend an urgent meeting just before lunch.

"Let me know as soon as he returns." Costas barks

What the hell is going on? Why did Mercator tell me these things about Howden?

Minion or Master

Puzzled and worried, Costas concludes that this information from Howden's office must mean that Mercator, his son and heir, has lied to him.

Why should he do this? What in the name of all the Greek Gods is happening to me?

Costas covers his face with his be jewelled hands and rests his elbows on the top of the table trying to think clearly. A tray of lunch brought up by room service lies untouched on the table. The silver cutlery, wrapped in a linen napkin, is undisturbed. The prime fillet steak, char grilled, medium to well done, has cooled. The fine bone handled steak knife with its six inch serrated steel edge is unused. Today Costas has no appetite. A loud banging on his suite door interrupts his dark, confused and troubled thoughts.

"Father, it's me Mercator. Let me in, father; father, let me in!" Mercator pleads outside the room his shrill excited voice penetrating through the thick cedar panelled door to reach at last the ear drums of Costas.

Hearing his son's voice Costas jumps up to open the door. Mercator pushes past and falls into a ball on the settee; he starts sobbing. Costas chases Mercator into the room; for a moment, he stares at his son. He notices the dishevelled appearance and the shadows under his eyes; he feels no compassion; just uncontrollable anger; the red mists of fear and greed takes over.

"What the hell is going on Mercator? Can you tell me?" Costas shouts taking no notice of Mercator's apparent distress.

"Answer me you little shit!" Costas losing his temper drags Mercator from the settee and pushes him against the table. Holding Mercator by his lapels Costas keeps shaking Mercator like a rag doll. So much tension has built up in

Costas this last twenty four hours that he cannot control his primal urges. His son Mercator has tricked him.

"Why did you tell me Howden has been charged with fraud. Why have you lied to me?" Costas screams as he continues to shake his son.

Mercator has taken just about as much as he can. He has been used by his father who has never loved him. His father ordered him to come to this stinking Island. It is his father's fault that he has been scared shit less by that FBI agent who has forced him to chose to be informer or drug offender. He has no choice. His father gave him no choice. The shaking and shouting continues. Mercator is sobbing, his arms are pushed back onto the table; Costas continues to shout in his face and shake him. Mercator's hands slide on the table trying to get some kind of support to stop the shaking. His right hand feels the outline of the bone handle. Taking a great gasp of air he grasps the handle of the knife and lunges at Costas screaming

"I hate you!"

The point of the steak knife digs into the neck of Costas. For one brief moment, the eyes of father and son lock onto each other; transmitting messages of terror shock and regret. In a split second Costas sees his life flash past; now his brain receives the shock messages. Costas lifts his hands to his neck; the blood starts spurting from the severed artery. Mercator, his face soaked from his father's blood, looks at the knife in horror and drops it onto the carpet. In shock unable to move, Mercator, watches as Costas falls to the floor his life blood draining away.

Al fills in Michael

Michael Gregory has been expecting Costas. Jamil El Hassan got a message to him early this morning. Watch and see what happens. Costas may do our work for us. Guessing that Costas would want to stay in a luxury suite Michael also booked a suite. The top floor of the Princess hotel had three suites available. Michael booked the middle one. Having sent Al Corsino off to find out more information about Sammy's killers Michael Gregory waits in the hotel.

Michael selected a table at the back of the spacious reception area where he can observe the comings and goings for his lunch. He does not wait long before he sees and hears Costas Tinopolis making a fuss at the reception desk. Quietly and unobtrusively, looking like a guest going to his room, Michael follows Costas and the security guard as they go to Mercator's room. Michael makes a note of the room number and disappears back to his lunch table. When Costas returns to reception Michael moves close to the reception desk pretending to study a tourist brochure and smiles smugly as he overhears the receptionist allocate Costas the suite right next to his.

Returning to his suite Michael opens the sliding doors which give access to the balcony. All three suites have a common balcony partitioned by six feet high walls. Michael had hoped that Costas would have his sliding doors open so that he might over hear conversation but no such luck. Costas's doors are closed.

It is just after two when Al Corsino returns to the suite.

"Jesus Al I knew your dress sense was not great but this outfit beats everything." Michael guffaws.

"That ain't funny boss. At least I got some info for us due to being dressed as a tourist." Al responds with no amusement in his voice.

"So what gives?" Michael asks getting straight back to business.

"I followed up the shark angle. Seems this fishing guy, the one who fished up the shark, with the banker's hat, knows the Rucker family. He and a guy called Charlie Rucker go back a long way. They were at school together. Then they played in a band together. Any how the fisherman tells me that Charlie's daughter Jasmine went to New York with Sammy, and get this, Charlie's other daughter Leonora is sweet on George Howden. It looks like Howden did go to New York and snatched Jasmine from Sammy. No one knows where this Jasmine is. What now boss? Do we get this Howden guy?" Al fixes himself a cold drink from the refrigerator.

"So that must be the link. I thought there must be a broad involved somewhere. I need to think this through." Michael Gregory starts to walk out to the balcony to see if he can hear anything from next door when the telephone rings. Michael Gregory answers and says nothing he just listens as his boss relays the information about "Ocean Star". After placing the receiver down on its cradle, very gently, Michael Gregory looks up at Al and asks

"This fishing guy do you think we could hire his tub for a few days?"

"Might be, I gave him a story about being a New York journalist. He liked the dollars I gave him. So I guess he would be for hire. Why boss are we going fishing?" Al Corsino asks with absolutely no humour.

"Two things, one, get the boat hired for two days immediately. Tell the guy your editor's come over. He likes the story line. He wants to check out the sharks and fancies a short vacation. Two, get some heavy duty weapons from the local low life. Something to make a big bang would be good."

"I'm on it boss." Al Corsino gets up and as he opens the door they hear a furious banging from the adjoining suite door. Swift as a cheetah Michael Gregory runs to the door and holds back Al Corsino. They both listen as Costas and Mercator argue and shout. Then there is silence. Michael Gregory checks no one is in the corridor and beckons for Al to come with him. The suite door is open. They see Mercator frozen to the spot standing over Costas. Swiftly Michael Gregory closes the door and runs to check Costas for a pulse. There is none. The knife is lying on the carpet; he signals to Al to pick up the murder weapon. Al gets a napkin from the table and picks up the knife being careful not to touch it himself.

"Who are you?" Mercator asks in a very timid frightened voice.

"We are your friends. We are here to make all this go away. It's Mercator isn't it?" Michael Gregory speaks soothingly and calmly as Mercator nods his head.

"I didn't mean to do it. The FBI made me. They will put me in Gaol." Mercator sobs.

"Everything will be fine. Let my friend take these clothes off you. So we can get you away from all this." Michael Gregory signals to Al to get the bloodstained clothes off Mercator. With unusual gentleness Al unbuttons Mercator's shirt.

"Ok Mercator let's go. Take off that shirt and remove those pants. We ain't got all day. If the cops come you are facing first degree murder." Al talks softly to Mercator.

The word murder brings out a reaction in Mercator as he begins to understand how much trouble he is in.

"Listen Mercator we work for a friend of your fathers. We can get you away. No way is your father coming back. You need to think of yourself now. You could inherit a fortune but you gotta get away, now, with us." Michael Gregory whispers urgently.

In a split second Mercator puts his father's death to a recess in his mind and starts thinking about how he will spend his father's money, greed and selfishness temporarily out weighing his fear and sorrow.

"The FBI said I wouldn't be able to fly off this damned Island. They control the airport."

"Yea well you ain't flying out. We got a neat fishing boat all lined up to sail you away this evening. But we have to move out of this room before anyone discovers the body with you looking like a bloodthirsty butcher. Do you understand? Let's go!" Coming to his senses, Mercator realizes he has no choice. He undresses and puts on a large bath robe. Michael Gregory places the bloodstained clothes along with the murder weapon wrapped in the napkin in a laundry bag. They place a "Do not Disturb sign" on the door of Costas's suite and go to Mercator's room.

Michael Gregory orders Al to get on with his errands and gets Mercator to take a shower and get dressed in warm clothes for the boat.

"It's not safe to stay in this room. We need to go up to my suite" Michael Gregory orders Mercator.

"How did you have a boat all lined up? You couldn't know what was going to happen in the suite. What's your angle?" Mercator having had time to think in the shower is suspicious.

"You are right. We are here on another job. Your father 'phoned our boss and said about his problems with his ship. So we got orders to help out. It was luck we were in the next suite. The boat is needed for our other job which we gotta get started on this evening. So you can ride along, after the job is done, we will take you to the US coast and get you away back to Europe. We got contacts all over the States. You ain't gonna have any problems once we get you away from here." Michael Gregory speaks with certainty as he looks at Mercator who is starting to smile.

"You must be from Uncle Jamil. Father spoke about him. Now Maybe I will deal with him direct. Now I own everything." Mercator boasts.

"That may well be. We never mention our boss's name. One more thing, tonight, we are Pressmen from a New York paper. You will have to be my assistant. Can you do that? Otherwise it will be difficult to get you on board without making the boat's skipper suspicious. As soon as we get aboard you plead sea sickness and get below deck out of the way, OK?" Michael Gregory gives out instructions in his quiet low key voice as if he were ordering a take away.

Chapter Twenty Nine

Petrus

Friday Evening 3rd June 1966

George comes clean

George is troubled. He had no luck persuading Adrian or his colleagues to help rescue Jasmine from "Ocean Star". It seems to him like a month has passed in just a few hours. Was it only yesterday that he thought he had at least two weeks before he needed to confront Leonora and Charlie with the news that Jasmine was not only a prostitute but a drug addict? Now events have overtaken his plans. George cannot hold off the truth any longer from Charlie and Leonora.

The waters in the Harbour Club swimming pool are gently rippling in the late spring breeze as the warm evening sun light shines down. George sits at a table near the pool. His hand fiddles nervously with a glass which holds a large gin and tonic as he recalls that this very table was where he sat when he first came to the Club and heard Leonora sing. It seems a lifetime ago. He is apprehensive about meeting Charlie and Leonora tonight but knows he has to tell them about Jasmine before they find out elsewhere.

George's heart misses a beat and his face flushes up when he sees Leonora walking with her father past the club bar. George cannot take his eyes away as she smiles at people she knows and then stops with Charlie at a few tables to speak with admirers asking her if she will be singing tonight. He is mesmerized at how fantastic she looks wearing a black mini skirt and a white blouse which shows off her coffee coloured skin and just a hint of cleavage.

Conversation at the table is kept casual and light until the trio finish their desserts. George by now has built up sufficient Dutch courage to speak confidently to Charlie and Leonora. Starting with his large gin then topped up by the best part of a bottle of red wine George's blood stream is sending relaxing signals via his nervous system into his brain.

So now is the moment let me get this over with

Before he can start, Charley, first looking into the eyes of his daughter, then across to George, sensing some kind of reticence within George, speaks.

"So now Howdy me and Lenny really thank you for all you have done for us since we first met. I know we have had troubles with our Jazzy but I guess that's not why you have gone to the trouble of wining and dining an old man like me. No, I have seen the looks between you and Lenny. I know she is a happier person buzzing around the house since she met you. I ain't beating about the bush; I like to say it how it is. As far as I am concerned I got no objections to you and Lenny going out together. Hell, I know there's some folks that think white and black should not mix. Well I ain't one of them. You got my blessing whatever you and Lenny do together is fine with me. You are very welcome at our house any time and I know I speak for Lenny too." Charlie smiles across at George and gives Lenny a gentle hug. George can scarcely believe what he is hearing, his heart is racing and his brain is working overtime.

My God did Charlie think I was going to ask for Lenny's hand tonight?

He looks across at Lenny who is grinning from ear to ear; her eyes locked into George's face. George's mouth is wide open; Charlie's words have left him dumbfounded and speechless.

For sure I never saw that one coming from Charlie. Come on George speak, say something nice don't spoil the moment!

"Oh, thank you so much Charlie. That is so sensitive and thoughtful. You have got me lost for words. Yes I have very strong feelings for Lenny and I am so pleased that she is here to hear what you just said. I am really all of a quiver." George looks across at Lenny who has a tear drop filling her eye. He watches as the drop fills up over the lid and runs down her cheek to rest on her lip.

"If it is possible, I want my friendship with Lenny to blossom and grow. I feel so happy when I see Lenny that I just can't bear to see her sad. It is a beautiful thing to see her smile and laugh. That makes me happy. Oh yes I am so glad I came to Bermuda and have met Lenny. Every day I thank my lucky stars for bringing Lenny to me." George pauses and laughs out loud as Lenny has got up from her chair and with tears streaming down her face rushes to George and plants a great slobbering kiss on his lips.

"Oh Howdy, you make me so happy. You just don't know. I never ever felt so much at ease with any one before. I want our friendship to grow too, Dear Howdy." Leonora plants another smacker on George's lips as they hold hands.

"This calls for a celebration, a bottle of champagne." Charlie shouts delightedly.

Minion or Master

After clinking glasses and toasting success and long lasting friendship to each other George decides he must come clean about Jasmine.

"Whilst we are all together there is some news about Jazzy I have to tell you. The ship she is on has been damaged in a storm. The ship is heading here and she should be here by Monday, all being well. Now I have just found out today that the ship is carrying a very dangerous cargo and tomorrow I am going to move heaven and earth to see if we can get Jazzy off that ship before Monday." George watches Charlie and Leonora's expressions as he relays this information. Their faces have taken on a more serious look but there is no sign of any hostility towards him. He continues

"Do you remember me talking about Sammy Santino?"

"That devil. May he rot in hell for what he done to my Jazzy" Charlie snarls.

"Its good riddance to him thanks to you Howdy." Leonora simpers at George.

"Yes well Sammy made Jazzy ill. It will take her some time to recover. We will all need to support her. I have been making some enquiries about a special clinic to help her re habilitate properly."

"What illness we talking about here, has she picked up something from those pimps and low life's? What clinic? Me and Lenny got no money for fancy clinics Howdy." A look of concern and worry has crept onto Charlie's lined face.

"There is no need to worry about the clinic cost Charlie. That will be taken care of with Sammy's own money. There is no easy way to tell you. You both know Sammy was a drug dealer. He got Jazzy hooked. That is how he got her to do the things she did. Now she will need special help to beat the addiction Sammy forced on her. If we all work together we can beat this evil." George places his hands palm down on the table relieved that at last he has brought out the truth.

"So now Howdy, let me see if I got this right. Jazzy is on a ship which is damaged with a dangerous cargo and she is probably feeling desperate and lonely as she experiences withdrawal symptoms from drugs. Is that it Howdy?" Leonora asks looking very serious.

"Yes. I have arranged for Captain Kato to look after her. He is a good man. I am so upset because it was my idea to rescue her by putting her on the ship. I had no idea it would be dangerous. My thoughts were to get Jazzy away from Sammy safely." George pleads.

"Well, dammit Howdy, if we is going to build our relationship I want to rescue Jazzy with you and I don't want to wait until tomorrow. Let's get on it right now. What do you say Howdy?" Leonora cries out.

Another day at sea

"Ocean Star" is limping towards Bermuda. She has over 400 miles to steam before reaching safety. Throughout the day the sea has remained choppy with a heavy swell. The violent storm has long gone from the area but it has left the sea angry and capricious. A westerly wind of fifteen knots is pushing sea water through the jagged gaping hole on "Ocean Stars" port side into hold five. The bilge pump has been working flat out. Kato wants to keep the water level low enough to prevent the loose crate from floating around and banging against the

Minion or Master

sides. He is worried this might cause adjacent holds four and six to be breached.

At times Kato thinks that the pump is winning the battle as no noise comes from the bowels of the hold; indicating that the crate is stationary. Then a crashing thump tells Kato that a heavy ingress of water, pushed by the wind and swell, has defeated the pump and the crate is crashing into the side of the hold. The banging is like a warning sound of death and destruction coming to those listening on deck.

Kato, looking tired and drained from lack of sleep, listens anxiously for another thud to send its warning message from the hold. For some hours Kato has worried over whether the bilge pump will break down. He knows it could easily get clogged with grain and then over heat. The pump has been on full power for over ten hours. There is still at least thirty four hours of sailing to go. His first duty is for the safety of his ship and crew. The cargo is of secondary importance. Kato is a seasoned sailor; he knows having a back up solution to any maritime problem is always a good thing. Kato makes his decision. He instructs the crew to set up the discharge pumps and suck out the grain cargo from each hold into the sea. The reduced weight will lighten "Ocean Star" and raise the hull sufficiently so that the sea water will no longer be able to enter. He needs twelve hours to raise the hull so that the hole in the side of the ship is above sea level.

Deciding he can do no more for now Kato goes to his cabin to take a few hours sleep he so desperately needs. On the way to his cabin he remembers he has not seen his number two since yesterday. Kato has been so occupied in dealing with the storm and the ship's damage he has forgotten about Petrus. Kato passes his own cabin and proceeds down the corridor to Petrus's cabin. The cabin door is not locked. Kato goes in; Petrus is not there.

Another charge to bring against him, how did I end up with this useless officer? Yes it was Costas Tinopolis. I had no say in the matter. He instructed me to take Petrus on as my number two. He wanted Petrus to gain experience. He told me Petrus was a promising young recruit from a good family in Piraeus. He said I was the best captain to train young Petrus. Well now Petrus has burnt his bridges. Just wait until I catch hold of him. His career is ended as far as I am concerned

Kato walks swiftly to the communications room to check if any further information has come from the US Coastguard.

Opening the door of the communications room Kato is surprised to discover that the radio operator is not at his desk. The radio is on; there is a faint voice coming from the speakers which Kato cannot hear clearly. He goes into the room and places his ear to the speaker in an attempt to hear the voice message. The only sound is the hissing of static. As Kato lifts his head up from the speaker an arm wraps around his neck and wrenches his head and torso back in a vicious arm lock. Kato sways his arms in an attempt to free himself from his attacker but bangs his head on the desk; he falls to the floor. The last thing Kato sees before he sinks into unconsciousness is the grinning face of Petrus.

Since bashing Petrus on the head Jasmine has stayed in her cabin. She is only too aware that Captain Kato has his hands full in dealing with the storm. Last night she snuggled under the giant sized duvet Kato had covered her with. Soon, she was asleep only to awake in the early hours of the morning. The erratic rolling of the ship coupled with noises from the wind and rain disturbed her. She stayed under the duvet wishing the storm would go away. Jasmine's mind has been concentrating on surviving this storm. She has not thought once about her need for drugs. Now, hearing Kato's muttering in the corridor she thinks she might be able to cajole Kato into giving her the remaining fix. She runs to the cabin door and peeps her head around the door jamb just in time to see Kato at the end of the corridor heading towards the communications room. Wearing her sneakers which George had bought her at the supermarket Jasmine follows Kato. As she rounds the corner at the end of the corridor she sees through the communications room window. She halts putting her hands in horror to her face watching Petrus wrestle Kato to the floor. There is no time for Jasmine to do anything. Everyone is on deck supervising the removal of the grain. Fearing that Petrus might spot her peeping around the corridor corner Jasmine withdraws back along the corridor. Afraid and lonely Jasmine feels helpless. She has no weapon. She has no friends. She has no allies on board. The only person on the ship she knows and trusts is Kato. She realizes she must take action. She racks her brains wondering what she can do.

Dusk Sailing

The heat from the sun is beginning to lose its strength as the earth's rotation gradually transforms Bermuda from day light to dusk. The shadows are lengthening as Al Corsino returns to the Princess Hotel. Al has a bulging ruck sack strapped to his back and he is carrying a very large suitcase.

"So what have we got Al?" Michael Gregory asks as Al carefully removes the ruck sack from his back.

"Seems all clear in the corridor boss, next door hasn't been disturbed; the "do not disturb" sign on the door is still there. I got the fishing boat coming at eleven tonight. I said we wanna be out for two days and to get plenty of food and fuel on board."

"O K that's good. So what have we in the sack and case?"

"What about him?" Al Corsino looks over at Mercator who is sitting in an arm chair staring back. Al Corsino is puzzled because Mercator's manner appears controlled and calm. A complete contrast from the trembling, gibbering and scared guy he saw just a few hours ago.

"You don't need to concern yourself over me. We are in this together. You get me away safely and I will see you are well rewarded and your boss's interests will be looked after in the future. I will be in your debt and in charge of the ships you need to use." Mercator answers Al's question, his stare moves from Al Corsino to Michael Gregory. His eyes then move to the suit case.

"That case, it is very big. My father could fit in there. Could he not?" Mercator questions as his mouth twists into a thin, cold smile.

"It's OK Al. Mercator has told me the FBI guy and the local cop will be looking for him tomorrow morning. He knows his only chance to get away is to go with us, he will co operate. I've filled him in on what to do. Come to think of it may be we could dump the body at sea. No body no charges." Michael Gregory looks thoughtful.

"Well yea I guess that would work. You said you wanted a big bang. I got dynamite in the ruck sack. The case is to hide the dynamite. I got a real big case to make like we have film equipment and cameras. I got one of those fancy little trolleys in the case to make it easy to carry around. Just like real Press guys Boss. I got labels and markers to write "Press" all over the cases. We don't want the fishing boat skipper to be suspicious." Al Corsino replies, his cold, ruthless manner giving no hint to either party listening that he is looking pleased with this bit of subterfuge.

"Let's get to work. We got under two hours before the fishing boat arrives. Al get to work prepare the dynamite with four minute fuses, Mercator, fetch that case and come with me!" Michael Gregory orders.

Costas Tinopolis lies where he fell on the carpet. The food ordered by Costas for lunch is still there, untouched, on the table. Only the steak knife is missing. Mercator looks at his father lying on the floor. His eyes are open staring into the room his flesh is cold to the touch.

I expected more blood on the carpet. I was covered in blood. His heart must have stopped when he fell

Only a few hours have passed since Mercator killed his father. At the time of the killing Mercator had felt a pang of guilt and remorse.

The look of surprise and fear in my father's eyes, the knowledge of imminent death, probably his last thought, is going to haunt me for ever. I will just have to live with it.

Mercator places his arms underneath his father's shoulders and with Michael Gregory holding the legs they cram the dead weight of Costas Tinopolis into the suit case. After they have cleaned the carpet of blood stains and dried it out with the hairdryer Michael Gregory instructs Mercator to bring his unused bath robe from his room to replace the one taken from Costa's suite. Whilst Mercator is on this errand Michael Gregory goes down stairs and picks up a steak knife from the dining room which, after carefully wiping any finger prints away, he places on the table next to the uneaten steak.

Eugene Jordan has brought "Sara's Pride" around the harbour to moor at the Princess Hotel's dock. The lights on the wharf pick out three men as they walk along the gangway with a large suit case being pulled along on a small trolley.

"Good of you to accommodate us skipper. This is my assistant and you know my reporter. Now skipper, to make this story work we need some excitement, some drama. So we want to see the sharks out there in the Bermuda Triangle. We heard on the radio that some ship got damaged out there. If we could get some shots of the sharks with the damaged ship that's what sells newspapers. You can be sure our readers will want more of that. It will be good for your business. Here's your money, one thousand dollars. If we get the shots and the story I want there will be a good bonus in it for you. OK skipper?" Michael Gregory sweet talks Eugene Jordan with his crisp bankers talk.

"It will be ten or twelve hours sailing south east to the area where that ship is. Are you sure you don't want to do some midnight fishing closer in tonight?" asks Eugene Jordan.

"If it's all the same to you skipper we would like to try for some sleep tonight. It's been a tiring day. You get us out to the ship area. Then tomorrow we will be ready to get a great story."

"Yes sir you are the boss." After counting his money Eugene shows them to the bunks then signals to Clyde, his assistant, to cast off. Eugene then concentrates on negotiating "Sara's Pride" from the hotel harbour.

It is past midnight, "Sara's Pride" is sailing south east at her optimum speed of ten knots. Eugene Jordan looks out from his cabin at the moon lit silver streaked ocean. He is apprehensive. His sailor's superstitious nature has been offended by these land lubbers talking of the sea and its creatures as some kind of spectacle.

At three bells Eugene Jordan will get his assistant to take over at the helm for four hours. Then they will be deep into the Bermuda Triangle. Eugene Jordan offers up a prayer to his marine Gods to watch over him and "Sara's Pride" on this voyage as they sail into the unknown.

George gets Afloat

"How far away is Jazzy on this ship of yours Howdy?" Charlie asks.

"She can only make ten knots an hour. So I guess she is probably four hundred miles south east of us. Why do you ask Charlie?" George wonders what is going through Charlie's mind. After his statement about Lenny nothing that Charlie says will surprise George.

"It may be a long shot but my pal Eugene might be able to sail us out for Jazzy. You know me and Eugene goes back a long way George. Eugene was the meanest saxophone player in our little group of four with me on the guitar and the two girls, my Emilia and Eugene's Grace, doing the singing, we had a ball. Ah those were the days." Charlie smiles with pleasure as he thinks of the good times he had enjoyed back in the late forties. The war was over the Americans were flooding the island. Every evening the group were out making music. Every night he made love with Emilia then in no time at all along came Jasmine and a year later Leonora.

"O K Pa so, go give Eugene a call! We got no time to dream. Let's get the show on the road!" Leonora urges. Charlie blinks as his daughter's voice penetrates through his dreaming of the past and without a word he moves from the table and strides purposefully over to the bar for the telephone.

"So that is where you get your voice from Lenny. Now it is starting to make sense." George smiles at Leonora.

"Yes Howdy. My ma had a wonderful voice. I loved hearing her sing so I guess I must have inherited the voice genes from her. I wish she was here to meet you Howdy I surely do." Leonora gazes into George's eyes, their hands entwine, as their lips move closer and closer.

"I say you two steady on. This is a British colony you know. Where is your stiff upper lip George?" Adrian chuckles as he passes the table.

"Do you want me to read him his rights George for interrupting a very precious moment?" Inspector Johnson queries with a twinkle in his eye as he stares at Adrian.

"Hi George, what's with your Limey friends spoiling your fun?" Duane drawls following his two colleagues.

"Hello fellers, you know Leonora. Jasmine is her sister and we are planning how to rescue her from "Ocean Star" Lenny meet Inspector Johnson and Duane Pickens from the FBI. I think you have already met Adrian Cuthbert from Government House." George introduces his colleagues.

"Well now gentlemen. Perhaps you can help get my sister back home safely instead of playing school boy pranks with George here, how about it!" Leonora stares at the men challenging them to prove to her that there is more to them than just bluster.

Minion or Master

"I am really sorry but Duane and I have a very important meeting tomorrow which means we have to stay on the Island. George knows how important it is." Inspector Johnson tells Leonora in his soft Scottish brogue but avoids eye contact with her.

The group are interrupted by Charlie returning from the bar. After brief introductions all around Leonora desperate for action to save her sister wants to know if Eugene can help them.

"I spoke to Grace. She told me that Eugene was pleased as punch. He got a surprise two day charter from some New York newspaper. He is sailing tonight, so no luck there".

"Where is "Pembroke Lady" now? Have you finished with her?" Adrian asks Inspector Johnson.

"She is still at the Police mooring. I have spoken with Henry Rucker at the bank. So far as he is concerned the bank want nothing further to do with the boat. Apparently it was Wayne Luther's idea to buy the boat. Old man Rucker was never keen on it."

"So is she free for charter?" George asks.

"So far as the police are concerned—Yes—but you will need the owner's permission." Inspector Johnson tells George.

"Leave that with me. Mr. Rucker has a soft spot for me. He got me my job in reception. Always says what an asset I am to the bank. Can you get her fuelled and ready to sail Inspector Johnson please?" Leonora asks.

"Aframe Shipping will meet all expenses. I want the crew and Jasmine to be safe as soon as possible." George tells Inspector Johnson who nods to confirm he will comply with Leonora's request. George continues

"Adrian? You sailed "Pembroke Lady" back with Inspector Johnson didn't you. How about coming with us?" George gives Adrian a look that says "remember you owe me one".

"Well, as it happens, I am free tomorrow. So, yes, I could come along and help." Adrian smiles at George and Leonora. Adrian knows that to refuse would leave his relationship with George in tatters. George's actions over the last week have surprised Adrian who has had to re—assess the quiet, sometimes shy young business man whom Adrian had first considered to be a conventional unimaginative numbers man.

"Splendid. Let's all meet at the Police mooring an hour before dawn so that we can be away at first light. In the meantime get some rest. It looks like tomorrow will be a busy day." George advises the group; surprising himself at how he has assumed control. George is beginning to appreciate that these powerful men appear to respect him.

Chapter Thirty

Invitation

Friday Night 3rd June 1966

Jasmine Hides

On returning to his room the radio operator sees Petrus bending over Kato who is now lying unconscious on the floor of the communications room.

"What's happened to the skipper?" the operator cries.

"The skipper lost his footing and crashed into the desk. He must be all in. He hasn't had a break for over twenty four hours. He needs some rest. Help me get him back to his cabin so I can take a look at him properly." Petrus orders the radio operator.

Jasmine stretches her head around the corner of the corridor. She sees Petrus gesticulating at the radio operator as they manoeuvre the dead weight of Kato. Jasmine retreats back towards her own cabin. On an impulse she decides to go into Kato's cabin. The door is not locked. Kato's cabin comprises one large working room with two smaller adjoining compartments. The first compartment houses a bunk and fitted wardrobe. The second compartment is the heads with a wash basin, shower and toilet. The main room has a large desk. At the other end of the cabin there is a sofa/settee, two arm chairs and a coffee table. The furniture is bolted to the floor. A large sea trunk with its lid secured with an iron clasp lies unbolted on the floor next to the cabin door.

In a panic, Jasmine searches each room for a hiding place. The shower cubicle is a possibility but she would easily be seen if any one comes into the heads. There is no space under or over the bunk for Jasmine to hide. The wardrobe is full of Kato's uniforms but there is room for her to squeeze in. The desk has a fitted cupboard with drawers containing charts and ships papers. No space to hide in there. She could just about hide behind the sofa which has its back to the wall or there is the sea trunk. The trunk has enough room to hide Jasmine.

Noise from outside the cabin makes Jasmine decide. Swiftly she lifts the heavy clasp from the side of the trunk and raises the lid. She jumps in and crouches on top of Kato's winter duffel coat and snow boots which lie in the bottom.

Moments after she lowers the trunk lid, she hears a heavy thwack as the clasp falls back onto its hasp. Jasmine hears the cabin door open and then the sound of Kato being dragged in by Petrus and the radio operator.

"Let's get him onto his bunk." Petrus says. Inside the trunk Jasmine can hear the two men grunting as they struggle with Kato.

"Right get back to your station! I'll look after the skipper now!" Petrus instructs the radio operator.

"Yes Sir!" There is something nagging away in the radio operator's mind as he leaves Kato's cabin. He has served with Kato for many years and even in the roughest of conditions he has never known the skipper to miss his footing. Nevertheless he knows that under maritime law Petrus is now legally in charge of the ship and the crew. Then there was the radio message earlier for Petrus from

Minion or Master

Monaco which he had taken to Petrus in his cabin. The message seemed innocuous merely advising Petrus that he was being considered for promotion to captain and he would need to attend an interview in Piraeus as soon as possible.

The instant the radio operator closes Kato's cabin door Petrus goes to work. Kato is lying on his back on the bunk and is still unconscious. His head is badly bruised from the bang on the desk. Petrus tears a large bed sheet into four strips. He twists each strip to make a thick cord and ties Kato to his bunk. Each arm and leg is tied to a corner. Next, he covers Kato with a large blanket which conceals the bindings and gives the impression that Kato is asleep.

Petrus checks his watch. The time is nearing mid night. One of the last messages Costas Tinopolis ever sent was a coded message for Petrus. Any message from Monaco to Petrus with the word Piraeus in it meant that "Ocean Star" must be sunk with out trace. Petrus's reward will be one hundred thousand dollars and command of his own ship. Kato must go down with the ship. He knows too much about me Petrus decides as he locks Kato into his cabin and walks to the bridge to assume command. Petrus knows that in twenty four hours the ship will be sufficiently close to Bermuda to ensure his rescue but the sea will still be deep enough to swallow "Ocean Star" and Kato.

In the dark of the sea trunk it is beginning to dawn on Jasmine that she is trapped. The problem with the sea trunk is the clasp. It has a side fitting. Jasmine needs someone to lift the clasp from the outside. There is no way she can penetrate the sides of the trunk made from hardened whale skin. Jasmine feels drained and exhausted. She needs a fix to get her head around this crazy situation.

She is angry at everyone especially the men who have manipulated and coerced her into the situation she finds herself in.

Sammy got me into drugs. He promised me the world. I believed him. Then George rescued me from Sammy by getting me on this damned ship with Kato. Now what? Me and Kato is in a cabin both helpless. Shit what a mess this is. Why did I believe Sammy? Why did I trust George? How the hell do I get myself out now?

Jasmine curls up in a ball in the bottom of the trunk and starts to weep tears of despair.

On the bridge Petrus advises the crew of the skipper's accident. He approves the orders of Kato to continue pumping out the cargo to raise the hull so that the hole in the side will be above sea level.

Might just as well keep everyone occupied so they have no time to think. By morning, the hull will be raised and the crew can take a well earned rest. Then I can get on with a spot of sabotage. Before that; perhaps I can have a little pleasure with that bitch woman of Kato's. Rubbing the side of his head Petrus has not forgotten he owes that whore more than just a brief seeing to. Petrus passes command to the senior deck hand and goes below looking for Jasmine.

Saturday Morning 4th June, 1966

Where is Mercator?

"Did George and Adrian get away this morning on "Pembroke Lady"?" Duane Pickens, with his mouth full of waffle which has been topped with a thick layer of maple syrup, asks Inspector Johnson. Whilst mouthing his query Duane brings a finger up to the corner of his

Minion or Master

mouth where a dollop of syrup has emerged and is starting to slither down the side of his face. Duane pops the sticky syrup laden finger into his mouth and then loads up with another helping of syrup coated waffle.

Inspector Johnson watches Duane with some distaste. His eating style does not bother Inspector Johnson in the slightest he saw far worse as a young constable on the beat around the Gorbals district in Glasgow. No, what Inspector Johnson cannot understand is how any one can refuse porridge and kippers for breakfast in the police canteen and, instead, opt for waffles. No accounting for taste, he thinks to himself.

"Aye, my sergeant told me by the time all the formalities were complete and the boat fuelled up they left at six this morning. By now they should be well outside the reef. Adrian is going to keep in radio contact with my sergeant."

"That's real good Jonno. I felt a bit mean last night not being able to go with the kid when George asked us but I really would love it if we can nail these Tinopolis guys." Duane answers with his eyes focussed down on his plate of waffles which are rapidly diminishing.

"Och Aye. If we can have them charged and found guilty the case will be really big; both in the States and in Europe. We could become famous. But, we are no where near that situation yet Laddie. First things first we need to find out if Mercator will give us any information that we can use. What time did you arrange to meet him?" Inspector Johnson queries as he places his fish knife and fork neatly together having devoured with relish every morsel of his kippers smoked the traditional Scottish way and despatched from Oban in West Scotland.

"Well now I told Murky that if he was not down in the restaurant at the hotel by nine thirty with something good for us then he could look forward to us questioning him again at the station and being kept here until I can get his ass transferred to the USA. Let's go and see if we have anything Jonno!" Duane gets up from the canteen table and moves away purposefully. He stops abruptly and returns for the last syrup laden waffle left on his plate which he wraps in a tissue. Inspector Johnson shakes his head in disbelief as he and Duane head for the Princess Hotel with Duane's last waffle leaving a trail of syrup spots on the floor of the Hamilton police canteen.

There is no sign of Mercator in the room. His suitcase lies empty at the bottom of the wardrobe. Looking at the crisp white sheet and blanket turned down neatly on the top of the bed, Duane thinks the bed was not used last night. Standing in the bathroom Duane exclaims

"He's done a runner Jonno. Look . . . there's no tooth brush!"

"Wait Laddie not so fast! Perhaps he stayed with his father."

"Guess you might have a point there Jonno. What's this?" Duane points to a blood stain on the inside of a bath robe hanging from a hook on the bath room door.

"Could be any thing, let's go to reception and find out what old man Tinopolis has been up to before we do anything else. Eh Laddie. Come on!"

"So, have you seen or heard either Mercator or Costas Tinopolis since yesterday?" Inspector Johnson questions the hotel receptionist.

"No Sir. There's a "do not disturb sign" on Mr. Costas's suite door and he is not answering the telephone. We have tried to connect several calls but he does not pick

Minion or Master

up." The receptionist looks up at the two detectives then looks away as she answers an incoming call

"Good morning Princess Hotel. How may I help you? Mr. Costas Tinopolis? Trying to connect you please hold the line." The receptionist holds up the telephone receiver to Inspector Johnson who snatches it eagerly then stoops his ginger haired head down towards the receptionist and with his cold blue eyes staring unblinkingly into her face he speaks into the mouth piece of the telephone

"This is Inspector Johnson from Her Majesty's Colonial Police who am I speaking to?" There is silence at the other end of the telephone. Inspector Johnson strains his ears concentrating hard trying to pick up any noise from the other end which might provide some clue as to the location of the caller.

"Hello I want to speak with Mr Costas Tinopolis this is his pilot speaking from the airport. Where is he please?"

"That is precisely what I would like to know. When did you last speak with him?" Inspector Johnson demands.

"Late yesterday morning. We were ordered to have his plane ready for immediate take off but since then we have heard nothing. It is most unusual. Has any thing happened to him? Why are the police involved?" The pilot responds cautiously not wanting to get himself into trouble either with the Police or his unpredictable boss.

"Please inform Hamilton police station as soon as you hear from either Costas Tinopolis or his son Mercator." Inspector Johnson instructs the pilot. Immediately after terminating this call Inspector Johnson orders the airport police to ban Costas Tinopolis's private aeroplane from taking off until further notice.

"That should get his attention when he hears about that. I'm just going to the John to wash this syrup from my hands then I guess we had better take a look at the old man's suite." Duane grins at Inspector Johnson.

"Yes, see how the other half live eh Laddie. What's the betting that he hasn't had waffles for breakfast?" Inspector Johnson chuckles.

"And you can bet your fine ginger head that he never had that white stuff looking like wall plaster and burnt fish you gobbled down." Duane retorts as he walks across the hotel foyer to the rest rooms.

"Guess Costas must be off his food. No breakfast and yesterdays food is untouched." Duane drawls then asks the security guard who has accompanied them to the suite to find out what time the steak dinner was delivered to the suite.

"I don't think he is here. His bed is not slept in. He hasn't even unpacked his clothes. That is odd though. Look!" Inspector Johnson, kneeling down, is staring at the carpet around the table where the morning sun light reveals a slightly different pattern to the rest of the area. He crawls up to the table and examines its legs carefully.

"Ah now, what have we here?" Inspector Johnson exclaims as he brings out a magnifying glass.

"What's with the Sherlock Holmes bit Jonno? I gotta tell you Jonno I prefer looking at your ginger hair than your big fat ass sticking up in the air." Duane guffaws as he walks across to the door to let in the security guard.

"Blood spots Laddie. There are blood spots on the table legs. Someone has done a clean up job here. That robe in Mercator's room. I want that stain compared with these spots. Let's see if we get a match. I am going to call my forensic people. There is something suspicious going on here. Can you deal with the security guard and make sure no one messes with this suite or Mercator's room?

This could be the evidence we need." Inspector Johnson gets up off his knees and moves to the telephone to summon help and his forensic officer.

Buried at sea

The cabin below the deck of "Sara's Pride" is small and cramped. Michael Gregory selects the more comfortable floor bunk for himself. Al Corsino climbs on to the higher bunk. The large suitcase, containing the body of Mercator's father, takes up all the floor space between the bunks and the opposite side of the cabin. There are just the two bunks in the cabin so Mercator has to rest as best he can on top of the suitcase. The air in the cabin is stale and rank. The smell of the sea and rotten fish combined with diesel fumes from the throbbing inboard engine together with the constant rolling of "Sara's Pride", in the Atlantic Ocean swell, make conditions in the cabin uncomfortable.

Al Corsino secures his rucksack, containing five sticks of dynamite complete with four minute fuses, to the inside of his bunk. He also has a spare stick of dynamite and a number of different length fuse wires in the rucksack. His six inch commando knife nestles in its sheath strapped securely above his ankle.

Michael Gregory lies on his back. A Berretta hand gun nestles in a holster located beneath his left armpit. A slim stiletto blade, honed to the sharpness of a Samurai sword, is concealed in his jacket sleeve. The back of his head rests on top of the laundry bag which contains proof that Mercator murdered his father. Just like any banker, Michael Gregory believes in having security. The evidence may be a life saver for him one day.

"How long before we can dump this case? The stink of my father's body is making me heave." Mercator, pinching his nose, asks Michael Gregory.

"We have been sailing for five hours. I guess in another six maybe seven hours we will be where we need to be. For now we sit tight and conserve energy." Michael Gregory speaks quietly, his eyes staring into the bunk above him.

"I'm gonna take a wander outside. It's getting light enough for me to inspect this tub's lay out. You can come up here for now! Just make sure you don't fool with my ruck sack!" Al Corsino nods to Mercator as he climbs off the bunk and gingerly negotiates his frame around the suit case.

After opening the cabin door Al stoops under the door frame and climbs the five steps to the deck hatchway. Fresh sea air and a pale orange light from the dawning sun hit Al's face when he climbs out on deck. A sea swell forces "Sara's Pride" to dip making Al lurch towards her bow. Al starts to walk around the perimeter of "Sara's Pride" taking in as much information as he can. In a few hours this boat will be at the centre of action; then he will need to know every detail. The homework he does now may save his life later.

He follows a narrow gangway along the edge of the deck. White painted guard rails with rust stains dribbling down the vertical struts line the edge. The main wheel house and observation cabin with the boat's radio and engine controls is located on the other side of the gangway. The wheel house exterior wall has a rope secured at waist height for grabbing on to. Used car tires attached by rope to the guard rail struts lie on the deck every few

Minion or Master

feet. The tires are used to act as a buffer between the boat and any object such as a harbour wall or another ship.

At the bow, Al manoeuvres around the anchor chain and capstan, he turns to look back towards the stern. He sees a small, two man dinghy, with a Mercury outboard engine tied in to the side. Al looks in to the wheel house and waves at skipper Eugene Jordan who is at the helm.

"Good morning Mr. Henry. Did you all get some rest last night?" Eugene Jordan shouts through the open wheel house window.

"When do we eat? My boss editor is feeling hunger pangs." Al shouts back, noticing the flat roof space above the wheel house, which houses big game fishing rods and gaffing poles.

"In one hour my mate Clyde will be up. Then we will cook eggs and hash browns. The galley is below deck from de wheel house here. You come. Make a brew if you want Mr. Henry." Eugene Jordan calls back.

"OK. That's not a bad idea. Some sweet black coffee will just about hit the spot right now." Al makes his way down the other side of the boat to the wheel house.

"What do you use the oil drums for skipper?" Al has seen several empty oil drums roped up with a large steel hook hanging from the lip of each drum.

"The hooks on de drums are baited up with old fish. De sharks come when we put fresh blood from a fish catch on de water. Then we drop the hooked bait in. When you feel a tug on the rope you dun got a shark on de hook Mr. Henry. You pull de shark up on de rope and drop in de drum. Den bang him on de nose with a hammer. You dun hit his brain. Now he dun be dead. You wanna try later Mr. Henry? Catch your own shark maybe? Make good story for your paper." Eugene Jordan is eyeing his client carefully; trying to assess his

strengths and more importantly his weaknesses. He can see from the awkward way he moves on deck that this client is a land lubber. Yet there is something about the man that disturbs Eugene Jordan. He cannot identify the reason but his seaman's instincts warn him to be wary.

"Did you get any radio message from the damaged ship? Are we on course still to intercept her? Man that sure will be something for our readers if we can get shark pictures with the ship as back ground." Al, laying it on thick, keeps up his pretence of being a reporter.

"We heard on the radio earlier this morning that "Ocean Star" is making steady progress. We should see her this afternoon".

"Can't this tub go any faster? Maybe we could rendezvous by lunchtime. My editor wants to be back in New York tomorrow night. Time is money. There will be an extra bonus for you. What do you say skipper?" Al cajoles

"Sara's Pride" is not a fancy speed boat. She's built for fishing and her engine will work all day at this speed. Any more and we will be asking for trouble. She could over heat then we'll have to stop and wait maybe a few hours until she cools. Worse case the engine could seize up. Then we will need rescuing." Eugene Jordan speaks with quiet determination as he stares intently at the icy unemotional facial features of Al. Corsino. Al stares back at Eugene Jordan for several seconds before deciding to hold back on any confrontation for the time being and walks away heading for the galley to make coffee.

A few hours later the air temperature has risen to a pleasant twenty two degrees centigrade. Al Corsino and Michael Gregory have left the cabin and are seated in

Minion or Master

the stern of "Sara's Pride". They have left Mercator in the cabin fast asleep.

"We need to speed things up Al. The skippers taking a rest, I'm gonna lean on the mate. If the skipper comes back out you know what to do." Michael Gregory gives Al a knowing look and strides purposefully into the wheel house cabin.

"How much dough is the skipper giving you for this trip? You know I'm gonna pay him two thousand US dollars. I'm guessing you ain't gonna get more than one hundred bucks." Michael Gregory stares into Clyde's face and sees doubt in his eyes.

"I'm right. I knew it. Now I'm in a rush to get this job finished so here is two hundred bucks." Michael Gregory waves four fifty dollar bills and watches Clyde eyeing the money as he waves it back and for

"All you got to do is get this old tub to top speed and get us to this damaged ship pronto. I'll give you a hundred dollars now and the rest when the ship is in sight. Your skipper is asleep so you are in charge. Do we have a deal?" Michael Gregory holds out the two bills and grins as the mate pockets them and pushes the throttle control to maximum.

Eugene Jordan is not asleep. This trip and these clients are puzzling him. Most clients are excited on their first night. Not these. They stayed hunkered up in their cabin all night. They didn't want to drink like most clients nor even come on deck to look at the stars. There has been no jokes, no small talk, no banter, such a contrast from when he first met Mr. Henry at the Harbour Club.

Why have they paid me well over the odds for this charter, why? It just doesn't make sense.

He sits on his bunk, his head cradled in his hands, looking at the deck, trying to make some sense of the situation. An alteration in the boat's engine noise grabs his attention. Eugene Jordan looks up, his seaman's senses on full alert. The boat lurches forward increasing speed. Eugene Jordan gets up and races for the deck. As he emerges from his cabin an arm wraps around his neck and he is pulled back.

"What the hell . . ." Eugene Jordan cries before he sees a blinding flash. Al Corsino has slammed his head against the cabin wall. Eugene Jordan falls to the deck unconscious. Al drags him back into the bunk. Eugene Jordan is gagged and trussed like a turkey with his body secured to the bunk. He cannot make any noise and he cannot escape. Al wanders back out on deck and reports to Michael Gregory.

"I guess its time to dump the body. Go and wake the kid to come and help take the case to the stern. I'll keep the mate distracted." Michael Gregory orders Al.

Getting the case, containing the body of his father, from the cabin up the five steps to the deck then pushing and shoving it to the stern required a massive effort from Mercator. He sits at the stern of the boat, his head between his hands. He is panting and sweating profusely. Michael Gregory saunters down from the wheel house and whispers to Al who heads back to the cabin.

"Do you have any last words for your old man?" Michael asks Mercator.

"May he rot in hell" Mercator pants out; venom tingeing his voice

"Can we get this over?" Mercator pleads looking desperate.

"I thought you might like him to go out with a bit of a bang." Michael Gregory remarks as he stares at Mercator, making him look even more uncomfortable, before swivelling his eyes towards Al returning from the cabin with the spare stick of dynamite and various fuses.

"Let's see," Michael continues looking at his Rolex

"It is twenty to twelve. Noon is an appropriate time. Don't you agree Al? I think a twenty minute fuse." Michael Gregory nods to Al who selects the fuse then inserts it carefully into the stick of dynamite. Michael Gregory opens the suitcase lid being careful to keep upwind and offers Mercator a lighter and the fused dynamite.

"Will you do the honours?" Michael looks at Mercator who gets up without a word. He snatches the dynamite and lighter from Michael and bending over the case he shoves the stick of dynamite into his fathers opened mouth and lights the fuse. As Mercator closes the case the stench of his fathers decomposing body wafts into his throat which makes his stomach heave until he is sick all over the case.

"Farewell Costas. I guess a burial at sea is a good way for you to go." Michael Gregory shouts as the suitcase bobbing up and down floats away from "Sara's Pride".

The Chase

Adrian is first to arrive at the Police wharf in Hamilton docks. The cathedral clock is just finishing chiming five in the morning as he walks purposefully along the pontoon to "Pembroke Lady". The duty sergeant hands over the keys. Adrian checks that the fuel tanks are full. On the dashboard Adrian reads a note from

Inspector Johnson requesting that he be kept informed of progress using the Police radio frequency. Charlie, George and Leonora soon arrive at the docks in Charlie's Morris Minor. They are dressed in identical yellow oilskins and seamen's boots.

"Good morning to the three of you. My you are showing me up. I didn't realise we were to wear uniform?" Adrian chuckles.

"Charlie borrowed them from Grace Jordan. She said that Eugene would have liked nothing better than a trip with his old friend Charlie but a booking is a booking." George advises smiling back at Adrian.

"There is a spare set in the car if you want?" Charlie offers as he gazes around and exclaims

"Oh my Lord this is some boat! What speed can she do? Look a harpoon gun!"

"Bring the spare clothes on board Charlie you never know they may be useful. My blue anorak and captain's hat will suit me just fine for the moment. We will see how fast the boat will go Charlie just as soon as we can get under way. I suggest you and your daughter get some rest. George and I will take the first watch. After breakfast you can all have a lesson at using the boat's controls and radio." Adrian takes command with nonchalant ease.

Once outside the reefs Adrian sets the compass bearing to match the co ordinates given by the Police Sergeant to intercept "Ocean Star" and pushes the throttle lever to full power. With a quiet sea and light following wind "Pembroke Lady" heads south east through the Atlantic ocean at a speed approaching thirty knots.

"Thank you for helping with this Adrian. You know how worried I have been about Jasmine since you told us about the Nitro-Glycerine on board "Ocean Star". I will be so relieved if we can get her back safely." George looks across from the co—pilot's seat to Adrian who is staring intently out to sea.

"It's the least I can do for you George. Might I say what you have done this last week has been extremely helpful. You are held in high regard by a number of people and I count myself as one of those people. I am glad we are out here working together. I know we are from different back grounds and are following different career paths but I believe that we might be able to help each other. You are able to act outside the constraints of the public sector scrutiny which I am subject to. I, on the other hand, can influence and sometimes manipulate the levers of power to great advantage. A small example has been how we have managed the inquest of Sammy Santino and the access to his funds. I think we might be able to do much more in the future to our mutual benefit. What do you think?" Adrian inquires casually continuing to look straight out to sea.

"I say Adrian. Are you suggesting we enter into some kind of secret pact? It sounds interesting and exciting. I think we have learned a great deal about each other this last two weeks. How would your idea work in practice?" George's enthusiasm brushes away any negative thoughts he might have.

"Well, if I have a problem, or, say, I need some information about someone, I might ask you to help. Outside the glare of public life, you are able to break a few rules which I can't do. I would only ask you to help for the greater good. It would not be for personal gain. You, in return, would have access through me to information and resources from the public sector. Such information could be of immense value to a young businessman like you. I would watch out for your interests." Adrian explains as if his proposal were no more onerous than ordering a pint of beer.

"Are you sure this is all legal?" George is now looking concerned and confused.

"Well, now George. Do you really believe that H M Government complies with every little detail of the law? Nothing would ever get done if that were so. The civil service is made up of thousands of minions who are there to carry out orders. They might be compared to worker ants in a colony. There are a few, such as myself, who are required to "think outside of the box" and act accordingly. We sometimes take unorthodox action. The prime mantra is not to get caught breaking any of the tedious rules set up for the minions. Our political masters want results. We are the brains in the system. Without us nothing would get done. We occupy a privileged position in society. We have access to state secrets and have the ear of powerful people. We cannot perform our roles for the good of society in isolation. Each one of us has to build up contacts, people we can trust to do the right thing. I am building up my web of contacts. I want you to be one of them. I think you are the kind of man I can work with. We are both young. We might work together for perhaps fifty years. Think of what we might achieve? That excites me tremendously. It is as simple as that. I am offering you access to power and privilege. There you have it my cards are on the table. Are you a minion or a master? Not everyone gets a choice." Pausing for effect Adrian finally turns his head towards George and whispers in his ear

"You have to choose today old boy!"

George sits in silence looking through "Pembroke Lady's" windscreen at the sea and the far horizon. The

Minion or Master

weather is good. Visibility is clear for miles. George's mind is far from clear. So many thoughts are racing through his brain.

What sort of commitment will I be making? Will I be corrupted by Adrian into becoming a criminal? Can I be a free agent with an obligation to Adrian? What do I want out of life? Should I settle for a quiet existence with rows of numbers or taste some action? Can I actually influence my destiny by a choice I make today? Shall I choose excitement and uncertainty or boredom and predictability? Is my choice that simple? Perhaps it comes down to one question. Do I trust Adrian? The evidence from this last two weeks, after our initial confrontation, is that he has supported me. If it hadn't been for Adrian rescuing me from Sammy in the Harbour club things might have turned out far worse for me.

George's heart is with Adrian. He likes Adrian. He respects Adrian. George's professional training screams at him to be cautious. Do not rush into a commitment. Check everything. George has to balance caution with boldness. He can choose safety or risk. He must decide the path life will take him on today.

"Your proposal requires serious consideration Adrian. I shall give you my answer today as you request. However, right now, I want to focus my attention on getting to "Ocean Star" and bringing Jasmine safely back to Bermuda. Only then will I be able to see my future clearly. I tell you now, though, that whatever is decided; what we have done and your part in it, I will never ever forget. That is going to stay in my memory for ever. Now what would you say to some breakfast?" George smiles at Adrian who nods in approval.

"Just one thing old boy. No coffee for me. I will make tea for myself if there is any on board! I can't stand that instant stuff." Adrian shudders and puckers up his nose as George laughs and goes off to the galley.

After breakfast Adrian gives everyone instruction in using the controls on "Pembroke Lady" and the short wave frequency radio. They all listen to Adrian speaking to the Bermudan police and learn that "Ocean Star" is on course with no further incidents reported.

Later in the morning, with the warm summer sun beating down, Leonora agrees to take over the controls. The three men with nothing to do for the time being relax.

"How do you like our little island of Bermuda then Adrian?" Charlie wants to know.

"It's my first posting overseas Charlie. Bermuda is one of our smallest Crown colonies so my bosses didn't think I would get into too much trouble here. The weather is good but I must confess I do miss London, the theatres, restaurants and hotels where they serve tea in bone china sets. What I wouldn't give for high tea in Claridges right now." Adrian dreams away.

"Well I guess me and Lenny in the Harbour Club can't compete with your fancy London night clubs I'll grant you that." Charlie responds.

"On the contrary your daughter has one of the finest natural voices I have ever heard. If she had a year of tuition in say the Royal Academy of Music in London she could be a world class singer." Adrian volunteers.

"Now come on Adrian. How is the likes of us gonna get our girl Lenny into such a fancy place." Charlie laughs out loud.

"Well that's easy to answer Charlie. I shall speak with my uncle. He is on the Board of Governors." Adrian advises with no trace of amusement in his voice.

Minion or Master

"Are you serious?" Charlie cries his mouth wide open as he looks astounded at Adrian. Before Adrian can reply a shriek comes from Leonora at the controls followed shortly after by the sound of a distant explosion. The three men look at each other in puzzlement before running to Leonora at the controls with George leading.

"What's up Lenny?"

"There was a flash over there!" Lenny points to the starboard bow where a puff of smoke is now hanging in the air.

"Steer towards the smoke and throttle back to slow speed Leonora!" Adrian orders then says

"Quick everyone let's see if we can spot anything! George take the bow, Charlie move over to starboard and I'll take port!" Adrian races to the port side of "Pembroke Lady".

George stands in the bow holding on to the stainless steel bow sprite guardrail and stares intently into the blue sea. The sun is high overhead and is reflecting back off the water making George squint. Slowly "Pembroke Lady" cuts through the water towards the area where the smoke was seen.

"Engage neutral Lenny! We are heading for some objects floating dead ahead." George shouts. "Pembroke Lady" slows right down her momentum still carrying her along.

"Yes I can see something. Fetch me a net!" Adrian shouts. Adrian trawls the net attached to a bamboo pole and finally succeeds in trapping the object. He lands the net and drops the object onto the deck.

"Over here Adrian quickly bring the net!" George shouts from the bow. Not waiting to inspect what he has landed Adrian races to the bow with the net.

"Look in the water there Adrian. My god! It's a hand!" George exclaims. Swiftly Adrian dips the net in to the sea and picks up the gruesome find which he carries back to the first object he landed. Everyone gathers around to look. Charlie picks up the first object which is a sodden piece of dark coloured material. Carefully Charlie unfolds the material which is frayed around the edges. Adrian inspects the hand. There is a gold ring on the index finger. The finger is swollen preventing Adrian from removing the ring.

"This material has a label sewn in. I think it looks like a C and a T in fancy writing." Charlie shouts.

Adrian picks up the hand and carries it in a cloth to the galley where he places it on a chopping board. Using a sharp kitchen knife with a serrated edge he carefully slices off the index finger above the ring and forces the ring off the severed finger. After washing the ring in the galley basin Adrian holds it up to the light from the porthole. He sees an inscription on the inside which reads "Costas Tinopolis for his 21st Birthday."

Adrian orders George to re engage power to "Pembroke Lady" whilst he radios in the discovery of the hand and the ring to Inspector Johnson.

Chapter Thirty One
Kato

Saturday morning 4th June 1966

Sprung from the chest

Petrus feels frustrated and angry. He has searched everywhere for Jasmine. He has checked her cabin on several occasions during the night and into the early hours of Saturday morning but he can find no trace of her. Returning once more to Captain Kato's cabin he walks across the main room to the bunk where he has confined Kato. Petrus peers down at his prisoner with a contemptuous look. The only sign of life in Kato is his shallow breathing. Unsure if he is unconscious from the blow to his head or whether he is now just asleep, Petrus, without a care whether Kato lives or dies leaves him tied to the bunk and locked in the cabin.

Curled up in the bottom of Kato's sea chest, wrapped up in his duffel coat, Jasmine has managed a few hours troubled sleep. Lying in the dark, trapped in the sea chest, she has been disturbed by noises in the cabin several times. Once more a noise in the cabin scares her. With her eyes shut tight she concentrates on trying to in⸺ the noises. Her nerves are frayed and stretch⸺ drum skin. She is on edge and scared.
on the linoleum lined floor of the cabin.

to the chest. Jasmine's heart misses a beat. Will the chest be opened to expose her trapped and vulnerable? She imagines seeing Petrus leering at her over the lid of the chest. She covers her mouth and nose with her hands. She trembles with fear anticipating the worst. The next sound is a "clunk" as the cabin door closes. Jasmine hears the door lock being set. She allows her body to relax from its tensed position and quietly she whimpers.

Silence stretches beyond minutes into an hour. Since jumping into the chest to hide from Petrus Jasmine has been desperately thinking what she can do. Should she scream for help? How will Petrus react if he finds her? Will he want revenge after she smashed the ash tray over his head? Can she get out of the chest by herself? She thinks back to when she jumped in. Where is the chest clasp? She feels around the edge of the lid until her fingers touch the raised hinges. The clasp must be on the opposite side of the chest to the hinges she concludes. What if I roll the chest so that the lid is on the floor? The clasp might release itself. She resolves to give that a try.

Moving her body to the side of the chest she raises her feet up to the inside of the chest lid. Keeping her body rigid she forces the chest to rock. At first the movement is slight but Jasmine maintains her stance and keeps forcing leverage by moving her body until sufficient momentum makes the chest rock strongly. As the chest rocks to the maximum angle Jasmine lunges and slides towards the fulcrum where her body weight tips the chest over. Now the lid is on a vertical plain and the clasp is horizontal.

Encouraged by her success Jasmine repeats her movements until the lid of the chest lies on the floor. Although the clasp is now lying vertical it is still stuck in its hasp. Calling on her last reserves of energy Jasmine starts to kick the side of the chest close to where the hasp is fixed. Eventually a dull thud on the side of the chest tells Jasmine the heavy iron clasp has been released. With her back resting on the lid Jasmine pushes the chest up with her feet. Gradually the open box structure is pushed up into the air until a big enough space is made between the lid and the box. Nimbly Jasmine rolls out from the chest. With the support from Jasmine's feet gone the box crashes back down onto the lid narrowly missing her foot.

Lying tensed up in a ball on the cabin floor Jasmine worries whether the noise from the chest crashing down might bring unwanted attention on her from outside. After a few minutes waiting and listening Jasmine begins to explore the cabin. The room is unlit but Jasmine's eyes, which have been accustomed to the greater darkness from being trapped in the chest, have no trouble in picking out the main features in the cabin. As she starts moving around she hears a muffled noise coming from the far end of the cabin. She stands rooted to the spot; tensed and ready to react. The sound repeats itself. Jasmine slowly twists towards the noise but sees nothing. Summoning up an inner courage she never knew she possessed she turns on the light switch located on the wall near the door.

Jasmine can now see the compartment at the end of the main cabin room where the sound has come from. Nervously she tip toes towards the compartment afraid, that at any moment, someone might jump out at her. She peeps around the compartment door, then, relaxes as she realizes the sound is coming from the blanket covered body of Captain Kato.

"Are you OK?" Jasmine exclaims as she rushes forward to the bunk. There is no reaction from Kato. Looking at Kato lying on the bunk, helpless, Jasmine feels mixed emotions. She is relieved that no one other than Kato is here. The fear of being discovered in the chest was acute and has drained her energy. Until now she has seen Kato more as her guard than as a human being with needs. She realises that she has been selfish, making things difficult for Kato, thinking only of herself. She has failed to recognise a decent man who has been trying his best to help her. He saved her from Petrus. Without him she would not have got away from New York. Who knows what might have happened to her if she had stayed under the influence of Sammy, Randy and that slime ball Artie.

"Oh Kato I am so sorry." Jasmine cries releasing the pent up emotions she has been experiencing. She reaches out to hold his hand then sees that his wrist is tied to the bunk.

"My God did Petrus do this to you? You poor man I'll soon get you free." Jasmine chatters as she unties Kato.

"Ah! My head! What's happened?" Kato cries. Jasmine's movements around the bunk have finally brought him out of his violence induced stupor.

"Don't you remember last evening? Petrus attacked you. He's tied you up and locked you in your cabin. What on earth is going on?" Jasmine questions, her voice trembling with fear. Kato swivels his body into a seating position on the bunk. He lays his head on one hand and massages the back of his head

"I really can't say Jasmine. Petrus was not my choice as a number two. He was forced on me by Costas Tinopolis. I can't remember the attack but I must have it out with him." Costas states with resolve in his voice.

"Petrus has locked us in here. Do you have a spare key to the cabin door? Let me take a look at that head of yours before you get into any more trouble." Jasmine responds examining the back of Kato's head.

"I have the key to my desk and in the locked drawer is my revolver. We will wait for Petrus to return then ambush him." Kato grins at Jasmine who has fetched a cold wet towel from the next door compartment and placed it on the bruised and swollen scalp of Kato.

The two wait. An hour stretches into two, dawn comes and goes. Time extends towards midday. They have had coffee and a few biscuits which Kato found in his desk. Hunger pangs are becoming more prominent. Both are feeling weak. Jasmine is experiencing a severe drop in her energy levels as the previous adrenaline surge from last nights events drain away. Kato keeps his old revolver with him and tries hard to ignore the pain racking his body. A noise at the cabin door spurs them both to move swiftly to their agreed positions.

After sleeping longer than he intended Petrus is inundated with managing ship business. The pumps have finished discharging the grain cargo so now Petrus has had to re assign the crew to new duties. "Ocean Star's" hull has risen sufficiently so that the hole in the side is now above the waterline.

Kato made the right decision about that. Now, I had better get below and make sure he is still tied up. I don't want him causing problems. When I start to sink this ship he can go to the bottom for all I care. I will get my money from Costas who will not be at all concerned if the captain is lost. Knowing Costas he will be pleased. He will claim insurance with out Kato as a key witness. That will make things go easier with the claim.

Petrus grins wryly at this thought as he races down the steps to the crew quarters.

At Kato's cabin door Petrus looks up and down the corridor. No one is around. He turns the key in the door lock and opens the door. The cabin appears the same as before as Petrus walks to the bunk. He raises the blanket to check on his victim.

"What the hell?" Petrus cries as he looks down at Jasmine lying in the bunk staring up at him.

"The game is up Petrus!" Kato cries as he steps in to the bunk compartment from the heads, his revolver pointed at Petrus's neck. Petrus turns to look at Kato. Jasmine, seizing her chance, jumps out of the bunk and releasing all her pent up emotions she crashes the heavy steel ash tray she had taken off Kato's desk smack down onto the neck of Petrus who slumps to the floor.

"That felt so good!" Jasmine cries as she rushes into the arms of Kato who holds her close. For a few brief seconds nothing else seems to matter to them. Reluctantly Kato ends the embrace.

"Let's get him tied up. When he wakes I want some answers from him. Now I have a ship to captain."

Saturday Afternoon 4th June 1966

Dumped

"Look over there! That's smoke. It could be "Ocean Star"." Al Corsino shouting to Michael Gregory points to the horizon beyond the bow of Sarah's Pride.

"It's time to call them on the radio Al." Michael Gregory, looking through binoculars, trying to spot the shape of "Ocean Star" under the smoke, intones with not a shred of emotion in his voice.

"Where's my money man? De ship is over there. I need dat money now man 'fore Eugene dun come back. He will wanna take over now we can see dat ship. I'm surprised he ain't come out sooner than this man? What's happening man?" Clyde shouts. Michael Gregory slowly puts his binoculars down and saunters over.

"Your skipper is indisposed. So that just leaves you to carry on for now. Steer towards that smoke."

"O K but I don't like being here wiv out Eugene. You know man?" Clyde speaks with doubt creeping in to his voice.

"Now, I am a man of my word. Here is your money." Michael Gregory holds two fifty dollar bills between the tips of two fingers. Clyde grabs the bills and stuffs them in his trousers.

"Everything will be fine. Just get us to that ship!" Michael Gregory steps behind Clyde who is watching Al start to fiddle with the radio controls.

"This is "Sara's Pride" out of Bermuda, giving out a May Day urgent signal. We got a leak and our pump is broken. We have an hour before we must abandon ship. Can any one help please?" Al operates the radio like a professional switching over from transmitting to receiving. Clyde has listened with his mouth wide open in disbelief.

"Hey man! What you doing, we ain't leaking, wot is your game man? I'm fetching Eugene right now!" Before Clyde can move Michael Gregory places his Beretta pistol into his ear. Clyde looks puzzled until it dawns on him what is sticking in his ear.

"Listen up! If you want to live do as you are told! This gun is small calibre, but, if I pull the trigger the bullet will enter your brain quicker than you can move. So take it easy. Throttle the engine back to cruising speed. I am watching you and my finger is on the trigger. Don't tempt me! Do you understand?" Michael Gregory whispers. Clyde nods his head and reduces power as ordered.

"Sara's Pride" this is "Ocean Star" we are thirty minutes away. You are on our radar. We can pick you up. We are inbound for Bermuda, over!" A reassuring voice comes out of the radio speaker. Michael Gregory gives a grin of satisfaction at Al Corsino who responds with his usual icy stare and with no emotion in his voice replies to thank "Ocean Star".

Al moves away from the radio. A few minutes later Eugene Jordan appears from his cabin. He is held in check by the knife which Al Corsino is holding firmly against his wind pipe. With the knife restricting any sudden movement Eugene is forced to shuffle slowly in the direction required by Al Corsino. Looking confused and worried Eugene Jordan sees Clyde at the helm with a gun pointed in his ear. He tries to call out but pressure from the knife, expertly handled by Al Corsino, stifles the shout before it is released. The two men continue their slow shuffle out onto the deck. As Eugene gets to the port side deck edge; with not a word and no warning; Al Corsino releases the knife pressure from Eugene's throat. Eugene, slightly off balance, turns to confront his captor. Al, anticipating this move, has swivelled like a professional boxer and with both his feet firmly planted on the deck he pushes at Eugene. With an expression of surprise mixed with anger Eugene topples over board. Within seconds "Sara's Pride" is twenty metres away from Eugene Jordan who is bobbing in the waves. Al Corsino cuts a rope holding a protective tyre and heaves it in the direction of Eugene who makes a desperate attempt to secure himself to it.

"OK sailor. You are next. You can go jump in right now. Otherwise I'll have you tossed in with a slug in your back. It's your choice sailor. What's it to be? You got until I count to five". Michael Gregory snarls at the mate who can't believe what he has witnessed.

"One . . . . Two . . . . Three . . . .

"OK Man I'll jump give me one of dem tyres man please an. I'll jump man." Clyde pleads. Al Corsino throws another tyre over board and at the same time Clyde hears the Beretta being cocked. He runs to the side of "Sara's Pride" and jumps into the sea. Clyde catches a brief glimpse of his skipper clinging to a tyre over one hundred metres away. Clyde swims with ease to the tyre floating nearby and heads towards his skipper.

"Get the dynamite ready Al!" Michael Gregory commands as he takes control of the helm.

"I'm on it boss. Where's the kid? Do you need him out here?" Al Corsino queries as he strides purposefully back to the cabin for his rucksack.

Mercator is in the cabin. He sits on the bottom bunk with his head in his hands going over recent events. He killed his father. In a moment of passion; a split second was all it took; one moment alive, the next, taking his last gasp of air. No way can it be changed. Now he must accept it. Only now in the silence of the cabin, with no one to interrupt does the enormity of what he has done sink in.

"Get your no good skinny ass up on deck! We got work to do!" Al Corsino shouts as he rushes in to the cabin and lunges up to the top bunk to release his rucksack.

"Come on dammit! Let's go!" Al pulls Mercator up from the bunk and pushes him out of the cabin.

"Don't push me around! You had better treat me with respect. Remember who I am." Mercator screams back at Al as he is pushed unceremoniously onto the deck.

"Ah Mercator, come here and take the helm. Keep on course for that ship! Do you see it?" Michael Gregory calls.

"Why should I? What's in it for me?" Mercator queries sulkily.

"Well now. I suggest you take a look astern. Let me help you." Al grabs hold of Mercator and force marches him to the stern.

"There are two men out there. They were on this boat just a few minutes ago. Would you like to join them? If you survive guess what? You'll be back in Bermuda answering a lot of questions. Now co-operate or face the consequences. We ain't playing here sonny boy." Al man handles Mercator back to Michael Gregory. Quietly Mercator takes over the helm. For now he decides to comply with these low life hoodlums but his face is scowling with rage.

"Sara's Pride" this is "Ocean Star" we are fifteen minutes away. We are reducing speed so by the time we come alongside we should be stationary to aid picking you up. Please acknowledge, over!"

Al acknowledges.

"Ocean Star" that's my father's . . . . I mean that's my ship. Howden was running it in Bermuda. She should be in the Indian Ocean. Why is she here?" Mercator questions his face now looking more suspicious than angry.

"Never mind that right now. Just keep us on course!" Michael Gregory orders. Gradually "Ocean Star" creeps closer. She is riding high in the sea. Michael Gregory studies her outline carefully. He sees the hole on her port side just forward of mid ships a few feet above the waterline.

"Perfect" he mutters and grins.

"Al, escort our friend back to the cabin. Then come straight back!" Michael Gregory takes over control of "Sara's Pride" and steers a course to be alongside the hole. With less than five minutes before "Ocean Star" is alongside Al returns.

"See that hole in the hull Al? Get the dynamite set in your pack. As soon as we are alongside I want you to chuck the pack in that hole. Then we get the hell away."

"OK boss. I'm working on it right now. The dynamite is all hooked up. All I got to do is light the fuse."

"Here we go two hundred yards, one hundred yards." Michael Gregory intones in his banker's voice, cool and unperturbed.

The radio blares out

"Sara's Pride" this is "Ocean Star" please have your crew ready to come on board via the ladder we are dropping now. We have not got much time please hurry. We will drop two lines to secure you to our port side, please acknowledge, over"

With just fifty yards to go Michael Gregory throttles right back so that the engine is just providing steerage way in the now calm sea. He takes "Sara's Pride" out in a circle to come alongside "Ocean Star" so that both ships are travelling in the same direction.

"Ocean Star" is twenty yards away, then just ten yards away. The rusty scratched and battered port side of the ship towers over "Sara's Pride". Al has climbed onto the cabin roof with his rucksack containing the dynamite. He lights the fuse. There is just fifteen feet between the ships.

Two ropes come crashing down onto "Sara's Pride" from "Ocean Star". Al and Michael Gregory ignore them.

"Sara's Pride" this is "Ocean Star" secure the ropes. Acknowledge." The radio voice is insistent with urgency.

Michael Gregory brings "Sara's Pride" alongside the jagged gaping hole. Al cannot see into the hole. There is just a dark forbidding emptiness. He checks that the fuse is well lit then with no further thought he heaves the dynamite into the hole and jumps down from the cabin roof.

"Sara's Pride" surges forward as Michael Gregory pushes the throttle to the maximum and steers away from "Ocean Star".

"Sara's Pride" this is "Ocean Star". What are you playing at? Please respond now."

Michael Gregory looks at Al who shows no emotion. Al looks at his watch which shows three minutes to detonation time. "Sara's Pride" is thirty metres away from "Ocean Star".

As warned by Eugene Jordan the engine of "Sara's Pride" has been overworked. It gives out a scream of protest, shudders and goes still and silent. The abused, ancient long suffering engine has seized up. "Sara's Pride" flounders in the ocean close to "Ocean Star". There are two minutes to go before the dynamite, so expertly prepared by Al, explodes in the bowels of "Ocean Star".

Thoughts about Kato

"Are you alright Sir; you took a nasty fall last night." The radio operator asks as Kato walks past the communications room on his way to the bridge.

"What do you know about that?" Kato gives the man a hard stare. He is intrigued to learn what story Petrus has been spreading. Kato has known the radio operator for many years and believes he can be trusted.

"Well Sir, I was returning from the heads. Petrus was in here bending over you. He said you tripped and hit your head. I helped carry you back to your cabin. Then Petrus dismissed me. He said he would take care of you. That's all I can tell you Sir, but I am very pleased to see you back on your feet Sir. We need your experience with the ship being in such a mess. I can't ever remember such a difficult voyage." The radio operator confides looking expectantly at Kato for his take on the events.

"Petrus is confined to my cabin. He has abused his position. He has no further authority on this vessel. When we get to port he will be charged with assault and unlawful kidnapping. I shall require you to provide a witness statement. Is that clear?" Kato stares intently at the hapless operator.

"Yes Sir. I must say I was doubtful when Petrus said you had tripped because I have never known you miss your footing . . ." before the radio operator can finish the radio erupts into sound. It is "Sara's Pride" with the may day request for help. Kato hears the message and enters the communications room.

"Do we have this boat on our radar? Is any other vessel in the vicinity?" Kato asks the bridge. Kato is informed that "Ocean Star" is the only vessel able to afford a rescue in the timescale reported. Saving souls in peril on the sea, the sailor's code, cannot be ignored. Kato knows he has to help. He orders communications to be transferred to the bridge where he takes charge.

On his bridge Kato is pleased that his plan to raise the hull has succeeded. The jagged hole in "Ocean Star's" port side is out of the water.

One problem solved. Now here comes another. At least this "Sara's Pride" is not far away and on our original course. It should be over quickly.

Kato gets ready to brief his crew on the rescue plan.

Jasmine has had a shower and something to eat. Sitting quietly in her cabin, drinking coffee, she is trying to make sense of the events from the past twenty four hours. In particular, she is going over that last hug with Kato. There was more to that embrace. Her womanly instincts remind her that whilst in his arms, although it was fleeting, she experienced a range of feelings. Why? Jasmine racks her brains for answers. Kato is much older than me. Perhaps he is a substitute father figure? No that's not it she decides. My feelings when I think of Pa are very different. In that embrace with Kato lasting less than a couple of seconds my heart fluttered, my skin tingled, my senses were heightened, I felt something exciting was about to happen. In the last few weeks we have shared experiences which have brought us closer to each other. Battling my drug dependency, escaping New York, fighting Petrus? So very different from the experiences with all the men I have known. Some made me laugh, a few were kind and courteous, very few were good in bed; most I cannot even remember what they look like.

So what is it that makes Kato different? He is handsome in a rough way. His thick grey hair, the white beard, blue eyes and his tanned seaman's face give him a distinguished look.

She shakes her head

This is not about looks. This is about how I feel. Right now I cannot explain why I feel like I do. Perhaps, more time will reveal the answer.

Jasmine stands up, stretches her arms and walks towards the cabin door. As she opens the door the background noise from "Ocean Star's" twin propellers drops off noticeably. "Ocean Star" has commenced her slowdown, within ten minutes she will be alongside "Sara's Pride" for the rescue operation.

Chapter Thirty Two

Dynamite

Saturday afternoon 4th June 1966

"Sara's Pride"

"Get those ropes over the side!" Kato orders as they near "Sara's Pride".

"We are not getting any radio response from them Captain." The radio operator calls out.

"What's going on Agios? Why have we stopped?" Jasmine, out of breath from rushing up the gangway stairs to the bridge wants to know.

"It's nothing to worry about Jasmine. We are picking up some people from this little boat "Sara's Pride". We should be on our way in a few minutes." Kato answers as he turns to the radio operator

"Try them on the radio once more!"

"Sara's Pride" is Eugene's boat. He's my Pa's friend. I'll see if I can spot him." Jasmine shrieks and rushes over to the port side of the bridge.

"Have those ropes been secured?" Kato queries with a tinge of impatience edging his voice.

"That's Eugene's boat alright. Eugene ain't there and I can't see Clyde his mate either. Those two go everywhere together. I can only see two strangers." Jasmine shouts across to Kato.

"They are ignoring the ropes Captain. It doesn't make sense. Someone's climbed onto the cabin roof. He's thrown a bag towards us. Now the boat is moving away." A deckhand relays by walkie talkie to the bridge.

"Do they want our help or not? What are they playing at? Try the radio again! Let's see if we can make some sense of all this." Kato pounds the bridge desk in frustration.

"Now they have stopped about thirty metres on our port side." the deck hand reports.

"Still no reply Captain." the radio operator reports.

"They are still stationary." The voice shouts out from the walkie talkie.

"Prepare the lifeboat to be launched, let's get over to them" Kato orders. Two deckhands rush over to the starboard side of "Ocean Star" where they free the lifeboat from its fastenings and commence winching the boat down towards the sea. Kato deputes two men to man the lifeboat and sail around to "Sara's Pride".

Explosive action

Kato watches with a professional eye as the crew start to winch the lifeboat out over the side. With no prior warning, Kato feels a violent tremor coming from below deck, followed by a dull boom sounding like a distant clap of thunder. Everyone on the bridge looks around curious to find out the source. They stare at each other with anxious expressions on their faces. Kato is the first to react. His sailor's instinct, honed over many years, senses danger. He knows that the hold is the source of his concerns but right now he does not understand what has happened. His leadership talents take over automatically.

"Sound the alarm emergency stations! Everyone put on your life jackets and helmets! Carry on with the life boat launch but have it stay close on station to wait further orders! The people on "Sara's Pride" will have to wait. Deck, get me a situation report on that hold!" Kato barks out his instructions calmly whilst also making sure that Jasmine has her life jacket and helmet properly fitted on her.

In hold five most of the force from Al Corsino's dynamite attack finds the exit of least resistance. The lethal blast emerges like an angry tornado through the jagged hole in the hull heading like a powerful death giving cluster bomb towards "Sara's Pride".

The force remaining in the hold smashes into the arms crate, splitting timbers and sending pieces with assorted munitions boxes hurtling into the sides of holds four and six. The badly damaged crate hurtles across the hold smashing against the ship's side. The nitro glycerine, stored deep in the centre of the crate, for maximum protection, is exposed to the elements. Fragments of splintered timbers penetrate the vacuum packs protecting the vials of nitro glycerine. Until now the pure nitro-glycerine has been stable. The un—diluted explosive maintained in a frozen state at ten degrees centigrade in the vacuum sealed packs was safe. Now, some of the packs are damaged; the nitro-glycerine's safety is compromised. The ambient temperature in the hold is twenty degrees centigrade. At thirteen degrees centigrade the material will start to become sensitive to movement. The faster it thaws the greater the risk of it becoming unstable.

"This tub is going nowhere. This engine is knackered" Al Corsino grunts. He stares impassively as he and Michael Gregory get the small dinghy with outboard engine into the sea and stow away provisions. Michael Gregory moves to the stern and prepares to get the engine started.

Al looks at his watch and whispers

"Any second now!" then he looks across the water towards "Ocean Star". He watches with satisfaction as the exploding dynamite rocks the ship. Neither Al Corsino nor Michael Gregory had anticipated the main force of the explosion to funnel out of the ragged hole in the hull. Within seconds, after the explosion, small armaments, wooden splinters, nails from the crate containing arms and jagged metal shards smash into "Sara's Pride". Pieces rip into the deck and hull. Al and Michael Gregory are peppered with debris. Mercator comes out on deck to find out what has happened. He sees the two men bent over clutching their faces in the boat.

"Where are you two going?" Mercator cries looking alarmed and puzzled.

"West, you can stay with this tub. There's only room for two in here." Michael Gregory answers casually.

"I'm damned if I will. I'm coming on board now. I give the orders. You people are just hired helps." Mercator retorts contemptuously and starts to move towards the dinghy.

"I said stay! Oh boy! You have got this coming to you." Michael Gregory tells Mercator and as nonchalantly as if he was lighting a cigarette he pulls out his Beretta and fires two shots in swift succession. Mercator stares in disbelief before collapsing on the deck clutching each knee in turn.

"Don't forget we got evidence how you killed your Pa." Michael Gregory calls waving the laundry bag from the Princess hotel. Mercator starts to whimper.

The life boat from "Ocean Star" is in the sea. The two man crew release her from the shackles linking her to "Ocean Star". The boat maintains position on the starboard side awaiting further orders from Kato.

"Now there is a third man. Two have got into a dinghy. They seem to be in some kind of trouble." Jasmine shouts.

"Well I'll be damned. That looks like Costas's son. What is he doing here?" Kato queries as he stares intently across at the figure on "Sara's Pride". His observations are interrupted after just a few seconds as "Ocean Star" is pushed up; almost right out of the sea. The stern end of the vessel housing the crew quarters and the bridge slump back as the explosive force from the nitro-glycerine travelling at thirty times the speed of sound pulverises the centre of the ship forcing it upwards. Before anyone can react the super intense air pressure pushed from the centre of the explosion hits the bridge with a tremendous ear splitting "whoosh" and smashes the windows sending shards of glass whizzing about. Kato and Jasmine along with the others on the bridge are sent flying. Every one is slithering, sliding or rolling across the deck. Their movements are uncontrollable until, one after another, they collide with the steel walls or the protruding edges of various desks. The crew are in shock, disorientated by the noise and debris scattered all around. Some are feeling pain from the violent bumping into physical barriers. Jasmine has bruised her legs and grazed her arms. Kato's order to don helmets has prevented serious injury. As Kato starts to pull himself up from the deck, the ship is dealt another devastating blow as the nitro-glycerine from hold four erupts with nuclear like power. This second lethal force concentrates its powers on the already badly damaged mid ships section. "Ocean Star" is split in two.

Life Boat

"Abandon ship send out a May Day signal." Kato gives the orders. So far as he can establish there have been no serious injuries just cuts from flying debris and bruising from everyone being thrown around. The bridge has all its windows blown away. Debris has smashed into equipment including the radio.

"The radio's bust skipper, I can't send a may day!" The radio operator cries out above the noise from the ship breaking up.

The front of the ship from holds five to eight has broken away and is filling with water. The stern end is tilting at an ever increasing angle towards the port side. Kato and Jasmine crawl and slide along the debris strewn deck to the gangway stairs.

"Don't leave me here! Mercator screams at Michael Gregory. Mercator looks at Al Corsino extracting an ugly looking splinter from his forearm as the shock wave from the nitro-glycerine explosion hits "Sara's Pride" with hurricane force. Glass is smashed, the oil drums for catching sharks are ripped from their fastenings and smash into the cabin. One drum hits Mercator on his side and sends him hurtling across the deck. Debris flying through the air from "Ocean Star's" holds smashes into the wooden boat making ominous rat a tat tat like noises. "Ocean Star's" violent movement from the first explosion of nitro-glycerine causes a large wave. This wave smashes into "Sara's Pride" at the same time as the explosive force from the second explosion of nitro-glycerine goes off in hold four of "Ocean Star". The wave catches the dinghy and sends it on its way with the two occupants hanging on for dear life. Mercator lies unconscious in the smashed cabin of "Sara's Pride".

"I must release Petrus or he will be trapped. Make your way to the starboard side and get in the lifeboat! Go now! There is no time to argue!" Kato shouts at Jasmine as they lurch from side to side with the ship's uncontrolled movement.

Jasmine stumbles into broken furniture as she staggers along the corridor to the hatchway exit onto the deck. On deck Jasmine is caught up in a maelstrom. It looks like a battle scene. Jasmine looks aghast at men clinging to rails to secure them selves against the list as the port side slips gradually into the ocean. Hose pipes lay scattered across the deck discarded when the crew realised the ship was doomed. Now they are being used as aids to climb up the steep incline to the starboard side. Jasmine grabs a thick red rubber hose which has been looped around the deck rail. Slowly she hauls hand over hand on the hose. Finally, gasping for breath from her effort, she reaches the edge of the deck. She gasps in horror as she peeps over the edge to see the lifeboat floating upside down in the ocean. Four crew men have clambered down the side of the ship. Secured by lines from the top deck they are frantically pulling on ropes trying to right the lifeboat. Jasmine can see that the water pouring in to the broken and fractured mid ships is creating an unstoppable momentum. Soon the rear half of "Ocean Star" will be side up in the sea and the starboard side will, for an uncertain amount of time, be lying horizontal before sinking into the depths.

It has taken Kato much longer to get to Petrus than he had expected. The listing of "Ocean Star" has made the corridor leading to the cabin an obstacle course. Some cabin doors have broken off and furniture has forced its way into the corridor and has then slid down to pile up at the end. Kato has to fight through the tangled heap then, hanging on to cabin door handles, he struggles up the steep incline to the end of the corridor.

Petrus has lost all trace of his former arrogance. He has been locked in Kato's cabin; powerless to take action. He is still dazed from the bang on his head but he heard and felt all the explosions. He started feeling seriously afraid as the ship started to tilt. He is very relieved to see Kato open the door.

"There is no time for explanations. We have to get out now!" Kato barks releasing Petrus from the shackles he had placed on him just a few hours ago.

"Skipper I am really sorry. I will make it up to you I promise." Petrus blurts out as they race out of the cabin.

By the time they get back on the open deck the list of the ship's stern has increased to thirty degrees. Kato sees Jasmine hanging on to the deck rail struggling to keep her balance. He scrambles up the steep incline using the fire hose to reach her. He is soon followed by Petrus.

"Keep that son of a bitch away from me Agios!" Jasmine cries.

"It's OK miss. I am so sorry for everything that I have done. I know you can't forget what I did but for now let me just help." Petrus implores.

"We must work together. There is no way that life boat will be righted. We will have to secure ourselves as best we can on the up turned hull. Petrus! Get the men to start weaving the ropes from side to side on the life boat for everyone to hold on to! Also see if they can rig up some shelter and a mast and sail. Tell them to hurry there is not much time!" Kato urges as he examines Jasmine's grazed arms.

"Yes Sir!" Petrus answers enthusiastically relieved to have something to do.

"You two, get provisions from the galley! Pack them in watertight containers! Make sure you bring plenty of water! Get blankets and warm clothes! Rendezvous back here as soon as you can! Get going Hurry!" Kato commands two of the crew. Jasmine watches with admiration as amongst the chaos Kato takes command.

After thirty minutes of frantic work the up turned hull of the life boat has been criss-crossed by a latticework of ropes. Each rope has been secured to the fittings by the men diving underwater. A canvas shelter has been rigged up. Two oars lashed firmly to the stern rudder fixings serve as a makeshift mast which has a canvas square attached. Every one has scrambled down the now almost horizontal side of "Ocean Star" to clamber onto the hull of the lifeboat and secure themselves to the ropes. There have been no fatalities. Three men have broken limbs. Everyone has cuts and bruises. Two men on each side have been deputed by Kato to be oarsmen. Kato checks everyone is secure in the ropes then gives the order to start rowing.

Kato's eyes go moist as he watches first the bow section of his ship, then the rear sink beneath the ocean. The hiss of air coming to the surface from the broken ship sounds like the dying gasps from a drowning man. Kato has never lost a ship until now. He feels numb as though he has lost a loved one.

The battered wreck of "Sara's Pride" drifting aimlessly in the sea, previously hidden from the lifeboat by the bulk of "Ocean Star", is now visible. Kato orders his men to row to the wreck.

Chapter Thirty Three

Radio

Saturday afternoon 4th June 1966

Message

"Hello Duane? It's Jonno here. I've just had a radio message from Adrian and George. You are not going to believe this." Inspector Johnson speaks in an unusually excited voice to Duane Perkins. Duane has gone back to McKinley airport frustrated that they could not locate either Mercator or Costas Tinopolis this morning at the Princess Hotel.

"Hmmm Jonno let me take a wild guess. Adrian "water melon mouth" Cuthbert has finally chucked out tea as a drink and agrees that sweet strong coffee is now his drink of choice. I'm right aren't I?" Duane Pickens drawls out.

"Or maybe I've got another dinner invite"? I just can't wait for you to tell me Jonno."

"No! No! Duane. This is quite bizarre. They saw a flash and some smoke then they picked up a piece of clothing in the sea."

"Jeezus Jonno! So what! We are getting no where with this. I can't justify my expenses staying here because your Limey mates found some rags in the Atlantic Ocean." Duane interrupts in exasperation.

"Duane if you would please not interrupt. The cloth they found has not been in the sea long. It has the initial "C T" stitched in. The best bit is they also found a severed hand, floating in the sea, with a ring on the finger. The ring has an inscription reading Costas Tinopolis for his 21st birthday." Inspector Johnson pauses, looking triumphantly down into the telephone receiver, expecting Duane to interrupt or shout. Instead there is silence.

"Duane did you get that?"

"I'm thinking Jonno. Do you think someone has bumped off Costas?" Duane enquires his tone much more respectful.

"Remember the blood spots in Costas's suite and the blood stained bath robe we found in Mercator's room? So, yes, something is definitely up. One more thing, one of my constables spoke with the night porter at the hotel and it seems that three people left with a boat called "Sara's Pride" last evening. He recognised two of them as being in the suite next to Costas."

"Did you get their details?" Duane interrupts.

"Yes. They have given addresses in New York. Can you get your guys to check them out? Inspector Johnson asks.

"Sure. What about the third guy? Who is he?" Duane questions.

"We don't know, but, Mercator is missing and it looks like Costas is dead so maybe the third man could be Mercator."

"So what's the plan now Jonno?" Duane asks.

"I shall keep in radio contact with Adrian. I am trying to speak with the skipper of "Sara's Pride". In any event "Sara's Pride" should return sometime tomorrow. Then I will have some questions for those on board." Inspector Johnson advises Duane.

"OK Jonno. Keep me posted!"

A life saved

Adrian has boxed the severed hand of Costas Tinopolis and placed it in the boat's ice box. Inspector Johnson wants it preserved for evidence.

For the last thirty minutes George has been at "Pembroke Lady's" helm with Leonora in the co pilot's seat. She is keeping a sharp look out for rogue waves. At the speed they are travelling any abnormal wave could flip "Pembroke Lady" over. They both know it is vital to keep a sharp look out so that avoiding action can be taken. The sea is now mostly calm so George is able to maintain "Pembroke Lady's" high speed whilst avoiding the few dangerous waves spotted by Leonora. He wants to meet up with "Ocean Star" as soon as possible so that Jasmine can be reunited with her family. Then, and only then, will George feel that he has honoured the trust placed in him by Lenny and her father.

"Look! Over there Howdy! There's something in the water." Leonora cries out pointing to an object on the port side some fifty metres away. "Pembroke Lady's" bow drops into the sea as George throttles back and steers the boat towards the object.

"Why have we slowed down George?" Adrian asks as he pops his head out from the galley. Charlie comes up from the cabin where he has been cat napping. He scratches his head as he wanders over to the port side of "Pembroke Lady", curious as to why the boat has slowed right down

"Oh! My Lord! Dat's Clyde he's Eugene's mate on "Sara's Pride". Clyde! It's me Charlie . . . Charlie Rucker.

Hang on! We'll get you out." Adrian, hearing Charlie's shouting, runs up behind him and seeing the man in the sea clinging to an old tyre reacts with lightening speed and jumps in. In seconds he is alongside Clyde who is crying and blubbering incoherently.

"It's OK old man. Calm yourself. You are safe now. Let's get you aboard." Adrian re assures Clyde as he pushes him to the side of "Pembroke Lady" where Charlie has fixed an aluminium ladder. With Adrian pushing Clyde is able to clamber up the ladder. On the deck he stands shivering dripping sea water onto the deck. Charlie wraps a blanket around Clyde's shoulders. Clyde is sobbing as he hugs Charlie the only word that Charlie can understand is

"Skee . . . . pa . . . Skee . . . . pa . . ."

"What is you bin doin' here Clyde? Where's Eugene? Where's de boat?" Charlie questions; desperate to know where his old friend Eugene is. With sympathetic persuasion from Leonora Clyde blurts out what happened.

"Charlie, take Clyde below and into some dry clothes. George, let's start searching the area for the other man Eugene. He can't be too far away if Clyde's account is accurate. I am going to radio Inspector Johnson." Adrian orders.

A Working Radio

"Secure the ropes to the side rails." Kato orders as the upturned lifeboat bumps alongside the debris strewn, pock marked hulk of ""Sara's Pride"". Kato and Petrus climb onto the deck and pick their way around loose oil drums, their seaman's boots crunch on broken glass, scattered across the deck, as they make their way cautiously, to the dashboard in the wheel house to search for the radio.

"Let's hope the radio on this wreck is working." Kato mutters to himself.

"Captain, there's a man behind this drum." Petrus shouts as he rolls the oil drum out of the way to examine the unconscious Mercator.

"What's he doing there? Ah here is the radio. Thank God. It's working." Kato calls as he flicks the power switch and sees the red signal light flash on.

"I am going to get a May Day signal off whilst there is power in this set." Kato shouts over to Petrus who is bending over the body.

"I don't believe this. It's Mercator, the boss's son. He's been shot in both knees. He needs help" Petrus shouts back at Kato.

"This is Captain Kato of "Ocean Star". This is a May Day message. "Ocean Star" has sunk after an explosion. There are ten of us, three wounded. We are one hundred eighty miles south east of Bermuda. Our lifeboat is upturned and we are tied up with a small fishing boat "Sara's Pride" with one man who has bullet wounds. We require urgent assistance." Kato switches the radio to receive and swivels around to look at Petrus.

"I saw Mercator from "Ocean Star". There were three on board. I wonder where the other two are. Is he conscious? Kato asks Petrus.

"No Sir. He is out cold. He is breathing. I'm going to get our first aid guy across." Petrus responds.

"Captain Kato this is Inspector Johnson of Her Majesties Colonial Police in Bermuda. We have received your message and have requested Motor Boat "Pembroke Lady" to give urgent assistance. She should be with you within an hour. I have requested them to contact you direct. Please maintain your position. Please confirm message received."

Gimme the Grumman

"Duane? It's Jonno here again. We have a new development. "Ocean Star" has sunk. The crew are on an upturned life boat and guess what? They are tied up to "Sara's Pride". Someone's got bullet wounds. There is definitely something very suspicious going on. Can we get out there on your sea plane?

"Gimme one minute Jonno. I'll get back to you." Duane slams the telephone down and races down the corridor to the office of U S Strategic Air Control where Colonel Jim Lucas is sitting at his desk dialling a number on his telephone. Duane bursts in, not observing the normal protocol of knocking the door before entering, and rams his hand down on the telephone.

"Hey Duane, what's gotten into you? Where's the fire?" Jim Lucas, keeping cool, although inwardly annoyed at Duane's barging in to his office, stares at Duane.

"Jim I'm real sorry for this we got a genuine emergency. There's a ship down one hundred eighty miles south with ten crew and a guy who's been shot. I need the Grumman pronto . . . please? It's the fastest way out to them." Duane pleads looking at Jim Lucas's face turning from indifference to interest.

"O K Duane. You got it. Get to St George's harbour. I'll scramble her. She'll be with you in thirty minutes."

"Jim I owe you one" Duane smiles as he races out.

"Jonno, its Duane. You got twenty five minutes to get your ass to St Georges. The sea plane's on its way."

Chapter Thirty Four

Rescue

Saturday afternoon 4th June 1966

Choose one or eleven

"If we can't find this guy in the next few minutes we will have to leave him for now. "Ocean Star" has sunk. There are eleven people needing our help. We have to get to them as soon as we can." Adrian shouts to George and Leonora who are scanning the sea desperately looking for Eugene.

"Have you any news of Jasmine? Is she safe? What about Kato? Is he with her?" George queries whilst Leonora looks aghast her hands covering her face.

"No news except there are three injured and it was Kato who sent the may day signal. So the chances are she is safe with Kato. Let's get them rescued and come back to look for this guy. We have to go with the odds. An eleven to one situation gives us no alternative." Adrian explains.

"Let's do it. It's like looking for a needle in a haystack out here. It's a tough call but you are right Adrian." George agrees. He turns the wheel to send "Pembroke Lady" south east and selects full speed.

"I'll see if I can call up Kato on the radio. Let him know we are on the way." Adrian advises.

Late afternoon Saturday 4th June 1966

Clyde feels guilt

"Hello "Sara's Pride" this is "Pembroke Lady". We are twenty miles away. Our speed is thirty knots. Request you discharge flares in thirty five minutes. Over" Adrian speaks into the radio as George keeps the boat on course with Leonora maintaining watch by his side. Charlie and Clyde are below.

Clyde is upset because he could not reach Eugene in the sea. When he was forced to jump into the sea there was just a few hundred metres separating him from Eugene. Being a strong swimmer Clyde, with all the naive arrogance of youth, never doubted that he would be able to reach Eugene. More experienced sailors know that the sea is fickle and can never be taken for granted. Winds and ocean currents are immense forces which can never be ignored when using the sea. After twenty minutes of frantic swimming instead of getting closer to Eugene the gap between them had increased. Clyde's falling energy levels compelled him to abandon Eugene. Now, sitting safe in the cabin of "Pembroke Lady", Clyde is overcome with guilt. If he had not taken that bribe maybe Eugene and he would still be on board "Sara's Pride". The fifty dollar notes he snatched in his greedy haste are sodden in his jeans pocket; a secret testimony to the betrayal of his boss who is somewhere on his own in the death zone known as the Bermuda Triangle. If Eugene is not rescued Clyde knows his burden of guilt will be too much to take.

"Adrian could you ask "Sara's Pride" if Jasmine is OK please?" George asks giving Leonora a re—assuring look.

Chapter Thirty Five
Marlin

Late afternoon Saturday 4th June 1966

Grumman and a heat seeker

"Well Jonno of the Yard now I've seen everything." Duane chuckles as Inspector Johnson hands the Police motor cycle crash helmet back to his sergeant who has ferried his superior on a death defying ride through Bermuda's narrow, winding lanes at speeds well in excess of the maximum speed limit.

"It was the quickest way to get here Laddie. Let's go! Lives are on the line!" Inspector Johnson gives Duane a look of impatience. They race down the dock steps and climb aboard the Grumman HU 16. The sea plane's twin engines throb loudly. As soon as the fuselage door is closed the sea plane moves quickly out of the harbour and accelerates to take off speed.

"We need to do a search some twenty miles from where "Ocean Star" went down. There is a man missing. He's been in the sea for over four hours. Adrian will be able to deal with the survivors from "Ocean Star" whilst we look for this guy." Duane informs Inspector Johnson as they don their life jackets in the sea plane. Inspector Johnson fingers the cold steel of his trusted Smith &

Wesson Model 36 Revolver in his jacket pocket. He wonders if it will be needed on this trip.

"This is the position we were given. Let's carry out a two mile search north to south then south to north. The new heat seeking equipment is gonna prove useful." Duane advises the pilot who is positioning the sea plane for its first search run.

"What's this new heat toy you Yanks have got Duane?" Inspector Johnson asks.

"It's kinda secret Jonno. We are experimenting with it here. It's been developed by NASA part of our man on the moon programme. The machine picks up heat discrepancies like body heat in the sea." Duane winks at Inspector Johnson giving him a conspiratorial look.

Marlin Attack

Two hundred feet beneath the hull of "Sara's Pride" two vacuum sealed containers, survivors from the explosions that ripped "Ocean Star" apart, are moved by air bubbles seeking the surface. A pocket of air is being released under pressure from the increasing weight of water crushing down on the sinking ship. The movement in the hold is slight but it is sufficient to move the yellow and black painted canisters, carriers of destruction, away from obstructions and set them free from the confines of the sinking wreck. The canisters rise slowly.

"Jasmine, come over! Your father is on the radio." Captain Kato shouts across to the upturned lifeboat where Jasmine is seated roped up.

"Pa, Oh my Lordy" Jasmine shrieks as she unties her self and starts to tip toe cautiously over the webbing of

ropes crisscrossing the upturned hull. Kato watches and waits at the guard rail on "Sara's Pride".

Nearing the surface the canisters glint from the strong sunlight penetrating the crystal clear sea water. The school of Atlantic Blue Marlins are attracted by the yellow colour of the glinting canisters. The lead Marlin weighs a solid eight hundred pounds and is accelerating to a speed in excess of fifty miles per hour. He senses a tasty late afternoon snack. Fifteen feet beneath the surface he smashes into the nearest canister his spear like snout penetrates the vacuum between the reinforced double skinned plastic. Still accelerating the Marlin soars towards the surface wanting to investigate the interesting dark patches he sees. Pushed to the surface by the Marlin the yellow canister now has warm sea water reacting with the nitroglycerin. The solid state nitroglycerin is heating up and becoming sensitive to shock waves. The sleek ten foot, eight hundred pound master fighter from the Atlantic Ocean flies out of the sea at sixty miles per hour. Soaring ten feet above the lifeboat the Marlin narrowly misses Jasmine who loses her balance and trips. Her fingers slip as she tries to grab a rope. Kato watches in horror, powerless to help, as Jasmine slithers into the sea.

The flying Marlin gives Kato a malevolent stare. Everything has happened so quickly Kato has no time to react. Instinctively he tries to duck from the oncoming giant fish. The lower fins, sharp as razors, scrape and lacerate the top of Kato's head. Stunned he loses balance and falls onto the glass strewn deck. Seconds later the explosive force from the nitroglycerin erupts from the sea ten feet away from Sara's Pride. The force smashes into the hull penetrating the timbers of the stricken boat.

Chapter Thirty Six

Lifeboat again

Late afternoon Saturday 4th June 1966

Fear and Panic

Shock and surprise mixed with fear were the emotions experienced by Jasmine as she fell into the sea between the sides of the lifeboat and "Sara's Pride". Afraid of being crushed between the two vessels Jasmine takes a deep breath and dives under the lifeboat emerging on the far side. She clings to one of the ropes attached to the underside. Petrus has seen her. He unties himself from the lifeboat ropes and goes to her assistance.

Pandemonium breaks out amongst the survivors on the lifeboat as the unstable nitroglycerin erupts. The explosive shock wave sets the lifeboat rolling violently in the sea. Petrus is thrown off the up turned lifeboat and he falls into the sea near Jasmine. The violent movement of the lifeboat forces her to let go of the rope. Both she and Petrus are pushed away from the security of the lifeboat which is drifting away.

Kato staggers to his feet. He rubs his head and feels sticky warm blood. He has lost sight of Jasmine. He cannot see Petrus on the lifeboat which is rising and falling on the disturbed sea. He has to act "Sara's Pride" is damaged. He knows the boat will not survive. He orders the two deckhands in the cabin to evacuate the injured.

"This is Kato on "Sara's Pride". There has been an explosion. We are sinking. Casualties are being transferred to the lifeboat. I will set off flares now, out." Kato closes down the radio and races past the deckhands bringing an injured seaman on deck. He fires all six of the flares.

"We must keep together Jasmine." Petrus shouts treading sea water as they both watch the lifeboat and "Sara's Pride" drifting further away from them.

"Why does it have to be you?" Jasmine splutters.

"I can make it back to the boat I am a good swimmer. I'll get them to rescue you."

"There's no way. They have their own problems. Didn't you hear the explosion?" Petrus screams.

"No. I'm going back!" Jasmine swims powerfully away as sleek as a seal just like when she tormented Wayne Luther off Carver Island.

"Jasmine, come back!" Petrus shouts despairingly.

Jonnos keen eyes

"No indications so far skipper. That's our third run." The co pilot declares.

"Roger that. How much more time do we have here Duane?" The pilot asks.

"I reckon we have fifteen minutes. Enough time for maybe a few more search legs skipper." Duane responds.

"Duane! Look on the starboard side at two o'clock. Do you see it Laddie?" Inspector Johnson stands up and points down to the sea where a splash of colour in the foamy white breakers created from the sea breeze has caught his attention.

"Lose some height skipper! Let's get a closer look!" Duane orders. The sea plane banks sharply throwing Inspector Johnson off balance.

"Don't take up dancing Jonno!" Duane grins.

"This is "Pembroke Lady". We are closing in on the wreck. There are casualties. We will need assistance. Five minutes to rendezvous." Adrian's voice penetrates into Duane's head phones.

"Aw, that voice, it's getting to me. Why can't young George speak on the radio? Give me a break" Duane grimaces as he and Jonno peer out of the window. The pilot has lowered the lumbering sea plane down to fifty feet above the sea. He judges that the waves are just about safe for him to touch down. The heat sensor beeps loudly.

"We got contact." The co pilot screams excitedly.

The pilot and co pilot struggle with the controls of the Grumman HU 16 sea plane as they negotiate a landing in the sea. Inspector Johnson and Duane Perkins tense up. Even though they are strapped in their seats they feel every lurch and bump from the giant vessel as it bounces in the sea. The pilots have the craft under control and are following the heat sensor signal.

"This is where the heat signal is strongest. Go take a look guys. We can't see down below from these cockpit windows." The pilot shouts into the cabin. Inspector Johnson and Duane Perkins unbuckle from their seats. When the cabin door is opened the intense afternoon light, reflecting off the ocean, floods into the cabin making them squint.

Inspector Johnson clings to a wing strut as he balances on the sea plane's float looking into the sea. A flash of yellow colour shows on the crest of a small wave forty feet away.

"There Duane I see something. Get the dinghy out."

Inspector Johnson and Duane Perkins work frantically to get the dinghy. The sea plane follows the dinghy keeping a safe distance. They see Eugene lying spread eagled over the tire. It is his bright yellow shirt that Inspector Johnson saw.

"This guy is in a real bad way. He looks completely exhausted. I can just about feel his pulse. Let's get him back to the sea plane." Duane orders. The help of the co pilot is needed to transfer Eugene from the dinghy to the shelter of the fuselage. Inspector Johnson strips off Eugene's sodden clothes. Duane gets to work vigorously rubbing Eugene's body, the blue tinge of the skin indicating that Eugene has started to go hypothermic. After ten minutes pummelling Eugene coughs up some sea water and groans.

"It looks like the laddie might make it." Inspector Johnson remarks as the seaplane gets airborne heading toward "Pembroke Lady".

Early evening Saturday 4th June 1966

Prepare for Rescue

"How many are left in the cabin?" Kato asks.

"Just the guy who has the bullet wounds in his knees." The deck hand answers as he helps a sailor with lacerations and a broken arm across to the lifeboat. Kato counts the number on the lifeboat. He sees five. There are two in the cabin helping Mercator off the bunk. So that makes nine with him. Kato realises the two people missing are Petrus and Jasmine.

"Sir, your head is bleeding badly; shall I get help for you?" The radio operator asks as he sees Kato on the deck of "Sara's Pride". The radio operator is helping another crewman to get Mercator off "Sara's Pride" Mercator is conscious. He has been given a pain killer and his knees have been bandaged tightly. He leans on the shoulders of the two crewmen as they shuffle past Kato. Mercator has met Kato several times in Europe with his father. He does not look Kato in the eye. Even though he is in pain, and has only recently gained consciousness, his instinct for self survival is sharp. Say nothing. Mercator decides is his best option. The failure by Mercator to make eye contact does not go unnoticed by Kato. He has too much to do and too many other problems at the moment but he will not forget the incident.

"No I'll be alright for now. Get this man secured on the life boat. We do not have much time before this boat sinks. We must all be on the lifeboat. Come on! Let's go!" Kato urges as he leads the way across the damaged deck towards the lifeboat where he waits in order to help the men transfer the sullen, uncommunicative Mercator across.

Why is he here? Why did he get shot? Kato wants to find out the answers to these questions but realises the mystery of Mercator will have to wait.

"There's a motor boat coming up fast." A sailor shouts.

"Untie those ropes before "Sara's Pride" drags us down with her and use them to tie us to the motor boat." Kato instructs his men whilst he gazes across at the rapidly approaching "Pembroke Lady". The only person he can identify is George. Kato guesses he must be trying to spot Jasmine. Kato knows the re union with George will be very difficult for them both.

He trusted me to look after Jasmine. Dammit where is she?

Kato clenches his hands together in frustration.

"Pembroke Lady" to the rescue

"No one answered the radio. I hope everything is OK." Charlie speaks to no one in particular trying hard to keep the disappointment out of his voice as he walks out from the cabin of "Pembroke Lady".

"We should be seeing the flares soon. Keep a sharp look out everybody." Adrian shouts. The late afternoon sun is strong; glistening on the aquamarine sea. Everyone is squinting, scanning the horizon, straining to see a signal. Each has their own special reason. Charlie is seeking his daughter. Leonora wants to see her sister. George wants to see Charlie and Leonora reunited with Jasmine. Adrian wants George to respond to his offer, which he will only do once Jasmine has been rescued. Clyde wants the rescue to be over quickly so they can resume the search for his skipper Eugene.

"There! There!" Leonora points at the flares climbing into the sky over a mile away.

"Hold on everyone" calls Adrian as he gets maximum power from "Pembroke Lady's" twin diesel engines. The sea is turned into a creamy white froth at the stern as she powers through the sea her bow heading towards the flares.

"Clyde will you go and help tie us to this floating wreck. Then help get everyone across here. Charlie and Leonora could you get the cabin clear for the injured and get as much food and clothing as we have." Adrian gives out precise orders in his unwavering clipped accent as if he were ordering a meal rather than taking part in a dangerous rescue.

"If it's all the same to you I want to see my Jazzy first." Charlie retorts.

"Yea, an' me, Adrian, I wanna give my sista a hug. Dat's why we come all dis way. Don't you know?" Leonora joins in the mini protest.

"Ok, Ok guys but hurry please! George? Will you go down to the cabin and start things off down there instead! We don't have a lot of time." Adrian gives in; realizing they will waste even more valuable time arguing.

""Pembroke Lady" this is Grumman HU 16 code name Oscar Sierra we are inbound to your position with an ETA of ten minutes. We have retrieved a man from the sea. Advise your requirements, over."

George and Adrian smile and Clyde gives a great whoop of uncontrolled relief when Charlie tells him his skipper has been rescued. Whilst everyone is busy Clyde secretly discards the sodden fifty dollar notes into the sea.

Chapter Thirty Seven

Missing

Early evening Saturday 4th June 1966

Where is my girl?

The sun is losing its intense heat. An early evening sea breeze is pushing the lifeboat farther away from Jasmine. She cannot swim any more. She surrenders to the sea. Her life belt keeps her afloat. The salt is crystallising on her face. She feels really scared. She doesn't want to die this way. Not saying good bye.

"Somebody, anyone, help me" Jasmine cries in desperation, tears streaming down her salt encrusted cheeks. No one hears.

"Where is Jasmine please?" Charlie asks the man who seems to be in charge of the lifeboat.

"I do not know at the moment. Who are you?" asks Kato.

"I'm her Pa and this is her sister. We need to see our girl mister!" Charlie implores. Kato's heart sinks down into his boots. At this moment he wishes the Marlin had speared him through the heart and dragged him down to the ocean floor. He cannot avoid the truth.

These two deserve to know at least some of what happened.

Kato forces himself to look in to Charlie's eyes he speaks slowly.

"Sir and Miss I am sorry. Jasmine is missing. She fell overboard about forty minutes ago. That is all I know. As soon as we get everyone on board your boat we can start looking for her. My First Officer Petrus is missing as well. Now I know you are upset but you must realise we have to first complete this rescue so please try to help us now. After that we can concentrate on looking for Jasmine and Petrus." Kato can barely look at Charlie and Leonora. The news he has given them has changed their mood from hopeful anticipation to one of despair and worry as they trace their way back onto "Pembroke Lady". They are so distraught they do not notice the hustle and bustle all around as the crew transfer the injured sea men. Adrian is concentrating on keeping "Pembroke Lady" under control. He wants to ensure that the minimum wave disruption is caused as people climb up one of two ladders to reach the deck of "Pembroke Lady". He fails to notice Charlie and Leonora as they make their way down to the cabin.

George is worried sick. He is getting on with the work Adrian asked him to do in place of Charlie and Leonora. He is below deck in one of the cabins but his thoughts are elsewhere. On the deck he had a quick look at the lifeboat and could not see Jasmine amongst the people.

She would have stood out from the rest of the crew being the only woman. What has happened to her? She has to be here somewhere. What has Kato done to his head and why did he not greet me? Something is up.

George feels powerless to do anything until this rescue is over.

"I am Captain Kato. Everyone has been transferred safely but we have two people missing. We had an explosion and they went overboard around forty five minutes ago. My guess is that if they are afloat, taking account of the trade winds and the local conditions, they will be four or five miles east of our position. If there is any chance of finding them we must move quickly please?" Kato implores Adrian. Adrian has not so much as shown a flicker of emotion or change in temperament at this news.

"I am Adrian Cuthbert from HMG Bermuda at your service. George Howden has mentioned you." With no time for small talk Adrian orders the ropes to be untied and requests Duane to carry out an immediate search with the Grumman HU 16 sea plane.

Despair

George knew it was not good news as soon as he caught sight of the anguish on Charlie and Leonora's faces as they entered the cabin.

"Jazzy is missin George. She dun fall into the ocean forty minutes back. No one has seen her since." Leonora, her voice choking, tries hard to fight back a flood of tears. George looks across at Charlie sitting on a bunk bed. The life has gone from Charlie's eyes. He sits like a zombie, a blank stare where once there was a twinkle. Lenny is trying hard to maintain a degree of composure. George says nothing. He stands up and holds Leonora in his arms. Leonora lets go of her fragile composure and gives out deep mournful sobs which get muffled as she buries her face into George's chest. Holding Leonora tightly, feeling her pain through her sobs, George feels despair and guilt. Despair because he knows there is nothing he can do to ease the pain of Leonora and Charlie, guilt because he has caused this to

happen. He is the author of this nightmare. Gently he takes Leonora across to her father.

Mercator wondered if Howden recognised him when he was brought down into the cabin.

Evidently not

Mercator muses as he lies quietly covered in blankets in a corner bunk. He has heard the news. He watched out of the corner of a blanket the grief and upset in the cabin. It's good to know that upstart Howden is getting some misery Mercator gloats.

Straight after his head wounds had been attended to Kato goes in search of George.

"George, I am so sorry, there was nothing any one could do, believe me, everything happened at lightening speed. Let us hope we might find her. There is still an hour's day light." Kato explains.

"It is my fault Agios. Why did I have to interfere, why, tell me?" George feels the guilt tearing into him eating away at his very being.

"That is not true George. You and I have been used. You know that Costas Tinopolis used us. We were compelled to act or just be treated as minions. I feel guilt over Jasmine. I have wracked my brains wondering if I could have stopped her falling into the sea. I do not think I could have done anything else George. Now there is more. Did you know that Mercator was on "Sara's Pride", he has been shot, I would love to know what happened. I bet Costas Tinopolis will not be laughing when he hears what has happened eh George." Kato hugs George trying to get him out of his dejection.

"Agios, you do not know, of course. Come with me I have something to show you." George races out to the galley with Kato in pursuit. Looking at the rings inscription and the frozen hand Kato mutters

"So Costas is dead. Mercator is shot. Perhaps we should ask him what happened."

"There is more Agios. The skipper and mate of "Sara's Pride" were dumped in the sea. Clyde the mate says there were two guys posing as reporters but they had a gun and a knife. They have disappeared. According to Clyde, Mercator was just a bit player.

As the two men walk from the galley the engines of "Pembroke Lady" slow right down. Adrian, assisted by Kato's seamen has been searching for several minutes in the area suggested by Kato. There is some thing in the water. George's heart misses a beat.

Please let it be Jasmine

Adrian puts the engines into neutral. "Pembroke Lady" moves slowly towards the object. The light is fading fast. Two sailors clamber down the side ladders to the surface of the ocean. George and Kato peer over the side straining to see in the fading light. The object is a body. The sailors carry the corpse up the ladder and lay it on the deck.

"That is Petrus." Kato says quietly.

A Prayer

George leaves the deck of "Pembroke Lady". He can do nothing to help Kato. Petrus is dead. He just hopes that Jasmine will not meet the same fate.

The two cabins below deck are taken up with injured seamen. The bunks are all occupied in the port cabin. Charlie and Leonora are huddled together comforting each other sitting on the floor of the starboard cabin.

Their backs are resting against the lower bunk. Mercator is in the bunk opposite. Leonora sees George.

"Why did we stop Howdy?" Leonora asks looking up at George her face is drawn. George's heart sinks as he looks at Leonora. He can't bear to see her look so helpless and strained from the worry over Jasmine. Should he tell her about Petrus or keep it quiet for now? Hearing Leonora speaking Charlie opens his eyes, he looks up at George and forlornly gives George a thin smile.

I can't keep back what has happened

"They picked someone out of the sea. No it's not Jasmine." George blurts out seeing first a glimmer of hope in Leonora and Charlie's eyes then dismay as the truth sinks in.

"Where is she George? Where is my Jazzy?" Charlie pleads. George just stands in the cabin his head bowed. So full of remorse and guilt it is all he can do to keep composure.

Kato steps into the cabin having overheard Charlie's cry.

"Jasmine is young and strong. She helped me on "Ocean Star". She is a heroine. We are searching the sea as I speak and there is also an aircraft searching. So, please do not give up hope."

"She can't be far away. My sister is out there all on her own. Jazzy keep safe. We want you back." Leonora offers up a prayer and huddles back into her father who just stares vacantly into space.

Chapter Thirty Eight

Air and sea Search

Saturday evening 4th June 1966

Air search

"How much time have we got before we need to head back?" Duane asks the pilot.

"No more than thirty minutes. That landing and take off to pick up your guy has eaten into our reserves." The pilot answers looking at his fuel gauges.

"OK this is the situation. There are two people missing from the wreck. Best guess is they are four to six miles due east from "Pembroke Lady's" co-ordinates at the rescue. Let's get over and do some searches with the heat sensor. We might strike lucky." Duane orders the pilot.

"Roger that but remember we do not have enough fuel for another landing in the drink." The pilot advises as he sets the Grumman on the heading calculated by the co pilot.

"Look! There is the motor boat!" Inspector Johnson's keen eyes are the first to see "Pembroke Lady". The pilot loses height.

""Pembroke Lady" this is Alpha Foxtrot Niner, we will commence our search pattern five miles to your east we have you on visual." Duane sends a radio message.

Several hours after the Grumman sea plane has left no one wants to admit the search for Jasmine has been unsuccessful. Night searching without proper search equipment such as searchlights has been difficult. Eventually the needs of those who have been rescued to have medical treatment have to be given priority.

Reluctantly Adrian steers "Pembroke Lady" onto a north westerly course to head back to Bermuda.

Charlie and Leonora are distraught. They can't bear to leave. They sense Jasmine is near but just out of their reach.

Floating

As the sun sets, a red hue glistens on the sea and reflects onto Jasmine's face. Jasmine's aim of returning to the lifeboat has long gone. The feeling of despair and fear when she realized she wasn't going to get back has been replaced by a quiet resolve to float, to survive. Treading water, conserving her strength, she will go wherever the wind and prevailing currents dictate. There is always a chance for rescue whilst she keeps afloat. She does not want to die but she has accepted that it is a possibility. Mentally she wants to survive the night. Tomorrow is another day.

"That's it. We have reached our fuel limit. We have to head back to Bermuda." The pilot advises Duane and Inspector Johnson who both look disappointed.

In the distance Jasmine hears the drone of an aeroplane's engines. The engine's sound fades away. Now, the only noise comes from the waves. Daylight has been replaced by a silvery moon.

To keep alert Jasmine thinks up tunes which she keeps repeating to herself.

Flotsam and jetsam from "Ocean Star" litter the sea. Wind and current move the detritus.

Something bumps into Jasmine. The tune running through her head gets interrupted. A wooden door, seven foot long, floats alongside her. The door is gently bobbing up and down in the waves. Jasmine hauls her tired, aching body onto the board. She lies down and gets some respite for the first time since she fell off the lifeboat eight hours ago.

Chapter Thirty Nine
Return to land

Sunday 5th June 1966

Governor

A hero's welcome awaits the crew of "Pembroke Lady" when at midday she cruises into the Great Sound. American and British warships anchored in the Sound blast away on their horns and sirens; signalling their congratulations for an historic rescue. A flotilla of small boats pursue "Pembroke Lady" through the Sound to her final docking point at the police berth from where she had left thirty hours before.

At Hamilton harbour ambulances await to take the injured sea men to hospital. Captain Kato goes to hospital for his wounded head to be properly attended to. Inspector Johnson pounces on Mercator before he is moved off "Pembroke Lady". Mercator is escorted by two police officers into a police van and taken under police guard to a secure room at King Edward the seventh hospital.

Sir Jeremy Mannerby Watson, resplendent in his full ceremonial Governor's uniform, salutes Adrian, George, Charlie and Leonora as they disembark from "Pembroke Lady"; a Royal Marines band play stirring military music. A crowd of local people and visitors wave and cheer.

Minion or Master

Sir Jeremy insists that "Pembroke Lady's" crew and Kato should come to Government House for lunch. The local press and some international papers have heard of the dramatic rescue. They are clamouring for information and pictures. Sir Jeremy has organised a press conference for four o'clock.

Coming off the boat Charlie and Leonora are completely drained of energy and have no enthusiasm to attend the governor's lunch. They do not want any attention. They just want Jasmine back. Duane persuades them to come to the reception so at least Charlie can meet his old friend Eugene, saved from the sea by the Grumman HU 16 sea plane.

Surprise Drop In

As everyone gathers in the grand reception room at Government House an equerry strides into the room and whispers to Sir Jeremy who then calls for silence and everyone's attention.

"I am informed that another guest is coming. A helicopter from U S battle cruiser John D Winter is on its way." the governor's announcement gets drowned by the sound of a Huey helicopter hovering over the gardens of Government House. Everyone rushes outside to greet the unknown guest. Admiral Steven A Becker Jnr. emerges from the helicopter. The admiral stands to attention in front of the crowd waiting for the engines to shut down.

"Your Excellency, ladies and gentlemen. On behalf of my crew I offer congratulations to your heroes from "Pembroke Lady" they have performed valiant work in accordance with the finest sea faring traditions. Last night we were privileged to have our navy seals take part in a search. Five teams of three using our small search craft were tasked from midnight until four in the morning to search a sector of ocean. My men are training for the moon landings taking off from Cape Canaveral scheduled for three years time. It is our role to search and find our brave astronauts landing in the sea in their space shuttles. Last night, we did not find an astronaut, but my men did find one very brave individual." Admiral Becker turns towards the Huey where a naval rating is escorting a young woman from the helicopter.

"It's Jazzy Pa!" Leonora shrieks and starts to race across the grass to her sister. Charlie hears Leonora's cry; he is standing with his old friend Eugene. George can't believe his eyes. He runs after Leonora he sees it really is Jasmine and races back to Charlie who is looking bewildered at Eugene.

"Jasmine is here Charlie. Come on!" George shouts and grabs Charlie by the hands pulling him towards the helicopter. At last the truth sinks in. Charlie sees Jasmine. He is not dreaming. As if a heavy cloak has been removed from his body Charlie's face lights up with a grin;

"I'm coming Jazzy I'm coming!" Charlie roars at the top of his voice.

George felt a profound sense of relief when he saw Jasmine emerge from the helicopter. Tears of joy welled up in his eyes as he watched Charlie and Leonora hugging her. Kato, also, was fighting hard to keep his emotions in check.

George and Kato stood shoulder to shoulder a few feet away from the family waiting their turn to welcome Jasmine back. As they each hugged Jasmine both remembered their special experiences with her. George thought how scared and helpless she had seemed trapped in the evil empire of Sammy Santino and how she had placed her trust in him to get her safely away. Kato remembered how beautiful and vulnerable she looked when he first set eyes on her; then, the incidents when she demanded drugs, the attack by Petrus, and the ghastly image of her falling off the lifeboat. Most of all he remembered their hug on board "Ocean Star" after she knocked Petrus out.

As she embraced everyone Jasmine's emotions were on a roller coaster ride of highs and lows. Happiness burst out like a spring flower when she saw Lenny and her Pa. As she hugged them she remembered vividly the feeling of despair she felt on her own in the sea, she had experienced a mental strength she never knew was in her as her will to live over came her fear of dying. She had taken a chance on George in New York. There had been something she could not explain. A quality of honesty and trust she found irresistible. She would never forget the intense almost profoundly religious feeling of thanks when the US Navy found her. As Kato came to hug her she noticed his eyes were moist. She tried desperately hard to stop her body from quivering as he held her.

It did not go unnoticed by Leonora that Jasmine clung to Kato longer than she thought necessary.

Chapter Forty

Aftermath

Sunday afternoon 5th June, 1966

George's Answer

"So George, a successful outcome I believe. Come and have some champagne." Adrian greets George and steers him towards the drinks table.

"We couldn't have made it without your efforts Adrian piloting "Pembroke Lady". I really have so much to thank you for. Now, we have a quiet moment together, I want to give you my decision on your proposal. I realise the dead line we agreed to on "Pembroke Lady" has passed."

"There were extenuating circumstances. I think we can allow you a slight overrun. Will you choose to be a master or a minion George?"

"I am not choosing to be a master Adrian." George speaks, carefully looking at Adrian's jaw drop as his words sink in.

"But if you want a loyal, reliable friend here I am." George smiles at Adrian. The two men seal their friendship with Sir Jeremy Mannerby Watson's finest Cristal champagne.

"You two guys look smug about something." Duane jokes.

"Me and Jonno can't stay. We're on our way back to Hamilton. We are gonna question Mercator. Boy has he got some explaining to do. Real glad everything has worked out for Jasmine. We will catch up with you guys later."

Sunday evening 5th June 1966

Questions

Mercator has been brought from the hospital to the interview room at Hamilton Police station. A police constable pushes Mercator sitting in a wheelchair into the room. Mercator instantly remembers the stale smell in the room and the unpleasant memories of his previous interview here.

"So Mercator, we meet again. I need you to explain why you were on "Sara's Pride"? We know you were with two other men. Tell us their names!" Inspector Johnson starts the questioning. Mercator keeps his mouth firmly shut and stares blankly over Inspector Johnson's shoulder.

"Why did you shoot yourself in the knees Murky? Why didn't you make a decent job of it? Like this!" Duane Pickens takes out his revolver and places it against Mercator's temple.

"Come on Murky you can tell us. Don't be embarrassed. I've seen guilty guys do a whole lot worse to them selves." Duane stares into Mercator's eyes. Perspiration is starting to run down Mercator's face. Duane keeps his revolver pressed against Mercator's head.

"Listen to me Mercator. If you will not co-operate and talk we will charge you. First off, conspiring with others to smuggle six million dollars of cocaine for US consumption, then, kidnapping and attempted murder of the skipper and mate of "Sara's Pride". They have been rescued and can't wait to testify against you. You are looking at ten to twenty years in prison here. After that we will send you over to the US to face charges there. If you tell us all you know it will be taken into account by the Courts. So come on, talk to us!" Inspector Johnson stares into Mercator's face who avoids eye contact. Inspector Johnson moves in closer confronting Mercator eye ball to eyeball and quietly whispers

"Finally, there is your father, where is he? You agreed to meet him and report back to us on Saturday morning. Did you see him? We know he checked in to the hotel" Inspector Johnson keeps staring into Mercator's face he sees doubt creeping in. The corner of Mercator's eye is twitching nervously. Duane removes the gun from Mercator's head.

"I don't know where my father is. Why should I?" Mercator cries and bangs the interview table. Inspector Johnson moves away from Mercator to the other side of the table and continues with the evidence.

"There is blood in your father's hotel suite. Someone tried to clean it up. They must have been in a hurry because they didn't do a very good job. The dressing gown in your room also has blood on it. Fragments of your father's clothes were found floating in the sea. You must have heard the explosion? Then, guess what, a severed hand, with a ring on one finger floated by "Pembroke Lady"." Inspector Johnson pauses.

"The hand got fished out of the sea. It was swollen. They couldn't remove the ring. So they cut the ring finger off the hand. Then the ring came off easily laddie. Look laddie! Here is the ring. Your father's name is inscribed on the inside" Inspector Johnson rolls the ring across the table. Mercator looks in horror at the ring. The blood drains from his face as though he has seen a ghost.

"I didn't do it. They came into the suite. They stabbed my father. They made me go with them on "Sara's Pride". They blew my father up with dynamite then they dynamited "Ocean Star", the engine seized on "Sara's Pride". They said there was no room for me in the dinghy. They shot me in the knees before they left. That's the truth. I don't know who they are. I have never seen them before. They scared me I do not want to see them ever again." Mercator rests his head down on the table and starts sobbing. Duane and Inspector Johnson look at each other. Duane shrugs his shoulders as if to suggest maybe this is the truth.

"OK laddie. We will check your story out. You are still held under suspicion. I will have you sent back to the hospital." Inspector Johnson responds.

Monday Evening 6th June 1966

So long

"I guess this is the end of the line for you and me Jonno. I gotta get back to the big Apple. We need to identify these two guys who have caused all this mayhem. It's a real pity we can't get Murky. I tell you Jonno that guy is as guilty as hell. I swear he's not telling us everything." Duane throws his hands up in frustration.

"Aye well the witnesses all say he was not involved on "Sara's Pride". There's no evidence laddie. Everything is circumstantial. I shall be releasing him. All in all I think we have had good results here. Let's not be too despondent eh laddie. There is fifteen minutes before your flight so how about a nice cup of tea?"

"Urr Jonno you know my answer to that one!" Duane looks at Inspector Johnson who is grinning from ear to ear.

"You Limeys crease me up. I'll call you if we find these two guys. So long Jonno."

Chapter Forty One

Futures

July 1966

Charlie

"Well Charlie, how do you feel about losing both your daughters? Lenny going to study music in London and who would have thought Jazzy would be going to Greece with Captain Kato?" Eugene queries as the two friends enjoy an evening drink at the Harbour Club after a day's fishing.

"I got no problem about it Eugene. I am mighty pleased for my girls and I can tell you very proud of them both. I just wish my dear Emilia could have seen her two girls grow into such fine young women. Since coming home I tell you Eugene I been seeing such strength in Jazzy. It's like all those bad experiences she had has brought out the best in her. Some folks might say Jazzy is too young for the likes of Agios but when you see them together; the way they look at each other; I know they is made for each other. They are going to see Agios's family. My heart misses a beat every time I see them together. I couldn't be happier for them. As for my girl Lenny well she and George is just great together. I got hopes that one day, when they are ready, they will tie the knot. George wants Lenny to concentrate on her singing in London.

She can stay with his Ma and Pa who live near London. So really everything couldn't be better. So how is you and Clyde getting on with the new boat?" Charlie gives Eugene a sly grin.

"We gonna change "Pembroke Lady's" name to "Sara's Pride" the second. I just couldn't believe it when George and Lenny said that the bank had no use for the boat and would I like it. I said to George that I could never find the sort of money those boats go for. You could have knocked me down with a feather Charlie when George said it would be a gift. How come? I asked. George said there was a big insurance settlement due to my boat being destroyed by "Ocean Star". Me and Clyde couldn't be happier. All we want now is for those bad guys who dumped me and Clyde brought to justice. We have given the police descriptions and they have made artist impressions so we is crossing our fingers on that one.

August 1966

George

"George, I do hope you will come out to Hong Kong and visit. You know Inspector Johnson is also transferring in September. So no excuses, there will be two people who will be pleased to see you in the old colony. By the way, my uncle has told me that he intends to take a personal interest in Leonora's progress. I have filled him in on what's been going on. The newspapers have tended to exaggerate the whole business. Do have some more of this Oolong tea my dear fellow." Adrian proffers the fine bone china tea pot but George shakes his head

"I might not be able to get over to visit for a while Adrian. I have promised Lenny I will get over to London as much as I can in the next twelve months. I am so excited for Lenny. It's a great chance for her. She really could make it big. It's all thanks to you and your uncle." George looks at Adrian who is engrossed in his tea.

"Don't mention it old fellow. If chums can't help each other what would this old world be like? Are you sure you won't try this tea? It takes the Chinese over twelve processes to make Ti Kuan Yin."

"How can I refuse a friend? Yes please Adrian. You know there is a possibility I may be able to get a business trip via Hong Kong. Kato and I are looking to get into the container shipping business. Demand is at an all time high due to the Americans shipping all but the "kitchen sink" out to Vietnam to give their boys a taste of home."

"That sounds exciting old boy. We will make a master out of you yet. Do you fancy a game of tennis later old chap?"

THE END

About the Author

Martin Smith started writing his first thriller "Minion or Master" two years ago after attending a creative writing course. He has written poetry and some walking and travel books. He attends a weekly literary group and is now busy working on "Minion or Master II" He runs a niche professional practice advising companies and individuals working in the media and other professions.

Martin worked in Bermuda in 1967. He now lives in a small mining village on the edge of the Brecon Beacons National Park in South Wales with his partner Hester and their two Jack Russell terrier dogs.

Hill walking has been a passion for many years resulting in many overseas trips. He has carried out sponsored walks for Cystic Fibrosis and BBC Sport Relief.